VARGAS' BREATH CAUGHT IN HIS THROAT

It was finished. There was no way to get back now. Raising his gloved hands over his helmet, Njombe showed that he was ready to surrender. *"Na zaluchene,"* said a Russian voice in Vargas' earphones. As the Venezuelan coasted close enough to touch the struts of its midsection, a rocket shell exploded against Njombe's chest. Vargas' helmet was sprayed with chunks of bloody flesh. He gagged and felt bile rising in his throat. Through the blood-smeared visor of his helmet he saw the Soviet soldiers hovering all around him some twenty meters away. And he suddenly realized what *na zaluchene* meant: "No prisoners."

The final rocket shell exploded squarely on his helmet.

Look for all these TOR books by Ben Bova

AS ON A DARKLING PLAIN
THE ASTRAL MIRROR
ESCAPE PLUS
GREMLINS GO HOME (with Gordon R. Dickson)
ORION
OUT OF THE SUN
PRIVATEERS
TEST OF FIRE
THE WINDS OF ALTAIR (trade edition)
VOYAGERS II: THE ALIEN WITHIN (in hardcover)

BEN BOVA
PRIVATEERS

A TOM DOHERTY ASSOCIATES BOOK

PRIVATEERS

Copyright © 1985 by Ben Bova

First printing: October 1985
First mass market printing: June 1986

A TOR Book

Published by Tom Doherty Associates
49 West 24 Street
New York, N.Y. 10010

Cover art by Boris Vallejo

ISBN: 0-812-53223-6
CAN. ED.: 0-812-53224-4

Library of Congress Catalog Card Number: 85-199387

Printed in the United States

0   9   8   7   6   5   4   3   2   1

TO
Stanley Schmidt

The only thing necessary for the triumph of evil is for good men to do nothing.

Chapter
◆ ◆ ONE ◆ ◆

The explosion was utterly silent.

Vargas hung in emptiness and saw the red finger of the rocket's flame lance out and find Carstairs. The shell hit the astronaut's jet backpack and exploded into a meteor shower of shredded fabric, metal and flesh. The young Venezuelan flinched inside his space suit, expecting the blast to knock him tumbling. But in the vacuum of space there was no blast, no sound. Just a surreal nightmare, hanging helplessly in weightless horror as Carstairs' helmeted head, severed from its trunk, spun past spewing blood into the black emptiness.

"It's a trap!" one of the others was yelling. Vargas heard it as a terrified screech in his helmet earphones. "Get back! It's a trap!"

But Vargas could not move. He was frozen, paralyzed with shock and sudden numbing fear.

The big Russian ore freighter hung in space, a massive sphere, a fat ovum, with the four needle-shaped flitters hovering close by like eager sperm cells. It was supposed to be easy, Vargas thought. A simple hijacking, like all the others. But instead of ores from the Moon, this Soviet freighter was carrying Russian troops armed with rocket-firing rifles.

A Trojan Horse. There had been no warning, no hint of danger. Vargas had piloted one of the four flitters from the space station *Nueva Venezuela* to intercept the freighter. It was supposed to have been unmanned, a drone ore carrier coasting from the Gulag mines on the Moon to the Soviet factories in orbit near the Earth. Dan Randolph had sent them out on missions like this half a dozen times.

But the spherical freighter had cracked open like a giant clamshell and disgorged two dozen armed cosmonauts. Their first shot had blown Carstairs apart and frozen Vargas where he hung unarmed and feeling very naked, between his own flitter and the advancing Russian troops.

They were asking no questions, showing no mercy. Two more of Vargas' companions were blown apart by rocket rounds. One of the flitters took a hit in its middle and its propellant tanks blew up in a brilliant soundless flash of flame.

"Get back to the ship!" Njombe's deep voice roared in his earphones. "Get the hell out of here!"

Vargas tried to blink away the searing image of the exploding flitter. His eyes burned and watered. He knew that he had to turn himself around, get away from the freighter and its space-suited soldiers. But he could not make his hands move, could not even flex his fingers. He was drifting toward the Russians, as the screams and curses of dying men filled his earphones.

A second flitter exploded as a rocket hit it. Vargas could see a space-suited figure suddenly flash into a smaller burst of flame as debris from the shattered spacecraft ripped into the oxygen tank of his backpack. A long agonized scream rasped in Vargas' earphones.

"I'm burning. . . . Helllp. . . ."

Another rocket shell reached out unerringly, trailing red fire like a malevolent meteor, and blew the thrashing man apart.

The sudden silence seemed to crush the breath out of

Vargas. His chest constricted. He could feel his heart trying to burst through his ribs.

"Vargas! Move it! Get back here, boy!"

Njombe's voice broke the shell of ice that seemed to encase him. He looked down at his hands, past the thick metal rim of his helmet collar, and saw that they were shaking uncontrollably.

"Come on, Paco! Move it!"

With every ounce of strength in him, Vargas forced his hands to stop shaking, forced his fingers to touch the buttons on the control arms of his jet backpack. But as he looked up, he saw the third flitter blow up. The Russian troops were swarming outward now, leaving the concealment of the freighter's shadow and jetting out into the sunlight. Their space suits were a light tan, Vargas saw; a part of his mind noted quite calmly what trivia the senses can observe in the midst of terror.

There were only two other astronauts left floating weightlessly between the freighter and the last remaining flitter, and the Russians were streaming out after them. Vargas turned himself around, the jetpack thrusters puffing out microscopic bursts of cold gas. Another astronaut sailed past him, racing at top speed for the last remaining flitter where Njombe waited, still bellowing into his radio microphone for them to hurry.

Vargas turned his head to find where the other man was, just in time to see a rocket shell reach him. He was one of the newcomers to Dan Randolph's little band of pirates, younger even than Vargas himself. A fellow Venezuelan. In the flash of a second before the shell detonated, Vargas had just time enough to register the kid's face, eyes wide with panic, mouth gaping, lips peeled back to show every tooth, legs churning uselessly in a mad impersonation of a man being chased by something horrifying. The flash of the shell's explosion blinded Vargas momentarily; everything turned hot white, then black. Something thumped against him and set him spinning, tumbling, head over heels, as the jetpack's thrusters struggled automatically to right him. Vargas squinted through painful eyes and saw what had hit him: an outstretched arm, the fingers of its dead hand reaching out in useless supplication.

The jet thrusters finally stopped Vargas' spinning, but he saw through the expanding cloud of blood and gas that had been a man just a moment ago that the Russian troops were flying toward him at full speed. Faceless behind their tinted helmet visors, they looked like robots: deadly, merciless killing machines. One of them propped the butt of his rifle against his hip. Vargas turned and tried to flee.

As if in a nightmare, he felt trapped in invisible quicksand. He could barely move. Far in the distance he could see Njombe standing inside the cockpit of the last remaining flitter, its transparent bubble of a canopy open, the spacesuited Kenyan waving both arms over his helmeted head, roaring at them in his native tongue. Ahead of himself, Vargas could see the other astronaut, the white metal of his jet backpack glinting in the harsh sunlight, its main thruster emitting a steady sparkling white plume of cold gas. Vargas did not know who the man was; he could not see his face.

Turning his head, the young Venezuelan saw the Russians gaining on him. No matter what he did, they were coming closer, closer. The one in the lead, the one with the rifle at his hip, was pointing it straight at him. Vargas saw the ugly muzzle of the gun yawning darkly, saw the flash as the Russian pulled the trigger.

The rocket leaped toward him. Instinctively Vargas ducked, pulling his head down inside the fishbowl helmet. The rocket lanced past him, missing by a good twenty meters, and he felt an overwhelming flood of relief.

The explosion flashed the other astronaut into flame as Vargas turned his head. It must have hit the man's legs, because he had time to scream hideously before he died. Vargas wanted to clamp his hands over his ears but knew that it would do no good.

He raced for the flitter, for Njombe standing there like a

beacon to guide him, for the safety that only the spacecraft could give.

If Njombe loses his nerve, Vargas thought wildly, if he kicks up the rocket engine and clears out before I reach him . . .

There were no others left. All the others were dead. The only way out of this carnage, the only way back home, was to get to the flitter and rocket out of here.

"Come on, Vargas!" Njombe urged. "Faster, man, faster! They're on your tail!"

Another rocket round flashed past him, a silent messenger of death. Vargas knew this one was not aimed at him; they were shooting at the flitter now, trying to destroy it.

Njombe was hunkering down into the pilot's seat, Vargas saw. Working the controls. The flitter jerked suddenly sideways, then lurched and pitched nose down. Vargas heard a babble of Russian voices in his earphones. More rocket trails lanced out toward the spacecraft. Njombe was maneuvering frantically, trying to avoid their shots without lighting up the flitter's main engine and zooming away. Desperately, he was trying to stay close enough so that Vargas could reach him.

A hundred meters away. Vargas' hands stretched out toward the spacecraft without his willing it, without his realizing that other hands had reached toward it scant seconds ago, in vain. Another rocket sizzled past, missing Njombe in the cockpit by millimeters.

Fifty meters. Njombe jinked the spacecraft slightly to the left as still another rocket round flashed harmlessly past. It seemed to Vargas as if he had spent his whole life trying to reach the flitter, straining to get to it yet unable to close the distance.

A rocket-driven shell hit the tail end of the shuttle and exploded. Not a big explosion. Not the kind of eye-searing flash of flame that a hit in the propellant tanks would have made. Merely enough to cripple the flitter, to make it a useless junkpile of beryllium struts and bulbous titanium tanks.

Vargas' breath caught in his throat. It was finished. There was no way to get back now. He saw Njombe stand up in the cockpit again; the plastic canopy was still tilted back, the Kenyan had never closed and secured it. Raising his gloved hands over his helmet, Njombe showed that he was ready to surrender.

"*Na zakluchene*," said a Russian voice in Vargas' earphones. As the Venezuelan coasted close enough to the flitter to touch the struts of its midsection, a rocket shell exploded against Njombe's chest. Vargas' helmet was sprayed with chunks of bloody flesh. He gagged and felt bile rising in his throat.

"*Na zakluchene!*" he heard again as he fought down the burning, retching horror. Through the blood-smeared visor of his helmet he saw the Soviet soldiers hovering all around him, some twenty meters away. And he suddenly realized what *na zakluchene* meant: "No prisoners."

The final rocket shell exploded squarely on his helmet.

Chapter
♦ ♦ TWO ♦ ♦

As his men were being slaughtered, Dan Randolph lay asleep in his cabin aboard the space station *Nueva Venezuela*.

He had seen the four flitters off on their clandestine mission, and as he watched them dwindle from view and become no more than four additional specks of light amid the star-flecked darkness of space, he felt a slight pang of regret at not having gone with them. Hijacking Soviet ore shipments from the Moon had become necessary for business, and it always pleased him to twist the bear's tail. But it was only really fun when he himself took part in the hijacking. The twenty-first century's premier pirate, Dan preferred to be at the scene of the action rather than sitting safely in an office.

But he knew the Russians were watching him now, following his every move closely. He could account for coming up to the space station from his headquarters in Caracas. There was nothing unusual in that, nor in his seeing a small flotilla of flitters off at the station's main loading dock. But the Russian sympathizers aboard *Nueva Venezuela* would quickly report that the American capitalist had gone venturing off in one of the needle-shaped spacecraft, and that would arouse immediate alarms in Moscow and aboard the Soviet space station, *Kosmograd*.

So Dan stayed at the Venezuelan space station and watched the flitters depart, just as if they were going off on a routine repair-and-refurbishment mission to one of the space factories.

He had gazed out the thick glass of the viewing port for a long silent while: a solidly built man in his late thirties, with light gray eyes that laughed at the world's foolishness and unruly sandy hair tickling the edge of his collar. His jaw was square and stubborn, his mouth often set in a faintly mocking smile, his nose slightly flattened, as if he had charged into one brick wall too many. In his plain blue coveralls there was no way to tell that he was one of the richest men on Earth—and certainly the richest one ever to work in space.

Long after the flitters had disappeared from view, Dan Randolph remained at the port, staring out at the red, blue and golden emblem and the big stenciled letters above the loading dock's main arresting collar. They spelled NUEVA VENEZUELA. After all these years, he still expected to see the Stars and Stripes of the U.S.A. Finally he gave a self-derisive little snort and pushed away from the window. He floated to the hatch that led ''down'' toward the normal-gravity part of the space station and his private quarters.

Nueva Venezuela had been built on the old ''wheels within wheels'' design: it looked like a set of bicycle tires nested one within another. The outermost wheel spun fast enough to create a sensation of full earthly gravity inside it. Two-thirds of the way ''up'' to the hub there was a wheel that spun just fast enough to simulate the gentle gravity of the Moon. The hub itself was effectively at zero gravity.

Dan pushed his way along one of the long narrow tubes that looked, from the outside, like the spokes of the nested wheels. As he made his way ''down'' from the hub, he could feel the sullen weight of gravity pulling on him once again. Within moments he was no longer floating, but stepping carefully, rung by rung, down the ladder that ran the length of the tube.

He worked for a while in his spare little utilitarian cabin, dictating memos and reviewing the month's production schedules on the display screen of a desktop computer. It would take six hours for the flitters to reach the incoming Russian freighter, he knew. His eyes began to feel heavy. He was still on Caracas time, and it felt like late at night. Clicking off the humming computer, he went over to his bunk and stretched out for a nap.

"Wake me when they make radio contact," he told the phone terminal. It said nothing, but its yellow COMMAND FUNCTION light turned on. It stared unblinkingly as Dan turned out all the other lights and fell quickly asleep.

At first, in his dream, he was floating in space, alone in utter darkness without even a star to light the void. He turned, though, and found himself in a parklike forest where stately trees were spaced generously and cool green grass stretched in every direction under a gentle summer sun. Like a Manet painting he had seen once, years earlier. The summer afternoon was filled with lovely women. And he recognized them, each of them. They all knew him. He walked among them, touching and being touched, as they smiled and chatted with him. He had slept with each one of them at one time or another, and they all looked happy to see him again.

Far off in the distance, through the leafy branches of the trees, Dan could see a white dome just over the horizon, with a statue of a stern female figure atop it. It was Jane, of course, and once he recognized her she was standing beside him in a flowing white robe. The other women backed away. Jane smiled at him, beckoning, her long coppery hair loose and flowing, her hands outstretched in greeting. But as Dan approached her, Morgan was standing beside his wife, holding her protectively.

Dan shook his head and turned away from them. Lucita somehow appeared before him, her beautiful childlike face with those haunting dark eyes utterly serious, her luscious lips grave and unsmiling. And Malik was with her, the cynical, ruthless, handsome Russian, holding Lucita in his arms, kissing her, caressing her.

And then it was Dan himself holding Lucita, fondling her, speaking to her as he had never done in reality as she gazed up at him with those fathomless midnight eyes, her rich full lips trembling, aching to be kissed. Dan drifted weightlessly with Lucita, the two of them all alone, totally removed from everyone in the world, far out in a featureless, empty nothingness. He laughed at the joy of it and she laughed too, happy and free in their private cosmos. They glided effortlessly, languidly, bathed in a warm crimson glow that had no source. Her naked skin gleamed as if oiled, her heavy curling black hair floated unbound.

Dan felt her warm smooth flesh, slid his hands across her soft breasts and down the curve of her hips. She sighed softly and her arms twined around him as he stroked the silky length of her thighs.

"I love you, Lucita," he whispered in his dream. He had never said it waking.

And in his dream she replied, "I love you, Daniel. I love you more than I can bear."

He held her slim young naked body in his strong hands. "I've loved you since the first moment I saw you, that afternoon in your father's house, the afternoon of the rainstorm. . . ."

Her dark, luminous eyes searched his soul. "You must not say such things, Daniel. The danger . . ."

He placed a finger on her lips. "What danger? Who cares? All they can do is kill me."

Lucita kissed his fingertip. "But if you die, *amado*, I will die too."

"No. You're young . . . too young to die."

"Daniel, I would not live without you. I adore you, my darling *Yanqui*."

He kissed her again and felt her body arching against his. Weightlessly they floated, intertwining, gliding through the silent emptiness.

18

"We can never let them know of our love," Lucita warned.

"Not let them know?" Dan laughed. "I want to tell the whole world! I want to write it across the sky in letters of fire!"

"No, no," she begged, frightened. "They will try to take me away from you."

"Never! We'll run away. Where would you like to live? New Zealand? Tahiti? Shall I buy the Taj Mahal for you and make it your palace? Or build a new world all our own, far out in space where no one can ever reach us?"

But she was very serious. "Daniel, we cannot run away. I will not be the cause of your giving up everything you have worked so hard to build."

"The only thing I want is your love," he told her. "Nothing else matters."

"You have my love, dearest one. You have all my love."

Her vibrant young body was flawless, irresistible. She stretched languidly as he stroked every curve of her. Slowly their bodies revolved around each other as their passion rose, skin glistening in the heat of their desire, endlessly floating in the sensuous weightless freedom from all restraints. They were alone in their own universe, nothing else existed: no world, no stars, neither night nor day. Only each other, the electric thrill of flesh on flesh, the whispered moans of delight, the musky scent of arousal climbing to its farthest peak. His mouth on her nipples, her hands sliding along his flanks. He gripped her buttocks and she threw her head back keening as he entered her hard and demanding in one insistent thrust and they heaved and writhed together as her warmth enveloped him and he held her thrashing, sobbing, shouting her pleasure and pain and mad, wild desire.

Dan's eyes snapped open.

For an instant he thought he was back on the construction gang, with the burly old Japanese foreman prodding him to get out of the bunk. But as he focused his sleep-blurred eyes, he saw that it was a stocky Russian captain in the red-trimmed uniform of the Strategic Rocket Corps prodding his middle through the sheet with the muzzle of a stubby pistol. Behind him stood two Russian soldiers holding ugly, snub-nosed machine guns. They fired fléchette darts, Dan recognized. The darts would not penetrate the fragile skin of the space station's hull, but they had more than enough power to puncture the thin sheet covering Dan's naked body and the living skin beneath it.

"Daniel Hamilton Randolph," said the captain in impeccable midwestern American, "I arrest you for piracy in the name of the Presidium of the Soviet Union and by order of Vasily Malik, chairman of the Soviet Combined Space Forces."

Chapter
◆ ◆ THREE ◆ ◆

In Paris it was drizzling again. Willem Quistigaard sipped at his aperitif, savoring the golden warming glow of the Pernod as he watched the gray, wet evening slip inexorably into the darkness of night.

"Once they called this the City of Lights," he said to his young aide, almost sighing at the memory. He was a tall, rawboned man, vigorously active although well into his seventies. His thick hair and mustache still showed traces of gold among the silver. His voice was deep and strong. His big-knuckled hands dwarfed the glass he was holding.

"The lights are on again," replied the aide. His youthful face looked puzzled. He had the bland, innocent features of a born bureaucrat. Quistigaard knew that the youngster had gone straight from college into government service. Never been in the real world at all; never experienced a day for which he did not have an agenda already prepared. In triplicate.

Quistigaard did sigh. It had been a long day, a long week, and now his flight back to Geneva had been delayed several hours. He sat under the awning of the hotel's sidewalk cafe and watched the few straggling pedestrians scurrying toward their homes in the cold drizzle.

"I didn't mean it literally," he told his aide.

"Oh. Sorry."

Quistigaard took another sip of the Pernod and felt its warmth spread inside him. But it didn't taste the same; not like the old days. Nothing was the same anymore.

"When I was your age," he said, "Paris was the most exciting place in the world. At this time of the evening the city was just beginning to come to life. The restaurants! The cars! The women!" He shook his head and gestured halfheartedly toward the emptying streets.

"If the weather were better . . ."

"It's not the weather. It's *not* the weather. It's here." Quistigaard tapped two fingers of his right hand against his breast. "The heart's gone out of Paris. Out of all Europe. It's all turned gray and dreary."

"You're tired," the aide murmured sympathetically. "Once the sun comes out and you get some fresh air into your lungs you'll feel differently. Tomorrow you'll be on the ski slopes. You'll feel better then."

"I'll have to fight my way past Russian tourists," Quistigaard muttered.

The aide laughed politely. Then, changing the subject quite deliberately, he said, "I thought the conference went rather well. Didn't you?"

The older man lifted his shoulders in a weary shrug. "Conferences always go smoothly when all the real work is done before the conference opens."

"You did a magnificent job."

I suppose there's some sincerity in that, Quistigaard thought. After all, his job is secure; he doesn't really have to butter me up.

But he leaned across the tiny table and said, "The International Astronautical Council is nothing but a rubber stamp for the desires and actions of the Soviet Union. Since I am chairman of the council, that makes me the inkpad for the rubber stamp. You are working for an inkpad."

"That's not true!" the young man blurted, astonished.

22

Quistigaard smiled inwardly, pleased to have penetrated his bland façade. If I'm an inkpad, he thought, what does that make my assistant?

"The conference resolved several very difficult issues," the aide went on, his voice at least half an octave higher than it had been. "The matter of allocating new orbital slots for communications satellites; the question of disseminating geological data from observations made from orbit . . ."

Quistigaard waved him to silence. "Tell me one issue that was decided in a way that the Russians did not approve."

The younger man blinked once, twice.

"You see?" Quistigaard almost laughed. "It was the Soviet government which organized the agenda for the meeting. Every item on the agenda was agreed upon before the first session convened. Every issue went the way the Russians wanted it to go. We shuffled a great many papers. We listened to a number of boring speeches. We sat for four days and held sixteen concurrent sessions."

"We accomplished a lot," the aide muttered, almost sullenly.

Quistigaard held up his right hand, the thumb and forefinger hardly a centimeter apart. "Not even that much got through that was against the Russians' wishes. Not one iota of disagreement was allowed. *They* run the IAC; you and I are merely figureheads."

The young man shook his head, frowning.

"Come on, son, admit it. The Russians *own* outer space; they run things exactly the way they want to. Just as they run all of Europe."

For several moments neither of them said a word. Quistigaard took a long pull on his drink. His aide sipped at his demitasse of coffee and tried to avoid the older man's eyes.

The chill was getting to Quistigaard, despite the yellow heat of the Pernod. He pulled his topcoat closer around him and slouched deeper into the rickety chair.

"They didn't have to fire a shot, you know," he muttered.

23

"Once the Americans backed down, they could have had Europe for free."

"It was the French," the younger man said. "They forced the Soviet retaliation."

"Bah! Do you believe what they told you in school? I was *there*, when it happened."

"The war?"

"It wasn't a war. It wasn't even a battle. The Americans announced their withdrawal from NATO. On the day it became effective, one hotheaded French submarine captain fired a missile—probably at the United States, if you ask me. Or maybe he was a Communist agent provocateur, working for the Russians. That thought occurred to me."

"That's impossible!"

Quistigaard smiled frostily at the young man's naiveté. "Was it? The Soviets announce that they have weapons in orbit that can shoot down ballistic missiles. The United States caves in to Soviet demands and quits NATO. One French submarine—part of their pitiful little Force de Frappe—fires one solitary missile from the middle of the Atlantic Ocean. A Soviet laser beam destroys the missile within three minutes of its launch. The Soviets then launch a missile of their own and detonate a small hydrogen bomb in space, over Paris. The electromagnetic pulse from that explosion knocks out almost all the electrical power systems and equipment from Iceland to Kraków. No electric lights, cars don't work, heaters don't work, telephones don't work, most of Europe is plunged into darkness and cold. And panic. People were throwing up in the streets out of sheer terror. Then three Soviet cruise missiles hit three French military bases with poison gas warheads."

"The French were preparing a counterstrike."

"So the history books say. I have my doubts. Most of those texts were written by Russians."

"No!"

"Perhaps I exaggerate," Quistigaard said, dryly enough to let the young aide know that he did not believe so.

"But there was no other fighting. There was no nuclear war."

"Of course not. With the Americans humbled and Western Europe groping in the dark, there was no need for fighting. The Soviets had made their point. Paris, London, even Bonn fell all over themselves in their eagerness to make their accommodations with the new political situation. The Cold War ended almost overnight. And now you see the result."

"Things are getting better."

"So I am told."

Gazing up and down the wide boulevard, the two men saw a dark, wet, chilly, empty street. A steam-powered bus chuffed by, lumbering and lurching. The sidewalks were bare of people, except for a couple of stocky men in long gray raincoats hurrying along. They looked like Russians to Quistigaard.

"The Americans," the young man whispered, almost as if he were talking to himself. "It's their fault. They abandoned Europe. They left us defenseless."

"Yes, that's true. But they made themselves defenseless first. Once the Soviets established antimissile weapons in space, the American nuclear forces became rather useless."

"But why? How could they have been so blind?"

Quistigaard lifted his glass again, only to find that it was empty. No waiter was in sight.

"The Americans got tired," he said. "They shouldered the burdens of the world for almost a century, and then they got tired of the job. They tried to take the easy way out. They never felt comfortable about world leadership. In their hearts, all they wanted was for the rest of the world to like them. Like little puppydogs. All they wanted was to be petted and told that they were good. They made several very poor decisions, and before they realized what had happened, the Soviets had a decisive military advantage over them."

"The antimissile satellites."

"That was the straw that broke the Americans' back," Quistigaard agreed. "But I think they were relieved to quit the race. I honestly think so. They were always isolationists at heart. They never had Europe's best interest in mind.''

"Well, they're certainly isolated now. They didn't even send a delegate to the convention."

"Why should they? They abandoned their space program. The Soviets have cut off almost all their international trade. They have to learn how to adjust their economy to exist on its internal market alone; for America, there is virtually no overseas trade. I haven't even seen an American tourist here in Paris. Have you?"

"It's not the season. . . ."

"No. They're done for. They'll strangle on their own bile. A nation that size can't exist without overseas markets. The United States will self-destruct within another generation, while the Soviets watch and laugh."

"And the rest of the world?"

"Oh, we go through the motions of being independent. China is still strong, but its missiles are just as obsolete as the Americans', against those lasers the Russians have in space."

"But Europe is rebuilding."

"Along Soviet guidelines. Even Paris is turning into a dull Socialist grayness."

"But the Third World nations are still going their own way. They operate their factories in orbit."

"At Soviet sufferance. And I wonder how long that's going to last. Did you notice the hubbub in the Russian delegation this afternoon? Something is happening, something big. Malik did not attend any of today's sessions. He wasn't even at the final plenary meeting."

"Yes," admitted the young man. "That did strike me as odd."

"Something's in the wind," Quistgaard said gloomily. "Something big is about to happen."

Chapter
♦ ♦ FOUR ♦ ♦

The Russians had seized the entire space station. Venezuelan national territory or not, it was now under Soviet control. The captain and the two soldiers watched stolidly as Dan pulled on his coveralls, then they marched him out of his cabin and down the long sloping corridor that ran the circumference of the huge, revolving wheel. The captain would not answer any of Dan's questions; none of the Russians said a word after the captain had awakened Dan and announced his arrest. They locked Dan in one of the storerooms and marched off, out of sight.

Alone, Dan looked around at his improvised jail cell. It was a bare little space, about the size of two telephone booths put together. Three of its walls were heavy wire mesh, the fourth the curving hull of the station structure, slightly cold to the touch despite its thick layers of insulation. The enclosure had been used to store electronics spare parts, Dan remembered. But the Russians had emptied it completely. Just like them, he thought. The first thing they do is turn something useful into a prison cell.

There was nothing at all in the enclosure: no bunk, no

bench, nothing but the bare floor and the overhead strip of fluorescent lighting. Looking out through the heavy wire mesh door, Dan saw that the Russians had set up a TV camera in the storeroom on the other side of the narrow walkway that ran the length of the storage area. He grimaced into the camera, hoping that whoever was monitoring him would be startled, at least for a moment.

They must have intercepted the flitters, Dan realized. I hope they're treating the crews all right. Their spy system must have been a lot better than I thought.

He sank down onto the floor, leaned his back against the stiff metal screen. So ends the illustrious career of the twenty-first century's premier pirate. It's all over. They'll stuff a sponge rubber ball in my mouth and put a bullet through the back of my head. I'll never see Lucita again. Never have the chance to tell her that I love her.

He felt more angry than afraid. Frustrated rather than fearful. His hands were steady, his insides calm. The finality of it was too real, too inescapable. There was nothing left to hope for. But so much to regret. So many things he still wanted to do. So many scores still unsettled. And Lucita. His mind kept coming back to her. He tried to tell himself that it would be better for her this way. He would have brought her nothing but pain and turmoil. Now she could marry the damned Russian and live her life and forget about him. Then he looked down at his hands and saw that they were clenched into fists.

He almost laughed aloud. You're not very good at being noble, are you?

It was laughable. A cosmic joke. And it was going to end very soon. The Russians would not take any chances. Bang, you're dead. And their problems with space piracy are solved. Their monopoly of space is preserved. The rest of the world gets shown who's boss. With one shot.

Lucita. Can it be that I've only known her for less than a year? Funny how time can stretch and contract. How a second can seem as long as infinity. How years can race past and disappear before you realize it. He rested his head against the wire screen and squinted up at the flickering fluorescent tube overhead. The day I met her. The very first day. It was raining. Yes. Poured all day. That's the day I met Malik, too. And Zach Freiberg.

" 'Like the drip, drip, drip of the raindrops,' " Dan quoted under his breath. Then, aloud, he grumbled, "Damn Cole Porter!"

His office window was leaking again. Nothing much, just enough to make an annoying dripping sound and form a soggy puddle in the thick carpeting. The rain teemed down with biblical fury. Dan stood impatiently at the wide, sweeping window of his office and stared out at the downpour. It was as if God were dousing Caracas with a celestial fire hose, pouring torrents of water, solid sheets of it, all over the city. Normally Dan could see the green hills that rose up beyond the city's boundary and the cable towers for the tramway that went over the mountain to the port at La Guaira. And the wretched squatters' shacks of cardboard and plywood that infested those hills. But not today. He could barely make out Bolivar Square, just a few streets away from his office tower, in the intensity of the downpour.

Brand-new building and it leaks like a sieve, he complained to himself. Where the hell's the damned maintenance man? Called him an hour ago. Christ, even in Houston the service was better than this.

His office was on the top floor of the tallest skyscraper in Caracas. It was the office of a man of enormous wealth and power, rich without being garish, imposing without being intimidating. Dan grinned at himself in the faint reflection from the rain streaked window. At least the roof doesn't leak, he thought. Then he added, Not yet.

He turned back toward his desk, a bulky, ornate heirloom of Victorian grotesquerie that his great-grandfather had acquired when he had been a young minister in rural Virginia. The office's couches, chairs and long polished conference table were all in the ultramodern Venezuelan style of leather, mahogany and chrome. The carpets were from India and China. One of them, richly woven with threads of gold, was a gift from his old friend Saito Yamagata. There were no paintings on the walls, but plenty of photographs. None of them were of people. Most showed spacecraft standing on launching platforms, silhouetted against dramatic skies. Others showed views of the Earth as seen from space. The largest one, taking up almost the entire wall opposite Dan's desk, was of the spidery wheels-within-wheels structure of the Venezuelan space station, *Nueva Venezuela*. Dan had taken that photograph himself. Just as he had built the station itself.

Behind his desk, on the wall over the low bookshelves built in there, was a framed page from a three-year-old issue of *Forbes* magazine. It showed a color photograph of Dan sitting at his desk in his old office in Houston. As a portrait, Dan found it amusingly deceptive. He was looking squarely into the camera, grinning boyishly, a grown-up Tom Sawyer playing business tycoon. His gray eyes sparkled, his sandy hair was tousled as if he had just been engaged in some strenuous action. He was in his shirt-sleeves, tie slightly askew, one hand reaching for the key pad of his phone terminal. Dan knew that he was no beauty, yet his rugged, unhandsome features seemed to intrigue women. It was the smile that got them, he thought. The smile and the eyes. His nose was too big for his own liking, and still slightly bent from the time it had been broken during a drunken low-gravity fistfight on the Moon. A Japanese mining engineer had made a wisecrack about American stupidity and Dan had tackled him and his three compatriots. He had never taken the trouble to have the nose straightened, even after he had become so wealthy. Dan told himself he was not that vain. His plentiful enemies said he was too vain to correct the imperfection.

The text of the article that accompanied Dan's picture had been written by a young woman who had thought herself a

30

hard-probing reporter, too tough and sophisticated to fall for a grown-up Tom Sawyer. She started the article by describing him:

"A throwback to an earlier era, Daniel Hamilton Randolph is probably the richest thirty-five-year-old industrialist in the world. Scion of a genteel Virginia family that traces its roots back to Thomas Jefferson, this former astronaut, former lunar mining engineer, has created the first multinational corporation to crack the billion-dollar-per-year mark entirely through space industries.

"Randolph is not a big man physically, but he has the inner toughness that comes from making his own way in the world. Unmarried and handsome enough to head *Playgirl* magazine's 'Ten Most Wanted Men' list, Dan Randolph has the brilliance, the drive, and the towering ego of a latter-day Ted Turner."

His desk phone chimed and Dan snapped his fingers in answer. The phone terminal spoke with the dulcet voice of a professional actress whom Dan had once admired enough to buy her an apartment in New York. Her voice, it turned out, had been the sexiest part of her.

"Dr. Freiberg to see you, Mr. Randolph."

Glancing at the growing puddle on the carpet by the window, he growled, "Where the hell's the maintenance man?"

Picking up on the key word, the phone replied, "Maintenance department was called one hour and thirty-seven minutes ago. Do you wish to call again?"

"You're double-damned right I do!"

The phone made no response. It did not understand Dan's vehement language. He huffed, then said slowly, "Yes. Call the maintenance department again. Repeat the same message and add that I will deduct any damage to my carpeting from the rent."

"Yes, sir," said the phone. "And Dr. Freiberg."

Dan nodded. "Right. Let's have Dr. Freiberg, by all means."

Zachary Freiberg, Ph.D., appeared almost instantly in the

chair at the left side of Dan's desk. His holographic image, projected by laser equipment built into the ceiling, scintillated slightly. It was solid enough to look real, although Dan knew that if he extended his hand, it would go through empty air. He could see, faintly, the photos on the far wall through Freiberg's three-dimensional image. The scientist was slouching slightly in the chair, cross-legged, his eyes focused slightly away from Dan.

"Hello, Mr. Randolph," said Zachary Freiberg. He was a youngish man, with curly strawberry-blond hair flopping down boyishly over his broad forehead. His face was round, apple-cheeked. An open-neck shirt, its pocket stuffed with pens, rumpled denims and feet bare except for sandals that were cheap imitations of Japanese getas. Dan got an impression of youth and lazy softness. He suppressed a frown, feeling suddenly overdressed in his own informal shirt and slacks.

"Dr. Freiberg." Dan forced a smile. "How's the weather in California?"

Freiberg grinned back at him. "Sunny and warm, what else?"

Unconsciously, Dan sniffed at the dank air of his office. No matter how much he spent on air conditioning, the place always smelled slightly fetid to him, as if the jungle beyond the city's limits were sneaking back in to reclaim the territory that humans had tried to steal from it. Not even Houston, for all its humidity, was as bad as this. Today, with the tropical torrent tumbling out of the skies, the air felt musty and almost chill. Dan knew it was more in his imagination than reality, but still he nearly shuddered.

"We're about ready for Noah's ark here," he said, making a joke of it.

"Yes," Freiberg said, "I can see the rain coming down past your window."

On both sides of it, Dan groused to himself. Aloud, he said, "Dr. Freiberg, I thought that you were all set to join us here at Astro Manufacturing. Now my personnel manager tells me there's a hitch. What's the problem?"

32

Freiberg's round face grew serious. His eyes strayed slightly away from Dan's, avoiding direct contact.

"Well, uh . . ." he stammered, "it's, uh . . . well, it's a little embarrassing."

Dan said nothing and waited for Freiberg to sort out his conflicting emotions. The scientist looked overweight to Dan, both physically and emotionally. Still wearing his baby fat. But Astro Manufacturing's chief scientist and personnel di rector both insisted that Freiberg was the best planetary geo chemist they could find. He was the man they needed, and therefore the man Dan wanted to hire. Freiberg had agreed to this appointment with Dan, so obviously the man was willing to talk. It would just take him a few moments to get over the hang-up of politeness. Dan had learned years earlier that most people would rather make asses of themselves than say something they considered impolite. They were trained from childhood to be pleasant and never utter a word that might upset someone. "If you can't say something nice, say noth ing at all," was the wisdom that long generations of parents instilled in their trusting offspring. So the kids grew up to tie themselves in knots, holding back their true feelings, smiling when they wanted to spit, and they wound up paying exorbi tant fees to psychologists or going to pop therapy courses where they finally liberated themselves enough to be able to say in public, "I've got to go to the bathroom."

Freiberg squirmed in his chair and twitched for a few mo ments, then said at last, "The problem is that all my friends tell me I'd be almost committing treason if I went to work for you."

"Treason?" Dan snapped.

"A lot of people here think that you're a . . ." Freiberg's face reddened. "Well, a traitor."

Chapter
♦ ♦ FIVE ♦ ♦

Dan leaned back in his leather chair and eyed the younger man carefully. He had expected something like this. At least it was out in the open now.

Carefully, calmly, he replied, "According to the Constitution, treason consists of giving aid and comfort to an enemy of the United States."

"That's merely the legal definition. . . ."

"Do you think I'm a traitor to the United States because I've moved my corporation's headquarters to Caracas?"

"You left the country."

Dan forced his voice to remain calm, reasonable. "In a sense, Dr. Freiberg, you could say that the country left me. I'm in the business of running factories in orbit. The United States government decided to close down all its space activities and revoke the operating licenses of all the firms working in space. I had no choice. It was either leave the country or go out of business."

"Yes, I know that, but . . ."

Dan made himself relax and grin. "Now look . . ." He almost added, "*kid*," but held it back. "My motto has

34

always been, 'When the going gets tough, the tough get going—to where the going's easier.' ''

Freiberg did not laugh. He merely looked more uncomfortable than ever.

Dan abandoned his attempt at humor. ''The American government gave up all its space operations at the insistence of the Russians. You know that, don't you?''

Freiberg nodded glumly.

''So, in a sense, if I'm working against anyone or anything, I'm working against the Kremlin. I'm carrying on the work that America would be doing if Washington hadn't caved in to the Soviets.''

''But it's not that simple,'' Freiberg objected. ''A lot of people think you just ran out because you could make more profits in Venezuela.''

Christ! Dan swore silently. Spare me this neoliberal twaddle!

''You left a lot of people without jobs here,'' the scientist added.

Dan said carefully, ''I brought as many people with me here to Caracas as I could. If I had allowed the American government to shut down Astro Manufacturing completely—as they were going to do—then *all* of Astro's employees would have lost their jobs. I really had no other choice.''

''There's still a lot of resentment here about you. A lot of hostility.''

''I'm sure there is. But are you going to let that kind of petty jealousy decide the future of your career?''

Freiberg started to reply, but hesitated.

''Look,'' Dan said, as sweetly reasonable as he could manage to be, ''the United States has agreed to halt all its operations in space. Washington turned over the American space station to the United Nations, and you know who runs the UN since they left New York.''

''There's still the scientific exploration of the solar system,'' Freiberg said, a little stiffly. ''We still build the finest scientific probes in the world.''

''But you have to launch them on Russian boosters. You

35

have to get approval from the Soviet Academy of Sciences or your beautiful hardware sits on the ground and rusts away. Right?''

"We work in cooperation with our Russian colleagues. Scientists don't get involved with politics.''

And rain makes applesauce, Dan thought. He reached across his desk and touched the screen of his phone terminal once, twice, then once more. "In the past four years,'' he said, glancing from the screen to Freiberg's solid image and back again, "your group has been allowed to place one vehicle aboard a Soviet shuttle. . . .''

"The Saturn orbiter,'' Freiberg murmured.

"Which is still at *Kosmograd* because the Soviets haven't granted you the high-energy upper stage you need to get it to Saturn.''

"There've been some delays. . . .''

"I'll bet there have. And your group's proposals for orbiters of Neptune and Uranus have been flatly rejected by the Soviet Academy. Your proposal for an automated prospecting mission through the asteroid belt was turned down. Your proposal for a Titan lander was turned down. . . .''

"I know, I know!'' Freiberg admitted. "They're squeezing the life out of us.''

That's what Dan wanted to hear. "Dr. Freiberg—may I call you Zachary?''

"Zach. My friends call me Zach.''

"Thank you. And my friends call me Dan. I don't have to tell you what my enemies call me.''

Freiberg grinned.

Feeling that he was thawing the youngster at last, Dan said, "Now listen, Zach. And think. Do you believe—I mean, really believe, down deep inside your guts—that the Russians are going to allow more of your scientific missions in the coming years, or fewer?''

"Well . . .''

"Don't you really think that they've just been picking your brains, learning your technology, and by the time they let

36

your Saturn orbiter go on its way they'll be ready to take over *all* future planetary missions for themselves?''

The scientist's round face grew somber. ''Where did you hear that?''

''I have sources of information,'' Dan replied. ''You'd be shocked at how easy some of these dedicated Communists are to bribe.''

''There've been rumors . . . I thought they were just the usual scare stories.''

''The future exploration of the cosmos will be done by Soviet spacecraft, lifted aboard Soviet boosters,'' Dan warned. ''When men go to Mars, and Jupiter, and Saturn and all their myriad moons, they will be Russians. That's their intent.''

Freiberg said nothing.

''The Russians think they've got it all sewed up. They keep telling themselves that they represent the inexorable forces of history. Bullshit!''

The scientist blinked at Dan's sudden vehemence.

''That's just a load of Soviet tripe, that inexorable forces of history garbage. *People* make history, Zach. What I do, what *you* do, what each of us does is important. Calories don't count, maybe, but people do. You're an important man, Zach. A very important man.''

''But I'm just one person. . . .''

''Of course. But you're not alone. There are others. I'm fighting as hard as I can,'' Dan went on, earnestly, coaxingly, ''to prevent the Russians from achieving a total monopoly on space operations. Even if the United States has been forced officially to abandon space, Americans can still carry on the fight, still explore the solar system.''

The scientist looked sharply at him. ''And make profits from it.''

Dan had been waiting for that one. He grinned. ''Zach . . . how do you think we pay for the research we do? How do you think we're going to finance our missions to the asteroid belt?''

''You're going to the belt?''

Now you've got him hooked, Dan knew. He's easier than you thought he'd be. Just reel him in, nice and gently.

"We plan to. We want to. With the Russians monopolizing the Moon and setting their own prices for lunar ores, we've got to look elsewhere for raw materials. The asteroids are the obvious answer."

"Yes, obviously."

"We need you to head the program, Zach. You're the only man who can do it for us." Flattery, Dan knew, but not too far from the truth. "If you don't come with us to head the team, I don't think we'll be able to pull it off." Then he grinned again and added, "Unless we can get one of the Russians to defect."

Freiberg visibly straightened in his chair, squared his pudgy shoulders, lifted his round chin.

"Will you help us, Zach? Will you help us to expand beyond the limits of the Earth-Moon system? If we wait for the Russians to do it, we'll both be dead and in our graves before the first asteroid mission goes out."

"I'll . . . have to talk it over with my wife, of course."

"Of course."

"She's a native Californian."

A mental picture of a lank-haired vegetarian who believed in astrology and the mystical benefits of cocaine flashed through Dan's mind. But he said, "Tell you what, Zach. You bring your wife down here for six weeks. Just to see how the two of you like living here and working with Astro Manufacturing. What does she do?"

"She's a social worker."

What else? Dan quipped to himself, thinking of the vast sea of unemployed and unemployable Californians. Half the state stood in welfare lines while the other half stood behind the desks ministering to them. Maybe they take turns at it, he thought, one week in line and one week running the system.

"She speaks fluent Spanish," Freiberg added, brightening.

I'll bet she does. Cautiously, Dan replied, "I wouldn't be

38

surprised if we could find something useful for her to do here in Caracas.''

"That sounds good. I'll tell her."

"Fine. I'll have my travel people get in touch with you. You won't have to lift a finger. They'll take care of everything.''

Freiberg nodded, smiling broadly now.

"I'll get an employment contract off to you this afternoon," Dan said.

"We haven't talked salary."

Waving an impatient hand in the air, Dan replied, "You fill in the salary number. If it's too much, we can haggle over it." Experience had shown Dan that most people, especially scientists, settled for far less than he was prepared to offer them.

"That's . . . very generous of you."

Time to bring him into the boat, Dan told himself. Hunching forward in his creaking leather chair, he said earnestly, "We need you, Zach. The exploration of the solar system needs you. Politics always snarls up the important things. But the exploration of the solar system is too important to let politics get in its way."

"You're entirely right," Freiberg said firmly.

"Okay. I'm glad we had this chance to talk. You'll get the contract form this afternoon. I'll be looking forward to meeting you in the flesh. And your wife."

"Thanks, Dan."

"Thank you, Zach."

The holographic image froze, then faded. Dan swiveled his chair and touched the phone terminal's OFF key. Then he grinned. "A pound of ego for every ounce of brains. And his wife's a social worker! She thinks she's worked with poor people. Wait'll she sees those shacks up on the hills. She'll puke!"

He glanced at the wide curve of windows to the right of his desk. The rain was still cascading down. If there are any shacks left after this deluge, he thought. But he knew that no matter how many were washed away, there would be new ones dotting the hillsides as soon as the sun came out again.

The damned puddle was growing into a miniature lake. And sending arms out toward his desk. Angrily, Dan leaned on the phone's ON pad.

"Where the hell's the maintenance man?" he growled.

"Maintenance reported six minutes ago that a service person is on the way to your office, Mr. Randolph," the phone said.

Dan thought briefly about talking directly to the maintenance supervisor, or his own secretary, or somebody human, anybody, just as long as he or she reacted with normal living emotions. The phone was fast and smart and efficient. But it was absolutely useless as far as emotional satisfaction went. You could not seduce it, or bully it, or even annoy it.

"Anything else, sir?" asked the phone, misinterpreting his silence.

Admitting defeat, Dan said more gently, "Yes. Transmit a standard employment contract to Dr. Zachary Freiberg. His number is on file. Term of contract should be six weeks, with a one-year automatic renewal clause. Copies to legal and personnel."

He thought a moment, then added, "When Freiberg sends the contract back and legal and personnel approve it, notify personnel to contact Dr. Freiberg and initiate procedures to move him and his household here to Caracas."

The phone replied, "Contract transmitted as specified, sir. Legal and personnel notified as specified, sir."

"Good."

"Anything else, sir?"

"No."

"It is three forty-three, Mr. Randolph," the phone reminded. "You are due at Señor Hernandez's reception at five P.M."   .

"Right. Thanks."

Hernandez's reception. To meet the new chief of the Russian space program. That ought to be interesting. It might even be fun.

A meek tapping at the door to the outer office caught his attention. His secretary did not wait for an answer, but opened the door a crack and announced timidly, "The maintenance man is here?" She was a strikingly lovely redhead, a stunning decoration for the office, but she made every sentence into a question, as though begging permission to exist. "To see about the leak?"

Dan nodded. "About time. Send him right in. I was just leaving anyway."

"The Hernandez reception?" the secretary said. "It starts at five?"

"I know. The phone just reminded me."

A potbellied, swarthy Venezuelan in grease-stained green coveralls frowned his way past the secretary. He waddled across the carpeting and went straight to the window, gazed down at the growing puddle, then looked up at the top of the window. He heaved a great wheezing, grunting sigh.

"I'm leaving," Dan said to his secretary. He patted her rump as he went by her, and she smiled compliantly.

"You're going to dress for the party?" she asked.

"Right." Dan glanced at his wristwatch. More than enough time. "Want to help me?"

She shrugged deliciously and wrinkled her nose for him. Without waiting to see if she were following, Dan headed for the private elevator that went down to his apartment, thinking happily of what the Russian's face would look like if he knew that Astro Manufacturing had just taken the first step toward tapping the mineral resources of the asteroids, resources that were thousands of times richer than the ores the Russians could scrape from the powdery surface of the Moon.

The secretary scampered after him and made it into the elevator just before the doors slid shut. She smiled sweetly for Dan. He wished he could remember her name. She had just started working for him a week ago. And she would be gone before long, he knew. Just like all the others.

Chapter
♦ ♦ SIX ♦ ♦

Rafael Miguel de la Torre Hernandez was Venezuela's Minister of Technology, a post of high importance and considerable delicacy. He felt himself in the grip of a powerful vise, constantly being squeezed by the boorish, imperious Russians on one side and, on the other, by the demanding, dangerous American expatriates led by Dan Randolph. But Hernandez recognized that, if he could survive this pressure, if he could successfully play the Yankee capitalists against the Communist bullies, he would one day be elected president of Venezuela.

So he bore the travails of his position with patience and good grace. He was a tall, stately patrician who looked perfectly at ease in a formal dinner jacket and the bemedaled blue sash of his office. His cheekbones were high and his nose as thin and finely arched as any true Castilian's. His hair was silver, although his trim mustache was still handsomely black. Only his eyes betrayed him. They were the color of mud, as flatly brown as a peasant's or Indian's, the eyes of a man whose schemes and calculations never rose further than his own personal ambitions.

He stood tall and haughty at the head of the reception line as Dan stepped from his limousine, safe from the torrential rain under the protection of the Hernandez mansion's marquee. He watched the American sprint up the front steps of the stately old house; no sense of dignity or refinement, the man had nothing in him except brashness and impatience.

As he hurried up the steps, eager to get out of the musty chill of the rainstorm, Dan saw Hernandez at the head of the reception line. Next to him stood Vasily Malik, the new director of the Soviet Union's space program. Malik broke all the stereotypes in Dan's mind about Russians. Instead of being dumpy, dour and déclassé, Malik was inches taller than Dan himself, glowing with robust good cheer, ice-blue eyes sparkling, longish golden hair curling slightly over his ears in the latest Western fashion. His dinner jacket fitted him perfectly and showed that Malik was keeping his broad-shouldered body in good trim. He was reputed to be something of an athlete and a martial arts buff. He was considerably younger than Dan had expected, several years younger than Dan himself. Quite a contrast to the usual Soviet octogenarian. Malik's smile was bright and seemed sincere. He was enjoying himself as he shook hands with the arriving guests.

Hernandez took Dan's hand in his own slightly limp, long-fingered grip. "So glad that you could find the time to join us," he said in English.

"I'm delighted that you invited me," Dan replied honestly.

"Comrade Malik," Hernandez said, turning slightly toward the Russian, "permit me to introduce you to Mr. Daniel Hamilton Randolph, the founder and chief operating officer of the Astro Manufacturing Corporation."

Before Hernandez could start the other half of the introduction, Malik grabbed at Dan's hand. "Ah, the American capitalist!"

"Ah," replied Dan, "the Russian commissar."

Malik laughed heartily. He held a glass of champagne in his left hand, a cigarette between two of his fingers.

"You have made Venezuela the leading space power among

43

the nations of the Third World,'' Malik said without a hint of mockery. His English was perfectly American, no trace of a European accent.

Dan answered, "Señor Hernandez and the people of Venezuela have accomplished that. I've merely helped them where I can.''

Malik feigned shock. "A modest American? Can it be?''

"It's no more rare than a Russian who appreciates the finer things in life," said Dan.

"I can see that you two will get along well," Hernandez said, his face pinched slightly with distaste, "despite your differences.'' It was his way of moving Dan off so that the guests behind him could get through the reception line.

Dan took the hint, gave Malik a slight nod and smile, then went down the line shaking hands with other Venezuelan and Soviet officials. At least the other Russians looked more like what Dan expected: squat, suspicious and ill at ease amid foreigners. Once he had finished the last one in the line, Dan shouldered through the chattering crowd and made his way to the bar.

He downed half a glass of champagne with his first gulp, then began scanning the crowd for people he knew. Hernandez had chosen to hold the reception in his own home rather than the ministry's sterile building, a good choice as far as Dan was concerned. The ministry was one of those modernistic architect's conceptions, all sharp angles and recessed lighting, like a state-built college campus hall. The Hernandez town house, on the other hand, had been built back in those gracious years before air conditioning, when labor was so cheap that individual peons were expendable, and a man could erect a gracious, high-ceilinged, ornately decorated monument to himself over the bodies of starving workers. Chandeliers dripping real crystal, hand-crafted draperies from Belgium, furniture of solid walnut and oak and mahogany. Nothing in this elaborate, crowded, noisy drawing room was less than a century old.

Almost all of Caracas society was here, Dan saw, from

ministers of government to the grande dames of the oldest families. The American ambassador stood gloomily by the tall windows, watching the rain while he knocked back straight rye whiskey. His wife, across the room, recognized Dan and waved at him. He smiled back but decided he was not in the mood for her. After a few drinks she became garrulous and indiscreet; Dan had no desire to participate in one of her scenes.

No one else from Astro Manufacturing had been invited. Aside from the ambassador and a few of his flunkies, Dan was the only American at the reception. He chatted politely with the people clustered around the bar, talking business with the men and fashions with the women. Everyone commented on the rain. Everyone drank Sr. Hernandez's excellent champagne. Off in the library, across the foyer, a quartet of musicians began playing dance music. Dan noticed that Malik, free of the reception line at last, attracted a crowd of admirers, including many of the younger women. He stood surrounded by them. No other Russians within twenty feet. That means either that he's wired with a transmitter, Dan thought, or he's so powerful inside the Kremlin that the KGB isn't allowed to listen in on his casual conversations. As if a Soviet official of his stature has any casual conversations.

The party was a bore. Dan had two options. Either he could make his farewells as graciously as possible and get back to his secretary, who was undoubtedly still luxuriating in his bed, or he could stroll across the room to join the crowd around Malik and start an argument. Dan thought it over for a few moments, came to the conclusion that he was not drunk enough to enjoy an argument with the Russian and made up his mind to make as inconspicuous an exit as possible.

He put his champagne glass down on a marble-topped table and turned to find Hernandez, his host. There he was, holding court next to the mantelpiece, under the big portrait of his sainted wife. The crowd around him was almost as

45

large as the one surrounding Malik, but a good deal older than the Russian's admirers.

Dan started off toward Hernandez, but stopped in his tracks when he saw a lovely young lady standing alone beside a splendid arrangement of tropical flowers. She was small, slight, with the large searching eyes of a waif. But the gown she wore was not the clothing of an urchin: it was a regal creation of gold and royal blue, modest yet splendid, the kind of gown worn by a princess in a fairy tale. And she was as beautiful as a princess should be, with midnight-black hair and full, tempting lips. Her expression was utterly serious, almost grave, as she scanned the room searching for— who? Dan wondered. Her eyes met his, hesitated a moment, then swept past. But in that moment Dan felt sparks flashing through him.

I wonder what she looks like when she smiles? He decided to find out.

He maneuvered past a pair of cigar-wielding old men who were pacing across the room locked deep in earnest debate, oblivious to the others around them. Seeing that the young lady held an empty champagne glass tightly in her two hands, Dan asked in Spanish:

"May I have the honor of getting more champagne for you, señorita?"

She looked surprised that he had spoken to her. "No, thank you very much," she replied.

"You really should move away from these flowers," Dan said.

"What do you mean?"

He gave her his best smile. "It's not fair to them when someone so beautiful puts them in the shade. You make them look very plain and dull."

He expected perhaps a blush. Instead she smiled, and it was even more splendid than he had hoped for.

"You are the *Yanqui*, are you not?" she asked.

"How can you tell?"

"Your accent, of course."

"Ah yes. I learned your beautiful language when I lived in Texas."

"So I can hear."

Dan said, "My name is Daniel Hamilton Randolph."

"Yes, I know."

He started to ask her name, then realized that she would prefer to be formally introduced by a third party. Scanning the crowd quickly, Dan saw the American ambassador's wife staring at them from only a few feet away. Before he could say or do anything, the woman advanced upon them.

"Why, Dan, I haven't seen you for weeks and weeks! Where have you been keeping yourself?"

Millicent Andrews needed only a few drinks to transform herself from a docile diplomat's wife into a raucous, raunchy refugee from the West Texas dustbowl. "Lucita," she asked the young woman, "how're you doing?"

In English, Lucita replied, "I am very happy to see you again, Mrs. Andrews. Are you enjoying the reception?"

"Call me Lissa, honey. All my friends do."

"Thank you. I am pleased that you think of me as one of your friends."

"Why sure! Why not?" She gave Dan a sidelong glance. "How long have you known this filthy rich rascal?"

"We have just met. We have not even been properly introduced."

"Oh!" Lissa seemed to be weaving slightly, even though her feet were not moving from where she stood. "Guess I ought to do the honors, then, huh?"

"Please do," Dan said.

Gesturing with her half-full champagne glass, Lissa said, "Lucita, may I introduce to you Mr. Daniel Randolph. Dan, Señorita Maria de la Luz Hernandez."

Dan felt a slight jolt of surprise. "You're related to the minister?"

"His daughter," Lissa blurted before Lucita could reply.

Lucita extended her hand and Dan took it in his. Feeling a

47

little awkward, he bent slightly and brought her hand to his lips. Her skin felt cool and smooth.

"I am honored," he said in Spanish.

Sticking to English, Lucita replied, "And I am very pleased to meet you, Mr. Randolph."

Lissa leaned toward the girl, spilling some of her champagne in the process, and said in a stage whisper, "Don't let him get you in a corner, honey. He's sneakier than an octopus."

"Mr. Randolph has a reputation for being a lover of women," Lucita said, smiling amusedly at him.

Dan smiled back. "How can a man resist being charmed by women as lovely as the two of you?"

"Ya see?" Lissa crowed. "Didn't I tell you? Smoother'n mayonnaise!"

"Is it true that you are a billionaire, Mr. Randolph?" asked Lucita.

"You better believe it," the ambassador's wife said.

"My accountants tell me that the company's assets are a little under nine billion," Dan said, trying to make it sound modest. "That's not my personal wealth, of course; it's the assets of Astro Manufacturing Corporation."

"But you don't go hungry, do you?" Lissa joked.

With a shake of his head, Dan answered, "Not very often, these days. Lissa, your glass is empty. Can I get you a refill?"

The ambassador's wife looked from her long-stemmed glass to Dan, then glanced at Lucita. A shrewd expression came over her. "I guess I can find the bar for myself. See y'all later."

Dan felt a wave of relief as she sashayed off, leaving him alone with Hernandez's daughter.

"She is a little drunk, I think," said Lucita.

Laughing, Dan replied, "She'll be drunker before the party ends."

"I believe she is not happy here."

"Lissa could be happy anywhere. It's her husband. Andrews is the unhappy one. He's dragging Lissa down with him.''

"How so?'' Lucita asked.

Dan searched across the crowded room, marveling inwardly that he could be alone with this lovely young woman in the midst of such a large crowd. Voices blurred into a general hubbub punctuated here and there by polite laughter, the clink of glasses and the rattle of ice cubes, an occasional roar of real merriment. He could barely hear the dance band; only the rhythmic thump of its Latin beat penetrated the party noise. The drawing room was getting hazy with smoke, despite the high ceiling and the air conditioning. Ambassador Andrews was still standing moodily by the windows, still staring out at the rain while he held a tumbler full of whiskey in his right hand. The rain continued to pour down as if it would never stop.

"All his life,'' Dan answered, "Andrews has wanted to be president of the United States. But he was beaten out of the job by a woman, and it's done a lot of damage to his ego.''

"But your *La Presidenta* appointed him ambassador to Venezuela, did she not? Isn't that a very prestigious position?''

"I think it is. But he doesn't. He sees it as being exiled to some remote wilderness. He doesn't realize that Venezuela is one of the most important countries in the Third World.''

"The poor man,'' Lucita murmured.

Turning from the solitary figure of Andrews to the crowd of admirers still clustered around Malik, Dan shook his head in dismay. "No use feeling sorry for the ambassador. Feel sorry for the nation he represents. His job here in Caracas is to maintain good relations between the United States and Venezuela. But it looks to me as if the Soviet Union is scoring all the points.''

Lucita followed his gaze. "The new chief of the Russian space program, you mean?''

"Your father's guest of honor.''

"Yes. My father wants me to meet him. I was waiting here for my father to introduce him to me.''

49

Dan turned his focus back to her. "Is that why you looked so unhappy?"

Her eyes widened. "Did it show?"

"You looked like a princess who needed to be rescued," he said. "I just didn't know what you needed to be rescued from."

"From a boring party that is merely an excuse for my father to introduce me to a prominent Russian who just happens to be unmarried and young enough to be a prospective husband for his only daughter."

"What? Your father . . ."

"It would not be a bad match, as far as he is concerned. It would bring him much prestige to have a son-in-law who is so high in the Kremlin. It would bring about closer ties between Venezuela and Soviet Russia. It would help him to impress the voters in the next presidential election."

"Presidential election? You mean your father . . ." Dan's mind was suddenly spinning. "I'll be double-damned. I never realized . . ."

"Of course," Lucita went on, "I have to meet the man first. And he has to propose marriage to me and beg my father for his permission."

She was angry, he realized. Beneath that flawlessly beautiful face there was blazing rage. She had not been frightened or worried when he had first seen her; she had been furious.

Dan offered his arm. "Let me take you away from all this. Shall we go outside for a breath of fresh air?"

"In the rain?"

"Surely a house as magnificent as this has a covered veranda somewhere."

A smile lit her face. "As a matter of fact, there are three." She slipped her hand into the crook of his arm and led Dan toward the door to the front hall. Glancing back over his shoulder, Dan saw that both Malik and Hernandez were still enjoying the attentions of their separate groups of admirers. Neither of them noticed Lucita slipping off with the American capitalist.

50

She led him toward the back of the house and out a French window that opened onto a broad covered veranda. The rain still poured down in solid sheets, so heavy that Dan could hardly make out the big trees and carefully tended shrubberies in the garden beyond the veranda's wooden railing. They were alone here, the two of them, as far away from the noise and smoke of the party as if they had moved to another world.

"I love the rain," Lucita said.

"I hate it."

"Don't you think it's beautiful? It makes everything look like a Japanese silk painting."

"Rain's bad for business. Makes it difficult to launch a booster. Tough to land in a storm, too. I prefer clear weather and lots of sunshine."

She looked up at him with laughter in her eyes. "Is that how a man gets to be a billionaire? By thinking of nothing but business?"

"It's not merely business, señorita. It's my life. I would be doing this even if I made nothing at all from it."

"Would you?"

"Of course." He grinned, remembering. "In fact, for many years that's exactly what happened. I worked hard and stayed poor."

"I find that hard to believe."

He felt himself frowning. I don't have to justify myself to this kid! But their conversation had run aground. He looked out at the rain, heard it drumming on the roof over their heads, gurgling through the downspouts, splashing in the swampy puddles that stretched across much of the garden.

Lucita was silent also. Then Dan saw that she was holding her arms clutched across her bosom. She looked chilled. He pulled off his dinner jacket and draped it across her shoulders. It was ridiculously large for her small frame; it went down to her knees.

"You'll be cold," she protested softly.

"Not while I'm near you." He did not take his hands from

51

her shoulders. She did not try to move away. Dan pulled her closer. She lifted her head toward him and he kissed her. For a long, breathless moment she melted into his arms.

But then she edged slightly back from his embrace. "I must rejoin the party. My father will be looking for me."

"To introduce you to the Russian," Dan said.

"Yes, I suppose so."

He got the wild urge to scoop her up in his arms and go dashing through the rain with her, somewhere, anywhere, so that they could be alone and away from everyone else.

But before he could act on the impulse Lucita slipped out of his jacket and offered it back to him. "Thank you. . . ."

"May I see you again?" he asked. "Can you come to dinner with me tomorrow?"

With a small, troubled shake of her head, "I don't think that would be wise."

And she turned and headed back for the party, leaving Dan on the veranda alone.

He got into the jacket again, then stared out at the unending rain for long minutes. She doesn't think that would be wise, does she? She's probably right. Then he laughed and said aloud, "But what the hell does wisdom have to do with it?"

Chapter
◆ ◆ SEVEN ◆ ◆

Feeling somewhat like an ancient Christian martyr marching into the arena to face a lion, Maria de la Luz Hernandez left the puzzled American and walked back into her father's house. As she approached the noise and smoke of the party, however, a tiny smile glimmered on her lips.

Daniel Hamilton Randolph. All the romantic rumors she had heard about the *Yanqui* billionaire had been true. He was a real devil of a man, the kind who could easily sweep a woman off her feet. *Just introduced and already he took me in his arms and kissed me! She marveled at the thrill of it. It had taken all of her willpower to break free. A dangerous man. Her heart pulsed wildly at the thought of him; her lips burned with the memory of his kiss.*

There was no one she could tell about this moment, no one she could turn to for advice. As she had virtually every day for all these years, Lucita wished that her mother were alive to hold her close and counsel her. She shut her eyes and saw it all again: her mother's beautiful face set in a determined frown of concentration as she drove the Mercedes through the worsening rainstorm; the leaves and branches littering the wet, puddled road as the wind howled and tore at the trees, bending them over so far that Lucita was terrified they would reach into the car and seize her; the truck stalled on the muddy curve; their car screeching as it spun over the shoulder of the road and into the rain-filled ditch.

Blackness. Cold and black. Lucita remembered how wet and chilling it felt in the ditch, with water seeping in through the shattered window and crumpled door on her mother's side. It was the cold and wet that revived her as she hung in the straps of a child's safety harness. Her mother lay sprawled across the seat beside her, head tilted back, mouth open, eyes staring sightlessly at the car's roof.

At first Lucita thought that her father was angry with her, as if he blamed his daughter for his wife's death. Gradually she realized that it was grief that made him so distant, so unreachable. And guilt. As she grew older, Lucita learned that her mother had been hurrying to get to their seaside villa in time to greet the guests due to arrive for one of her husband's political dinners. Slowly, gradually, with the unconscious instinct of a child, she won her father back to her, made him realize that she loved him and needed his protection and the assurance that he loved her and did not blame her for the tragedy that had bereaved them both. They grew closer, consoling each other, helping each other to ease the pain without forgetting their loss, to face the future together, happy to have each other.

Lucita was thirteen when she realized that her father was a sexually active male. Suddenly she saw him as an attractive, vigorous man in the prime of his life, and she was terrified of the strange new feelings that surged through her. He must have known, or felt similar feelings of his own, because he suddenly decided to send his only child off to a convent school, far from Caracas. She went willingly, leaving her home, her father and all that was familiar to her for the discipline and austerity of gray stone walls and severe nuns who prayed, spoke and even scolded in whispers.

But her visits home were triumphs of pampering. Her

father, as if to prove that he could love her as a father should, treated her to parties and dinners and dances in her honor. Nothing she asked for was denied her. Lucita lived a schizophrenic life: ascetic discipline among the nuns and a vibrant social whirl with her father.

By the time she left the convent to return home and begin thinking about attending a university, she knew that her father was having affairs with women. She accepted this, telling herself that no matter what Holy Mother Church instructed, a man of her father's virility could not be expected to live as a celibate. Nor did she. Lucita quickly found, once she returned to Caracas, that the young men—and some older ones as well—found her powerfully attractive. She surrendered her virginity to a bold young Brazilian army officer who was serving at his nation's embassy. He returned home a few weeks afterward and she never saw him again, nor cared.

Now her father thought of her as a valuable possession, a piece of property that could be traded off in marriage to his advantage. Where once she had been frightened that she loved her father too much, now she found nothing in her heart for him but contempt. She would meet this Russian, this powerful foreigner whom her father wanted for a son-in-law. Yes, she would meet him and spit in his face.

She returned to the party, sipped champagne and spoke demurely to her father's guests, laughed at their insipid jokes and nodded when she was supposed to. It seemed like hours that she stood there, bored, angry, wishing that they would all go away and leave her in peace. The younger men gathered around her, as they usually did, but she did not enjoy being the center of their attention. She danced with a few of them, but always returned to the drawing room, where the Russian and her father held court in separate corners of the room, both of them paying her no attention whatever.

She thought about the *Yanqui*, Dan Randolph, again. He was a bold rascal, just as Mrs. Andrews had said. Not pretty; not even handsome, really. But the devil twinkled in his eyes. How old is he? Lucita wondered. His light brown hair showed no trace of gray, although an American billionaire would not be above dying his hair or even wearing a toupee if he were balding. But she did not believe Dan Randolph would do so. He did not seem to be vain about his looks. He was younger than her father, of that much she was certain. It will be easy enough to find his biography and read it.

"Lucita, there you are." Her father's strong, deep voice broke her out of her reverie. The men clustering about her melted back as Rafael Hernandez approached. The Russian was at his side.

"Lucita, I have the great honor of introducing Comrade Vasily Malik, chairman of the Council of Outer Space Activities of the Union of Soviet Socialist Republics." Turning slightly, Hernandez continued, "Comrade Malik, my daughter, Maria de la Luz Hernandez."

The Russian had a good face, Lucita had to admit to herself. Broad, strong cheekbones, clear blue eyes, a boyish smile. Hair the golden color of ripening grain. He took Lucita's proffered hand and touched his lips to it.

"I am delighted to meet you, Señorita Hernandez."

Lucita smiled back at him. "It is an honor to meet you, señor."

"I had been told that you are the most beautiful woman in Caracas," said Malik, still holding her hand. "That was an understatement."

Trying to sound unimpressed, Lucita replied, "You flatter me."

"Not at all," he insisted. "Would you care to dance?" Before Lucita could reply, Malik turned to her father. "With your permission?"

"Of course!" Hernandez beamed. "Of course!"

The Russian monopolized her for the rest of the evening. None of the other men dared to interfere. Lucita danced with him and listened to his talk. She noted that he drank sparingly, unlike other Russians she had met, who swilled vodka until they were stupefied and falling down.

To her surprise, his talk was interesting, fascinating.

"You've never been in space? What a shame! You must come to the Soviet Union and take a ride on one of our space shuttles. I can arrange for you to spend a week or more aboard a Soviet space facility. Properly chaperoned, of course." He laughed. "We Russians have a strong sense of propriety; we're downright prudish, in fact—officially."

"And unofficially?" Lucita asked, accepting the bait.

Malik made the corners of his mouth turn down. "I'm afraid there is nothing in the entire Soviet Union that is unofficial. Whatever is not specifically authorized by a law or a regulation is absolutely forbidden."

Despite herself, she found it impossible to dislike this Russian. Until she asked:

"Is it true that your mines on the Moon are run with slave labor?"

For just the tiniest flash of a second Malik's face hardened. He made himself smile almost instantly, but Lucita recognized the steel beneath the velvet.

"They are prisoners, yes. But hardly slaves. They are Soviet citizens who have broken the law, and have been sentenced to work on the Moon. When their sentences have been served out, they are returned to their homes and reinstated in society, just as you allow convicted prisoners to return once they have served their sentences."

"Then they're not exiled to the Moon for the rest of their lives?"

"You've been listening to anti-Soviet propaganda; I understand that there are American capitalists here who spread such slanders."

"I first heard such stories when I was in school," Lucita countered. "In a convent."

Malik's smile looked brittle. "The Church still tries to stir up trouble. No, dear lady, we do not exile people to the Moon for life. And the lunar mines are not a modern version of the old Siberian salt mines—which were another capitalist myth, by the way. The prisoners on the Moon live comfortably and work with highly automated equipment. There is not a pick or a shovel in the whole complex, believe me."

"I am glad to hear it."

The party officially ended at nine o'clock, although most of the guests had already left by then for their dinners. Malik and the other Russians were the last to leave. He kissed her hand again and promised to call on her before the week was out. Lucita smiled graciously and said she would await his call.

Her father walked Malik to his waiting limousine. The rain had finally stopped. He chatted amiably with the Russian for several minutes, then watched as the long black car pulled away from their front door.

Hernandez walked slowly up the steps. A servant shut the heavy oak door behind him.

"Well," he asked his daughter, "what did you think of him?"

"He is very charming," Lucita answered.

Heading for the dining room, Hernandez said, "More than charming, Lucita. Powerful. Important. Very important. He will make an ideal husband for you."

"No, Father," she replied. "He will make an ideal husband for *you*."

He stopped and looked down at her. "Merely because it would be advantageous to me is no reason to reject the prospect of marrying him."

"Father," she asked, "will it be necessary for me to love him? Or is that unimportant to your plans?"

He threw up his hands. "Love! Women always talk of love."

"You expect me to marry him, to sleep with him and bear his children. Shouldn't love be considered?"

"You will love him, in time."

"I will not marry a man I do not love," she said.

He gave a disgusted snort. "But you have loved several men that you have not married."

"What has that to do with it?"

"Everything! I didn't raise my daughter to be a whore!"

It was as if he had slapped her face. Lucita staggered back, feeling her cheeks burn. She had no words; her voice caught in her throat.

"When I think of how your sainted mother must be shamed by your behavior . . ."

"My sainted mother?" Lucita found her voice. "How do you think she would feel about your escapades?"

"My . . ."

"I know about your women! I've known for years! Have I ever reproached you for your behavior?" She felt tears stinging her eyes.

"It is not your place to reproach your father," Hernandez said icily. "In any case, a man's standard of conduct is different from a woman's."

"How convenient," Lucita spat. "How self-serving."

Her father's voice turned iron hard. "I will not put up with your abominable behavior any longer. You will marry this Russian. It is already arranged. You will marry him with dignity and prevent our family's fine name from being dragged in the mud."

"Never!" Lucita shouted, and she ran off toward the hallway stairs that led to her room.

Slamming the door shut, she threw herself on her bed. But she did not cry. There was no time for that. She was thinking, furiously racking her brain for a way to thwart her father's plans for her. For the first time she realized how deadly serious he was. It was not merely marrying her off for his own political advantage; he had learned about her adventures, and was determined to put a stop to them before scandal could threaten him.

He was a powerful man, and it would be almost impossible to get away from him. But I must, Lucita told herself. I must escape; somehow I must get away from Caracas and live my own life. But how? Who would help me? In all of Caracas, who would lift a finger in opposition to my father?

She thought of Dan Randolph. The *Yanqui* had been bold

with her, but he seemed kind as well. He will help me, if I ask him to, Lucita thought.

But a nagging memory tugged at her. The *Yanqui* was rumored to be in love with the American *Presidenta*. The whispers in Caracas were that he had fled to Venezuela because he had been in love with the wife of his best friend. That friend had been President of the United States. He had died in office, and his wife had taken his place, the first woman to become president. Soon, the rumors claimed, she would call Dan Randolph to her side, to rule what was left of the United States with her.

But before she did, Lucita resolved, Dan Randolph would help her to escape from Caracas, from her father's domination and from this powerful Russian who was so temptingly handsome.

Chapter
◆ ◆ EIGHT ◆ ◆

"But it's an *official* request." Pete Weston stressed the word. "You can't ignore it and you can't turn it down."

"Who says I can't?" Dan snapped.

He had been out at the launch center all morning, clambering up the spiderwork towers where the heavy boosters stood, striding through the control stations where intense teams of men and women directed the shuttles that were heading for the space station and those that were returning to Earth. Dan spent at least one day a week out at the center, which had been built on a man-made island in the Caribbean between La Guaira and Catia La Mar, just off the coast where the old commercial airport had been.

Now he stood on the uppermost platform of the original launching pad's tower, the bright hot sun sizzling the steel deck and railings. The tower was used as a meteorological station now; no rocket had taken off from this pad since the new heavy lift boosters had entered the company's service.

Dan had torn through the morning at double his usual hurried pace, driven by a seething inward restlessness that surprised him with its intensity. The little entourage that accompanied him on these inspection tours looked absolutely frazzled. Dan had been rattling off orders and demands faster than they could record them on their tape machines: Tell maintenance to upgrade the electrical service to the flight control center before somebody blows all the circuit breakers with their double-damned coffee brewers. Why can't purchasing find seals that won't leak oil all over my coveralls? Look at them! And I want that ant colony down at the bottom of pad five *exterminated*; this is the last time I'm going to tell you. If I see another red ant chewing on the insulation down there, I'm going to stake out whoever's responsible and let the ants chew on him! Can't anybody build a structure that doesn't leak? We shouldn't be getting rainwater through the roof of the assembly shed, for God's sake. When is MacReedy going to spray these handrails with plastic? For Chrissakes, we can build heat shields for space shuttles, but I still burn my hand every time I touch the railing up here!

Pete Weston squinted through the dazzling morning sunshine at his boss. "Nobody says you can't," he answered, "but I'm telling you that you shouldn't. It wouldn't be smart to turn him down."

Dan felt the sun burning into his neck and shoulders. After yesterday's interminable rain, it felt good. He stood spraddle-legged on the open steel platform, dressed in plain white coveralls and a baseball cap, fists on hips, his face set in a quizzical, puzzled expression. He felt something driving hard inside his guts, but he had yet to figure out what it was. And why.

"You tell that handsome young commissar to go take a flying leap."

Weston sighed deeply. He was a lawyer, a freckle-faced, balding, soft-spoken corporation lawyer who seldom left the air-conditioned quiet of Astro's offices in Caracas to come out to the field. Perspiration beaded his forehead and upper lip; his summer-weight suit was visibly wilting and wrinkling in the humidity and heat, even though the sea breeze wafted his tie over his shoulder now and again. The five others with

Dan, three men and two women, stood off to one side of the high platform, back where the anemometer and other weather instruments hummed away. They were in coveralls and caps, but their boss's furious pace this morning had soaked them with perspiration, too. Dark pools of sweat stained their white uniforms.

"Dan, please. Calm down and listen to me," Weston urged. "You pay me to give you legal advice, at least listen to what I have to say with an open mind."

Dan scowled at him.

"The request came through the Ministry of Technology, from the Russian embassy. As formal and official as can be. The new director of the Soviet space program would like to visit Astro Manufacturing Corporation's launch facilities while he's in Caracas. Would it be convenient for him to come out here this afternoon, after lunch?"

"No!"

"Why not?"

"Because we're busy," Dan snapped. "We don't have time for VIP tours. This isn't Disney World. And besides, that double-damned bastard is only interested in seeing what we've got here; he's on a goddamned snooping mission."

Weston sighed again, then asked patiently, "Boss, don't you think the Russian surveillance satellites take pictures of this facility? Don't you think their people up in their space stations watch what we're doing?"

"That doesn't mean I have to let them onto the grounds!"

"I ought to remind you," Weston added, "that legally, this facility is on property owned by the government of Venezuela. Legally, Astro Manufacturing operates under Venezuelan license and is subject to Venezuelan jurisdiction."

Dan hesitated a moment before replying. Then he said, "You're telling me that the Russians could lean on the Venezuelan government to force us to let them in here."

"That's what I'm telling you."

"Yeah, Hernandez would roll out a fucking red carpet for them," Dan muttered.

"They're going to get in here, one way or the other," Weston said softly.

"That doesn't mean I have to like it."

"You don't have to be anywhere near here," the lawyer said. "You can be back . . . back at . . . Hey . . ."

Weston's knees went rubbery and his eyes rolled up into his head. Dan grabbed him as he collapsed, held him up by his shoulders. The others rushed to them.

"Too much sun," Dan realized. "Get him to the elevator, quick! Bring some water."

They half carried, half dragged the lawyer to the shade of the elevator cab and lowered him gently to the scuffed tile floor. One of the women handed Dan a plastic cup full of tepid water. He held it to Weston's lips. Someone else pressed a paper towel soaked in water across his balding, freckled dome.

"He'll be okay."

"Gonna have a beaut of a sunburn, though."

"He's not used to being outside."

"Better get him a salt pill."

Weston opened his eyes. "Wha . . . How did . . ."

Dan held the water to lips. "Shut up and drink this. For Chrissakes, if you want me to let the Russians in here, you just had to ask me to do it, not pull this dying swan routine on me."

The lawyer sipped at the water, then said weakly, "All in a day's work, boss."

Malik brought his own little entourage with him, of course. Dan watched from the second-story window of the launch facility director's office as three black limousines, each bearing little red Russian flags on their front fenders, rolled up to the visitors' parking area. Dan counted an even dozen men entering the reception building. Malik was easy to spot: not only was he taller and blonder than the others, he was the only one wearing a decent suit, a very modish light mocha-colored outfit of Italian silk. Looks like a goddamned movie star, Dan grumbled to himself. The other Russians looked like extras. Heavies.

Dan personally led the tour, much to Malik's apparent delight. The Russian smiled and laughed his way through the afternoon, charming the women he met as well as the men. Dan smiled back, even told a few jokes along the way. But in his mind he thought he could hear the constant click of miniature cameras and the hum of tape recorders secreted on the bodies of the Russian visitors.

It was hard to dislike Malik, though. The man seemed outgoing, friendly and genuinely impressed with the launching facilities.

"Marvelous, marvelous," he kept saying.

Dan responded, "Your base at Tyuratam is much bigger."

"Yes, but not as modern. These new boosters . . . how many tons did you say they lift?"

They were standing on the floor of the mammoth vertical assembly tower, where the heavy lift boosters were checked out before being trundled out to their launching pads. Two of the boosters, rising as tall and broad as Sequoias, loomed up before them. Far above, a welder was showering sparks; he was so high overhead that the flashes from his torch looked like meteors streaking across the sky.

"Three hundred tons, to low orbit," Dan replied. His voice echoed in the metal-walled building.

"Three hundred tons," Malik repeated. He seemed impressed.

"Is that metric tons?" one of the other Russians asked.

"Metric tons. Right," said Dan. He imagined he heard the whirring of a tape recorder coming from the man's suit jacket.

"And you disassemble these boosters once they reach orbit?" Malik probed.

"Right. We only use these big dumb boosters to lift very heavy loads. Complete machine assemblies, for example. Or a new smelting system. If we tried to put that heavy stuff up with the shuttles, it would take a dozen flights. Old Dumbo here can lift it in one shot.''

Malik grinned at him. ''And then Dumbo is broken apart, after it has done its job.''

Nodding, Dan explained, ''The booster can't fly back to Earth, like a shuttle can. It's not reusable. So we break it up and use the metal as structural material for housing the equipment the booster lifted. We send the rocket engines back on a shuttle; they're too expensive to throw away.''

''Very ingenious,'' Malik said.

''You knew we were doing that,'' said Dan.

''Yes, I have read the reports about it. But still, it is very good to see it with one's own eyes.''

Finally the little group reached the meteorology tower and Dan took them up to the top. ''From here you can see everything,'' he said, his outstretched arm sweeping out the view.

Malik turned slowly in a full circle, squinting against the brutal afternoon sun. The other Russians looked distinctly uncomfortable, even a little fearful. Maybe they'll pass out, like Pete did, Dan hoped. Maybe they'll all get sunstroke and die.

''A tropical paradise,'' Malik said. ''I envy you.''

''It is pretty,'' Dan agreed.

The Caribbean glittered alluringly under a sky of brilliant blue. Stately cumulus clouds towered like the turrets of some giant's castle, row after row, sailing slowly across the afternoon. The sun was a molten glowing eye blazing down at them. Turning to take in the panorama, Dan saw the lush green mountains that stood between the coast and the teeming city of Caracas. They hid the city and the ugly sprawl of squatters' shacks that huddled around it. The old airport lay across the narrow channel from the man-made island where they stood. Its long concrete runways were used only for space shuttle flights now. A massive double-decked shuttle was trundling slowly down to the end of the runway as they watched, the roaring whine of its jet engines no more than a thin keening at this distance. Riding atop the swept-wing lifter was the stubby, fat orbiter with its delta-shaped wings and big rocket nozzles poking out from under its rakish tail fin.

The double-decked craft hesitated at the end of the long runway for a moment, seemed to gather itself, then lumbered down the two-mile-long concrete strip, gathering speed, its engines thundering with undeniable power as it lifted its nose off the runway and then raised itself and its piggyback orbiter off the ground and arrowed up into the blue.

Dan glanced at his watch. "The lifter will be back in half an hour. And there'll be an orbiter landing in about an hour, if you want to go over to the field and watch it come in."

"What will it be carrying?" Malik asked.

Frowning slightly, Dan pecked at the tiny keys on his wristwatch. He held it to his ear so that he could hear the information he had asked for, then repeated:

"Mixed cargo of pharmaceuticals, high-strength alloys and electronics components—mostly gallium arsenide microchips, I suppose."

The Russians glanced uneasily at each other and began to mutter in their own language.

"That's La Guaira over there." Dan pointed toward the port. A tourist cruise ship was in the harbor, its red funnel bearing the hammer and sickle insignia. It was impossible to make out the cable car tramway that led up into the mist-shrouded mountains and then down the other side into Cara cas, but Dan knew it would be packed with Russians and Eastern Europeans today.

Malik was smiling like a video star. "You picked a perfect location for your operation. A perfect location."

Where else could I go, Dan fumed silently, after you forced America to give up space operations? Aloud, he said merely, "It's near the equator. That gives us some advantage from the Earth's spin."

"And the Venezuelan government is very cooperative," the Russian said.

Dan sensed a trap ahead. "This entire operation," he answered slowly, "belongs to the Venezuelan government. To the people of Venezuela, since this country is a democracy. Astro Manufacturing Corporation operates this facility under contract to the government. This is not a privately owned facility." Otherwise, he added silently, you would never have gotten past the front gate without a squad of tanks.

"Yes, of course," Malik agreed easily, still grinning. "But you manage to make a profit from all this, even though it belongs properly to the people of Venezuela."

"I manage to eke out a living," Dan replied, smiling back at him. "And so do the people of this country. This space manufacturing operation accounts for as much of Venezuela's gross national product as her oil exports, and twice as much as her agricultural exports."

"But how much profit do *you* make?" Malik asked, his smile looking slightly sardonic now.

"As much as the government allows."

"And how much is that?"

"Ask Señor Hernandez. He has the figures."

Malik would not be deterred. "Enough to feed the poor people living in those miserable hovels outside the city? Would you say that your profits could help to feed the poor, rather than making a very rich man even richer?"

"This operation makes jobs for thousands. . . ."

"Of engineers and tax accountants."

"And butchers, bakers, telescope makers"—Dan found himself enjoying the challenge of argument—"cooks, babysitters, auto mechanics, salespeople of all kinds, gardeners, truck drivers—you name it. We bring money into this country, and each bolivar that space operations produces gets spent eight or ten times over, within the country's internal economy. That's a considerable multiplier, and it's fed more Venezuelans than all the damned welfare programs the government's ever funded!"

Malik laughed derisively. "And yet there are still many hungry people, while you live in luxury."

Dan started to reply, but held himself in check for a moment. He saw something in Malik's eyes, something crafty and dangerous. The other Russians were watching the two of them; even those who claimed they could not understand English could see the sparks that the two men struck off each other.

"You really want to feed those hungry people?" Dan asked coolly.

"Yes, certainly."

"Then lower the prices you charge us and the other Third World space operations."

That caught Malik by surprise. "Lower the prices for the ores we mine from the Moon?"

"Right," Dan said with a grin. "All the Third World space manufacturers—even the Japanese—have to buy their raw materials from the Soviet Union. You control the lunar mines and you set the prices for the ores."

Malik nodded. The smile was gone from his face, replaced by a skeptical, almost worried expression.

"Lower the prices for our raw materials, and we can lower the prices for the finished manufactured products. That means we'll be able to sell more of our products. Which means we can increase production. Increased production means more jobs. More jobs means fewer hungry people. So if you really want to feed those hungry squatters . . ."

"No, no, no!" Malik waggled a finger in Dan's face. "You would not hire those unskilled men and women to be astronauts or engineers."

"Maybe not. But we'd hire some of them to drive trucks and do maintenance work. Others would get all sorts of jobs in the city, working in restaurants, driving taxicabs, all sorts of things. And we could help to build schools for their children, so that *they* could become astronauts and engineers."

"Capitalist propaganda." Malik smirked.

Dan laughed. "Propaganda or not, friend, that system has

produced more wealth for more people than all the Socialist planning in the world.''

The Russian shook his head.

"Try it!'' Dan urged. "Try it for one year. Just twelve months. Lower the prices you make us pay for the lunar ores, and I guarantee you that those shacks on the hills will start to disappear.''

"No,'' Malik said. "That is not the way to end poverty.''

"Then how do you propose to do it?''

His handsome smile returned. "In the proper Socialist manner, of course. The Soviet Union will increase its voluntary contribution to the International People's Investment Council. That will provide more funds for alleviating hunger in nations such as Venezuela.''

"Increase their dole, eh?'' Dan grumbled. "Make them more dependent on the Soviet Union's largesse.''

"We will feed the hungry,'' Malik said firmly. "Of course, to do this, it is necessary for us to generate more revenues for the Soviet treasury.''

Dan saw it coming, but it was far too late to do anything about it. He felt like a tenpin in a bowling alley, watching the inevitable rolling toward him.

"And to generate such increased revenue,'' Malik was saying, his grin widening, "it will, of course, be necessary to *raise* the prices charged for lunar raw materials.''

"Raise them,'' Dan echoed.

Malik nodded smugly. "You may not like it, but that is the decision that the Council of Ministers reached last week. The prices for all lunar ores will be increased by approximately twenty-five percent, as of the first of next month.''

Dan's first impulse was to take a swing at the Russian. Then he shrugged and laughed. It was all nonsense, a game that they played. The pious pronouncements they made about feeding the hungry and helping the poor was nothing more than a sham; the Russians' *real* goal was to drive the last vestiges of capitalism out of the orbital factories and to monopolize every aspect of space industries. He knew it;

Malik knew it. But still they maintained the pretense. What else was there to do but laugh?

Malik's dour-faced aides glanced uneasily at each other. Here the American capitalist had just been told that his costs for raw materials were going to be increased by twenty-five percent, and he was laughing. Even Malik looked surprised. Laughter was not what he had expected.

Chapter
◆ ◆ NINE ◆ ◆

When he was angry, *really* angry, Dan took a shower. It was a trick he had learned the hard way, back in the years when he had been an astronaut working on the earliest primitive space platforms, where water was so precious that even a sponge bath was something worth fighting over.

He had cut short the tour with Malik as gracefully as he could and turned the Russian group over to one of his assistants, who headed them off toward the airfield. Dan's smile evaporated as he went by helicopter to the roof of his office tower in Caracas and rode down the elevator to his apartment. Stalking past the robot butler before it could finish reading off the messages waiting for his attention, Dan went straight to the bathroom and stepped into the shower stall still fully clothed. The household computer sensed the presence of his body in the shower and turned on the water at precisely the mixture that Dan preferred.

For long minutes Dan stood unmoving and let the steaming hot water bake the knots out of his tensed shoulders and neck. He kicked off his sodden loafers, then slowly stripped off his soaked coveralls and underwear. Alone in the shower he could shout, bellow, curse until he got his equilibrium back. He could pound the marble walls if he wanted to. Instead, he found himself laughing sardonically at the madness of it all. The world and everybody in it was crazy, and he was the craziest one of them all. He nudged the pile of soaked clothing to a corner of the shower stall with a bare toe, then stood luxuriating in the fact that he could have all the hot water he wanted, for as long as he wanted it.

Finally he felt calm enough, in control of himself enough, to step out of the shower and begin toweling himself dry. The water turned off automatically; the heat lamp in the ceiling glowed as long as he stood on the floor plate beneath it.

Freshly shaved and dressed in a pair of light slacks and an open-neck shirt, Dan went to the desk in his study, followed at a respectful distance by the butler robot. It was a squat fireplug of a machine that rolled across the thickly carpeted floor on noiseless trunnions. As a butler it was more of a curiosity than a servant: it could carry a tray of drinks or hors d'oeuvres, it could gather up empty glasses and take them back to the kitchen, but it was useless as a dresser or housecleaner.

"There have been several phone messages, sir," it said in the cultured voice of a distinguished British actor, long deceased. The robot's inner computer was electronically linked, of course, to the phone and the household computer.

"Hold them," Dan commanded, "and get me a glass of sherry."

One good thing about a robot: it never argued, never insisted. "The amontillado, sir?"

"Right. Straight up. Make it a double."

"Yes, sir." The machine trundled off toward the bar.

"Phone!" Dan called.

"Yes, sir?"

"Get me Saito Yamagata, wherever he is."

The phone was silent for the flicker of a second, then said, "Sir, it is six-ten in the morning in Tokyo."

"Sai's an early riser. Get him."

"Yes, sir."

Dan's apartment was the home of a man who could buy anything that struck his wide-ranging fancy. It was filled with electronic gadgetry and so highly automated that he could live in it for weeks without allowing another human being to intrude on his privacy. His office was little more than an alcove off the spacious living room, but he could screen it off at the touch of a button on his desk. The living room itself was built for meetings and parties, dramatically designed with slashing diagonal beams framing the windows and forming intimate alcoves. Small sofas and comfortable chairs dotted the carpeted floor, and a large round polished teak conference table dominated one corner of the huge room. The windows gave a panoramic view of Caracas, and there was a marble fireplace that was utterly useless in the climate-controlled building, but which Dan had insisted on. Another, smaller fireplace was in his bedroom. He slept on a waterbed because it was as close to sleeping in weightlessness as he could find on Earth. The big mirror over the bed was also a television screen. There were cameras behind the mirror, too, in case Dan got the urge to watch an instant replay.

He could have virtually any woman he wanted, and he chose many of them. But they seldom lasted more than a few weeks, at most. The apartment was often filled with visitors, businessmen, friends, people seeking help or interviews or jobs or money or advice or influence. The long marble-topped dining room table was frequently lined with glittering guests, powerful and famous men, beautiful and willing women. Yet Dan actually shared his home with no one. He treasured solitude, although he knew the uses of society. He shared his life with no one, not since he had left the States, not since Morgan Scanwell had died and he had fled from the wife of his best friend because she was too needing, too vulnerable, too strong a temptation.

More and more, lately, Dan ate alone in his sumptuous dining room and kept the apartment empty of other people. He did not even like the presence of human servants; only the

74

unavoidable cleaning crew, and they worked under the strictest of rules never to be present when he was in the apartment. Sometimes, when Dan remained in his rooms for several days on end, the clutter accumulated to the point where it drove him out so that the crew could set things right again. He paraded a succession of exquisite women through his bedroom, but even sex was becoming meaningless to him; he had not bothered with the video camera above the bed for months.

Now, as he sat at his desk and drummed his fingers, impatiently waiting for the phone to connect him with his old Japanese friend, Dan realized that his insistence on privacy was slowly turning him into a recluse. Solitude is one thing, he thought; loneliness is very different. You're going to end up as crackers as Howard Hughes was, if you're not careful.

"Mr. Yamagata, sir," the phone's soft voice announced.

Dan touched the ON pad on the phone keyboard and Saito Yamagata's image appeared before his desk. His round face, usually as jovial as a chubby Buddha's, looked puffy and still half-asleep. Sitting on his heels, he was wrapped in a midnight-blue kimono decorated with white herons, the family symbol. Sai's getting old, Dan thought, remembering when the two of them worked as construction engineers on the first solar power satellite project, back at the turn of the century. Sai had been whipcord lean in those days and as agile as a kung fu master. But the years of easy living had fattened him, softened him.

"Did I wake you?" Dan asked.

Sai's old grin snaked across his jowly face. "Does the sun rise in the east?"

"You used to be up and around before the sun," Dan said.

"And you, old friend, were once a penniless engineer."

They both laughed. Their friendship went back to the days when Dan had to use his fists as well as his wits to gain the grudging respect of the Japanese construction crew. Americans had not been welcome on the solar power satellite project; Dan earned their respect by working harder, taking more chances and fighting better than any of the Japanese.

"Times have changed," Dan said.

"They have and they have not," replied Yamagata. "You always had more than your share of audacity. Calling me before six-thirty in the morning! I'd have the head of any employee of mine who dared to disturb me at this hour!"

"I hope I haven't disturbed anyone else." Dan knew that Sai's wife, the eldest daughter of a very ancient and noble family, slept in her own quarters. And that Sai seldom slept alone.

Yamagata made an elaborate shrug. "That is of no consequence."

"Your son is well?" Dan asked.

"Nobuhiko has risen to the position of foreman in our oldest and biggest factory."

"So? You must be very proud of him." Unconsciously, Dan slipped into his quasi-Japanese mode of speaking, even though the two of them were conversing in English. He could speak Japanese well enough, although Yamagata's English was much better than Dan's Japanese.

"He is a good son. One day he will take my place at the head of Yamagata Industries."

"Not for many years."

Yamagata nodded and shrugged, as if to say. *I will be content, whenever the time comes*. Aloud, he asked Dan, "Your solicitude for my family is gratifying, but is it the only reason for calling me at this early hour?"

Dan started to grin, but the recollection of Malik's smug ultimatum soured him. "I've just had a chat with the new head of the Russian space program."

"Comrade Malik," said Yamagata. "I have not yet had the honor of meeting him."

"He's raising the price of lunar ores—"

"Twenty-five percent. Yes, I know."

"What are you going to do about it?" Dan asked.

Yamagata smiled amiably. "Do? What is there to do? We must pay their price or close down our factories."

"There's got to be something else."

Clasping his hands over his round belly, Yamagata lapsed into silence.

"Now don't go inscrutable on me, Sai," Dan growled. "There's got to be *something* we can do to get around this . . . this . . . highway robbery."

With a slight shake of his head, the Japanese magnate said, "My old friend, there are some trees that not even the typhoon can blow down."

Dan gave him a disbelieving look.

"Accept the inevitable," Yamagata advised. "It is wiser than destroying oneself by trying to fight what cannot be altered."

"That sounds curiously like the ancient advice to a woman facing rape."

"Accept the inevitable," Yamagata repeated.

"Just let them screw me?" Dan snapped. "I'll be double-damned to hell and gone before I let them get away with that!"

Yamagata's round face took on a sorrowful look. "Ah, Dan, my impetuous friend, in all these years that we have known each other, I have failed to teach you the wisdom of the Japanese outlook on the world. You remain hopelessly American."

"I accept the compliment."

With a small wave of one chubby hand, Yamagata suggested, "Accept, instead, an invitation. Come here to visit me."

"To Tokyo?"

"To my country estate, in the mountains near Sapporo. You need a change of scenery, my friend."

Feeling suddenly annoyed, Dan answered, "I'm in the middle of—"

"In the middle of a forest." Yamagata raised his voice

enough to make Dan silent. "You see one large tree, but you overlook the others. You need a change in perspective, a chance to relax, to be away from the cares and pressures of your office. Join me at Sapporo. The trip will be worth your while, I assure you."

Dan leaned back in his chair and studied his old friend's eyes. Yamagata was trying to tell him something that he would not, or could not, put into words. Why not? Dan asked himself. Because he's afraid of being overheard. Phone calls are relayed by communications satellites. They can be tapped easily enough. Especially by the government that operates most of the commsats.

"I've never seen your place in Sapporo," Dan said.

Yamagata's smile returned. "I acquired it only a few years ago, when Nobuhiko became a fanatic for skiing. After living for so many years in Texas and Venezuela, you will enjoy seeing snow once again, I'm sure. Very invigorating."

"I'll come out for the weekend," Dan said.

Yamagata's eyes shifted slightly away from Dan for a moment. "My computer tells me that I am obligated to appear at a family dinner this weekend. My in-laws." He grimaced. "Come tomorrow! Spontaneity can be very rewarding."

"Tomorrow?" Dan echoed.

"Yes! I will tell Nobuhiko to join us. You will enjoy two or three days in the fresh, crisp air of Sapporo, I promise you."

Within his own mind, Dan was trying to translate Yamagata's words into their true meaning. Spontaneity. His estate all the way to hell up in the mountains of Hokkaidō. He wants to talk to me in person, as far away from his office and mine as we can make it. And he wants to meet with me quickly, before anybody can arrange to bug our meeting place.

"I'll leave tonight," Dan said, "and be there in time for lunch."

"Good!" Yamagata beamed happily. "I will make the necessary preparations and meet you at the airport."

His image faded into nothingness, leaving Dan sitting alone at his desk once more. For several moments he remained there, silent, unmoving. The butler robot trundled up to the desk.

"Sir, messages for you are accumulating."

"I'll look them over on the phone screen," Dan said.

"Señorita Hernandez . . ."

"She called?"

"No, sir. She is here. She arrived eighteen minutes ago, while you were showering. She has been waiting in the solarium. . . ."

"Why the hell didn't you tell me?" Dan snapped. He pushed out of the desk chair so quickly that it nearly tipped over and made his way through the big, empty living room toward the solarium. It had originally been a balcony running the length of the apartment, when the tower was first opened. But Dan had it enclosed with glass panels that could be polarized at the turn of a dial to go from complete transparency to a dark smokiness that kept the sun's heat out of the room. The glass was all of the highest optical quality, so that Dan could use the squat little astronomical telescope he had set up at the solarium's far end without opening the panels to let in the insects that hummed through the night air.

An exotic collection of flowering plants lined the solarium's glass wall, except for the area around the telescope. Dan had originally ordered shrubs and small trees from his native Virginia, in the hope that at least this little slice of his living quarters would bear a reminder of home. But the plants could not face the fierce tropical sun, even through the polarized glass. They withered and browned. Dan had them removed, and a botanist from the University of Caracas installed a preciously contrived microcosm of local flora. It was breathtakingly gorgeous. Dan hardly ever noticed it.

Lucita was sitting in one of the cushioned wicker chairs

dotting the solarium's tiled floor, watching the flaming sunset coloring the sky over the mountains southwest of the city.

"Señorita Hernandez," Dan said as the glass doors to the solarium slid shut behind him. Like the airtight bulkhead hatches in a space station, the solarium doors were programmed to close automatically, sealing the air in the solarium from the cooled and dehumidified air of the rest of the apartment.

She got to her feet and extended her hand. "I'm sorry to intrude. . . ."

"Not at all," he said. "The idiot robot shouldn't have stuck you out here in this heat. Come inside."

"No, thank you. I prefer it here. I like to watch the sunset, and the heat does not bother me. I thrive in it."

"You certainly do."

She wore a simple sleeveless frock of butter yellow that made her look fresh and cool and lovely in the tropical air. Her thick dark hair was coiled and pinned up, off her neck. Dan noticed a single stubborn strand curling down just behind her ear, and wondered what she would do if he reached out to tuck it up where it belonged.

But he kept his hands to himself and waited for her to speak. Finally Lucita said, "You must be wondering why I have come here, unannounced."

It was difficult for Dan to remind himself that she was merely a child, especially when he gazed into those wondrous eyes. "Just the fact that you're here is enough for me. I'm delighted."

"You are very gallant."

"And you are very beautiful, Señorita Hernandez."

She smiled prettily. "You must call me Lucita."

"I will. And my friends call me Dan."

Her eyes flashed at that. "What do your enemies call you?"

Laughing, "A young lady should not hear such words."

"Am I intruding?" she asked more seriously. "I realize that you must be very busy."

"No! Not at all." He really was delighted that she had come, he realized. "Can I offer you a drink? Do you have any plans for dinner?"

"Something cold," Lucita said. "I'm afraid I must be home within the hour."

"Hudson!" Dan called to the microphone hidden in the wall. "Champagne, please."

"Not champagne. . . ."

Turning back to her, "Why not? It's well chilled, and quite light."

Lucita wiggled a finger against the tip of her pert little nose. "It makes me giggle."

"Ah. I see. You're much too dignified a lady to be seen giggling in public."

"You're making fun of me."

"You didn't giggle at your father's party yesterday, and you were drinking champagne."

"No, I did not giggle then." Her face grew solemn and Dan cursed himself for breaking the mood they had created.

The glass doors slid open and Dan felt a finger of cold air touch him as the robot butler trundled into the solarium carrying a tray that bore a bottle of champagne in a hammered silver ice bucket and two frosted crystal tulip glasses. Lucita watched in silence as Dan wormed the cork out of the bottle. It popped loudly and bounced off a glass overhead panel. She jumped at the noise.

"Happy New Year," Dan said.

"What?"

"Nothing." He poured the champagne and handed her a glass. "*Salud, bella señorita.*"

"*Gracias, señor.*"

"*De nada.*"

Lucita barely sipped at the champagne.

"May I ask why you came to see me?"

She looked up at him, her large dark eyes giving her waif's face a look of mixed guilt and hope. "I want to leave Caracas, get away from Venezuela entirely. . . ."

81

Dan saw the problem instantly. "But your father won't permit it."

"Exactly."

"You don't like the Russian?"

"He has nothing to do with it," she said.

"Really?"

"I will not have my father barter me off like some prize heifer!" Lucita said angrily.

"And he will not allow you to leave Venezuela."

She turned to look out at the sunset. "You have private planes. You could fly me to Brazil or Europe or even to the United States."

"I'm going to Japan tonight," Dan heard himself say, casually, almost carelessly, as if it didn't matter to him one way or the other. "Would you care to come with me?"

She whirled to face him again. "To Japan? Tonight?"

"It's only a quick business trip, a couple of nights at most."

"Tonight? When?"

He glanced at his wristwatch. "The flight takes a couple of hours. I thought I'd leave around ten tonight; that'll put us in Japan by midafternoon, their time."

"You would take me with you?"

He thought briefly about her father and the difficulties the Minister of Technology could cause. But he said, "Sure, if you want to come."

"I do!"

Dan felt suddenly giddy. "Okay," he said, grinning. "Meet me at the old airport between nine-thirty and nine forty-five. I'll leave word at the gate for the guard to expect you."

"Oh, wonderful!" Lucita seemed as excited as a little child on Christmas Eve. She put her champagne glass down on the edge of the planter by the window and headed past the inert robot, toward the doors. "I must pack a bag and see that my car is ready. I'll tell my father that I'm visiting my Tía Teresa—she can be my duenna for the trip."

"Duenna?"

"My chaperon. I could not go without a chaperon, of course. You will like her. She is a wonderful person."

"I'm sure."

"A phone. I must use your phone. May I . . . ?"

Dan pointed toward the living room. Lucita dashed off, leaving him standing there with his glass of champagne in his hand, feeling rather foolish.

Chapter
♦ ♦ TEN ♦ ♦

Aunt Teresa turned out to be not much older than Lucita herself. Two girls barely out of their teens, Dan thought. Lucita drove a low-slung sports car out onto the runway apron and parked it with a squeal of brakes next to his own limousine. She and her chaperon climbed out, excited as schoolgirls, as one of Dan's technicians took the car keys from Lucita and opened the trunk. At least they've packed sensibly, Dan saw; only four bags between them.

Lucita was wearing a loose-fitting jumpsuit of powder blue, cinched at the waist with a wide silver mesh belt. Her hair was neatly tied back into a girlish ponytail. Her duenna wore a peasant's wide skirt, dark purple decorated with tiny embroidered flowers, and an off-the-shoulder white blouse that accentuated her full bosom. The ground crew men ogled the two of them; even the women of the crew stared openly. Lucita ignored them, but Teresa seemed to notice their attention and enjoy it.

The hypersonic plane was parked at the edge of the apron, its silvered skin glittering under the airport floodlights. It was a smaller version of the passenger liners that crossed the

Pacific in an hour, taking off like a normal airplane, then lighting off its rocket engines to arc high above the ocean in a ballistic trajectory and finally reentering the atmosphere like a space shuttle to land at a commercial airport.

Dan welcomed the two young ladies and personally escorted them to the plane. Teresa could not be more than a year or two older than Lucita, he thought. Some chaperon. She was good-looking, with the typical dark coloring of the Latin woman, an inch or so taller than Lucita and noticeably rounder, the kind of woman who would be on diets all her life. She would have looked very attractive to Dan if she had not been accompanying Lucita.

Stop thinking about it, Dan commanded himself. She's just a kid. A breathtakingly beautiful kid who probably thinks of you the same way she thinks of her father. You're an older adult to her, not a romantic possibility. But another voice in his head countered sardonically, It would be fun to teach her otherwise.

He showed the two girls around the plush interior of his plane while the pilots were checking out the engines and controls. They marveled at the deep leather seats that could swivel in a complete circle, and the pull-out tables and computer terminals and phone consoles built into the bulkhead by each chair.

"How does a man get to be so rich?" Lucita asked. Teresa barely suppressed a giggle.

Dan replied seriously, "None of this belongs to me personally. My own real wealth is comparatively small, I'm afraid."

"Really?" There was a challenge in Lucita's eyes, almost a mockery.

With a slow smile, Dan answered, "Really. I'm barely a millionaire."

She laughed, and he enjoyed it.

"But tell me truly," Lucita insisted, "how did you achieve all this?"

Teresa had already lost interest in this subject, Dan saw.

85

She went up forward to strike up a conversation with the pilots as they checked out their instruments.

Feeling a little awkward, Dan motioned Lucita to a chair and took the one facing it.

"You were not born rich," she said. The teasing tone had left her voice. Her face was earnest now. "I have read about your life. You were an astronaut. . . ."

Nodding, he said, "I went to Japan to work on the first solar power satellite. Even back then, the United States wasn't moving ahead in space as fast as other nations."

"And then you lived on the Moon?"

"Before the Russians took over all the facilities there, yes."

"But how did you become so wealthy?"

Dan was tempted to evade her question, to crack a joke and get off the subject. But instead, he heard himself say, "Two ways: slowly at first, and then very quickly."

She waited for him to explain.

"While I was working in space and on the Moon I earned a very good salary. And bonuses. I invested almost all of it in space industries. By the time I left the Moon to return to Earth, I was able to convince a few bankers to loan me enough money to start Astro Manufacturing Corporation. The first few years were difficult, but once we started delivering zero-gee alloys and pharmaceuticals to markets on Earth, the corporation became very profitable. I sunk most of my earnings back into the corporation, to help it grow."

"I see," Lucita said. "You are a man of vision."

Dan accepted the compliment with a shrug. He did not mention that the man who convinced the bankers in Houston to invest in this unknown astronaut-engineer was Morgan Scanwell, who later became president of the United States. He did not tell her that he moved his corporation to Caracas when Scanwell was forced by the Russians to dismantle all American space activities. He did not tell her that his widow, now the first woman to be president, blamed him for her husband's death. Or that the two of them had been lovers behind his best friend's back.

Instead, Dan pushed all those memories away and politely asked the young Venezuelan girl, "Have you had dinner?"

Lucita said no, so Dan asked the stewardess to fix her and her aunt something from the galley. Teresa came back from the flight deck and Dan gave her the chair he had been sitting in, glad to get away from Lucita's questions and the pain of the past.

"Anything for you, sir?" the stewardess asked, giving Dan her best smile. She was tall and tempting, a drama student who had applied for work at a Los Angeles agency that specialized in hiring temporary help for major corporations.

He shook his head. "I'm just going to try to take a nap," he said.

Dan took a chair farther back near the tail of the plane, buckled his safety belt and leaned back into the soft leather upholstery. Lucita and her aunt sat across from each other, chattering rapidly in Spanish as the plane taxied out to the runway, hesitated a few moments, then hurled itself down the concrete ribbon with a furious roar of sheer power, angling steeply up into the night sky. Dan saw the lights of Caracas flash past, then felt the surge of even more insistent power as the pilot cut in the rocket engines that would thrust the plane high above the sensible atmosphere. He glanced at the girls. They were still gabbling away, oblivious to the plane's speed and angle of climb.

Kids, Dan told himself. Well, at least she's not afraid of flying. He closed his eyes and tried to sleep, while either Lucita or Teresa turned on the plane's entertainment system to the loud, thumping beat of the latest *latino* reggae-rock music. Dan willed himself not to dream, and if he did dream, at least he remembered nothing of it when he awoke.

Four hours later, Dan sat on the straw mats of Saito Yamagata's living room floor, sipping hot Japanese tea and trying to convince himself that it was four o'clock in the afternoon and not three in the morning. The room was virtually bare of furnishings; nothing but an exquisitely lacquered low table bearing the tea service, and a pair of matched silk paintings on the walls to either side. Through the triple-glazed glass shoji screen that formed one side of the room, Dan could see the snow-covered mountains that sparkled in the afternoon sunshine. None of them was as perfect as the divine cone of Fujiyama, but the mountains were very pretty. They reminded Dan of Colorado and years gone by that could never be recaptured.

"It was good of you to come all this way to see me," said Yamagata. He wore a Western-style business suit, perfectly tailored for his burly, short-limbed build. His round, smiling face had lines etched into it that Dan had not seen before, marks of worry.

"I'll never phone you at six A.M. again," Dan said wearily. "Your revenge is too swift."

Yamagata laughed, a hearty belly-shaking bellow that reminded Dan of the old days.

"I got the feeling," Dan said, "that you wanted to talk to me in private."

The Japanese magnate grew serious. "Yes. It was necessary for us to have absolute confidence in the privacy of our discussion. This house is guarded by men whose families have served my family for many generations. We can speak here without fear of being overheard."

"Good."

"You are concerned about the Russians' decision to increase the price of their lunar ores."

"More than that," Dan said. "It's their stranglehold on us that bothers me. By controlling the mines on the Moon they control the raw materials that we use in our orbital factories. They've got their hands at our throat every minute of every day of every year."

Yamagata closed his eyes and nodded.

"Sooner or later they're going to shut us down completely. You know that, don't you?"

His friend said sadly, "They may close down your factories, Daniel, but not mine. You are an American. . . ."

"Expatriate."

"But still an American. They fear you. They hate you."

"So do most Americans," Dan muttered.

"Nevertheless," Yamagata went on, "the Russians would be happy to close down your space operations. Only the fact that you have worked under the flag of Venezuela has stayed their hand—so far."

"They don't want to make the Third World mad at them, I know."

"But they will find a pretext for closing down all the other nations' space stations and all their factories. It is merely a matter of time."

"That includes you," Dan pointed out.

"Perhaps not," said Yamagata. "The Japanese space stations are under the informal protection of the People's Republic of China. Not even the Soviet Union has the courage to displease the Chinese."

"Not yet."

"Not for some time to come. China never relied so heavily on its nuclear missiles that it became powerless once the Russians perfected their space defenses. The Chinese still believe in manpower."

"With their population, why not?"

"A billion and a half, at latest count."

"Christ, they could walk to Moscow and the Russians wouldn't be able to stop them."

Yamagata pursed his lips. "The situation is not that simple, but suffice to say that for the foreseeable future the Russians do not desire to antagonize the Chinese, and China looks favorably upon Japan's space-based industries."

"They're your principal market, aren't they?"

"For products manufactured in orbit, yes, of course. We sell quite a bit to India, too, despite their own space factories. We underprice them!" He laughed again.

"So you're safe."

"For the time being," Yamagata repeated.

"And this Russian price increase?"

"We are attempting to negotiate an exception, although I don't think we will succeed. If not, then we will simply pass the cost on to our customers."

"That's something I can't do," Dan muttered.

"You mean that the government of Venezuela will not allow you to do it."

Dan smiled at his old friend. "Right. I don't own the operation, I just make the decisions and run the show."

"A twenty-five percent increase in your costs would undoubtedly drive your operation into the red."

"And how!"

"Then what do you propose to do?"

"Get around them."

"How?"

Dan turned his gaze from his friend's careworn face to the snowy mountains in the distance, then looked back at Yamagata again. "You know me, Sai. When the going gets tough, the tough get going. . . ."

"To wherever the going is easier," Yamagata finished for him. "Yes, I remember your motto. But where will the going be easier for you?"

"The asteroids."

Yamagata drew in his breath with an audible hiss. "Ahh. I should have guessed."

"For every ounce of raw materials on the Moon, there's tons and tons of the same stuff in the asteroids."

"And heavy metals, as well."

"Damned right! Enough iron in one little asteroid to feed Japan's steel industry for twenty years."

"And there are thousands of such asteroids."

"Millions of 'em!" Dan said. "Sai, some of the smaller ones—just a few hundred meters across—are worth ten billion dollars apiece, easily. Not to mention what the mile-long ones are worth."

"An expedition to the asteroids will be very costly, though,"

Yamagata mused. "And time-consuming. They lie beyond the orbit of Mars, don't they?"

"Most of them," Dan agreed. "But a few of them come closer. A lot closer. Some of them even cross Earth's orbit."

"So? You propose to reach one of these closer rocks?"

"Yes. Reach it and bring it back to *Nueva Venezuela* for processing."

"A daring plan. I had expected nothing less from you, my old friend."

Dan accepted it as a compliment. He took a sip of the hot, clear tea, then put the fragile cup back on the tray before him. His thighs were beginning to ache slightly; he had not sat cross-legged like this for so long in many years.

He took a deep breath, almost letting the air hiss between his teeth in the Japanese way of showing respect. "You probably know what I'm going to ask for next, Sai."

Yamagata gave a grunting, chuckling laugh. "Money, what else?"

"I need your help."

"Yes. Even to capture a nearby asteroid will require a considerable investment."

"I thought perhaps Yamagata Industries and Astro Manufacturing could go half and half. . . ."

"Yamagata Industries can do nothing," the Japanese said. But before Dan could object, he smiled and raised a placating hand. "There are certain delicacies to be observed, you see."

Dan raised his eyebrows.

"I too am faced with a government that is reluctant to incur the anger of the Soviet Union. Even with Chinese protection, the government of Japan moves very cautiously in such matters."

"The goddamned Russians have got everybody bullied," Dan grumbled.

"But there are certain affiliates of Yamagata Industries which operate in Okinawa and the Philippine Islands," Yamagata explained. "They, in turn, have associates in Europe. You would have no objection if your funding comes from a Swiss bank, would you?''

Grinning, Dan replied, ''None whatsoever. Not even the Russians have been able to buffalo the gnomes of Zurich.''

''Good. We can discuss the exact terms and other details later.''

''I'm heading back to Caracas tomorrow, Sai.''

''Yes, I thought you would be. I must attend a director's meeting tomorrow, in Osaka.''

''So we'll have to talk out the details before we both head our separate ways.''

Yamagata nodded. ''After dinner, then. For the present I want you to meet my son.''

''Nobuhiko? I thought he'd be out skiing.''

''He is here.'' Yamagata clapped his hands once. ''We have been quite alone, Daniel. The sound activates the house's intercom system.'' In a louder voice, he called his son's name.

Dan reached for his teacup again. It was blood red, with a tiny white heron painted in flight. Before he could put the cup down, the light paper shoji screen to his right slid back and a tall, slim, smiling Japanese youth in his early twenties stepped into the room. For an instant Dan blinked in surprise. The young man's face was exactly how Saito had looked years ago, when Dan had first met him, up at the construction site of the first solar power satellite project.

Nobuhiko Yamagata made a deep bow. Dan scrambled to his feet, grateful to stretch his legs after sitting on the floor so long.

''Nobo . . . you're a grown man!''

Nobuhiko grinned and bowed again. ''Mr. Hamilton, it is such a pleasure to see you once again.''

The young man wore skintight ski pants and a windbreaker, both bright blue with white stripes running down the sleeves and legs. His face was youthfully lean, but still the round, flat-nosed shape of his father's. His cheeks were

92

reddened by a morning spent out in the cold and wind of the ski slopes.

Nobo sat on his father's left, facing Dan, with his back to the view of the mountains. The robot servant rolled in with a fresh pot of tea and a cup for the young man. Yamagata did the pouring in silence, with great care.

After they had each sipped the scaldingly hot tea, Yamagata said, "Nobo has been working for the past year as a deep-space pilot. But there is little for him to do at Yamagata Station."

"I've flown our orbital ferries," Nobo said. His voice was a clear, pleasant tenor, full of energy and eagerness.

"But the Russians won't let you handle any of the lunar craft, will they?"

"No, they won't allow anyone to pilot a spacecraft between geosynchronous orbit and the Moon. They handle all those missions themselves."

"I thought," his father said slowly, "that perhaps you might find useful employment for Nobo at *Nueva Venezuela*."

Dan glanced at his friend. The old fox is making his son part of our deal, he realized. Is he doing it to keep an eye on me, or does he just want to get a rambunctious son out of his hair for a while? Probably some of both, he decided.

Aloud, he asked Nobuhiko, "Are you qualified to pilot a shuttle?"

Nobo's nod turned into a small bow. "*Hai!*" In his excitement, he lapsed into Japanese to tell Dan of his various professional pilot's ratings.

"Excellent," Dan replied in Japanese. Turning to Saito, he said, "I am certain that we can find interesting work for your worthy son at Astro Manufacturing. Perhaps there will even be an opportunity for him to pilot a deep-space vehicle even farther than the Moon, one day."

Nobuhiko hissed with pleasure and gratitude. His father merely smiled and said, "We should prepare for dinner now."

Chapter
◆ ◆ ELEVEN ◆ ◆

Lucita looked doubtfully at the little wooden tray placed on the table before her. It held half a dozen small pieces of what looked suspiciously like raw fish. She glanced at Teresa and saw that she was hesitating, also.

No one had warned her about the rigors of a Japanese dinner. Both she and Teresa had dressed in their usual informal evening wear. Lucita wore a simple but elegant full-skirted chiffon dress of soft lavender with beautifully embroidered sleeves. Teresa had wanted to wear something equally eye-catching, but Lucita had insisted that her chaperon should not compete against her for attention. So Teresa wore a plain white outfit with a pleated skirt and high mandarin collar, and a gold rope belt that twined around her waist twice. It was attractive enough, Lucita thought.

But she had not expected to sit on the floor! Dan had not warned her. In fact, he had paid her no attention whatsoever since they had taken off from Caracas. Lucita and Teresa had found themselves in the care of Japanese house servants, about evenly divided between squat bulky robots and equally short roundish women who wore sky-blue kimonos and spent most of their time bowing and hissing.

Teresa was Lucita's aunt by virtue of being the youngest daughter in a family of thirteen children. Lucita's father had been the oldest son. Grandmother Hernandez had dutifully borne her husband this baker's dozen of offspring, and died while pregnant with a fourteenth. The fetus died with her. Everyone in the family had thought it quite an unlucky omen to die after thirteen children.

Lucita's mother had not made that mistake. She had been a modern woman, the daughter of one of the new oil millionaires who had made his fortune when the once mighty OPEC had raised the world price for petroleum. Mama had been educated in the United States, where she learned of feminism and equal rights for women before returning to Caracas to be married off to the rising young politician, Rafael Hernandez. She had borne one child and then killed herself in an automobile accident. But not before she had instilled in her five-year-old daughter a fierce thirst for independence and freedom from the strictures of Latin American family politics. Hernandez had genuinely loved his headstrong wife, even though she had failed to bear him a son. He loved Lucita, too, and she knew it. But it was the love of an owner for a possession, and Lucita knew that her father was perfectly capable of using his possession to further his own ambition.

Lucita had declared her independence by fleeing Caracas in the company of the dashing American billionaire. What better way to show her father that she would not be cowed by him, or allow him to sacrifice her life on the altar of his political ambition? But she had been careful to bring Teresa along; no one could say that she had failed to observe the proprieties. She was independent but not a wanton. Teresa, like Hernandez's many other sisters and brothers, had not shared in the wealth he had acquired through his marriage. They lived modestly, either jealous of their brother's good fortune or subservient to it, as their individual natures dictated. Teresa, the youngest, was of the subservient kind. She made a good chaperon: compliant and discreet. This was not the first time the two of them had gone off adventuring.

There were no utensils on the low table except chopsticks. One of the woman servants showed Lucita and Teresa how to hold them. It was less difficult than Lucita had thought it would be. Somehow she choked down a few morsels of the raw fish. She felt better as the meal progressed to more palatable dishes of sliced steak, steamed vegetables and rice. She was surprised that the sake poured into their tiny cups was warm; at home wine was almost always served chilled.

Dan Hamilton and his host were joined at the table by a younger Japanese, introduced as their host's son. She had expected the natives to wear splendid oriental robes, but they were both dressed in ordinary business suits, just as Dan was. None of the men paid much attention to Lucita or Teresa. They talked among themselves, ignoring the women. Somewhere in the back of her mind Lucita recalled reading that Japanese men usually ate by themselves, served by their women, who ate afterward. She seethed with sullen anger at the thought.

Kimono-clad women served the table, and kept the sake cups full. Lucita saw that the father and son, and even Dan, slurped the rice wine noisily. She thought that disgusting and made it a point to sip hers with great dignity.

It was a great surprise to her when, after the meal was concluded, she needed help to get back onto her feet.

"My legs . . ."

Nobuhiko was at her side almost instantly, while two of the women servants assisted Teresa.

Dan grinned apishly at her. "Too much sake," he said, the first words he had aimed her way since the dinner had begun. "It melts the bones."

"Perhaps," said the elder Japanese, "the lady is not accustomed to our way of sitting. I apologize, señorita. It was thoughtless of me to force you to endure such discomfort."

It took an effort of will for Lucita to realize that they were speaking in English. "I'm all right," she said slowly. "My legs seem to have fallen asleep."

"I'll help you," said the younger Japanese. He held Lucita's arm and placed his other hand at her waist.

She began to protest, but noticed that Dan had already turned his attention back to their host.

"Oh, thank you," she said to the young man. "If you could show me to my room . . ."

"Of course," he said.

Dan watched Nobuhiko assisting Lucita out of the dining room, followed by Teresa—who was walking without aid, although one of the women servants followed her at a respectful few paces.

"She is very beautiful," Yamagata said, raising his cup for more sake to be poured into it.

"A child," replied Dan.

"Nobo seems quite taken with her. He seldom reacts so gallantly with women his own age."

His own age echoed in Dan's head. Tearing his gaze away from the now closed screen where Lucita had departed, he saw that his own cup had been refilled again. He drained it with one swift gulp. The servant, blank-faced as always, poured still more wine for him.

"Now that I have you properly dazed with food and wine," Yamagata said with a good-natured grin, "we should discuss the terms of our agreement."

Dan looked back at the translucent screen and realized that Nobo was one of those terms. The kid would come to Caracas for an indefinite stay. Now that he'd met Lucita he would probably come to Caracas even if he had to swim the entire distance.

"The terms?" Yamagata repeated gently.

Dan snapped his attention to his old friend. "Yes, the terms," he muttered. He had never felt less like discussing business in his life.

Yamagata produced a miniature tape recorder from his suit jacket and placed it on the lacquered table as the women

cleared away the dishes. Once they had left, he and Dan
swiftly worked out the financial arrangements for the asteroid
mission. Dan could keep no more than half his mind focused
on their negotiation. He kept wondering what Lucita and
Nobo were doing. She's got her aunt with her, he told
himself. She'll be okay. She's chaperoned. She'll be all
right.

Yamagata clicked the tape recorder off, then got to his
feet. "I will have my computer make hard copies of this
agreement for our signatures."

"Sure," Dan said absently. "Of course." He slowly got
up and followed Yamagata as the Japanese slid back one of
the shoji screens and led him down a narrow corridor. Their
getas flapped softly on the bare polished wood floor. Yamagata
pushed another screen back, and they stepped into a modern
office, furnished in Western style with a richly carved teak
desk and comfortable cushioned chairs.

One entire wall of Yamagata's office was made of *garasu-
shoji,* sliding screens fitted with glass panels rather than
opaque paper. Dan saw that the ski slopes off in the distance
were ablaze with lights. The sky was dark and featureless; no
moon in sight, not even the steady bright gleam of a space
station visible. Too far north, Dan thought. Still . . .

"If I recall correctly," Yamagata said, "you prefer
Armagnac to cognac."

"That's right," Dan said, making himself smile.

Yamagata bobbed his head once in a nod that was almost a
bow. It made his fleshy face produce several chins, and Dan
realized anew that his old friend had allowed his body to get
sadly out of shape. With a surprised pang of regret, he
recalled how the wiry young Yamagata could scamper among
the spiderwork beams and cables of the first solar power
station back in the days when they were constructing it.

> *So we'll go no more a-roving*
> *So late into the night,*
> *Though the heart be still as loving,*
> *And the moon be still as bright.*

"This Hernandez woman," Yamagata said, handing Dan a snifter with a splash of dark amber liqueur swirling in it. "Whatever possessed you to bring her with you?"

"She wanted to get away from Caracas," Dan said lightly.

"Are there no commercial flights? Or private planes to charter?" Yamagata went to his desk as he spoke, put down his own tumbler of unblended Scotch and inserted their tape cassette into the computer terminal sitting on an L-extension of the desk. He flicked his fingers over the keyboard for a moment, and the computer hummed and buzzed in response.

"Her father would have prevented her from using the regular flights or a charter."

Yamagata's eyes narrowed. "Then she *is* the Technology Minister's daughter. Is it wise to antagonize a man who is so crucial to your operations?"

The computer printer sprang to life, chugging frenetically as it typed out the taped agreement at an inhumanly mad pace.

Dan sipped at his Armagnac before replying, "Hernandez wants his daughter to marry the new head of the Russian space program. She wants no part of it."

"So she fled to your arms for protection." Yamagata smiled crookedly.

"No, it isn't like that," Dan said. "She's just a kid."

"You have no romantic interest in her?"

"No, I'm just a convenient source of transportation for her. I'm old enough to be her . . . well, her older brother, I guess."

"I think you must return her to her father," Yamagata said.

"She'll go back when she's ready to. She's just a child who's having an argument with her father."

Yamagata studied Dan's face for a long moment. "I have never known you to place yourself in the middle of a family argument."

With a relaxed grin, Dan explained, "The Russian's involved, too. Don't forget him. He's altogether too self-confident. This ought to take a little of the wind out of his sails."

The Japanese industrialist shook his head. "Ah, Daniel, my old friend, the years have not changed you in the slightest. You are still as impetuous and foolhardy as ever."

Dan felt his brows knit into a frown. "I haven't done so badly," he said.

"It is we Japanese who are supposed to be rushing toward death, yet that is what you have been doing all your life."

"You get philosophical when you're drunk, you know that, Sai?"

Raising a stubby finger, Yamagata insisted, "I remember the chances you would take on the construction in orbit. And on the Moon. Now you are willing to attack the Russians—and antagonize your friends in Caracas at the same time."

"I don't have any friends in Caracas," Dan muttered. "Just politicians who're getting rich off what I'm doing."

"You are a man who is seeking his true destiny," Yamagata said. "I hope you find it before the quest kills you."

Dan gave him a long look, then broke into a grin. "Getting there is half the fun, Sai."

The printer stopped, beeped once, then fell silent. Yamagata put his drink down and lifted the sheets of paper from the printer's tray. He held them at arm's length, squinting in the light from the desk lamp as he read them over. Dan saw that they were in English. Later they would be automatically translated, he knew, into Japanese. And eventually into Russian.

"I believe this states our agreement accurately." He handed the papers to Dan, who read them swiftly and nodded. He saw that the computer had printed two copies. Pulling the pen from his jacket pocket, Dan rested the papers on the desktop and signed them. Yamagata took a felt-tip pen from his desk and signed his name both in roman script and Japanese *hiragana* characters.

"Dan," said Yamagata as he handed over one set of the signed papers, "you cannot afford to antagonize the Minister of Technology. How far do you think this asteroid mission will go if Hernandez decides to oppose you?''

Dan scowled, unable to think of a quick response.

"And placing yourself between this girl and Comrade Malik is like putting yourself between the jaws of a tiger. If you want the woman for yourself, that is one thing. I can understand the foolishness of romantic ardor. But if you are doing this merely to spite the Russian . . .'' Yamagata shook his head like a worried father.

And Dan realized that he *was* a worried father. Even though everything that Yamagata said was true and made sense, there was a deeper motive behind his words. He's trying to make sure that Nobo has a clear path, Dan realized. He wants to keep me out of the way so that his son can get close to Lucita without causing a conflict with me.

"You're right, Sai," he said aloud. "She'll be nothing but trouble for me. I'll bring her back with me tomorrow.''

Yamagata smiled and clapped Dan on the shoulder. "There are better ways to spite the Russians than to get involved in a romantic triangle,'' he said. "We must not allow a woman to get in the way of our new project!''

Dan nodded, thinking, Especially when your son's practically drooling over the woman. But he smiled back at his old friend and raised his glass.

"To the asteroids,'' he toasted.

Yamagata clinked his glass against Dan's and they drank. Then he proposed, "Ten thousand years of good fortune!'' They drank again. By the time their glasses were drained, they had toasted the Emperor, Robert Goddard and Sir Isaac Newton.

Yamagata personally escorted Dan to his sleeping room, which contained a Western-style bed rather than Japanese mats and headrests. He handed Dan a palm-sized control box. "You can summon a robot servant with the green button, or a human servant with the yellow one. The human will be a very attractive young woman who will be happy to satisfy your every desire.''

101

Dan had expected nothing less, knowing what Japanese hospitality was like. But he said, "Sai, all I want right now is to get some sleep. My internal clock feels like it's running backwards. And the sake and brandy didn't help much, either."

"I understand. Still, if you want anything . . ."

Looking down at the tiny control unit, Dan repeated, "Green for robot, yellow for woman. Wait, what about all these other buttons?"

"Oh, those? For TV, naturally." Yamagata pointed to a large armoire. "Seventy-centimeter screen. One hundred fifteen channels. My rooftop antenna picks up eleven satellites."

Dan laughed. "Great. But what I need is some sleep."

"Have a good night, then. I will arise very early. I must be in Osaka by eight-thirty."

"Then I won't see you tomorrow morning."

"I am afraid not."

Dan put his hand out. "Thanks, Sai. For everything."

Yamagata took Dan's proffered hand in both of his own. "It was good to see you again, Daniel. Very good. We will twist the bear's tail, won't we? The asteroids! Yes, we will twist the bear's tail for certain. And make a lot of profit, too!" He laughed his way down the corridor.

Dan closed the bedroom door wearily, thinking that since bears don't have tails it's damned difficult to twist them.

He was drifting in that shadowy half-world between consciousness and sleep when he thought he heard a tap at his door. Dan turned over and told himself he had imagined it. Yamagata, always the perfect host, had outfitted this room with a king-sized waterbed, knowing Dan's preference. Dan felt the warm softness enveloping him. . . .

And that damned tap-tap at his door again.

Muttering to himself, he sat up and touched the lamp on the bedtable once. It glowed softly.

"Who is it?" he called.

The door swung open and Lucita stepped into his bedroom. Her robe was buttoned from chin to hem, her feet demurely slippered. But her long black hair hung free about her shoulders. She seemed wide awake.

"Were you asleep?" she asked, almost whispering.

"Just about."

She stepped into the room and closed the door behind her. Feeling slightly ridiculous, Dan pulled the bedsheet up to his chest.

"Are you angry with me?" she asked, walking across the bare floor to stand beside his bed.

"No," he said automatically, realizing that it was not entirely the truth.

"You did not speak to me at all, during dinner."

"I was discussing business."

"I thought you were upset with me. Perhaps I said something that upset you."

"No. Nothing."

"I see." Lucita sat silently for a moment. Then she said, "It is merely your custom to ignore a woman when there is business to be discussed."

He was surprised at the sudden sharpness of her tone. "It is my custom," he said with a smile, "to conduct business and allow children to find their own entertainments."

"I'm not a piece of luggage that you can take off your airplane and put in a closet!"

"What's that supposed to mean?"

"I'm not in the habit of being ignored," Lucita said. "Your behavior toward me was very rude."

"You seemed to get all the attention you wanted," he said.

"Teresa and I sat through that wretched dinner while you *ignored* me!"

"So you got Nobo to take you to your room."

Her eyes flashed. "He, at least, has some sense of propriety. He knows how to be kind to a woman."

"Propriety?" Dan almost laughed. "You hitchhike halfway around the world with a man you just met a day earlier, and then march into his bedroom to complain that he didn't pay enough attention to you during dinner. Some propriety!"

"You're impossible," Lucita snapped.

"No, I'm bare-assed naked under this sheet. And if you don't march yourself the hell out of here, I'm going to get up and drag you back into this bed with me. Will that be enough attention for you?"

She stood her ground. "You wouldn't dare! My father . . ."

"Your father probably thinks I've kidnapped you. I'm going to have a tough enough time with him. I'm bringing you back with me tomorrow."

"Never! I won't go!"

"You'll go whether you like it or not," Dan said.

"You can't force me."

"The hell I can't."

"I'll tell my father that you raped me."

"Okay. Fine. Do that," Dan snarled. "I might as well be hanged for a goat as a sheep."

He swept the sheet off his body and swung his legs over the edge of the bed. He expected her to turn and flee for the door. But instead Lucita stood there before him, unflinching, unmoving, her jet-black eyes fixed upon him. He stood up, looming over her tiny frame. She did not run. There was no fear in her eyes.

Wordlessly he reached for the collar of her robe and opened the clasp, then began to undo the buttons, one after another. She stood mutely, unresisting. She wore nothing beneath the robe. He slid it off her slim shoulders and let it drop to the floor. Lifting her slender body in his arms, he carried her to the bed and gently put her down on its softly undulating surface.

"We're both crazy," he said, his voice a husky whisper.

"Yes," she said. "Completely insane." But she laced her fingers into his hair as he slid his body over hers and kissed her with all the longing that a man can have for a woman.

Chapter
♦ ♦ TWELVE ♦ ♦

In the morning she was gone.

Dan awoke slowly, lingering for a long while in that half-dreaming twilight world between sleep and full wakefulness. When he realized that he was alone in the bed, though, he sat up abruptly, sending waves spreading through the waterbed.

Lucita and her duenna aunt had left the house just after dawn, Nobuhiko told him over a Western-style breakfast of eggs, fruit and coffee.

"My father had already departed for Osaka," he told Dan from across the breakfast table, "so I had one of the chauffeurs drive them to the airport and see that they got the accommodations they desired."

"Where did they want to go?" Dan asked.

Nobo took a long sip of black unsugared coffee before answering, "It would not have been polite of me to ask. But I believe they intended to go to Rome. That is what I gathered from what they said."

Rome. Easy enough to check it out, Dan thought. He laughed inwardly. Left without so much as a good-bye kiss.

Not even a note. At least there's no entanglement. No tears, no scenes. Wham, bam, thank you, sir. Except she didn't even say thank you. Nobuhiko looked much more upset about her abrupt departure than Dan felt.

"Well, Nobo, that's women for you. Unpredictable."

The young man nodded, sighing. He could not hide his emotions any more than his father could. Saito was the least inscrutable Oriental that Dan had ever known.

"Are you ready to come to work in Caracas?" Dan asked.

Brightening, Nobo bobbed his head eagerly. "I am prepared to leave whenever you wish."

"Might as well come back on the plane with me."

"*Hai!*" said Nobo.

Rafael Hernandez was furious, of course. Dan had expected it, and was hardly surprised when his redheaded secretary told him in her apologetic singsong way that the Minister of Technology had been on the phone constantly for the past day and a half.

"He wants you to come to his office?" she said, standing before Dan's desk with her electronic memo pad clutched tightly in both hands. "He said he expects you there as soon as you return?"

Dan looked up at her. "Honey, I don't go to other people's offices. Especially if they're going to try to put me on the carpet. They come to me. You tell Señor Hernandez that I'm back from my business trip—and be sure to say *business* trip. Tell him that I will be happy to see him here, in my office. At his convenience. Tell him that I've instructed you to change my schedule to accommodate him. Whenever he wants to come over here, I will be happy to see him."

The redhead got it all down on the memo pad, which recorded voices and transcribed them automatically onto computer tape.

"What's he so all-fired worked up about?" she asked.

Dan grinned at her. "His daughter. She hitched a ride to Japan with me."

The secretary's mouth pursed into a round little "Ohh."

"The Latin father, upholding the honor of his family," Dan said. "You'd better have security check him out for weapons when he gets here."

"D'you mean that?"

"You bet I do! But have them do it discreetly. Use the remote sensors. I don't want them patting him down; he must be pissed off enough as it is."

"He certainly was angry," she said.

Dan felt impressed. It was the first time he had ever heard the redhead speak a declarative sentence.

He had spent the two hours in flight from Sapporo getting Nobo squared away with living quarters, employment forms and briefings on his new duties as an employee of Astro Manufacturing. All done by computer linked to Astro's office systems in Caracas. By the time they landed in Venezuela it was evening, and Dan spent most of the night at the desk in his apartment, catching up on the work that had accumulated while he had been away. A dozen separate messages from Hernandez were waiting for him, amid all the other things. Zachary Freiberg had sent back his employment contract, signed, with a salary figure written in that was about fifteen percent less than Dan would have been willing to offer him. And an official notification, on paper embossed with the red hammer and sickle of the USSR, that prices for lunar ores would be increased across the board by twenty-five percent, starting the first of the month.

By one A.M. Dan was ready for a few hours' sleep. He entered his office that morning slightly before nine. The redheaded secretary was already at her station, reaching for her memo pad as he breezed past her and entered his own office.

After she left, and Dan gulped down his first cup of coffee from the gleaming stainless-steel automatic brewer on the side table in the corner behind his desk, he instructed the phone to set up a conference with the chiefs of his engineering, research, cost accounting and security departments.

"And add Nobuhiko Yamagata to the conference," he said. "He's a new hire."

"Understood," said the phone. "Is this to be a telephone conference call or a personal meeting?"

"Personal meeting," Dan replied instantly. "Top priority and top security." He had no intention of risking a leak to the Soviets about his plans for an asteroid mission.

His secretary's pretty face appeared on the phone screen. "Mr. Hernandez will be here in fifteen minutes?"

"Fine," Dan said. "Show him right in when he arrives and then hold all calls. I don't want us to be disturbed." With a slight chuckle, he added, "Unless you hear a gunshot."

Her eyes widened. She did not laugh.

"And one other thing," Dan added. "Get Ambassador Andrews and set up a private meeting for me, preferably this evening at his home. Informal. I don't want to be seen at his office or have him seen coming here. Got it?"

"Yes, sir."

Hernandez was half an inch short of being livid with rage. His eyes blazed, his nostrils flared, his mustache bristled. Even his stiff-backed posture and abrupt, angry pace radiated fury as he crossed the carpeted floor of Dan's office and took the chair in front of his desk.

"Could I get you some coffee, sir?" the secretary asked.

"No. Nothing. Thank you."

Dan waved her away. She closed the door softly behind her as Hernandez sat silently, ramrod-straight, glaring at Dan.

"She's gone to Rome with her aunt," Dan said, without preliminaries. "She was properly chaperoned. She and her duenna were the guests of Saito Yamagata, the head of Yamagata Industries and one of the oldest and most respected families in Japan, at his home in the mountains of Hokkaidō, roughly eight hundred kilometers north of Tokyo. She was not on the Ginza visiting nightclubs."

Hernandez blinked, took a deep breath, but before he could speak, Dan added:

"Yamagata's son came back with me to start employment here with Astro Manufacturing. He was at dinner with his father and me, and your daughter and her duenna two nights ago. You can ask him about it, if you like."

"You have made a fool of me," Hernandez said in an angry whisper.

"I had no intention of doing that. Your daughter came to me and asked for a ride. . . ."

"You knew that I did not want her to leave Caracas!"

Dan put on a careless grin. "All I knew was that a lovely young child asked me for a favor. Your own daughter. How could I refuse? I didn't ask her why. I'm not interested in your family disagreements."

"You did not have to ask her. You knew!"

Dan shrugged.

"You slept with her, didn't you?"

The smile faded. "A gentleman does not discuss such matters, not even with the lady's father."

"You did! Don't deny it!"

"Are you afraid that the Russian won't accept her?" Dan asked. "From the information I've heard, that won't matter to him. He's quite a liberal fellow, for a Russian."

Hernandez's eyes narrowed. "It is a mistake, Señor Hamilton, to make an enemy of me."

"I certainly agree," Dan said smoothly. "I don't want to be your enemy. I'm not your enemy. Your daughter is a very headstrong, willful young lady. If I had refused her request, who knows what she might have done? It would have been easy enough for her to take her car and drive to Georgetown, in Guyana. Or rent a boat at La Guaira and go to Trinidad. Who knows what would have happened to her?"

"You— "

"This way," Dan continued, "she was safe from strangers, and stayed in the home of a highly respected and honorable family. She flew in a commercial airliner to Rome, where she is registered in a first-class hotel. With her duenna."

"So I should thank you, is that it?" Hernandez's face showed bitter scorn.

"No. I should apologize to you. I realize that now."

The Venezuelan huffed disdainfully.

"To tell the truth," Dan admitted, "I never even thought of the distress this escapade might cause you. Your daughter told me that she wanted to get away from the Russian, and the idea of spitting in his eye was too much for me to resist."

Closing his eyes as if struggling to maintain his self-control, Hernandez said, "You have placed me in an impossible situation."

"You know your daughter better than I. Wouldn't she have gone anyway?"

"Nevertheless, the fact is that she went with *you*. Both Comrade Malik and I hold you responsible."

Dan leaned back in his desk chair and ran a finger across his chin. "I suppose you're right. If Malik is that eager for her, though, he'll fly out to Rome and surprise her there. Might do him some good."

"He must return to Moscow today."

"He could stop off at Rome. That's what I'd do, if I were in his place. That's what *you* would do, wouldn't you?"

Despite himself, Hernandez almost smiled.

"But I do feel responsible," Dan admitted. "If your daughter is incurring expenses that are a burden to you, I would be happy to help you. . . ."

"That will not be necessary," Hernandez replied stiffly.

Dan hunched forward, leaning one arm on the desk, and the older man leaned toward him slightly without consciously realizing that he was unbending a little.

"Rafael," Dan said earnestly, "I am truly sorry that this matter has come between us. We should not be enemies. That can bring nothing but pain to both of us."

"What you did was not the act of a friend."

"It was unthinking, I agree. But I did not intend to hurt you. We have too much in common; the great goals that we share should not be endangered by this misunderstanding."

110

"She is my only daughter."

"She has not been compromised," Dan insisted. "And it would be a shame to allow this Russian to drive a wedge between us. That could do nothing but damage our chances to make Venezuela the most important nation in space industry."

Some of the stiffness seemed to go out of Hernandez's back.

"The Russians would like nothing better than to make the two of us enemies," Dan went on. "That would destroy the Venezuelan space program. And that would mean the end of your dream."

Hernandez said nothing.

Swiveling slightly away from him, Dan pointed toward the view through his window. "The rainstorm wreaked havoc with the squatters' shacks. You can see where they've been washed away."

"More than a hundred were killed," Hernandez said.

"I would like to donate some money to help them," Dan said, turning back to face the older man again. "Perhaps a hundred thousand bolivars?"

Hernandez's mud-brown eyes had lost their angry spark. Now they went flat as he made a quick mental calculation.

"A hundred thousand would hardly make a dent in the problem. A quarter of a million would be necessary, at least."

Dan hesitated just long enough to let him feel that he was getting the better of the deal. "A quarter of a million." He pursed his lips, scratched his chin, swung the chair around toward the window again and then back to face the minister.

"All right," Dan said at last. "A quarter of a million it is."

Hernandez nodded once in silent acknowledgment of Dan's generosity. They spoke for a few minutes more, but they both knew that the words were merely formalities now. Dan had made the best of a bad situation. It had cost a quarter million bolivars, approximately half of which would go into

Hernandez's own pocket. God knows where the rest will end up, Dan thought. Those poor bastards in the shacks on the hillsides will never see any of it.

Hernandez left, mollified. He was embarrassed that his daughter had disobeyed him, but satisfied that her reputation had not been tarnished. But Dan had no illusions about Hernandez. He had made an enemy out of the Minister of Technology, there was no doubt in his mind about that. Taking the bribe merely confirmed the fact: Hernandez was now solidly on the side of the Russians.

"It was a very foolish thing to do," said Quentin Andrews. "Extremely foolish."

He, Dan, and Andrews' wife, Millicent, were sitting in the ambassador's library, a snug little room lined with bookshelves and dark oak paneling. The rest of the ambassador's residence was light, open and airy, but Andrews had created this little refuge for himself, this room that simulated the feeling of his family home in snowy Buffalo, New York.

Lissa, sitting on the plushly cushioned love seat with her feet tucked under her and a snifter of brandy in one hand, eyed Dan craftily. "You didn't fly her all the way to Japan just to spite that Russian, now did you, Dannie boy?"

Dan gave her a shrug. "Actually, yes, I did."

Andrews was standing between the love seat and the armchair where Dan was sitting. He had a cut-glass tumbler in his hand, half-filled with whiskey. Dan realized that he had not seen Andrews without a glass in his hand for the better part of the past year.

"It was extremely foolish," he repeated. "Stupid, even. Relations with the Soviets are difficult enough, these days, without you throwing romantic entanglements into the equation."

"Our relations with the Russians aren't that difficult," Dan countered. He was drinking sherry, amontillado, his favorite ever since he had read Poe's tales when a teenager.

"Not difficult? Do you have any idea—"

Dan interrupted, "Come on, Quentin. The Russians tell us what to do and we do it. What's so difficult about that?"

Lissa made a snorting, laughing sound. Andrews frowned at her, then turned back toward Dan.

"It's all well and good for you to be so smug about it, but the fact of the matter is—"

"The fact of the matter," Dan said, unwilling to listen to another one of the ambassador's pointless speeches, "is that I have to see Jane, and I have to see her right away."

"The President? What makes you think she'll have time to see you?"

"It's important," Dan said.

Sitting up straighter on the cushions, Lissa said, "I thought you two were finished for good."

"This has nothing to do with our personal feelings," Dan said. "It's strictly business, and it's *vital* that I see her, soon. Before the week is out, if it can be arranged."

"Impossible!" Andrews flapped his free hand in the air.

"I said it's vital," Dan repeated.

"She can't be seen with you, you know that."

"Then something clandestine has got to be arranged. Like tonight. Nobody knows I'm here except your butler and your security chief."

"And the KGB," Lissa cracked.

Dan laughed. "Still cleaning bugs out of the walls?"

"The walls, the floors, the ceilings . . . we even found some in the books in here."

Andrews dismissed his wife's candor with a shake of his head. "Dan, I am not going to ask *that woman* to find the time to see you."

"Not even as a favor to a fellow American?" Dan asked, grinning slightly.

"You gave up your American citizenship when you moved your corporate headquarters here, remember?"

"It wasn't my idea! That silly law required it."

"Still, she won't take the chance of being seen with you, and I'm not going to lower myself by asking her to."

Dan drained the last sips of his amontillado and put the tulip-shaped glass down on the coffee table in front of his chair.

"All right, Quentin," he said lightly. "I've gone through official channels and been turned down. Now I'll contact her through unofficial channels. You had your chance; don't say I didn't come to you first."

He got to his feet, leaned down to peck Lissa's cheek and strode out of the room.

Chapter
◆ ◆ THIRTEEN ◆ ◆

The President of the United States felt close to crying.

She was sitting at her usual place at the long, gleaming table in the Cabinet Room, flanked on her right by the Secretary of Agriculture, on her left by the Secretary of State. The other Cabinet officers were arrayed around the table, a neatly picked balance of whites, blacks and Hispanics, men and women.

The Secretary of Agriculture, who once owned a chain of farm equipment dealerships in Nebraska and the Dakotas, was shaking his head mournfully. He had the round, slightly florid face of a born used-car salesman, but lately his optimistic smile and glib patter had been replaced by a somber, almost frightened look.

"That's the bottom line," he said. "The Russians set the international prices for wheat and corn, and they've set them eight percent lower than last year."

The President lifted her chin a notch and held back the anger and frustration that was welling up inside her. For long moments no one around the table said a word. Through the French doors at her back, the President could hear a robin singing, out in the Rose Garden. She glanced up at the portrait of Franklin Roosevelt over the fireplace at the far end of the room.

How I wish I had your boundless confidence, Jane Scanwell said silently to the jaunty FDR. Nothing to fear but fear itself: if only it was that simple.

The Vice-President, sitting directly across the table from her, was scowling like the New England schoolteacher he had once been. He had been the Senate majority leader, and a power to be reckoned with. Once Jane had succeeded her husband, she had plucked this scrawny, severe, latter-day Daniel Webster out of the Senate and made him Vice-President, where he could do her no harm. She was beginning to realize, though, that he could no longer do her any good, either.

"Eight percent lower," the Vice-President muttered. "But they can't—"

"Yes they can," Agriculture snapped. "The damned Commies set their price and the rest of the world market falls right into line with them."

The Secretary of Defense, once a post so important that he always sat at the President's right hand, said from the foot of the table, "We could refuse to sell at that price. Hold back the grain until the price goes up a little."

Agriculture shook his head. "The other food exporting countries will undercut us . . . Argentina, Australia, Canada . . ."

The President turned to the Secretary of State. Like most of the Cabinet officers, he had been her husband's appointee; she had not replaced them with her own choices. Not yet.

"Can we negotiate agreements with the other food exporters?" she asked.

"Bilateral agreements with each individual nation?" he asked. He was a former Dallas banker, a slim, elegant Hispanic with distinguished silvery hair and deep brown eyes that had a strange, slightly oriental cast to them. Jane thought of him as a department store mannequin, a figure of wax that dis-

116

plays clothes well. She imagined that he slept in a three-piece pinstripe suit of gray or navy blue.

"I was thinking," she replied, "more of a multilateral situation, sort of the kind that the oil-producing nations had back in the seventies."

"You mean OPEC?"

"Yes, that's it. An OPEC for the nations that export food."

He pursed his lips, as if seriously considering the idea for a moment, then said flatly, "The Russians would never allow it."

"You don't think . . ."

He gave the President a patient little smile. "The men in the Kremlin would never permit anything that interfered with their ability to set the world price for grain and other foodstuffs. To think we could get around that in some way is idle dreaming."

You condescending little prick, the President raged inwardly. It's smug little bastards like you who got us into this mess in the first place.

The Treasury Secretary looked up from the pocket computer he had been fiddling with. "An eight percent drop in the price we get for food exports is going to mean a *significant* increase in unemployment."

The President leaned back in her chair and let them take up that theme. They don't understand, she told herself. They can't see far enough to understand. If we can hold out, if we can just hang on for long enough, we'll win. In the long run we can win—if we don't destroy ourselves first. While the Cabinet officers argued hotly over just what percentage of the nation's work force would be laid off, and what this would mean to the national economy and the value of the deflated dollar overseas, and to her chances for reelection in November, she let her mind drift to the message she had received that morning.

I knew he'd come crawling back, Jane Scanwell told herself. It's taken more than three years, but he's finally begging to see me.

Maybe begging is too strong a word, she warned herself. Dan Hamilton never begs. He's too proud to bend his knees. But he wants to see me. He needs my help.

Cold anger seeped along her veins like a river of ice engulfing her. He needs my help, she repeated, savoring the thought. When I needed his help he ran away, left the country, left Morgan to die and me to carry on alone. Now he wants to come back, to be forgiven.

Never, she told herself. I'll see him burn in hell before I lift a finger to help him. I'll see the Russians hang him in Red Square first.

Dan Randolph hovered weightlessly, his boots a good four inches off the "floor" of the locker room, as the two technicians checked out his space suit. His helmet floated before him within easy reach, turning and drifting ever so slightly, like a severed head slowly turning its face away from him.

It's been months since I've been up here, Dan realized. I shouldn't let so much time pass between visits.

It had surprised him that he had felt slightly queasy for the first few hours in zero gravity. After all the hundreds of times he had flown into orbit, he thought he had left the butterflies of zero-gee far behind. That's what you get for staying on the ground too long, he told himself. It's your punishment for sticking in the mud instead of being up here where you belong.

In the few hours since his shuttle had docked at the space station the uneasy malaise gradually disappeared, to be replaced by the euphoria and pleasure of weightlessness. Dan felt as if he had left all the cares of Earth far behind him; he was in a new world now, in his own element, free and happy.

"Can't you guys go any faster?" he complained.

The chief technician, a toothsome blonde with a healthy tan and the confident smile of a woman who knew her business, gave him a disarming smile.

"Mr. Randolph, sir," she said, "we're responsible for

your safety. We don't want the Big Boss to get killed because we missed a pinhole leak in his space suit, now do we?"

"We don't want the Big Boss to die of old age before he gets out the airlock, either," Dan jabbed back.

She laughed. "We're careful, boss, not slow."

He grumbled and muttered good-naturedly as they completed their check of his suit, its radio, its life-support backpack and the jet maneuvering unit that embraced him like the back and two arms of a chair that had no seat or legs.

At last Dan put on his helmet, sealed the collar and slid the visor down and locked it in place.

The crew chief flashed him a toothy grin and said, "You are cleared for EVA, sir."

Dan barely heard her from inside the helmet, but he had learned to read lips years ago. He floated over to the inner airlock hatch and entered the round metal chamber. Airlocks always reminded Dan of stainless-steel wombs. This one was bigger than most, large enough to accommodate half a dozen astronauts at once or a fair amount of bulky equipment. Its metal walls were dulled by years of scratching and scuffing, but the labels on the inner and outer control panels had been freshly sprayed on: Dan could read them clearly.

He knew them by heart, of course. The technicians inside the space station were monitoring the airlock; automatic fail-safe systems would not allow a neophyte to kill himself by opening the hatches in the wrong order. It was a common understanding among the men and women who worked in space that a person who was careless enough to get killed probably deserved it; but the sloppy sonofabitch usually took somebody else with him, sometimes more than one other person. An airlock accident could wipe out everybody on the other side of the inner hatch, so both human and machine monitors watched the airlocks constantly.

The air pumped out of the metal womb and the control panel light next to the outer hatch turned green. Dan drifted over to it and leaned a thumb against the glowing plastic button. The hatch swung open without a sound and Dan glided out into the emptiness of space, a newborn leaving the womb.

For a breathless moment he hovered just outside the open hatch, reveling in the glory of it. The Earth revolved slowly, immense, filling half the sky, incredibly clean and glowing, purest blues and greens of the shining seas, swirls of dazzling white clouds that hid whole continents beneath their vast expanse. Dan gazed at it, the home of the human race. It looked so serene and beautiful from this distance.

It took a real effort of will to pull his attention away from the endlessly fascinating world that lay before him, and focus on the factory that hung less than five kilometers away.

It was an ungainly, almost ugly collection of metal pods, cylinders, connecting tubes, crisscrossing beams and big paddle-shaped solar collectors that stretched their arms out to the unfiltered sunlight like the dark rectangular leaves of some alien extraterrestrial tree, drinking in solar energy and converting it silently, efficiently, to the electricity that the factory needed.

In a way, the factory reminded Dan of an old typesetting machine that he had once seen in an ancient printing shop back in rural Virginia, when he had been a child; a clinking, clanking collection of moving mechanical arms and vats of molten lead.

The heart of the space factory was the smelter, where ores from the Moon were refined into pure elements: aluminum, titanium, silicon, oxygen. The factory itself had been built mostly of lunar metals. Now part of the factory made alloys that could not be manufactured on Earth, alloys that were stronger yet lighter than any earthly metals could be, because they had been made in zero gravity, where the molten elements could mix perfectly. Other sections of the factory manufactured special plastics, crystals for electronic equipment, pharmaceutical products that cured diabetes and other hormonal diseases.

But none of that interested Dan at the moment. Working

the control studs on the arms of his jetpack, he made his way from the slowly rotating wheels of the space station toward the graceless utilitarian clutter of the factory. As he approached it, Dan could see several shuttles hovering at the factory's loading docks, taking on cargo for return to Earth. Space-suited astronauts scurried back and forth around the shuttles like silvery ants busily working at their tasks.

Dan identified himself to the traffic controller at the factory's monitoring center and heard her calm, sure voice in his helmet earphones, acknowledging his call and giving him clearance to approach. He jetted past the loading docks, through the maze of interconnected struts and beams that linked the factory's various components together, and headed straight toward the odd collection of shapes that floated a few hundred meters beyond the factory's outstretched solar panels.

The asteroid ship was taking shape out there. It was a weird-looking assemblage of parts: a bulbous metal egg that housed the crew's living quarters, a collection of propellant tanks that would be filled with nothing more than water, plastic pods for holding tools and equipment, and a small oblong metal box, about the size and shape of an oversized coffin, which contained the nuclear power plant that delivered the electricity for the spacecraft and its propulsion thrusters. The various modules of the craft were painted gleaming white, except for the lead-shielded nuclear power plant, which had been daubed blood red.

"*Dolphin One*," Dan called into his helmet microphone. "Dan Randolph coming aboard."

"Welcome aboard, Mr. Randolph." He heard the voice of Nobuhiko Yamagata, clear and strong, in his earphones.

The spacecraft looked anything but like a sleek dolphin. Its name came from the fact that the dolphin was one of the disguises of the Greek god Apollo, and the mission of this ship was to intercept one of the small asteroids that passed relatively near Earth in its orbit—the astronomers called such pieces of rock the Apollo class of asteroids.

Dan expertly throttled his braking thrusters to kill his

forward velocity. He reached the crew pod's curving hull with a feather-light touch, worked the push-button controls to open the hatch and pulled himself inside. Once he had cycled through the airlock and stepped through the inner hatch, there was a technician waiting to help him out of the cumbersome space suit. Clad in white coveralls that were unmarked except for his last name stenciled over the left breast pocket, Dan made his way through the pod's central corridor in the easy swimming motion of zero gravity.

Nobo was sitting in the engineer's station, a clipboard thick with papers floating at his left elbow as he checked out the intricate panels of indicator lights and switches.

He dipped his head in an informal version of a respectful bow. "It's an honor to have you aboard, sir."

Dan automatically nodded back. "How's it going? How's the reactor behaving?"

"We haven't run it up to full power yet."

"I know. Your report last night said there was a glitch with the control system."

"Ah. That is why you've come here."

"I don't like troubles with something as important as the main power plant. Especially a nuke."

Nobo smiled. "You Americans have still not overcome your fear of nuclear power, have you?"

The smile and the tone of voice appeared overly tolerant, almost condescending. Dan replied, "We're not as fatalistic as you Japanese."

"It isn't fatalism, it's a matter of national survival. Hiroshima was a long time ago. We have learned to live with nuclear reactors. We had to. Especially since the Russians started marking up the price of oil and natural gas."

It was an argument Dan had played out with Saito Yamagata many times over the years. Japan had decided to go heavily into nuclear power rather than buy either Russian oil and natural gas or American coal. Despite the very real fears of accidents and radiation, the Japanese had opted for nuclear— and won. Their electrical power systems were the best and safest in the world, and with the extra power they received from their solar power satellites, even their automobiles were electrically powered. The air quality in Tokyo and every other Japanese city was unmarred by the carcinogenic smog that came from burning fossil fuels.

"So what's wrong with the reactor?" Dan asked.

Nobuhiko gave him another tolerant smile. "Nothing, really. It's a good piece of Japanese technology. But the control rods were manufactured by a Swiss contractor. They passed inspection in Kyoto and actually they performed within specified limits in yesterday's test. But barely within the limits."

Dan ran a hand across his chin. Nobo had won the assignment to be flight engineer for the asteroid mission. He had worked hard over the past two months and shown more intelligence, drive and dedication than even Dan could have hoped for. The job was his. And the responsibility. But Dan had to give him the power to make and enforce decisions, too. That went with the responsibility. If Nobo said the reactor system was no go, the mission was postponed. Or perhaps canceled altogether.

"I contacted the manufacturer last night—"

"Not from up here!"

"No, no." Nobo raised a placating hand. "I did not compromise our security. I placed a call from *Nueva Venezuela* to Caracas, which was relayed to Kyoto, and from there to Bern. As far as the Swiss know, their control system is being tested on an experimental reactor at the Yamagata Research Institute in the University of Kyoto."

Dan let out a long breath. "Okay. The Russians are suspicious enough already. Security is important."

"I understand." Nobo jabbed a stubby finger at a green light glowing steadily in the upper right quadrant of the big monitoring board. "The control system is now working within the limits that I have set. The problem was very minor; just a small adjustment was necessary."

Dan gave him a happy grin. In the eight weeks he had

been working for Astro Manufacturing, the young Yamagata had earned himself something of a reputation for insisting on well-nigh perfect performance from every piece of equipment he touched. The technicians joked that there were three sets of specifications for all the equipment delivered for the asteroid mission: the manufacturer's original specs, the natural limits that God set on how well the equipment could work and the performance that Nobuhiko Yamagata demanded from the equipment. Of the three, Nobo's was the most severe. "Yamagata's tougher than God," the technicians said. Not all of them were happy about Nobo's lofty standards, but they all respected him for it.

"Has Dr. Freiberg picked out our destination yet?" Nobo asked. "The last time I spoke with him, he was undecided among three possible asteroids."

Dan said, "He's narrowed it down to two, and we'll make the final decision in a day or so."

"When is the earliest possible time of departure?"

"The nearest window is the end of the month," Dan replied. "I don't have the exact time, but it's ten days from now."

Nobo nodded solemnly. "We will be fully prepared to go by then."

"Good."

"Will Dr. Freiberg accompany us?"

"No. Not that he doesn't want to go. But he stays at *Nueva Venezuela* during the mission."

"Security?"

"Damned right. His cover story is that he's setting up an astronomical observatory at the factory."

"But even if the Russians knew about this mission, what could they do about it?" Nobo asked. "We have a right to fly out to an asteroid; there is no international law against that."

It was Dan's turn to smile tolerantly. "Son, you'd be surprised at how fast laws can be written. The Soviets wouldn't hesitate to use force to stop us, and then get a law written afterward.''

Nobo shrugged his shoulders but said nothing. The motion lifted him slightly out of his chair.

"Freiberg stays here," Dan repeated. "Hell, if it weren't for the goddamned Russian snoops, I'd go along with you myself."

The young Japanese smiled appreciatively. "Yes. My father has told me many times of the days when the two of you worked together in space. I thought this mission would be very tempting to you."

"It is. But it's too important to risk for a personal whim." Dan felt that he was doing the wise thing, the prudent thing, the necessary thing. But a voice in the back of his head asked silently, If you were a couple of years younger, would you still elect to stay behind?

He spent most of the day inspecting the spacecraft, and saw that Nobo and the rest of the crew would have it ready well before the earliest possible departure date. Carstairs, the rowdy Australian, would captain the mission. And he had picked one of the younger Venezuelan astronauts, Vargas, as his first officer. Dan was satisfied that the ship and its crew were in good shape.

But as he jetted back to the space station he turned his thoughts to other problems. The biggest one was that Jane Scanwell had for two solid months refused every attempt he had made to contact her. Dan could understand that the President of the United States would find it politically unpalatable to meet with an American who had renounced his citizenship and run off to another country to set himself up in business there. He could even understand how the widow of his best friend would be furious with him for turning his back on her when she needed him most.

But this is important! he told himself. It goes beyond politics, beyond personal feelings.

Yes, he answered himself. But how do you get *her* to understand that?

Locked inside his space suit, alone in his private universe as he jetted across the emptiness between the sprawling space factory and the stately wheels of *Nueva Venezuela*, Dan mulled over his next course of action. The asteroid mission would be carried out under the flag of Venezuela. Astro Manufacturing bore the financial burden; no matter how rich the asteroid turned out to be in minerals and metals, this first mission would be of no profit. But it would prove that mining asteroids was feasible, and the profits to come in the future would be enormous. More than that, though, was the fact that the asteroids were beyond Soviet control. The Russians could not monopolize them, as they had monopolized the Moon.

Or could they? That worried Dan. That's why he wanted the United States to be involved in this first mission, even if it was only as an observer. Dan knew that Venezuela could never muster the power to stand up to a Russian challenge, if the Soviets chose to claim the asteroids for themselves. Maybe the United States would knuckle under, too, as they had with the Moon and with space in general. But he had to give Jane the chance to make a stand, he had to give her the chance to let the U.S. regain some shreds of its self-esteem and dignity.

He saw the airlock hatch of the space station coming up toward him, with the Venezuelan flag and the stenciled NUEVA VENEZUELA running along its curving flank. Inside his helmet, Dan made a wry little smile. You're still a goddamned patriot, aren't you? They hate your guts, but you still love the old States, you damned fool.

Or is it Jane that you love? he asked himself silently. Maybe she's wiser than you think. Maybe she's protecting both of us by refusing to see you.

He reached out his gloved hand and caught the metal bar grip alongside the airlock hatch. I've got to see her, he knew. There's no way around it. I've got to go to Washington and see her in person, face to face. No matter what.

His mind started turning over schemes for getting into the States incognito, making his way to Washington and meeting with the President. In secret. Not a small order. Even for a man of his means, it would be difficult.

As he wormed out of the space suit and made his way "down" to the outermost wheel where the gravity felt Earth-normal, he puzzled out ways to get the job done. It was quite a shock when he opened the door to his private quarters and found Lucita Hernandez standing by the window, waiting for him.

Chapter
♦ ♦ FOURTEEN ♦ ♦

That night in Sapporo, after they had made love, Lucita lay sleeplessly on the waterbed beside Dan Randolph and stared out the bedroom window at the cold distant Moon. It seemed to be laughing at her.

Her mind was a turmoil of conflicting emotions. She could see her father's angry face as he snarled the word "whore" at her. She had fled to the American billionaire to escape from her father's stifling clutches, to get free of his relentless plan to marry her off to the Russian. And to punish her father. To make him pay. A whore, am I? I'll show him!

She had expected Dan Randolph to treat her like he treated all women: to be flattering and attentive and generous. A seductive man; that was his reputation. And once he had seduced a woman, he forgot about her, ignored her, moved on to his next conquest. But Lucita had no intention of becoming another victim on Dan Randolph's long, long list. She would use him, rather than the other way around. He was nothing more than a convenient means of transportation for her, a means for escaping her father's clutches. How easy it was to make him agree to spirit her away from Caracas! All she had to do was mention the Russian, and the billionaire rolled out his private jet plane for her.

But the man did not behave the way Lucita had expected. Dan Randolph did not try to seduce her, he did not even pay her any attention, not until she brazenly went to his room and practically threw herself into his bed.

His lovemaking had been wondrously gentle, not the self-centered machismo that she had expected. He knew how to be patient with a woman, how to please her, how to arouse her to heights of near frenzy. Lucita had smothered her screams of passion against his hot powerful flesh as her mind dissolved in the shuddering, wild rapture of orgasm.

Now she lay silently and gazed at the snowy mountain peaks gleaming in the moonlight. She had given no thought to the repercussions of her actions. She had thought only of herself. Dan had agreed to help her escape from Caracas without a care for the consequences. He had not lusted after her; he had acted out of simple kindness. Despite all the tales about him, Lucita was convinced that Dan Randolph was basically a simple, honest man whose only impulse, when she had asked for his aid, was to help a lady in distress.

She knew that her father would be furious with him, and as Minister of Technology he could set about to ruin Dan's business. Then there was the Russian, Malik. Lucita had seen a glimpse of the steely ruthlessness behind his smiling mask. Such a man could kill, or order others to kill for him.

As the Moon slowly sank behind the snow-topped mountain crests and the sky turned milky gray with approaching dawn, Lucita sat up in the bed and made her decision. She looked down at Dan Randolph sleeping beside her, his ruggedly handsome face relaxed into the gentle smile of a little boy.

The feelings she felt surging through her body frightened Lucita. It would be so easy to fall in love with this dashing man, to surrender her heart and soul and flesh to him, to offer him her life forever. So easy. And so dangerous.

Quickly, silently, she got up and donned her robe, then

made her way to the bedroom where she and Teresa had been ensconced. She woke her erstwhile duenna and together they showered, dressed and had the Yamagata household servants prepare them an early breakfast. It was an easy matter for Lucita to get Nobuhiko—so polite and anxious to impress her—to arrange a car to take them to the airport. By nine that morning the two young women were on their way to Rome. Lucita stared out the plane's tiny thick window as they left Japan far behind them, and Dan Randolph too.

Rome should have been exciting, wonderful, happy. The Eternal City with its ancient monuments and handsome men. The Vatican, the Pantheon, the sublime works of Michelangelo, Bernini, Rafael, Titian, the ancient Roman Forum silent and noble in its ruin despite the streams of tourists babbling through it in Japanese, Polish, German and Russian. How many conquering hordes had come and gone through these ancient stones, Lucita thought to herself. Nights on the Via Veneto, being admired by the brutally beautiful young men with their smoldering, pouting looks and their carefully crafted casualness.

Lucita and Teresa allowed themselves only a little danger, and they quickly found that the Roman males could accept a refusal with a rueful grin and a whispered, "*Domani.*" They bought Italian ices at midnight from the vendor at the foot of the Spanish Steps. They splashed their bare feet in the fountain of Trevi. They attended Mass at St. Peter's and allowed themselves to be picked up for a wild motorbike ride out to the Villa d'Este and its thousands of cascading fountains.

Yet every day, every night, Lucita found herself thinking of Dan Randolph, wondering if he had ever seen Rome, if he had ever allowed himself the freedom to relax and savor this magnificent city. She knew that he had not been born to wealth, and she realized that creating such an immense fortune as his allowed scant time for ordinary pleasures. But she could imagine how much he would enjoy being in Rome, free with nothing to do but explore the city and its delights.

She could imagine how much she would enjoy having him here with her, and it made her heart ache to think of it.

After a week of being busy tourists, of doing nothing except seeing the sights by day and being seen by the virile Italian men at night, Lucita began to think about returning home. Teresa seemed to be wearying of their exhausting whirl; more each day she talked about home and family.

The two of them were returning from a day-long tour of the Vatican and an audience with the pope they had shared with seventeen hundred other tourists. At Lucita's insistence they had walked through the hot sunshine of late afternoon all the way back to their hotel. The cool shade of the marble-floored lobby was a welcome relief.

As Teresa went to the desk to get their room key, a burly, broad-shouldered man in a dark suit and even more somber face approached Lucita. Not an Italian, she knew instantly. Not a tourist. He frightened her.

"Señorita Hernandez, you will come with me, please," he said in grotesquely pronounced Spanish.

"Who are you? What do you want?" Lucita demanded. She could see, past the man's shoulder, that another just like him had taken Teresa by the wrist and was bringing her to them.

The man reached into his ill-fitting jacket's inside pocket and produced an identification card sealed in discolored plastic.

"Commissioner Malik has invited you to dinner at the embassy of the Soviet Union," he said. "We are to bring you there."

"Dinner? Malik?" Lucita's mind spun giddily. "He's here in Rome?"

"He flew in this afternoon and insists on having dinner with you—both of you."

"But I'll have to change. . . ."

"Your clothes will be brought to the embassy. You are to be the guests of the Soviet Union."

He reached out a heavy, thick-fingered hand. Lucita shrank back from him. He hesitated, then gestured toward the front

131

door of the lobby. A black limousine waited just outside. Lucita scanned the hotel lobby desperately. No policeman or guard was in sight. The room clerk was busily ignoring them. The concierge, at his delicate little desk, had his back turned to them and his ornate telephone to his ear. The Russian made an impatient, urging movement of his hand. Feeling trapped, Lucita started for the door, trailed by the two men and Teresa.

"I bring you greetings from your father," Malik said, smiling broadly.

He was standing by the sun-streaming windows in one of the embassy's huge, high-ceilinged drawing rooms, his golden hair lit by the radiance. He looked strong, confident and pleased with himself.

"He's very upset with you, you know," Malik added.

"I have written to him," Lucita replied as she crossed the long carpeted floor toward the Russian. "He knows where we are staying. He could have telephoned, or written back to me."

Malik took her hand and pressed it to his lips. They felt cool to Lucita's skin.

"Is it true," he asked in a lower voice, "that you ran away from Caracas to escape from me?"

She wanted to say, "Do not flatter yourself." But she felt afraid of this man who had the power to whisk her out of her hotel at the blink of an eye.

"I left Caracas because I needed some time to think, some freedom for myself," she replied.

He nodded, as if accepting her excuse for the moment.

"I have instructed one of the women servants to help your aunt unpack your things. You will have adjoining rooms on the third floor. I think you'll find them quite comfortable."

Lucita said, "I was planning to return to Caracas in a few days."

His eyes widened in genuine surprise. "Oh, no, you mustn't.

132

I won't hear of it. I have planned a trip for you and your aunt to Moscow. Your father has kindly given his consent.''

''To Moscow?''

''Yes, and perhaps Leningrad, if you like.''

Lucita looked deep into the Russian's ice-blue eyes and suddenly realized that, for all intents and purposes, she was Vasily Malik's prisoner.

Chapter
◆ ◆ FIFTEEN ◆ ◆

"What are you doing here?" Dan blurted as he stepped through the doorway into his quarters.

Lucita turned from the window and the panorama of the vast and beautiful Earth passing below.

"I am on my way home," she said. "I am returning to Caracas and my father."

She looked different. No longer defiant and angry. The fire in her eyes had been replaced by something that Dan could not quite define: bitterness, fear—despair? She was wearing soft, loose-fitting slacks of deep blue that tucked into low-heeled boots and a silver mesh blouse with a high mandarin collar and buttoned cuffs. Her gleaming black hair was pulled back and tied into a long ponytail. In all, Dan thought, she seemed quieter, more guarded, more mature.

"You've changed," he said.

"I have been to Russia. Vasily took me to Moscow, and to his home in Orel. We even went to the rocket launching center at Baikonur." Not a smile as she spoke. Not a hint of gladness.

Dan went to the liquor cabinet that stood behind his desk. "Would you like a drink?"

"Anything but vodka," Lucita said, and a wan smile flickered across her lips.

"You didn't like Russia?" He found a bottle of amontillado, not his favorite brand but the best he had up here at the space station.

"I was treated like a princess everywhere I went."

Pouring two glasses, Dan said, "Malik gave you the royal treatment."

Lucita sat wearily on the small curving sofa next to the window. Dan leaned across his desk and touched the control button that darkened the polarized glass. Newcomers to the station had been known to get nauseated from seeing the Earth lumbering by, out of the corner of their eye. He brought the glasses of sherry to the sofa, sat down next to her and handed her one.

"*Salud*," he said.

"*Zah vahsheh zdahrovyeh*," Lucita replied.

"You've learned some Russian."

"More than I will ever want to hear again."

"You didn't enjoy being in the Workers' Paradise?"

Her eyes showed a spark of their former fire, then she saw from the grin on Dan's face that he was being ironic.

"As I said, I was treated like a princess. I was guarded night and day. Not allowed to set a foot anywhere unless it had been planned and prepared for ahead of time. Vasily was a wonderful host, and it is clear that he is a very important and powerful man. But there is no freedom in Russia. Not for me, at least."

Dan sipped at his drink.

"Have you ever been there?" Lucita asked.

"No. I was all set to go, once, years ago. I was still working for Yamagata Industries then, nothing but a salaried mining engineer who had put in a tour of duty on the multinational mining facility on the Moon. There was a big international conference on developing extraterrestrial resources, being held in Moscow. I was invited to attend. Sent in my reservations and had everything confirmed."

"What happened?"

He laughed. "In the six months between getting my reservations confirmed and the opening of the meeting, I made my first million dollars."

"So you didn't attend the conference?"

"No, no." The laughter died. "They wouldn't take me. I was a filthy capitalist. They wouldn't let me in."

Lucita looked surprised.

Dan explained, "The Russians had pressured the United Nations into letting them take over operations of all the lunar mines. The multinational corporation that had been operating them was squeezed out, and it went into bankruptcy. I got some Texas friends of mine, including Morgan Scanwell. . . ."

"The President?"

"He wasn't president then, just governor of Texas. We bought up the multinational's assets for something like two cents on the dollar."

"And that made you rich?"

"The corporation had an asset that was worth billions: a UN approval to establish a factory in orbit for processing lunar ores."

"Ahh." Understanding dawned in Lucita's eyes.

"By the time the conference in Moscow was ready to convene, my share in the old corporation's stock was worth more than a million. It was all paper, of course, but to the Soviets I was suddenly persona non grata."

"So they refused to allow you into the conference."

Dan laughed again, more bitterly this time. "They didn't even allow me on their goddamned SST. My ticket with Aeroflot vanished from their computer's memory bank. My hotel reservation was mislaid. My entry visa suddenly had to be reexamined and wouldn't be ready until after the conference would be finished. They still owe me the cash deposit I had sent them in advance, the cheap sonsof—"

The sight of this Yankee billionaire being still indignant over a few dollars after so many years made Lucita laugh.

Dan grinned back at her. "That's better. I was afraid they had taken the laughter out of you."

"They did," she admitted. "I've just gotten it back again, thanks to you."

"Was it that bad?"

She grew serious again. "I felt as if I was being smothered. Every day, every night—I could feel them watching, listening to every word I said. It was frightening."

"I had thought they were loosening up," Dan said. "They've got nobody to be afraid of now. They've won the Cold War and nobody can possibly dare attack them."

"We were in Moscow," Lucita told him, "and Vasily took me shopping to a magnificent department store. It was incredibly beautiful, with crystal chandeliers and the most luxurious things I've ever seen—jewelry, perfumes, clothes . . ."

"A government store?"

She lifted one hand in a gesture that said, *Let me go on.*

"A young policeman stood on duty outside the main entrance. He must have been new, perhaps this was his first day on the job. I noticed him, as we were looking at jewelry at the counter just inside the store's front windows. He was staring in at us—but not at us, really; at the merchandise. His eyes were as big as saucers."

Dan nodded. "Never saw anything like it before, I guess."

"I didn't think anything of it," Lucita went on. "We spent almost two hours in the store. Vasily was showing off, he offered to buy me anything I wanted. I had to be careful not to show too much enthusiasm over anything, because he would order the clerk to wrap it up for me and send it to my hotel."

"At the taxpayers' expense," muttered Dan.

"As we were leaving, it must have been time for the police guard outside the store to be changed. There was an older policeman there, talking with the young one. It seemed to me they were arguing, but their voices were too low for me to tell."

Dan finished his sherry and started to get up to refill his glass. But Lucita put her hand on his to hold him at the sofa.

"The young policeman," she said, suddenly intense with the memory of it, "started to go into the store. His partner tried to hold him back, but the young one pulled free of him and opened the door to go in."

"Uh-oh," said Dan.

"He got about three steps inside the door when a pair of store guards ran up to him and began shouting at him. He shouted back. They tried to push him out and he began to push back at them."

"What was Malik doing?"

Lucita said, "His limousine had pulled up and he was helping me into it when all the shouting started. He turned around once I was seated inside the car. The older policeman from the street rushed into the store and grabbed the younger one from behind. It took all three of them—the two store guards and the older policeman—to force the young one out of the store and back onto the sidewalk."

"And Malik?"

"He went up to them and started speaking with them. The young policeman was very angry by now. He shouted at Vasily and pointed into the store." She stopped, her eyes focused on the scene in her memory.

"Then," Lucita resumed, "Vasily lifted one finger, as if he was trying to catch the attention of a waiter in a very fine restaurant. Three very big men in dark coats suddenly appeared—just as if they had risen out of the sidewalk. They took the young policeman away with them."

"It was a special store," Dan realized, "reserved for foreign shoppers and upper-echelon Communist party members."

"Not quite," Lucita said. "It was reserved for high government officials. Not even foreigners were allowed into it, unless they were the guests of an official."

"And no ordinary citizens could get in," Dan said.

"No. From what Vasily said, the young policeman suffered a nervous breakdown."

"I'll bet. If he didn't have one then, he's certainly had it by now. He's probably sitting in a mental hospital somewhere, juiced to his eyeballs with the latest brain-benders."

138

A small shudder went through Lucita. "I will never return to Russia. Not willingly, at least."

Dan's eyes widened. *So she understands that she can be forced to do things she doesn't want to do. She's grown up enough to get that through her skull. Malik's helped her to become a little more adult, in his own way.*

"Let me fill your glass," he said.

"Thank you, but no. I must go. The shuttle leaves in half an hour and I must be on it."

"Going back to Caracas."

"Yes." She smiled wanly. "My tour of the world is finished. Now I must get back to reality."

Lucita got to her feet and Dan stood up beside her. She looked small and fragile and very vulnerable. He wanted to take her tiny hands in his and keep her with him. But he knew that he could not. There were too many other things he had to do. She would be in the way. And she could get hurt.

Her dark waif's eyes were looking up at him, searching, hoping, expecting.

"I'll see you off at the shuttle dock," he said.

The light in her eyes faded. She stepped slightly away from him. "No," she replied. "That will not be necessary."

"But I—"

"Please. I have made it this far alone. I can find the shuttle without your assistance."

Something in the way she said "alone" made Dan ask, "And your aunt, your duenna —how is she?"

"Teresa?" Lucita's beautiful face became as cold and distant as the Moon. "Teresa committed suicide a week ago. We were aboard the Soviet space station when it happened. *Kosmograd*, they call it."

"Suicide?" Dan felt it like a blow to his stomach. "How . . . what happened?"

But Lucita shook her head and went to the door. "I don't want to talk about it now. I am bringing her body back to Caracas with me. Good-bye."

She almost ran to the door, leaving Dan standing alone in

the middle of the small room. He wanted to go after her, to bring her back and keep her with him. But he shook his head and told himself it wouldn't be wise.

"You're on your way to the States, old boy," he muttered to himself. "The last thing in the world you need is her tagging along with you."

Two days later, Dan arrived at New Orleans International Airport amid the pushing, yammering, frenetic influx of tourists who were thronging into the city for its annual Mardi Gras celebration.

It was utter foolishness to return to the States, Dan told himself. Pete Weston had argued adamantly against it. The few staff people he had informed had all been stunned at his decision to do it. Dan himself knew it was risky, at best, and more than likely to be a totally useless and even dangerous move.

But as he dug his exquisitely forged passport out of his shoulder bag, Dan was beaming inwardly. The airport was teeming with arriving tourists, roaring with the noise of jet engines and thousands of human voices. Dan smelled perspiration and perfume and the harsh scent of the powerful disinfectants the cleaning crews used as he jostled his way slowly through the long, sweaty, impatient line that had piled up at the immigration barrier. The airport was not air-conditioned, despite the heat of the crowd. Air conditioning was a luxury reserved for the summer, and even then only if the electricity-rationing board permitted it.

The customs officer's cheap-looking uniform was stained through with perspiration. He looked about fifty, bald, bored, irritable. Barely glancing at the passport, he asked Dan:

"Where is your place of residence, Mr. McKinley?"

"Minneapolis. Just coming back from vacation," Dan lied. "Been to see Havana. Terrific town. Just terrific. You oughtta see what they've been able to do since Castro died."

The man nodded glumly and handed the passport back to Dan. He stepped past the booth, overnight bag slung over one shoulder, garment bag in the other hand, and stood for a moment to get his bearings. Someone bumped into him from behind.

"Hey, move it, willya?"

Dan laughed and got out of the man's way. He hadn't heard an angry, impatient bleat like that in years. He was home again.

The President of the United States was scheduled to make a speech in the New Orleans Civic Auditorium that evening. Rumors were that she had more bad news to break; this time it was the expected drop in prices for American grain and livestock. On the commercial airliner from Havana—where Dan had flown by chartered jet from Caracas—he had overheard grumbling conversations among the American tourists on their way home, complaining that their dollars bought practically nothing, that the best hotels and best restaurants were filled with Russians and East Europeans, that Jane Scanwell had gotten into the White House on a fluke and she will never win an election in her own right.

For years Dan had seen reports on all these matters and many more, every morning in his daily session with the computer that digested all the intelligence reports his corporate hirelings gathered for him. But to hear the people themselves griping, to feel the intensity of their complaints, to touch the reality of it with his own hands—that was far different from reading neatly typed impersonal reports on a computer screen.

He took the airport bus into the city. On this trip he was moving with the people, no longer the wealthy industrialist who traveled by limo and private jet. He was an ordinary guy again, taking the cheapest means of transportation available. Just one common man in the midst of a sea of common folk; they were his disguise and his protection.

And his source of information. Dan listened to their conversations as the bus lumbered toward downtown New Orleans. Most of the homeward-bound Americans had either gone on to other flights at the airport or taken some other mode of ground transportation. This bus, heading for the major tourist hotels in and around the Vieux Carré, was filled mostly with European and South American visitors, chatting in Spanish, German, French, Russian and other Slavic languages. And, of course, the inevitable Japanese.

"You must be very careful of drinking the water," a Russian voice said in the seat behind Dan.

"I have no intention of drinking water," said his companion, a bored-sounding woman.

"No, seriously, they have such toxic wastes here that even bottled water can be dangerous."

"Who cares? It's the air that I'm worried about."

"Not as bad as the air in Smolensk."

"Bad enough."

Looking out the untinted glass of the bus window, Dan could see the dirty brown haze that hung in the air, the product of burning coal to generate electricity. Without nuclear power, and with oil and natural gas prices set higher by Moscow each year, the United States had returned to its most abundant fuel. But the price for using coal was paid by degrading the quality of the air. And by the people who died of lung cancer, asthma and the resurgence of tuberculosis of a new and deadly virulent strain.

Dan got off the bus at the downtown transportation terminal. Most of the foreign tourists stayed on, heading for the fancy hotels. The bus terminal was seedy, filthy. It stank of urine and vomit. Panhandlers shuffled around, dressed mostly in rags. Bag ladies huddled in every corner. Helmeted police marched through the terminal in pairs, shortsnouted shotguns clipped to their thighs, German shepherds walking unleashed between them. They skirted the sleeping or unconscious figures sprawled on the worn, littered tile floor.

Poverty, Dan saw. The kind of poverty that once was confined to the worst ghettos of the biggest cities. It was spreading all across the country.

"Everett McKinley?"

Dan wheeled to see a short, scruffy man with graying hair and a two-day growth of beard looking at him.

Remembering the identification phrase, he said, "Well, I ain't the pope."

The man grinned at him, showing bad teeth. "Okay, you're the one. Let's go."

Instead of taking the risk of renting a car that could ultimately be traced to him, Dan had arranged for a local driver. The man, who knew nothing except Dan's alias, the identification phrase and his destination, took Dan's garment bag and led him through the reeking bus terminal to the parking lot. Under the watchful eyes of uniformed security guards, they made their way to a dilapidated four-door GMota Corsair. It had once been bright red, but rust and age had dulled its finish. The driver tossed Dan's bag onto the back seat, muttering that the trunk lid no longer opened.

"You know where I want to go?" Dan asked as he sat on the tattered upholstery.

The driver grinned at him. "It ain't the Vatican."

They drove off through city streets filthy with litter. Idle men seemed to cluster at every corner, white and black alike. Poverty had brought a brotherhood that affluence had never achieved. Half the buildings seemed empty, abandoned. Traffic was only a fraction of what Dan had remembered from the old days, most of it hissing steam buses and trucks that belched black diesel fumes.

Once they got onto the interstate, the old car showed surprising power. The driver, squinting into the afternoon sunlight, said, "She might look like a shitbox, but she got a lot of cubes under th' hood." For the first time, Dan noticed the trace of a Cajun accent in the man's voice. "She can outrun the cops, you know. When I carry stuff from the boats. That's why the trunk don't open. Full of radar spoilers. At night, they can't even find me from helicopters, you know?"

"What do you carry?" Dan asked.

The driver glanced at him, narrow-eyed. "Oh, stuff. From Mexico. From Panama and all. You know."

Dan nodded. Dope, illegal electronics parts, even bottles of propane heating gas—from what he had heard, the local black market made its money by evading the protective tariffs against imports. Smuggling even shoes could make a man moderately wealthy these days.

"Fuckin' government, don't make money worth anything," the driver complained. "T'ree dollars for a cup of coffee. T'ree dollars! Medicare ain't worth shit. Taxes keep goin' up. Got to do something to make ends meet, you know."

"Sure, sure," Dan said.

"You know, I used to be a building contractor. Had my own company. Made damn good money, too. Started out as an apprentice. Then master carpenter. Then made my own company. Built houses, office buildings, whole shopping centers. Damn fine construction. Those buildings last, I tell you. Then everyt'ing went to hell. Whole country caved in. Nobody building nothing now. Most of my people out of work. Hungry, I tell you."

The driver mumbled on about the impossibility of finding work, and how a man had to scratch and scramble to provide for his family, as they headed out onto the highway that ran across Lake Pontchartrain toward Baton Rouge. Dan was going to meet the President in the evening, after her speech in New Orleans. No one had told Dan where she would spend the night; that information was kept in strictest security. But he did not need to be told where Jane Scanwell would be that night. He knew.

Chapter
◆ ◆ SIXTEEN ◆ ◆

With the spotlights in her eyes, the President could not see the vast audience that filled the huge auditorium. But she did not need to see them. She could feel their presence, hear their voices, sense their emotions as if they were one gigantic single beast lurking in the darkness out there.

The beast had been hostile when she had taken the podium. The applause had been perfunctory, a duty owed to the office of the President. They were angry with her, blaming her for their troubles, burdening four decades of slowly accumulating disaster onto her shoulders.

Jane felt their displeasure, their sullen, smoldering frustration and the gnawing fear that lay beneath. It was her task to transform them, to tame the beast hunched in the darkness, to harness their energy. She was their leader, whether they liked it or not. Whether they voted for her or not, she was their teacher, their guide, their high priestess.

She began her speech and listened even as she spoke at how the beast quieted down, how their coughing ceased and their feet stopped shuffling and they no longer rattled programs or fidgeted in their seats. As her amplified words boomed across the mammoth auditorium, the beast that was her audience began to be soothed, appeased.

Yes, America is no longer the leader of half the world, Jane Scanwell told them. And better for it. We no longer need to bear the burdens of being the world's policeman. We no longer need to send our sons off to foreign battlefields to fight other people's wars. We no longer live under the threat of nuclear annihilation. We no longer pay the taxes to support a bloated, ever-growing defense budget. We live in peace, and we are no nation's slave.

Yes, our technological leadership has been overtaken by others. But we still lead the world in the production of food. And as long as the world's population keeps growing, there will be markets for America's grains and livestock. World prices may fall temporarily, but in the long run they will rise again. We must weather the bad times and prepare for the good.

Yes, unemployment is severe. But we have beaten recessions in the past and we will beat the one that faces us today. (But she did not remind the audience that more Americans were unemployed now than ever before in history.)

"There are those," the President concluded, "who look longingly to the past, seeking faded glories and a way of life that we have outgrown. There are those who look to the future with despair and fear."

She hesitated, took a breath. Not a sound from the audience. The beast was holding its breath, waiting for its mistress to tell it what to do.

"I look to the future with hope. With an optimism born of the strength of the American people. I have a vision of a new America—free, secure from the terrors of war and the burdens of overseas entanglements, threatening no one and being threatened by none, growing more prosperous with every year as we learn to live within the natural boundaries that God has given us, using the abundant resources that reside in our own lands and in our own hands and hearts and minds.

"We will move forward and rebuild our nation. We will

146

purify its air and waters as we purify our own souls with the dedication that every generation of Americans has within them. God is with us. Our strength is boundless. We are moving toward a new era of peace and prosperity for all. We have taken the hardest and most difficult steps of all—the first ones. We will persevere. We will triumph. Thank you."

They came to their feet applauding, pounding their hands together, smiling, cheering, calling to her, shouting their approval and encouragement. The big auditorium was swept by a tossing, heaving sea of applauding people.

The President stood at the podium, gripping its sides in her two hands, smiling back at them, just the hint of a tear of gratitude glistening in her eyes.

Two hours later, after the heavily guarded reception and precisely orchestrated press conference, after her staff and even most of the reporters told her what a wonderfully inspiring speech she had made, after the long, quiet drive in the dark shadows of the limousine out across the dilapidated highway, with the governor of Louisiana apologizing to her for every pothole and then renewing his plea for federal funds to rebuild "my infrastructure," Jane wondered if Dan would show up.

She had made no move at all to contact him. She had ignored his attempts to contact her. She had maintained a tighter-than-usual security guard for this trip, surrounding herself with grim-faced young men and women who just might shoot Dan Randolph dead if he tried to get past them.

But he would be at the plantation, she knew. Dan will be there. There was no doubt at all in her mind. Years ago, when life had been so much easier for them all, she and Morgan and Dan and whichever girl he had picked up for the occasion would drive all the way from Houston to Knottaway Plantation and spend a quiet weekend sipping mint juleps and watching the Mississippi go by. It was the perfect place to relax, as far removed from the real world as Tara or Camelot or Xanadu.

Now, as she bade the governor good night in the gracious

foyer of the old plantation house, and followed her trio of personal security guards up the stairs to the old master bedroom suite, she wondered how far Dan would get.

It was no surprise to her when she saw him sitting calmly on the silk damask-covered sofa at the head of the second-floor landing.

Her guards—two men, one woman—instantly pulled out their snub-nosed machine pistols. Dan sat unmoving on the sofa, his eyes on Jane.

She smiled. "It's all right. I was expecting him."

The guards relaxed and put their guns away. Slowly, though. Grudgingly. They did not like the idea of a stranger suddenly appearing, someone they had not been told about in advance.

One of the young men opened the door to the bedroom suite. Two more guards were inside. They stepped out as the President invited Dan into the suite with a wordless gesture.

She closed the door behind her. "We're alone now. There are security agents on the roof and patrolling the grounds, but nobody else in here."

Dan grinned at her. "Aren't you afraid of being compromised?"

Jane did not smile. She was a tall, stately woman, with coppery red hair and skin as smooth and white as ivory. Dan saw that the years since he had last been this close to her had taken their toll on Jane. She was still beautiful, with the sculptured flawless face of a Norse goddess and those cool green eyes that he had known so well. But she was President of the United States now; her eyes were warier, they probed more deeply; her mouth was set in a distrustful, almost suspicious frown. She was dressed in an off-white suit that was tailored severely enough to look businesslike, yet took advantage of her tall, full figure and long legs. Scant jewelry: merely a choker of pearls with matching pearl earrings, and the diamond-studded gold wedding band that Morgan had given her so long ago.

Beautiful enough to be a screen star, Jane had earned her law degree in her native Seattle, where she met a lanky, bashful Texan named Morgan Scanwell. He was an agent for the Federal Bureau of Investigation. Jane went into corporate law, and when she helped Morgan to get a new assignment in Houston, she went to Texas with him. They married, he left the FBI and went into politics, with Jane guiding his every move and helping to overcome his natural shyness. They met Dan Randolph in Houston: an eager, impetuous, blithely reckless former astronaut driving hard toward his first millions. Dan raised money for Morgan's campaigns. They became close friends. So close that Jane and Dan flirted in and out of an affair that started and stopped time and again, only to start once more. If Morgan knew, he gave no indication. And Jane pretended not to notice her husband's occasional dalliances.

Morgan became governor of Texas. Then a senator. And then he ran for president as the ultimate confrontation of the Cold War took shape and the dark clouds of nuclear annihilation gathered on every horizon. One of the women on their public relations staff came up with the idea of having Jane run alongside her husband for the vice-presidency. Dan thought it was little more than a gimmick. But the gimmick won almost every woman's vote in the country. When Morgan took the oath of office as president, his running mate became vice-president. When Morgan died in office, little more than a year later, the victim of Soviet pressures and the collapse of American will, Jane Scanwell became the first woman president in the history of the United States.

And by that time, Dan Randolph had renounced his American citizenship and fled to Venezuela.

"Just out of curiosity," Jane asked him, "how did you get in here? Security was supposed to be airtight."

"Yes, I know. They checked out every member of the staff very carefully."

Her eyebrows lifted in a wordless question.

"When I found out that you were going to give a speech in

New Orleans, I bought this place. I'm the owner. Technically speaking, Madam President, you are my guest." Dan made a sweeping, old-fashioned bow.

Jane could not help laughing. "You rogue! So when the security people checked out the staff . . ."

"They checked out the owner as well. All I had to do was show up and prove to your trigger-happy guards that I actually am Everett McKinley of Minneapolis, the owner of this noble and ancient house."

They were standing in the suite's morning room, furnished in cushioned white wicker chairs. Decanters of wines and brandies stood on the serving table next to the door that led to the actual bedroom.

Heading for the liquor, Dan asked, "Can I pour you something? That was quite a speech you gave; I watched you on television."

Jane sat on the settee next to the curtained window. "What did you think of it?"

"You were incredible," Dan said, pouring two snifters of brandy. "The country's flat on its back, so you told them they've got noplace to go but up. Quite a performance."

Her green eyes went cold. "You're being sarcastic."

Handing her one of the snifters, he replied, "Not really. I don't think you could do anything else. They all know that things have gone to the dogs. They look to you for hope."

"That's right, they do."

Dan lifted his glass and muttered. "*Salud.*"

"You're not in South America now."

He grinned sheepishly. "I forgot. I'm getting accustomed to the place."

They sipped at the brandy. Dan made a sour face. "Cheap crap! I'll have to raise hell with the staff."

"It's my favorite brand," the President said. "Your staff checked with my people."

"Your favorite? This garbage?"

"Yes. And it was Morgan's favorite, too."

Dan felt his face tighten. "He never was much of a drinker."

150

"But you are. You're a man of the world, aren't you, Dan?"

Better to let that one pass you by, he told himself. Yet as he pulled one of the smaller wicker chairs up close to the settee and sat in it, Dan said, "There wasn't anything I could do to help. You know that."

"You could have stayed by him," Jane answered in a low voice. There was anger in it, even after years. "He needed every friend he had. God knows there were few enough of them."

"I came to the funeral," Dan said. "I wasn't invited, but I snuck in anyway."

"A lot of good that did."

He took a long pull on the brandy, despite its acrid roughness, remembering how Morgan preferred raw bourbon to twenty-year-old Scotch, well-done steak to veal cordon bleu.

"So you thought my speech gave the people hope," Jane said. Her tone was determinedly brighter; she was trying to put the past behind them, Dan saw.

"Yes, I did."

"And?"

He looked at her.

"Come on, Dan. What else? What do you *really* think?"

Shrugging, he replied, "You came into office to govern a nation that's turned its back on its responsibilities. They've stuck their heads in the sand, Jane. They got tired of the tensions and the pains of being a world leader. They let their fears rule them—fears of nuclear energy, fears of weapons, fears of war, fears of inflation, fears of taxes . . ."

"They had a right to be afraid of those things."

"Sure they did. They had a right to be afraid of the Russians, too. But their other fears overpowered that. Morgan's predecessors gave our power away, piece by piece. We abandoned Israel. We got out of Latin America. We gave up on nuclear power. We froze our missiles. We let NATO break up."

"Morgan wanted to change that. The people elected him to bring us back to greatness."

"They elected him by the thinnest majority since Kennedy squeaked past Nixon. And the day of his inauguration the Russians announced their missile defense satellites were operational, and what was left of our strategic missile force was useless."

Jane said quietly, "Morgan had his first heart attack that night."

Dan felt a pang of surprise. "I didn't know."

"No one did. Not even the Cabinet or most of the White House staff." Her green eyes drifted into the past again. "He never really was president. I was, from that very first day. . . ."

"And now you're going to stand for election."

"I'll win," she said flatly. The mist in her eyes disappeared.

"I heard a lot of citizens complaining, out there," Dan said, jabbing a forefinger in the general direction of New Orleans.

She almost smiled. "What else is new? It's their right to complain."

"They claim there are Russians in the White House, telling you what to do."

"Nonsense!"

"But the Soviets *do* have a pretty effective veto on anything you want to do, don't they?"

"Certainly not!" she snapped. "This nation is free, and we'll remain free. Anyone who thinks otherwise is a fool or a malicious liar!"

He smiled at her. "Good. That's the answer I was hoping for."

"What are you driving at, Dan?"

"A way out of the mess we're in. A way to help bring this country back to greatness."

She gave him a quizzical, almost unbelieving look. The United States was not prostrate, they both knew. It was merely impotent. The people's fear of Armageddon had faded. In its place was America the second-rate power; America the debtor nation; America the coal-burner, who could not afford

152

to buy oil, whose major export was food, who had to import high-technology products such as computers and jet airplanes and electric automobiles; America disarmed, its obsolete nuclear missiles dismantled under the watchful eyes of international inspectors (Russian, Eastern European, and—most humiliating of all—Cuban), its troops mustered out of service, its vast panoply of weapons sold to other nations or left to slowly rust away in the southwestern deserts.

And it was America the unbrilliant, as well. Six years had passed since the last American had won a Nobel Prize. The Brain Drain worked in reverse: bright American scientists and engineers went overseas to find career opportunities. Dan himself had been part of the earliest wave in that flow, seeking work as an astronaut in Japan's space program when it became clear to him that the United States was abandoning space.

"It's a little late for your kind of help," Jane said.

"But—"

"I know what you're after. You're going to send a mission out to an asteroid, to prove they can be sources of raw materials for your factories in space."

He sagged back in his chair, a shock of alarm racing through him.

Jane broke into a smile. "We're not without our sources of intelligence, Dan."

He recovered and grinned weakly back at her. "So I see. Congratulations. But if you know . . ,"

"Do the Russians? No, I don't believe so. There are people who are friendly to us and not to the Russians. You know how the top dog is hated. Now that we're not top dog anymore, we have lots more friends than we used to."

Dan kept the smile on his face, but his stomach felt as queasy as the first few minutes in free fall. If she knows, the Russians must know, he thought. Our security isn't as tight as I thought it was.

"What do you want me to do about it?" Jane was asking. "How can your space mission help the United States?"

153

"We can leapfrog the Russians," he heard himself reply. It was almost as if someone else were speaking and Dan was an eavesdropper, listening to the stranger's speech while his own mind was running through the implications of the breach in his company's security.

"Leapfrog?"

"They have a monopoly on cislunar space. Everything from the Earth's surface to the Moon's orbit is theirs."

"By UN agreement, they operate—"

"The Treaty of New York," Dan said. "They shoved it up our ass and gave it a full turn."

If the President was shocked, she gave no indication of it. She merely picked up her brandy snifter and sipped from it, her eyes never leaving Dan's face.

"We have the technology to go to the asteroids for raw materials. This mission I'm sending out will prove that. It'll open up a source of natural resources bigger than Africa and Asia *and* the Pacific put together. It'll be the biggest bonanza in human history."

"And what has that got to do with the United States? We have no space operations at all."

"But you could have," Dan answered. "You could establish trading relations with Venezuela, with Japan and China and all the Third World countries. Europe would come in on it, if the States showed enough guts to do it."

"And what would the Russians do?"

"If they were faced with an alliance that included the States, Japan, China and most of the Third World? What could they do? Not a damned thing."

The President shook her head sadly. "Dan, perhaps you're right and they couldn't do anything once such an alliance was formed. But do you have any idea of what they can do to *prevent* us from even starting to make such agreements?"

"They could threaten to cut off the last of the oil, I suppose," he muttered. "Cut food prices again."

"They could also stop all our electronic communications which are relayed through their satellites," the President said. "They could seize our overseas assets . . ."

"What's left of them."

"They would get Venezuela to close down Astro Manufacturing."

"Not if you granted Astro a license to operate out of Hawaii," Dan said.

"They'd send troops to seize your launch centers, wherever they are. They'd occupy your factories in orbit."

"Not if we defended those facilities!"

"Defended them?" Jane's face showed horror. "Do you mean with soldiers?"

"Yes. What else, Girl Scouts?"

"A military confrontation? Then what's to stop the Soviets from wiping out Washington with a missile? Or Caracas, for that matter?"

Dan suddenly found that he was out of answers. "It always comes down to that, doesn't it? They still have their hydrogen bombs and missiles; we don't. They don't have to invade us, or bomb us. Just the threat is enough to make us dance to their tune."

"It won't work, Dan," the President said, her voice softening. "It just won't work."

"It won't work because none of you has the guts to make it work."

Her eyes flashed. "You want me to risk a nuclear holocaust so that you can make another billion or two?"

"This has nothing to do with money, for Chrissake!"

"Everything you do has money behind it!" Jane snapped. "You left Morgan alone, left your best friend to die, so that you could run off to Venezuela and make more *money!*"

"That's not—"

"And now you want me to put the cities of the United States at risk of a nuclear attack. You're crazy, Dan! Insane! Money mad!"

"I'm sending that mission out," he replied stubbornly. "Whatever the consequences, we're going to get ourselves an asteroid."

"You're going to get yourself an asteroid. I hope it makes you very happy. I hope it's made of solid gold."

"We can make this country great again. . . ."

"I'm not going to let you endanger the United States," the President said. "If you want to send a mission to the asteroids, or to Mars, or to hell, for that matter, go ahead and do it. But don't ask me to help you."

Dan drained the last of the foul-tasting brandy and leaned over to put his snifter down carefully on the wicker table next to the settee.

Straightening, he asked, "Do you think Morgan would have taken the same position?"

Jane's alabaster face grew even whiter, like an ice sculpture. But her eyes flamed. "If you had helped him when he needed you, he would still be alive."

"And that's the real reason you won't help me now, isn't it?"

The President got to her feet. "This is pointless. You'd better go now."

Dan stood up and realized all over again that she was almost as tall as he, and one of the most beautiful women he had ever met.

"It never worked out right for us, did it?"

"No," Jane said, her eyes still angry. "And it never will."

Dan turned and went to the door, his mind already casting ahead to the mission that would reach an asteroid. So the Russians know about it—maybe, he said to himself. And Jane won't lift a finger to help. But I'm going ahead with it anyway. The hell with them and everybody else. I'm going ahead with it!

Chapter
◆ ◆ SEVENTEEN ◆ ◆

"It's a matter of security," Dan said. "I want the entire team to stay on *Nueva Venezuela* until the launch."

Nobuhiko Yamagata tried to keep his face impassive, but failed. Dan could read unhappiness, discontent, almost misery in the young engineer's dark brown eyes. They were walking under the hot morning sun at the launch center, crunching along the gravel path from the parking area to the concrete bunker at the edge of the pad where a huge unmanned booster stood massively, like a pillar upholding the sky. A damp breeze blew in from the sea. Both men were sweating freely in their coveralls.

"I understand the need for security precautions," Nobo replied, his voice serious and respectful.

Dan squinted up at the looming booster. It was loaded with new machinery to replace worn equipment in the main orbital factory. Packed in with the machinery that was listed on the official manifest was the final set of electronics spares and a ton of liquid oxygen for the life support system of *Dolphin One*.

"Look," Dan explained, "the Russians probably already know what we're up to. God knows which of our people around here are reporting to the Soviet embassy."

Nobo did not show the slightest surprise. He merely asked, "Then why all the extra precautions?"

"Because they probably don't know *when* we're going, and exactly what we're going to do. And the less they know, the less likely they are to try to stop us."

"You believe that security will be easier to maintain aboard *Nueva Venezuela*?"

"We can control all the radio transmissions from the space station," Dan said. "It's a lot tighter than here on the ground."

They reached the heavy steel door of the bunker. As he reached for its handle, Dan saw the agonized look on the young man's face. He let his hand drop and leaned against the concrete wall, grateful for the scant slice of shade it provided.

"What's the matter, Nobo?"

"A personal matter. I shouldn't allow it to get in the way of this mission, I know, but . . ."

"Who is she?"

His head dropping low, Nobo replied, "Señorita Hernandez, the one you brought to Sapporo."

Dan felt his eyebrows climb toward his scalp. "Lucita?"

With a barely discernible nod, Nobo said, "Lucita. I've had several dinners with her since she's returned to Caracas."

"Dinners." Dan felt like a stupid echo.

"While you were away last week we made plans to sail over to Aruba for the weekend. But if I have to go to the space station . . ."

A wave of resentment, almost anger, washed over Dan. But it ebbed away almost as quickly as it came. What did you expect? he asked himself. She's young, she feels trapped, her father's turned into an enemy, her best friend killed herself. And you've been off wooing the Ice Queen to no avail. Did you think she was going to sit around and wait for you to notice her? Nobo's her own age. And he's far from home. Probably pretty lonesome. Why shouldn't they find each other and be together? He laughed at his own feelings of

158

surprise and indignation. What does she mean to you, except more trouble than you need? Better that the two of them get together. Forget about her, there's an infinite supply of women. Why get emotional about her?

But even as he thought it, he heard himself saying, "Nobo, I've decided to push the launch schedule up by at least a week, more if we can do it without taking too many risks. The whole crew will have to be up at the station by Friday, at the latest."

The young Japanese closed his eyes in acquiescence. "I understand. Is it all right if I see her tonight or tomorrow, before going to the station?"

"Sure," Dan replied generously. "Go right ahead. But don't tell her anything more than you have to."

With the woeful expression of a disappointed lover, Nobuhiko made a slight bow and said, "Of course not. Thank you."

Dan felt only slightly guilty as he pulled open the bunker's door and stepped into its icily air-conditioned interior.

He gave a party at his apartment that weekend, after Nobo, Carstairs and the rest of the *Dolphin*'s crew had shuttled off to *Nueva Venezuela*. Good cover, he told himself. Throw a party, make everybody think you've got nothing terribly important on your mind. He made certain that his human and robot secretaries invited the Russian ambassador and key members of his staff. And the American ambassador and his flunkies, of course. Plus most of the other ambassadors, and the cream of Caracas' literary and artistic set. A few carefully selected news reporters and columnists. And top members of the Venezuelan government, naturally. Including the Minister of Technology; it would be unthinkable not to invite Señor Hernandez. And his daughter, too.

Dan played the perfect host, affable, friendly to everyone, even the Russians. He flirted with Lissa Andrews and instructed one of the human butlers to make certain that the American ambassador did not drink so much that he made a fool of himself. Videotapes of the newest Hollywood productions were run continuously in the screening room, and Dan had flown the leading ladies of two of the steamier ones in for the weekend. The Russian ambassador, stiff and distrustful at first, melted under the combined influence of vodka and the voluptuous attentions of the more spectacularly endowed of the two actresses.

Hernandez arrived, very late, without his daughter. Dan greeted him casually; the Venezuelan replied with cold formality.

"Is your daughter well?" Dan asked over the noise of the party. A live jazz band flown in from New Orleans was making the walls vibrate. A robot server, little more than a wheeled tray guided by a microprocessor chip and a video eye that allowed it to thread its way through the crowd, stopped at Hernandez's side and beeped for attention.

The Minister of Technology looked down at the tray of drinks, selected champagne and then turned his calculating brown eyes back to Dan. The robot, sensing one drink removed from its burden, rolled off into the throng.

"I understand there was a tragedy in your family," Dan said. He was practically yelling into Hernandez's ear.

"My youngest sister died," the Venezuelan said. Dan read it off his lips; the man's voice was lost in the party noise.

"My condolences."

"Thank you."

"And your daughter? How is she taking this loss?"

"It was a great shock to her, but she will recover."

"I hope so."

Hernandez sipped at the champagne, his eyes searching the noisy, frantic room.

"How did it happen?" Dan asked. "I understand they were on *Kosmograd*."

"Excuse me," replied Hernandez. "I must say hello to the Soviet ambassador."

"Of course," Dan said graciously, adding silently, You bastard!

The party was still blazing away at full intensity when midnight struck. Dan slipped away, unnoticed, and rode the elevator up to the top floor. He made his way through the carpeted corridors and empty offices to the communications center where, among other things, there was a desktop computer terminal linked directly to the laser receiver mounted on the building's roof. He looked at his wristwatch: in thirty seconds it would be exactly 12:10. A message was to be beamed by laser from *Dolphin One* to the rooftop in Caracas. No electronic eavesdropper could overhear the message, because it rode on the laser's narrow beam of light. *If* a snooper could position himself within a city block or so of the roof with the proper equipment, and *if* he knew exactly when the message would be transmitted, he might be able to intercept it. Even so, he would then have to decode it.

Exactly as the digits on Dan's watch flicked to 12:10:00, the computer screen flashed and showed a momentary string of black dots dancing across its phosphorescent face. Before Dan could blink his eyes, the dots were replaced by the decoded message: *All systems go. On schedule.*

Dan hadn't realized he'd been holding his breath until he let it out with a long, heartfelt sigh. That was the last transmission he would receive from Carstairs, Nobo and the rest of the crew, unless something went wrong. Everything was on schedule. They would be on their way in forty-eight hours.

He pressed the terminal keys that would erase the message from the computer's memory. Then he made his way back down to the party. The elevator doors slid open and a solid wall of noise slammed into Dan. He stepped out, took a glass of straight Scotch from a passing robot server and noticed Zach Freiberg staring at him from across the crowded room with questioning eyes.

Our security leak? Dan wondered. Freiberg would not be a conscious informer, he knew, but the scientist was not the tightest man with information. Dan nodded to him and raised his glass slightly. Freiberg broke into a big, boyish grin. If anybody's looking for a clue, Dan told himself, there it is.

Dawn was well advanced before the last of his guests straggled to the elevator and left. The Soviet ambassador was among the finalists, propped on either side by hefty unsmiling men who were utterly sober.

"A delightful party," he told Dan blurrily. "Leave it to the capitalists to throw a wonderful, decadent party. I must get the name of that actress. . . ."

His two bodyguards dragged him into the elevator. The last Dan saw of the ambassador, the old man was giggling and waving to him with both hands as the guards held him up between them.

"You must sober me up quickly," he mumbled to the guards in Russian. "Comrade Malik is arriving today. . . ."

The doors slid shut.

Malik! Coming back here. Dan stood for a long, silent moment, staring at the closed elevator doors. Why? he asked himself. What's he up to? How much does he know?

Making a mental note to have his intelligence people tweak their sources inside the Soviet embassy, Dan made his way through the litter and stale smoke of the dead party toward his bedroom, wondering what he could do to improve the security of the asteroid mission. Malik here in Caracas, less than forty-eight hours before the spacecraft's departure. That's not good. Double-damn it to hell, that's not good at all!

He found both actresses in his bed, wrapped in each other's slithering arms and long smooth legs, oblivious to him and everything else except each other. There's nothing I can do about Malik right now, Dan told himself. With a shake of his head, he decided that there would be time enough later on to comb out the bugs that the Russians had undoubtedly strewn around his apartment. They probably stuck a few thimble-sized video cameras here and there, too.

If they want to see capitalist decadence, this ought to make their eyes pop. He quickly stripped and joined the two sweaty, drug-dazed women on the big, delicious waterbed.

Chapter
◆ ◆ EIGHTEEN ◆ ◆

Hernandez had arrived home from Dan Randolph's party early, shortly after midnight. But then he went out again and did not return until nearly dawn.

Lucita, sleeping fitfully in her room on the third floor of the rambling old house, heard his comings and goings and knew that he had been to see one of his women. He keeps a harem, she said to herself as she combed her hair that morning, sitting at her dresser. The good Lord alone knows how many women think that he loves them. When he dies, half the women in Caracas will wear black.

She put the brush down and stared at herself in the dresser mirror. There was no makeup on her face. She had just showered. Her eyes were not puffy, but dark rings of sleeplessness marred them. It had been a long time since she had laughed, or even smiled. Not since she had last seen Dan Randolph. And even then . . .

She shook her head, dismissing such thoughts from her mind. Or trying to. Getting up from the dresser, she crossed the broad, sunny bedroom and went to her clothes closet. Opening one of its triple doors, she saw her full-length reflection in its long mirror.

Lucita slipped off her robe and let it drop to the floor. Naked, she examined her image closely. A little bird, she thought. A plucked chicken. Scrawny, almost. Your legs are too thin, your hips too narrow. Your breasts are small—But she turned sideways, profiling herself. Not that small, I suppose. At least they don't sag. And your backside isn't as big as most of the girls'. Some of them look like they're carrying watermelons around with them.

Still, she ached for the tall long-legged exotic good looks of the mestizo girls she saw in the city. Smooth skin the color of old ivory, high cheekbones and almond eyes, they somehow got the best of their mixed Indian, Spanish and black blood. I'm just a short, pale, plucked chicken, Lucita thought.

Carefully she selected a pair of jeans and a sleeveless light pink blouse, then tugged on the most elevating pair of rope sandals in the closet. She was putting on a touch of lipstick, back at the dresser, when her maid tapped timidly at the door.

"Enter," Lucita called out.

"Your father wants to speak with you," the maid said. She was an older woman, in her thirties, plump enough to show that she did not work terribly hard.

"He's awake?"

The maid smirked. "I think he has a hangover. The cook said he refused to take anything at breakfast except coffee."

Lucita asked, "Do you know what he wants me for?" She and her father had been living a sort of distant truce, sharing the big house while meeting each other as little as possible. Teresa's death hung between them like a barrier of pain. Despite what had happened to Teresa, Hernandez was going ahead with his plans to marry his daughter to Vasily Malik.

"There was a telephone call," the maid replied. "From the Russian embassy, the butler said. Your fiancé has arrived. . . ."

"He is not my fiancé!"

The maid shrugged. "Your intended."

Lucita shot to her feet. "You will tell my father that I was already gone when you came into my room."

"Gone? Where?"

"Out! Away from here. Away from *him* . . . both of them!"

Hastily filling a small leather pocketbook with her necessities, Lucita shooed the maid out of her room as she hurried to the back steps and raced down to the garage. She startled the chauffeur, sipping a late morning cup of coffee as he chatted idly with one of the cook's young helpers. Striding past the gleaming limousine and the smaller Mercedes, Lucita went wordlessly, tight-lipped with angry determination, to her own MG convertible. It was nearly six years old, and its transmission was as cranky as the mother superior at school. Lucita would allow no one to drive it except herself, and even then it needed the constant attention of a mechanic. But she loved her forest-green little convertible, had fallen instantly in love with it when she had first seen it and begged her father to buy it for her. It had been her birthday present when she turned sixteen.

Now she slid behind the wheel, slammed the door shut and gunned the engine to life. The bellow made the garage ring. She backed out, the sudden hot sunlight feeling strong and good on her shoulders, swung around on the driveway and roared out onto the road.

Out of the corner of her eye she saw her father standing at the long window of the living room, looking out at her. He was too far away for her to read the expression on his face.

She drove aimlessly, out onto the highway that ran around the city's perimeter. I must create a life of my own, she told herself. I must get away from my father and this marriage he has planned for me. Yes, but how? she asked herself. Where? How can you earn a living in this world beyond your father's walls? You have no skills. You know nothing except what the good sisters taught you: how to become a docile Catholic wife and mother.

Something made her glance at the rearview mirror as she

raced down the broad highway. The same black sedan that she had seen several miles back was still behind her. The highway was busy with four full lanes of huffing trailer rigs, overloaded buses and cars that ranged from dilapidated junks to brand-new Mitsubishis, made at the assembly plant in La Guaira. Yet this black sedan, a BMW, was still just behind her. Police? Lucita wondered. But why?

Then she thought, My father is having me followed!

Suddenly furious, she downshifted and cut in front of an approaching minivan to get into the left lane, then leaned on the gas pedal until the other traffic was only a blur as she whizzed past. Let's see them follow me now!

By the time she reached the cable car terminal the black sedan was nowhere in sight. Lucita parked her MG, bought a ticket and got onto the big, boxy car. It was almost empty, so she was able to take a seat on the front bench, with the full width of the front window to herself. Now she could be alone for half an hour as the cable car rode up into the cloud-wrapped mountain and then down again, to La Guiara. There was a little restaurant at the foot of the mountain, where she could have lunch alone, unbothered.

The car moved smoothly up the green mountain, swaying only slightly as it glided high above the squatters' shacks of cardboard and plywood. Lucita saw ragged children playing down in the weeds and bare, worn ground between the shacks. Goats were tethered here and there; the area was filthy with litter and piles of garbage.

Looking up, though, she saw the blessed gray mist of the clouds that clung almost always to the mountain's upper slopes. Oblivion. She wished the car would hurry into it.

But once surrounded by the gray featureless mist, with nothing to see but drops of condensed moisture trickling past her own dim reflection in the window, Lucita's mind returned to that terrible night in the Russian space station.

Her visit in Russia had been happy enough, although she could never escape the feeling of being watched every moment. Teresa was enjoying herself, and Malik seemed determined to show her that he was an attentive, urbane and charming host. It was clear that his position in the government was very high; Lucita found herself being treated like royalty.

She had never been in space before, and when Malik asked if she would like to visit one of the Soviet space cities, she agreed eagerly. Not until that night, when she and Teresa were alone in the luxury apartment that Malik had obtained for them, did she learn that Teresa was terrified of the idea of leaving the Earth.

Lucita laughed at her young aunt's fears and the two of them, accompanied by Malik and a handful of his young aides, rode a Soviet shuttle to *Kosmograd*. It was like an airplane ride, nothing more, except that there were no windows to look through. The space station was much larger than Lucita had expected, and after a few days, even Teresa had to admit that she felt almost as if they were still on solid ground.

They tried zero-gravity gliding in the space station's huge, spherical gymnasium. Lucita found it wonderfully exhilarating Teresa got sick and had to return to their cabin where gravity was normal.

Malik made overtures to Lucita, but she thought they were more formalities that he believed were expected from him rather than signs of real ardor. It was like an old-fashioned, old-world courting, where the swain might hold the young beauty's hand—but only under the watchful eye of her duenna. Lucita found it amusing. Malik appeared to expect nothing more. He even seemed surprised when she kissed him good night at her cabin door after they had spent the evening watching the Earth glide by through the big window in the space station's main observation center.

After three days, Malik had to return to Moscow. At Lucita's insistence, he made arrangements for the two women to go home to Caracas. Since there were no direct flights from *Kosmograd*, the Russian arranged a transfer to *Nueva Venezuela*; from there they could return home easily.

Their last night together, Malik invited Lucita to dinner in his quarters, alone. She hesitated long enough to let him know she considered this very forward, then agreed. He was utterly polite, to the point where Lucita wondered if there was any passion for her in him.

He smiled from across the candlelit table and, as if reading her thoughts, told her, "I hope you understand how much self-control I have had to exert these past few weeks."

"Self-control?" Lucita echoed.

His pale blue eyes sparkled in the candlelight. "I am not accustomed to the formalities of a Latin courtship, you know. We Russians are generally more . . . um, impetuous in our wooing."

Lucita reached for her wine goblet and took a sip before replying, "Have you swept many women off their feet with your impetuousness?"

"You're laughing at me," he said. There was no rancor in it.

"Vasily," Lucita replied, "we have seen each other every day for more than two weeks now, but we are still little more than strangers."

"Yet we are to be married."

"Someday," she admitted. "Perhaps."

"I . . ." The smile faded from his lips. For just a moment he looked troubled. "I have been very formal with you. I understand that you will need time to get to know me, and to accept the fact that we will be man and wife—someday. I don't want to do anything that would offend you, or your father. Yet . . ."

She waited for him to finish the thought. When he did not, she prompted, "Yet?"

Reaching across the table to take her hand in both of his, Malik said, "You are very beautiful, Lucita. And very desirable. I want you very much."

For an instant her pulse quickened. But then she saw something in his pale eyes, something that not even candlelight could disguise, something cold and calculating.

"What would my father say?" she asked, almost in a whisper.

He released her hand. "Yes. I know."

"I think I should go back to my room now," Lucita said.

"Damn politics!" Malik slammed his napkin to the floor. But he got to his feet and escorted Lucita back to her cabin door. She stood on tiptoe to kiss him good night. He held her around the waist and pressed her close, the first time he had done so.

"I want this to be more than a political marriage, Lucita," he whispered. "I want you to love me."

She closed her eyes and thought of her father and the other marriages of hypocrisy she knew in Caracas, where the wives accompanied their husbands on social occasions and seldom saw them otherwise, where the men could be seen in nightclubs with their young mistresses while the wives stayed home with their broods of children.

"It takes time, Vasily," she whispered back to him. "Please don't rush me."

He smiled and took her hand and kissed it like a cavalier of old, then walked away. As she opened the unlocked cabin door, Lucita began to wonder if the calculations she saw in his eyes concerned her or something else.

Teresa lay sprawled on the floor of the cabin, her skirt torn from her body, her blouse bunched up at her shoulders. There was blood on her bare thighs, bruises across her naked torso. The imprint of a hand welted one bare breast. Shreds of panty hose clung to her calfs.

Her eyes fluttered open. "Lucita . . ." she moaned.

A scream caught in Lucita's throat. But she could not make a sound, horrified though she was. She dropped to her knees beside her young aunt.

"What happened? Teresa, what happened?"

"They raped me. . . ."

"Mother of God! Who did this? How could they . . ."

She lifted Teresa's head from the floor. One eye was swollen shut. Blood crusted her lips.

The rest was a nightmare. She phoned Malik for help as Teresa mumbled her nearly incoherent story. Two young crewmen. She had taken dinner in the station's main galley. They had sat at the same table with her. They spoke no Spanish, Teresa spoke no Russian. She said nothing to them. She ate and returned to her cabin. They followed her and called after her as she hurried down the corridor. There was no lock on the door; they burst in. She tried to phone. She tried to fight them off. They beat her brutally and took turns raping her.

Malik arrived, white-faced with rage. A doctor came. An officer in uniform. They tried to question Teresa, but she was shaking with terror and shame now. The officer was some sort of policeman. He and Malik conversed in low, urgent voices and he left. Lucita and the doctor helped Teresa to her bed. The doctor gave her an injection to make her sleep.

"We'll find the men who did this," Malik said, his eyes glinting like the steel blade of a knife. "I promise you, they will be found and punished."

After all the men left, Lucita sat up in her bed next to Teresa's and watched the sleeping young woman. She did not move, barely breathed. Lucita drowsed, her head slumping down to her chest, her eyes too heavy to keep open.

When she awoke, Teresa's rumpled bed was empty. Startled, Lucita jumped to her feet. She saw that the light in the cubbyhole of a bathroom was on. Teresa was huddled in the shower stall, both wrists slashed open, her agonized face staring sightlessly up at Lucita, her life's blood already turning brown and crusty as it seeped down the shower drain.

The cable car broke out of the gray mist and bright Venezuelan sunshine flooded in through the big windows. Lucita squeezed her eyes shut, and the vision of Teresa's dead body melted away like the drops of condensed moisture on the glass before her. She took a deep, shuddering breath and brought herself back to the world of today.

The car glided to a stop in its terminal at the foot of the

mountain and its pneumatic doors slid open. The eight other people aboard shuffled out slowly, almost silently. Lucita was the last to leave. And standing there on the concrete platform, waiting for her, was the tall, blond figure of Vasily Malik.

Somehow, she was not surprised. Lucita knew that there was no place on Earth, or even beyond it, where she could hide from this man.

He was wearing a military uniform of tan with red trim at the collar. It made him look more handsome than ever. A dozen yards away, two men in dark civilian suits stood watching. Bodyguards for Vasily? Lucita wondered. Or jailers for me?

"Lucita . . ." He reached out a hand toward her, tentatively.

"Hello, Vasily." She decided not to ask him how he had found her there. The black car following her on the highway had been Russian, not police. They had followed her to the cable car terminal, and Vasily had helicoptered to the other end of the line, obviously.

"You left *Kosmograd* before we had a chance to apprehend the . . . those who . . ."

"I brought my aunt's body back to her home. We buried her last week."

"I never got the chance to tell you how sorry I am, how much I regret that this happened."

"I'm sure you do, Vasily."

People were making their way across the platform to enter the waiting cable car. Malik put out his arm to guide Lucita back toward the rear of the platform, where the steps led down to the parking lot. She moved before his hand could touch her. He let his arm drop and walked alongside her.

"We caught the two men responsible. A pair of Ukrainian mechanics." He said it as if he were describing noisome vermin. "They were drunk and they thought that your aunt was . . . well, they made the mistake of their lives."

"Are they still alive?" Lucita asked coldly.

Malik said, "Yes, but they both wish otherwise by now,

171

I'm sure. I had them sent to the lunar mines. Hard labor. They'll never see the Earth again."

As they stepped out of the cool shade of the concrete-roofed terminal and into the burning noontime sun, Malik said, "I hope that this terrible tragedy doesn't come between us, Lucita. I hope you don't blame me for what happened."

She looked up at him as they walked down the concrete steps and saw that he was very grave, very sincere. "No, Vasily. I know it wasn't your fault. It was mine."

"That's not possible!"

As she spoke the words, Lucita realized that they were true. "It *was* my fault. All my fault. I dragged Teresa around the world with me. I left her alone that night. I fell asleep when I should have been watching over her. I killed her."

He stopped in the middle of the long stairway and turned to her. "You mustn't think that. The victim is not responsible for the crime. It was the fault of two drunken louts, and they are paying for their outrage."

And I must pay, also, Lucita told herself. I must stop running away from my responsibilities. I must become an adult and accept the duties that have fallen to me. There is no escaping it. I will marry this man whether I love him or not. Whether he loves me or not. There is no escaping it.

Chapter
◆ ◆ NINETEEN ◆ ◆

For more than two months Dan went through the motions of leading a normal life. Normal for him. He worked at his office in Caracas. He visited the launch center off the coast at least twice a week. He changed secretaries almost regularly; the joke around the office was that no secretary of Dan Randolph's lasted longer than her menstrual cycle.

He traveled up to *Nueva Venezuela* regularly, but stayed at the space station only briefly each time before riding a slim, needle-shaped transfer craft over to the factory. A new module had been added to the orbital manufacturing facility: a smallish metal globe that was connected to the factory's control center by a jutting length of tube which served as a corridor to connect the two.

The new globe had nothing to do with the factory's operations. It was a control center, small and stripped down by comparison to the control centers the old NASA once operated at Houston and the Jet Propulsion Laboratory in Pasadena, but immediately recognizable by its banks of video screen monitors manned by intense men and women with earphones and pin mikes clamped to their heads.

Hanging in mid-air weightlessly next to the mission controller, a big, athletic-looking Angolan named Njombe, Zach Freiberg looked almost like a fugitive from a nursery. But Freiberg put in more hours at the control center than anyone. He was the scientific leader of the asteroid mission; he was living aboard *Nueva Venezuela* and spending eighteen-hour days in the control center, following every move, every breath and heartbeat of *Dolphin One*'s eight-man crew.

Dan would pop in for a few minutes, see that the spacecraft was coasting on schedule toward the chunk of rock floating through space, listen to the routine chatter between the crew and the mission controllers, and return to the space station to put in the semblance of ordinary business. If the Russians actually knew about the asteroid mission, they were not giving any hint of it. All Dan's intelligence probes and bribes had returned no information, no sign that the Russians were aware of what was going on.

Freiberg would return to the space station every few days with a batch of videotapes, and at night he would play the edited highlights of the past days' communications for Dan, behind the locked door of his quarters aboard *Nueva Venezuela*.

"All's well as can be expected," Carstairs reported on the mission's fortieth day. "Electrical power's down six percent from nominal; I've scheduled an EVA for tomorrow to check the solar panels. Might be a micrometeor cracked one of the cells. Or maybe dust coating 'em." His Australian accent said "mybe."

The voice of one of the mission controllers said, "We copy the tail off in electrical power. EVA is approved." He said it over Carstairs' continued talking, because it took his laser-borne words slightly more than a full minute to reach the spacecraft, nearly twelve million miles away. Because of the time lag in communications, there were no conversations between the spacecraft and the control center; they had two nearly simultaneous monologues instead.

"The bloody toilet's acting up again," Carstairs was complaining. "In all these years of battin' about in space you'd

174

think somebody would come up with a zero-gee toilet that actually *works*. And the air scrubbers are gettin' marginal. Nothing the instruments will show, but it's startin' to smell foul in here. Damn tight living, y'know.'' Carstairs grinned. "I think I'm fallin' in love with Halloran."

Halloran, the young geochemist from Chicago, happened to be just behind Carstairs at that moment. His beefy face turned as red as his brick-colored hair.

"Don't let him fool you, Halloran," said the mission controller, "it's just a shipboard romance."

But while the joke was speeding toward the spacecraft on the laser beam, Halloran—still red-faced—spluttered a denial laced with as much profanity as he knew. Which was neither large in quantity nor original in quality.

Dan laughed, sitting in his darkened cabin, lit only by the TV screen. Freiberg grinned too. Dan had insisted that all the crew members be male and heterosexual. He wanted no romantic entanglements of any kind during this long, difficult mission. He did not bother asking his company psychologists about it: why risk a security leak when he already was convinced of what he wanted? Thinking back to his own days as a working astronaut, he remembered that masturbation is much less damaging than murder.

With the inexorable precision of astronomical mathematics, the spacecraft made its rendezvous with the asteroid. Dan spent that whole day in the crowded, tense control center, in the back of the hot, sweaty room where he could survey the entire chamber easily. The circular chamber was dimmed, lit mainly by the glowing TV screens and banks of lighted control studs that lined each controller's desk.

It was one thing to read a report that the asteroid was not much longer than a football field. It was quite another to see this enormous boulder tumbling slowly as it glided through space. It was only slightly oblong, almost as thick as its length, and *big*. Its dark, brooding ponderousness dwarfed the approaching spacecraft.

Dan watched in rapt silence. The control center crackled with nervous electricity. Freiberg, down at the center of the string of monitoring desks, was literally quivering with excitement. Dan could see that the scientist could hardly stay still; his hands were fluttering like a pair of large moths drawn to the light of the TV picture in front of him. He jittered as he dangled weightlessly in front of his monitor screen, jouncing and bouncing so much that he occasionally floated too far off the floor and had to pull himself down again. He had grown so accustomed to the zero gravity of the factory that he hardly noticed his own antics. But Dan laughed to himself. *Better put a safety tether on Zach or he'll float right out of here.*

The mission controllers were watching their instruments and muttering into their headsets in the muted whispers of worshipers in a cathedral.

Christ, I wish I was there, Dan said to himself as he watched the main display screen, which took up most of the room's front wall.

The spacecraft's outside cameras showed views of the massive, looming asteroid. It was black and pitted, its surface lumpy and irregular. It reminded Dan of a huge chunk of coal.

"Isn't she beautiful?" Freiberg's voice sang through the darkness. "Isn't she gorgeous?"

A few low chuckles answered.

"She's metallic all right," Freiberg said, loud enough for everyone to hear. "Got to be. Look at her. Nickel-iron, or I'll eat it. Enough good steel in her to run this factory for ten years. Maybe more."

The second shift of controllers came on the job as Carstairs, Vargas and Halloran were emerging from the spacecraft's airlock for their first EVA jaunt to the asteroid. The original shift relinquished their posts grudgingly. None of them left the control center. They clustered in the back, around Dan, eyes glued to the display screen. Dan could feel the heat of their bodies in the darkness, smell the excitement in them.

Somebody passed a tray of coffee and soft drinks as the three-astronaut team jetted across the hundred yards or so between the spacecraft and the asteroid. They looked like tiny white midges next to the pitted dark bulk of the huge rock. Nobo was in charge aboard the spacecraft now, Dan knew. He saw the craft's manipulator arms extending slowly, like a sluggish metal spider extending its many limbs.

Carstairs was the first to reach the dark, pitted asteroid. His space-suited form reminded Dan of a knight in white armor. Vargas was carrying a video camera and he got a good close-up of Carstairs planting his boots on the rock's barren surface. He came in slightly too fast, though, and bounced off. The jets of his backpack puffed briefly and he settled down on the bare, airless rock like a deep-sea diver gingerly touching bottom.

"I name this little worldlet"—Carstairs' voice sounded faint and slightly muffled inside his helmet—"after the man who made this voyage possible: *Randolph One*. And may there be thousands more like it."

Dan let out his breath. He had not thought about giving the asteroid a name. In the shadowy darkness of the crowded control center, he heard mutters from the men and women standing around him.

"Carstairs is bucking for a raise, boss," somebody said.

"He's got it," Dan shot back.

It turned out to be a metallic asteroid, just as Freiberg had predicted. Halloran set about testing samples of it, chipping off pieces and carrying them back to the small analysis lab aboard the spacecraft. Almost pure nickel-steel, about four million tons of it. Among the impurities he found over the next two days was platinum.

"I estimate there's somewhere between fifty and seventy-five tons of platinum in her," Halloran reported, his florid face grinning into the TV camera.

Dan grinned back at the geochemist's happy image. Platinum was somewhere around $500 per troy ounce, he recalled. Fifty to seventy-five tons, he calculated swiftly, would come to $600 to $900 million. *That pays for the mission all by itself! With a bit of profit besides. Sai will be ecstatic.*

The question then was whether or not the crew should attempt to alter the asteroid's orbit so that it could be "captured" by Earth's gravity and swung into a permanent orbit between the Earth and Moon, where it could be more easily reached and mined. Back when *Randolph I* had been nothing more than a numbered speck of light in an astronomical catalog, Freiberg had picked this particular asteroid for their first mission because it was close enough to reach, it appeared to be a metal-rich body and its orbit was such that it could be maneuvered into an Earth-circling orbit.

During the two days that Halloran and the other crew members spent assaying the rock samples and filling the spacecraft's storage tanks with them, computers in Caracas and California (thanks to Freiberg's friends at Cal Tech) checked every facet of the orbital maneuver to twelve decimal places.

"I don't want to send a four-million-ton spitball into an orbit that'll crash into the Earth," Dan insisted.

"You just don't want to lose all that platinum," Freiberg kidded back.

"Check it again, Zach."

"Figures don't lie, Dan. And they're not going to change."

"Check it again."

The alternative was to allow the asteroid to continue on the orbit it had been following for millions of years, swinging out past the Sun and returning to Earth's vicinity every three years. If the astronauts altered that orbit, *Randolph I* would end up circling the Earth at about the same distance as the Moon—a tiny new moonlet.

The numbers checked and checked again. Dan still felt a gnawing uneasiness about the idea. He could accept, intellectually, that the asteroid would not crash into the Earth. But something deep in his guts was warning him that it was unwise to push the rock out of its natural path around the Sun.

Nine hundred million dollars, he argued with himself, from the platinum alone. And enough nickel and iron to allow us to start a whole new operation here at the factory. The Russians don't have any of the heavier metals; there aren't any on the Moon.

Reluctantly, still feeling vague forebodings, he gave the order to push the asteroid into an Earth-circling orbit. Nearly twenty million miles away, the astronaut team unrolled huge aluminized sheets of plastic—Reynolds Wrap, Dan always called them—and fitted them to the prefabricated frame of a concave solar mirror. They set it up at a mathematically chosen spot on the asteroid's bare, dark surface. Sunlight, focused to an intensity that boiled metal, jabbed its searing finger at the asteroid's body. The boiling metal acted like the jet exhaust of a rocket engine, exerting a force on the massive rock that altered its trajectory slightly. For two more days, as the astronauts made their preparations to leave the asteroid and return to Earth, Freiberg and a picked team of astronomers watched the asteroid carefully.

"It all checks out," the scientist told Dan. "She's swerving slightly, right on the predicted course. Eleven months from now the Earth will gain an extra moon, and you'll have a billion-dollar platinum mine at your disposal."

Dan smiled and shook Freiberg's hand. "Mission accomplished," he said. But he still had that uneasy feeling in the pit of his stomach.

He had two more months to wait while the *Dolphin One* made its way back to Earth. Two months to pretend to be doing business as usual, paying the Soviets their increased prices for lunar ores, playing the role of the billionaire bachelor, partying and being seen in public with the world's most beautiful women.

Everything in Caracas seemed to be normal. Too normal, Dan worried. The only unusual thing he could detect was that

179

Malik seemed to be visiting the city every other week. His ostensible reason was to court Lucita Hernandez. But what's his real reason? Dan asked himself. He decided that there was one person who might know: Lucita Hernandez.

Chapter
◆ ◆ TWENTY ◆ ◆

Their meeting had to appear casual, yet private. Dan was under no illusions. The KGB watched every move he made, as a matter of course. He was accustomed to that. And he suspected that Malik had a team of people watching Lucita, too.

"Two can play at that game," Dan muttered to himself. Phoning the director of the Astro Manufacturing division that operated the company's Earth resources satellites, Dan soon had detailed photographs of Caracas playing across the wall-sized TV screen in his office.

The pictures were taken by satellites that kept their exquisitely sharp camera eyes and other sensors focused on the Earth, from altitudes that ranged from a few hundred to one thousand miles up. The data they recorded on videotape was sold to customers around the world who were willing to pay for such information. Commodities speculators wanted to know how grain and other crops were growing, all over the world. Geologists looked for rock formations that promised the presence of oil or other natural resources. Environmental protection agencies wanted to see sources of pollution. Commercial fishermen needed to find schools of fish. Railroad managers used the satellite data to keep track of their trains and even individual cars. The city planners of Caracas used the pictures to see, day by day, how their zoning and building laws were being obeyed.

Much of the data that Dan's company sold around the world was illegal. International law forbade giving up any data about a nation that had not been previously approved for release by that nation. And almost every nation in the world stoutly refused to release *any* data about its own territory. Some of the individual governments, such as many in Africa, refused because they did not want foreign nations or corporations to know about their mineral wealth; they had a long history of foreign exploitation, and no desire to continue it. Other nations, like the Soviet Union, were secretive to the point of paranoia; any pictures taken of their territory were regarded as spying. Still others, such as some of the jackboot dictatorships in Latin America and Southeast Asia, did not want the world to know how harshly they were treating their own people, and how poorly the people were faring under military rule.

Yet Astro's satellites orbited placidly over every nation on Earth, beaming pictures and other forms of data to the corporate headquarters in Caracas. And the company sold the information to almost every nation—even those that protested the loudest against such "spying." The entire operation was known to all. And although it was as illegal as reproducing the pages of a library book in a copying machine, or secretly videotaping a new Broadway production, it went on anyway. The protests were formalities. The reality was that nations, corporations, even private individuals were willing to pay for the satellite data. They were willing to pay for it because they needed it, for their businesses, for their national welfare and security.

Dan needed the pictures of Caracas for a slightly different reason. With computer enhancement, he was able to watch the Hernandez home and see, day by day, when Lucita's forest-green MG left the house and where it went. Because it was a convertible, he could even enlarge the pictures electronically to the point where he could see that the driver was dark-haired.

"Look up," he muttered late one night as he stared at the pictures on the huge screen in his office. "Smile for the camera."

Within a week he—and the computer—had determined Lucita's pattern of movements fairly well. She was by no means a creature of habit, he saw. But there were some things she did almost every week. The problem he saw was that her little convertible was never alone for very long. At least two cars almost always accompanied her, one ahead and one behind. Possibly she did not know about her escorts; the Soviets changed cars daily, so that she would not notice the same ones from one day to the next. But Malik was having her followed, either because he wanted to protect her or because he did not trust her.

Dan smiled to himself in the shadows of his darkened office. "I'll bet the Russian doesn't trust her," he muttered. "Why would he have her followed, otherwise? She's in no danger here; this is her home. What's there to protect her from—except me?"

The morning dawned hot and clear. Lucita dressed quickly in shorts and halter and hurried down to the small dining room to be certain to catch her father before he finished breakfast and left for his office.

He was just dabbing his damask napkin to his lips, his coffee cup drained, the platter before him holding nothing but crumbs and the rind of a quarter melon.

"Good morning," Lucita said, beaming at him as if they had never been estranged.

Hernandez almost frowned, a reflex of disapproval at her scanty costume. But he held the scowl in check.

"Good morning, Lucita."

She perched on a corner of the heavy, stiff-backed chair

at her father's right hand. "It is a beautiful morning, isn't it?"

"Yes," he answered warily, almost suspiciously.

"Father"—she reached for his hand—"we have been angry with each other long enough. What is past is past, and we cannot change it."

A surprised smile unbent his lips.

"I am finished mourning for Teresa," she went on. "Actually, I was mourning for myself, I think. I was being a spoiled, stubborn child. I ask you to forgive me, Papa. I want you to love me again."

Hernandez drew in a deep, delighted breath. "I have always loved you, Lucita. Even when you caused me pain."

"I'm sorry for that, Papa." Her eyes dropped.

He reached out and lifted her chin slightly, so that he could look directly into her eyes again. "It must have been painful for you, also."

"Yes, it was."

"Can you truly put it all behind you?"

"Yes. I want to."

He studied her for a long, wordless moment. "Last night, you went to dinner with Vasily again?"

With a little smile, she replied, "He visits every other week, he asks me to dinner each night he is here, and I accept his invitation every time."

Hernandez arched an eyebrow. "Like a dutiful daughter."

"I will be more than dutiful from now on," she promised. "If he still wants to marry me, and you still want me to, I will agree."

She had thought that her father would be elated by her decision. But his face was somber, his flat brown eyes held no spark of joy.

"When you were in Russia, and then at *Kosmograd*, did Malik . . . was he a gentleman at all times?"

Lucita laughed. "A perfect gentleman. And he still is. Sometimes I wish he weren't. . . ." The laughter died off. "Papa, this is a political marriage for him, too. Perhaps we can learn to love each other; I think he genuinely is attracted to me. But . . ."

"Are you attracted to him?"

She started to reply, hesitated, then shook her head. "No. Not the way a romantic schoolgirl wants to feel. Not with the kind of passion that makes a woman behave foolishly."

"But you agree to marry him?"

Lucita wanted to ask, What choice do I have? Where can I go in the world that I can escape from him? How can I avoid him when my own father has offered me to him?

Instead, she replied meekly, "Yes, Papa, I will marry him. And bear his children. And live in Moscow or some Asian desert or even on Mars, if that's where his career takes him."

She wanted her father to be taken aback by that, to falter, to show some slight discomfort at the idea that he might never see his daughter again. But he did not even blink an eye. He took both her hands in his and held them firmly.

"You will learn to be happy with him, Lucita. I know you will."

She saw the vision in his eyes: not his daughter's future, far from home and family. It was his own future that Hernandez was foreseeing: president of the Republic of Venezuela. And then, who knows, perhaps with the help of the Soviet Union he would make Venezuela the most powerful nation in the Western Hemisphere.

Lucita pulled her hands free and ran from the dining room, leaving her father happily dreaming his dreams, oblivious to his daughter's needs.

She returned to her bedroom only long enough to grab the tiger-striped beach bag, then dashed down the back stairs to the garage, threw the bag onto the seat beside her and roared off for the beach in her MG. Reaching into the glove compartment as she swung the convertible out of the tree-shaded driveway and headed for the main highway, Lucita pulled on a pair of sunglasses. She pressed the gas pedal to the floor and the nimble little car leaped ahead, weaving from one lane to another as Lucita passed everything on the road. A pair of dark sedans tried to keep up with her for a few miles, but she outpaced them and soon left them far behind.

The wind felt good pulling at her hair, the air was clear and clean. She never noticed the unmarked helicopter droning high above, its tiny video camera aimed squarely at her.

She drove to the beach club, changed into a white string bikini that would have made her father frown his darkest and let one of the beach boys set up a chair and umbrella for her on the warm white sand. She stretched out on the reclining chair, soaking up the sun and staring at the gentle surf that curled in, wave after wave, endlessly. As gentle and relentless as Vasily, she thought.

It was quite a surprise to her when Dan Randolph came walking straight up to her, rising out of the sea like some ancient water god and trudging through the sand directly to where she sat.

"Good morning," he said, dripping. Lucita had forgotten what a hard-muscled body he had. The water sluiced down his arms, his legs, his flat belly, darkening his body hair.

"What are you doing here?" Lucita blurted.

"I've come to invite you to lunch," he said, grinning down at her. "First an invigorating swim, and then a pleasant lunch . . . at sea."

He pointed seaward and Lucita saw a trim little sloop riding at anchor out beyond the breakers. It was painted sky blue and gold.

"It's too early for lunch," she said.

With a laugh, he said, "Not if you have to catch it first!" He reached out his hand, and before she even thought about it, she lifted hers and allowed him to clasp it and pull her up to her feet.

"My bag . . ." she said.

"No problem." Reaching into the waistband of his skin-tight briefs, Dan pulled out a pencil-slim roll of clear plastic. It opened up into a thin flexible pouch big enough to take Lucita's handbag.

"We manufacture this stuff up in orbit," he told her. "Solocrystal is the trade name. Amazing stuff. Waterproof, too."

He took her hand again and they trotted to the water, waded in, then dived over a breaking wave. Side by side they swam to Dan's sloop. Lucita saw the name stenciled across her stern: *Yanqui*.

She stretched out on the forward deck to let the sun dry her, but soon turned and propped her head up on one hand, watching fascinated as Dan set the sails and hauled up the anchor: all with the help of computer-directed servo motors. The big dazzling sails filled with wind and the graceful ship bit into the water, nosing away from the beach and out to sea.

Dan broke out light fishing tackle, beckoned Lucita back to the cockpit and baited the hook for her.

"You catch us some lunch while I mind the radar," he said. "I want to make sure your Russian friends aren't following us close enough to eavesdrop."

"My . . ." Lucita's eyes widened. "What do you mean?"

She looked genuinely surprised. "Don't you know that Malik has a team of people following you whenever you leave your house?"

"No! I don't believe it."

Shrugging, Dan said, "It's true."

Lucita turned away from him and angrily cast the fishing line into the sea. Dan checked the display screen: radar showed no boats or planes suspiciously nearby, sonar gave no echoes of underwater craft. The horizon looked clear and bright, the sky as brazen as hammered brass. He had forgotten how quiet it could be on a sailboat, with nothing but the wind in your ears, and the slap of the waves against the hull. Even in space there was always the hum of electrical equipment or the whir of air fans. Silence up there meant quick death. Here, it was a pleasure.

She was no fisherman, Dan found. Lucita quickly hooked something; it would be hard not to, this far out. Her line bowed and she shrieked happily. He went to help her. She was excited but hadn't the faintest idea of what to do next. Under Dan's guidance she reeled in her catch. He netted it and brought it flopping and flapping onto the deck: a nice-sized sea trout.

"I'll clean it and you cook it, okay?" he suggested.

She gave him a waif's sorry, almost frightened expression. "I have never cooked a fish."

Dan pretended to scowl. "All right. I'll clean it and *I'll* cook it. How's that?"

"Who will sail the boat while you do?"

"The computer," Dan replied carelessly. "Trims the sails better than I ever could."

"Is there something I could do?" she asked.

He jabbed a thumb toward the hatch that led down into the galley. "Find the fridge and open a bottle of white wine. Glasses are in the cabinet above it."

Lucita hesitated.

"You do know how to use a corkscrew."

"I think so."

"Give it a try. If you get cork in the wine, I'll have to make you walk the plank."

She opened the galley hatch and ducked down into the darkness below.

There was cork in the wine, but not enough for Dan to complain about. They feasted on the broiled fish and frozen beans and carrots that Lucita thawed in the galley's microwave oven.

"I understand you're seeing a good deal of Comrade Malik," he said after the first glass of wine had gone down.

"Yes. Vasily comes here every chance he gets."

"To see you."

She nodded. Doesn't look too happy about it, Dan thought. Watching her as she sat on the padded bench that ran across the back of the cockpit, the Caribbean wind playing with her dark thick hair, he thought briefly of what fun it would be to sail on for days, for months, never setting eyes on land, just sailing the Spanish Main like the buccaneers of old with this lovely Latin prize as his beautiful prisoner.

He reached for the wine bottle, slanted in a frost-covered electronic chiller. Don't be a romantic idiot, old boy, he told himself. This is a business trip. Tax deductible and all that. Keep your mind on business.

"You don't blame Malik for what happened—"

"No, I don't," she snapped before he could finish the sentence. "Vasily was very supportive, very helpful. The men who killed Teresa are being punished severely."

"The Gulag," Dan said.

"The mines on the Moon," she said, as if correcting him.

"I suppose I'll end up there someday."

"You? Why would you be arrested by the Russians?"

Watching her face carefully as he spoke, Dan said, "They'll find some reason, sooner or later. They don't want anybody operating in space but themselves."

"Are you doing anything against the law?"

Grinning, "Every day."

"Truly?"

"Lucita, dear child, it's impossible to do anything that makes a profit that isn't against some law they've written, somewhere."

"But the Russians would never arrest you. They have no reason to. Do they?"

He shrugged. "Has Malik ever spoken about me? Has he discussed my operations at the *Nueva Venezuela* factory with your father?"

"No," she replied, shaking her head. "Not that I know of."

"Are you going to marry him?" Dan heard himself ask. He had not intended to; the words came from his lips before he had thought about them.

"Yes."

Just the one word. Without a smile. Without any trace of joy or anticipation or any warmth at all.

"But you don't love him," Dan said.

189

Her chin went up a stubborn notch. "How do you know who I love and who I do not love?"

"You *do* love him?"

"That is my affair, and not yours."

Dan pursed his lips. Then, "So you're going to marry him, whether you love him or not."

"I am going to marry him."

"Why?"

He saw turmoil in her eyes. A molten flow of conflicting emotions. Then she sat up straighter, as if forcing herself to regain control of her passions.

"He is the only man who has asked me," she answered coldly, almost mockingly. "After all, I am not getting any younger."

"And neither is your father," Dan said. "He wants to be president of Venezuela pretty damned badly, doesn't he?"

Anger flashed in Lucita's eyes, but before she could respond, the emergency beeper on the radio pulsed its shrill signal. Dan spun around in his swiveled deck chair and hit the audio switch.

"Randolph here," he said.

"Dan, it's Pete Weston." The lawyer's voice sounded agitated, frightened.

Dan touched the scrambler button, but it popped back up to normal mode. Weston was not scrambling the signal; he was speaking in the open, where anyone could hear him and understand. Dan frowned. Usually the lawyer scrambled even the most routine communications.

"What is it, Pete?"

"We just got a kind of garbled transmission from *Dolphin One*. They've been boarded by Russians!"

"What?"

"Radar and telemetry have been tracking them routinely until this morning. Looks like a Russian spacecraft burned in on them in a *very* high energy trajectory and made a rendezvous with them at approximately ten-thirty A.M."

"The Russians boarded them?"

"From what we were able to get out over the radio link, yes. Then the link went dead."

"Was there a fight? Is anybody hurt?"

"Don't know. All we've got for sure is that the Russian spacecraft came from the Moon, intercepted our ship, and now it's heading back to Lunagrad—with *Dolphin One* in tow."

Dan felt the breath sag out of him.

"Did you hear me, boss? The Russians are taking our ship back to the Moon with them. And our crew—or whoever's left alive among them."

Chapter
◆ ◆ TWENTY-ONE ◆ ◆

"Are you certain that your information is accurate?" Njombe's deep voice sounded almost like a growl in Dan's earphones.

He turned to face the Angolan, although all he could see was a featureless gold-tinted visor set into the helmet of the black man's space suit. Like the five others of his desperate little band, Njombe looked somewhat like a knight decked out in white armor. But Dan saw that the "armor" was dingy here and there, and the heavy boots they wore lacked spurs.

"For the amount of money I bribed that little code clerk with," he answered, "the information ought to be golden—literally."

The six of them were hovering inside the big, sepulchral sphere of an empty Soviet ore freighter, one of the dozens of globular unmanned spacecraft that regularly plied the route between the mines on the Moon and *Kosmograd*, where the ores were transshipped to their buyers among the Third World space factories.

They had boarded the empty Russian freighter when it had been less than twelve hours away from its landing center at

Lunagrad, the Soviet base on the Moon's *Mare Tranquillitatis*, the Sea of Tranquility, not far from the abandoned site of the old *Apollo 11* "Tranquility Base," where men first set foot on the Moon's dusty surface.

Dan had swiftly decided that he had no option but to force the Russians who ran Lunagrad to give up their prisoners. And it had to be done while the men from his *Dolphin One* spacecraft were still on the Moon, before they were transferred to the Soviet Union for trial as pirates. He had left Pete Weston and his other corporate lawyers to argue with the Soviets, the UN and Hernandez's Venezuelans. While they talked, Dan acted.

Nobuhiko Yamagata was a Soviet prisoner. Dan could not allow that. He was responsible for Nobo. It wasn't that Saito would blame him for Nobo's danger; the youngster had been eager for the asteroid mission, no matter what the risks. But Dan felt personally responsible for his old friend's son. There was no escaping that. It was his fault that Nobo and the others were being held prisoners at Lunagrad. And Dan Randolph met his responsibilities, paid his debts, one way or the other.

He had sailed the sloop directly to the launching center on the man-made island off La Guaira and ordered a helicopter to fly Lucita back to her beach club.

"Tell your father what's happened," he commanded Lucita, "although I suspect he already knows. Tell him that I expect the government of Venezuela to protest in the strongest possible terms. There are four Venezuelan citizens among the crew of *Dolphin One*."

"But what was the spacecraft doing so far away from Earth?" she asked, confused.

"I'm sending a man around to explain the whole mission to him. It was a private venture of Astro Manufacturing, but there were Venezuelan nationals on board."

He bundled her onto the helicopter, after getting one of the women from the administration center to find a pair of coveralls that Lucita could put on over her skimpy bikini. As the helicopter clattered off, Dan dashed back to the administration building and began asking his best and most experienced astronauts to volunteer for a rescue mission.

Njombe was the first man he asked. The big black man stared goggle-eyed when he heard what Dan had in mind.

"Raid Lunagrad and get the men back? That's crazy!"

"You have a better suggestion? The Soviets have eight of our men. They're going to try them for piracy. *Piracy!* Double-goddammit to hell, they're threatening to hang them!"

"They can't do that," Njombe said.

"They're not going to get the chance to. We're snatching them back. And you're going to help me do it."

The big Angolan started to frown, but it came out smiling. "Not me. I'm not crazy."

"I thought those men were your friends," Dan snapped. "Vargas, Carstairs . . . they'd come through for you if you needed help, wouldn't they?"

"That's not fair, boss."

"Since when have I been fair? It's an unfair universe, friend."

Scowling, Njombe said reluctantly. "All you're going to accomplish is getting more of us taken prisoner by the Russians."

"We're going to need five or six others," Dan said.

Njombe started to say, "I'll pick—"

"No, *I'll* pick them," Dan snapped. "I'm leading this mission, and I'll pick the team."

"You're going yourself?"

Dan felt surprised that Njombe would think otherwise. "Certainly."

The Angolan broke into a grin. "Shouldn't be any trouble getting half a dozen men to go with you. After all, if the boss gets himself killed, who's going to sign the paychecks?"

They had shuttled up to *Nueva Venezuela* that night, after several hours of computer runs to check out the best way to implement Dan's plan. With barely an hour's layover, seven astronauts—led by Dan himself—left the space station packed aboard a single needle-shaped flitter. But instead of going to the factory, they angled off on a high-energy boost to one of the empty Soviet ore carriers plying its way placidly back to Lunagrad.

Boarding the empty freighter had been easy. Now they waited for it to land, under remote command from the controllers at Lunagrad, on the roiled dusty surface of the Moon. Their flitter rode behind them with no one left in it except Goldman, whose job was to put the spacecraft in orbit around the Moon and stay there until Dan brought the rest of the crew and the captives up to him.

The flitter coasted in the radar shadow of the big spherical freighter. But Dan knew that once the freighter started its descent and Goldman moved their spacecraft into a Moon-circling orbit, it would become immediately visible to the Soviet radars at Lunagrad.

"Have you thought about what Goldman's going to do if they start shooting at him?" Njombe asked.

With nothing to do except hover inside the dark interior of the freighter's vast, spherical cargo hold, waiting for the giant eggshell of a spacecraft to touch down on the Moon, Dan and his team had plenty of time to worry over every detail.

"No antisatellite weapons at Lunagrad," said Kaktins, the lanky, wild-haired Latvian engineer who had left the Soviet Union for a vacation in Sweden four years earlier and never returned. Dan recognized his heavily accented English; in their space suits, they were almost indistinguishable from one another, except for gross differences in size. The names stenciled on their suit chests had all been painted over.

"No weapons?" Njombe sounded unconvinced. "You're certain?"

"No antisatellite weapons," repeated Kaktins. "Guns for shooting people—plenty."

"Hey, that's a big load off my mind," wisecracked Elger, the smallest of the six, and the only woman among them. "Goldman's safe as in bed; the only guns they got are for us."

She had literally fought her way onto the team, taking one of the male astronauts in two straight aikido falls when he had challenged her fitness for the mission. Most of the astronauts had eagerly volunteered to help rescue their friends from Lunagrad, once they knew that Dan was going. He had been surprised by their fervor.

"What I could never figure out," said O'Leary, "is why the Russkies use these stupid freighters. Why don't they just catapult the ores off the Moon?"

"You mean with a mass driver?" Njombe asked.

"An electric catapult system, yeah."

"That's the way we would do it," Dan said. "It's cheaper and more efficient. But the Russians aren't worried about cost or efficiency. Somebody in their bureaucracy must have written a memo about the safety hazards of flinging bucketloads of dirt off the lunar surface and having them flying around between the Moon and the space stations."

"But they'd move along perfectly predictable trajectories, just like any spacecraft."

Dan shook his head inside his helmet. "Astronomical laws and common sense don't count with bureaucrats. Only rules and regulations."

"And memos," Elger added. "The longer and harder to read, the more points you earn."

"It's stupid!" O'Leary said.

"Not altogether," countered Njombe. "These freighters are powered by rockets that burn powdered aluminum and oxygen, both obtained from the lunar soil. It's almost as cheap as an electric catapult system would be."

"Not by a factor of ten, I'll bet," said O'Leary.

Dan let them debate. They were talking out their nervousness. He had gotten them to volunteer quickly, before they could really think about the risks involved. Now, with nothing to do but wait, the realities of this mad escapade were catching up with them.

And with Dan. There were a thousand ways this mission could go sour. Seven people to attack a Soviet base housing hundreds of Russians. Seven against Thebes, he said to himself. Six, really. All we've got going for us is surprise. Maybe it'll be enough. Maybe. If not . . .

A sudden lurching feeling.

"Retrorockets," Njombe's bass voice rang. "We're on the way in."

Dan looked at the luminous numerals of the watch on his wrist, then turned on his helmet light to study the schedule taped just above it. On schedule.

The astronauts floated down to the floor of the big empty chamber. Strange, Dan thought, how even the slightest pull of gravity brings back all your Earthbound concepts of up, down, floor, ceiling. Tensely, they sat on the grimy metal plates, silent now, waiting for the final thump of landing. Several times they felt staggering lurches as the retrorockets fired brief pulses.

"Sloppy work," Elger muttered.

But with only the Moon's gentle gravity to contend with, the bursts of thrust were small, light, almost trivial. Dan turned his suit radio to the frequency used by Lunagrad's ground controllers, but nothing more than a hiss of static penetrated the spherical shell of the freighter. A final surge of thrust made him feel almost heavy, and then the craft thumped once and became still. For an instant none of the six moved. Dan felt the old familiar tug of the Moon's gravity.

He got to his feet carefully, remembering that he weighed only a sixth of his normal weight on Earth. Njombe, who had never been on the Moon before, overdid it and bounded upward like a giant frog. But he had time to get his legs straightened and landed on his feet in a lunar slow motion.

"Terrific," somebody said. "Can you do *Swan Lake*?"

"Just be careful," Dan cautioned. "You've all worked in zero-gee. Don't let the feeling of weight fool you; we're not on Earth."

Slowly, almost hesitantly, they clumped across the metal floor plates to the man-sized hatch. The entire freighter could split open like a giant egg when it was being loaded with cargo. Dan's information, obtained over several years of carefully cultivated contacts around the world, was that the standard procedure at Lunagrad was to send an inspection team out to the newly landed freighter to check it out before loading it with a new shipment of ores.

But how long before the inspection team gets here? he wondered. Minutes, or hours? And a voice in his head asked, Or days?

It seemed like hours, but only twelve minutes had elapsed on Dan's wristwatch when they "heard" the hatch being opened. The interior of the freighter was an airless vacuum, just as the lunar surface outside. But Dan could feel the vibrations of the hatch's mechanism working through the soles of his booted feet, coming up from the deck plates. The others "heard" it too; they flattened out along the curving bulkhead on either side of the hatch.

Two men in space suits stepped inside, the lamps on their helmets throwing pools of light into the dark interior of the cargo hold.

"She's the best lay in Tyuratam," Dan heard one of them saying, over the suit-to-suit radio frequency.

"That's what you say. . . ."

Their conversation never got any further. Dan's men overpowered the two Russians and quickly wrapped their arms to their sides with long strips of Velcro while Njombe and Kaktins squeezed the Russians' air hoses—not enough to really harm them, just enough to make them understand what might happen.

"Be quiet," Dan commanded in Russian, "don't struggle, and do what you're told. Otherwise you'll be dead men."

With tools from their belt kits, Elger and Kaktins disconnected the Russians' suit radios. Then the six astronauts left the freighter and closed the hatch behind them.

"How much air in their tanks?" Dan asked Kaktins over their suit-to-suit frequency.

"Four hours, if they filled tanks as regulations say," answered the Latvian as he climbed up into the cab of the little tractor parked outside the freighter. He added, "And if suits working hokay. They don't check out equipment too good sometimes. Lazy stupid."

The five others clambered up onto the tractor as Kaktins briefly scanned its dashboard, then grasped the two control levers and pushed them forward. Dan felt the electric motor vibrate as the tractor lurched into motion. Hanging on to its rear fender, Dan swept his gaze around the lunar horizon. It was night on the Moon; the Sun would not rise for another nine days. But the Earth shone bright and huge in the dark starry sky, aswirl with white clouds against living blue, bathing the barren lunar landscape with soft light. The big blue marble, Dan thought. At this distance it seemed to be an oasis of life set in the implacably cold and black emptiness of the universe.

The ore freighter looked like a giant metal bubble balanced delicately on three spidery legs. The undulating dark gray plain of the waterless Sea of Tranquility was pockmarked with countless craterlets, some no bigger than a fingertip's poke. Worn old mountains, sandpapered smooth by aeons of microscopic meteors falling out of the sky, broke the flatness of the horizon off to Dan's left. The tractor's treads lifted dust from the barren soil, and the clouds hung lightly in the gentle gravity of the Moon.

Beyond the freighter they had landed in, three more of the big spherical ore carriers stood. One of them was being loaded: a train of four treaded cars was pulled up alongside it and a conveyor belt, angling steeply upward like the arm of a crane, was moving powdered rock up to a large hatch in the sphere's top and spilling it into its interior. A grayish plume hung over the sphere, like a cloud that clings to a mountain peak.

Dan fiddled with his suit radio to find the frequency the Russian loading crew was using. They were talking casually, completely unaware of what was happening a few hundred yards away. Dan grinned, inside his helmet. One of the Russians was complaining about the food they were getting.

Turning, he looked past the shoulders and helmets of the other space-suited figures and saw the low domes of Lunagrad, the Soviet base. Most of the living quarters and offices were underground, Dan knew, protected by many feet of solid rock against the harsh radiation and occasional meteor shower that peppered the unprotected lunar surface. Even the domes here on the surface were partially covered with rubble bull-dozed from the top layers of lunar soil.

Standing just outside the little cluster of domes was a trio of squat spherical spacecraft. To Dan they looked like smaller versions of the ore freighter. But he knew that they were personnel carriers, capable of taking off from where they stood and going all the way back to Earth in an emergency. Our return tickets, he told himself.

Kaktins drove the tractor right into the biggest dome, following a trail of tractor tracks that led to a huge airlock hatch. The big metal doors swung open soundlessly as they approached; Dan could not tell if Kaktins had sent a signal from the tractor's instrument board or if the hatch worked automatically whenever a vehicle came near. They drove inside, the outer hatch closed and Dan could feel pumps start to rumble from somewhere beneath the big metal chamber. It took an agonizingly long time, but at last he could hear air hissing around him.

"Keep your voices down and keep using the suit radios," Dan commanded. "Let's give them as little information about who we are as possible."

The inner airlock hatch slid open as Dan's crew got down from the tractor. On the other side of the hatch stood three young Russian technicians in faded, stained coveralls. They looked surprised to see six space-suited figures aboard the tractor. Before they could raise an alarm, Dan and his team overpowered them and marched them into the narrow, hot little control room from which the airlock was monitored. Two more technicians were sitting at the controls, conversing casually together.

Dan yanked the pistol from his belt and ordered them in

Russian to stand up and put their hands on their heads. Shocked speechless, they did as they were told. While Kaktins and Njombe bound and gagged the five men, Dan swiftly scanned the control panels. Several were not functioning; one of the consoles had its front panel removed, showing the wiring and circuitry in its guts. Somebody's half-eaten lunch was strewn on the floor; crumbs and an empty unlabeled bottle littered the control board's work surface. Inside his suit helmet, Dan's nose wrinkled in disgust. Slobs. Just plain slobs. I'd fire anybody who dirtied up their work station like this. But another part of his mind was telling him, If they're this lax, you've got a chance to surprise them. You've got a chance to get away with it.

He left Elger in the cramped little control room to guard the five bound men.

"This is our escape route," he told her. "You've got to keep it open for us. If you have to, shoot them."

He could not see her face through the helmet's tinted visor, but he could sense her nodding. "I'll check out the getaway vehicles while I'm here, make sure they're ready for us."

"Good." It had not occurred to Dan that they might not be ready for a quick escape.

As the rest of them headed for the ladderway that led down into Lunagrad's main areas, Dan saw the bantam-sized astronaut sit in front of the video screens that showed the personnel vehicles outside the airlock. She carefully slid the pistol she was carrying from the tool pouch at her waist and rested it in her lap. The five bound and gagged Russians stared at the gun.

"Go get 'em, boss," Dan heard her in his earphones. "Everything here will be just fine."

Laughing, he made his way down the ladder to catch up with the others.

With Kaktins' guidance, they clumped down the dimly lit corridor toward the base's main control center, where technicians stood watch over Lunagrad's electrical power and life support systems. Control them, Dan knew, and you control the whole base.

The corridor was narrow and almost empty. And low. Dan instinctively ducked his head as they made their way along it. Oppressive. Depressing. They passed three Russians along the way: a man and a woman walking together, and a man alone. All were dressed in faded gray coveralls. All looked surprised at the sight of five people in space suits. None of them said a word; they squeezed past Dan and his crew in silence. Good Soviet training, Dan thought. When in doubt, keep your mouth shut and your eyes averted.

No guards. No sign that the Russians were aware they had been invaded. Business as usual. Lunagrad ran on Moscow time, and Dan had picked a freighter that landed at two A.M. for his Trojan Horse. Catch them in their sleep.

Kaktins, striding at the head of their group, lifted a hand to signal a halt.

"There it is," he said. Dan read the Cyrillic letters on the door: CENTRAL CONTROL—AUTHORIZED PERSONNEL ONLY.

Without a word of command from Dan, each of the five men pulled out their slim, deadly black automatic pistols. As he flicked off the safety catch and cocked his, Dan reminded them, "Nobody is to fire unless I do. I don't want to hurt any of these people; I just want to get our guys back."

He heard their muttered agreement. Taking a deep breath, he reached for the door latch with his left hand and pulled it open.

There were eight men and three women inside the control center, most of them sitting at consoles, watching instrument dials or display screens. One of the women was at an electric samovar, pouring herself a glass of tea. Two of the men were in a corner, playing chess. Like the airlock control station, this center also looked grimy, overused and undercleaned, to Dan. The Russians all froze with shock as he and his crew marched in and closed the door behind them.

"Take your hands off the controls and put them on top of

202

your heads," Dan commanded, loudly enough for them to hear him through his helmet.

They herded the Russians into a corner and made them sit on the floor, hands clasped behind their heads.

"Who's in charge here?" Dan asked.

They glanced at each other. The only gray-haired man among them, heavyset, with fatty jowls and tiny, angry eyes, glared up at Dan. "I am."

"Get up," Dan said. Picking up a phone handset as the Russian got laboriously to his feet, Dan ordered, "Call the base commander. Tell him there's an emergency and you need him here."

For the flash of an instant, Dan thought the Russian would resist. But after only a moment's hesitation he took the handset from Dan and punched out a four-digit number.

"My pardon for waking you, sir," the Russian said in a voice that was suddenly unctuous. "This is Ustinov, in the control center. We have . . . eh, something of an emergency here. It requires your presence. . . . Yes, sir, now, if you please. . . . Yes, it is quite serious. It calls for decisions that I am not empowered to make. You are the only one who can do it. . . . Yes, sir. Thank you, sir. I appreciate it, sir."

Handing the set back to Dan, his tone went back to flat hardness. "He will be here in five minutes."

Nodding inside his helmet, Dan said, "Good. Now where are the prisoners?"

The Russian looked at him blankly. "The prisoners?"

"The prisoners!" Dan snapped, lifting his hand so that the muzzle of his gun pointed at the Russian's bulbous nose.

"We have twelve thousand prisoners here," the Russian said. "Which do you want?"

Twelve thousand? Dan's mind reeled. Twelve thousand. I had no idea they had brought so many up here. They can't all be working the mines. Most of them must be just rotting away up here, exiled forever.

He forced the picture from his mind. "The prisoners that

203

were just brought in from a private spacecraft. They're not Soviet citizens. . . ."

"The capitalists," said the Russian.

"Yes," Dan said. "The capitalists. Where are they?"

"In a holding cell, two levels down."

"How are they guarded?"

He shrugged his fat shoulders. "I don't know. That's none of my business."

The door swung open and Dan reflexively turned toward it, gun pointed. So did the other four of his crew.

Vasily Malik stepped through the doorway and stopped, his eyes instantly taking in the situation. He was wearing spanking-new coveralls, the trousers still creased, the collar opened casually. His mouth dropped open in surprise.

"This isn't the base commander," Dan growled.

"Who are you?" Malik demanded. "What is going on here?"

"Why are you here? Where's the base commander?"

Malik's eyes went crafty. "I came here a few hours ago to supervise the transfer of a group of thieving pirates to the Soviet Union, where they will be tried by an international court."

Dan realized that his finger was curling around the trigger of his pistol. With a deliberate effort, he eased the pressure.

"I want those prisoners freed," he said.

"I won't release them," Malik replied. "They are in the custody of the Soviet Union and they will remain so."

Dan strode over to the control boards. "Which of these panels monitors the air to the living quarters? Do you want me to shut it off? Or turn off the heat? Or overload the main generators so badly that they'll burn out and leave the whole base dead?"

Malik's eyes were studying him, trying to pierce through the gold-tinted visor to see the face behind it. Dan was speaking in Russian, and his voice was muffled by the helmet, but he could see that Malik was straining to identify him.

"I'm not playing games," Dan shouted. "I'll wipe this base out completely if you don't release those prisoners."

The Russians sitting on the floor were all looking at Malik, eyes wide with fear. Dan could see that fat Ustinov had begun to sweat. But Malik did not move, did not say a word; he stood his ground and glared angrily at Dan, ramrod stiff, fists clenched.

Feeling rage boiling up within him, Dan whirled and quickly ran his gaze down the line of control switches and knobs on the board before him. He reached out and clicked off one switch, then a second.

"Electrical power to the communications center just went off. And to the food storage lockers." He took two steps along the long row of panels. "Life support for the sleeping quarters. Do you really want me to turn off their air?"

The tension seemed to flow out of Malik's body. His hands unclenched, his face relaxed almost into a smile.

"I'll get the prisoners for you," he said. "But I want it clearly understood that I do so under protest, and merely to save the lives of innocent Soviet citizens."

"Go fuck yourself," Dan snapped. He stepped toward Malik and prodded him toward the door with the muzzle of his pistol. To Kaktins, he said, "Zig, you come with me." Then, pointing to the hulking form of Njombe, "Take charge here. If there's the slightest sign of trouble, shut down all the life support systems for their living quarters. Destroy the controls if you have to."

He heard Njombe's deep-throated chuckle in his earphones, "I'll make them breathe vacuum if they try to fight."

With Malik in the lead, Dan and Kaktins clumped along the low-ceilinged corridor, then down a ladderway two levels. The corridor here was even narrower, lower, but brilliantly lit. The glare was almost painful. It was lined with blank metal doors on both sides. How many prisoners were being held in those cells? Dan wondered. How long had they been locked in there? And for what offenses? Speaking their minds? Trying to get out of the Soviet Union? Failing to fall on their faces when the Kremlin ordered them to?

Some fifty feet up the hallway, Dan saw a pair of uniformed guards, armed with pistols holstered at their hips. It was the longest fifty feet he had ever walked. From behind the visor of his helmet, Dan watched the guards' faces. They registered surprise that Comrade Malik would be approaching them at this hour of the morning with two men in space suits accompanying him. Surprise, but not alarm.

He could not see the expression on Malik's face, because he was behind the Russian, holding his pistol in the small of his back, hidden from the guards.

Malik stopped in front of the guards' desk. With only a slight prod from Dan's gun, he said, "The new prisoners—release them from their cell."

The guard seated at the desk started to tap on the buttons of the keyboard in front of him. The other, though, peered hard at Dan, trying to see through the gold-tinted visor. Kaktins slid over to one side and casually took his pistol from his tool pouch.

"Do what he told you," Dan commanded, "or all three of you will be shot."

The seated man glanced questioningly at Malik.

"Do as he says."

He finished punching out the combination. Behind them, Dan heard the faint click of a lock. He turned and saw Carstairs push open the door closest to the desk. There was a swelling bruise beneath his eye, but as soon as he saw the space-suited figures he broke into an immense grin.

"What'd I tell you?" he called over his shoulder. "Come on!"

Nobo was the last to leave the cell, and Dan let out a relieved breath when he saw that the young Japanese was unharmed. Carstairs and Vargas helped themselves to the guards' guns, and the whole squad of them started back toward the control center.

"How'd you—"

"No questions and no talk," Dan snapped. "Just keep moving and do as you're told."

"Righto, boss," answered the Australian.

Dan marched the little band back to the control center, where Njombe and the others still had the crew sitting on the floor. He studied the control board, swiftly deciphering the Cyrillic letters taped alongside each dial and switch. The entire layout became clear to him. He could destroy the whole Soviet base with a few touches of his fingers. And the twelve thousand prisoners they had exiled here. They would die too. Damned clever of the Russians; the prisoners guarantee their safety—unless the shit hits the fan.

"I don't think I could have lasted another hour," Halloran was babbling, unable to stop talking. "They had all of us jammed into that lousy little cell. There wasn't any air, no lights—"

"Cut it!" Dan snapped, once he was certain that he understood the controls. "Let's get the hell out of here."

He punched down the switches that shut the airtight hatches between every section of the living quarters on the levels below. Emergency Klaxons hooted, but Dan knew that the Russians below were trapped in their quarters, locked in by heavy steel hatches that sealed the corridors every twenty meters, and they would stay locked in until someone turned off the switches on the control board.

They took the entire control center crew with them, together with Malik and the two soldiers, as far as the airlock. Elger was waiting for them, and reported that she had run one of the emergency personnel rockets through its countdown. It was ready to lift off. Dan forced Malik to get into a space suit with the others and go out to the getaway rocket with them. They packed the eight *Dolphin* crewmen and his six raiders into the one spherical spacecraft, leaving Malik standing on the lunar soil just outside the airlock hatch.

Dan was the last to go up the ladder. He knew that Malik would sprint for the airlock as soon as he turned his back. The Russian would not wait to be caught in the blast of the

207

spacecraft's rocket engines. Dan also knew that by then there was nothing that Malik or any of the others could do to stop them from getting away and making their rendezvous with Goldman and the spacecraft orbiting above them.

"Don't think you're getting away with this," said Malik as Dan backed toward the ladder. The Russian's voice sounded tightly furious, even through Dan's helmet earphones.

"It looks to me as if we are," Dan replied lightly.

"I know who you are, Dan Randolph. You haven't fooled me."

I ought to shoot him right here and now, Dan thought. Wonder if the pistol works in vacuum?

"There's nowhere you can hide, Randolph," Malik went on. "I'm going to track you down and personally see to it that you are hanged!"

Dan laughed at him. "You're welcome to try."

He bounded up the ladder, taking four rungs at a time in the gentle lunar gravity, and ducked through the hatch. The spacecraft's interior was Spartan, little more than two dozen acceleration couches slung in triple tiers, like bunks. Njombe was already in the pilot's seat. Dan could not tell who the space-suited figure was beside him, possibly Carstairs, from the size.

"Lift-off in five seconds," Njombe's deep voice called out.

Dan sat on the nearest couch as the slight jolt of lift-off made the spacecraft shudder. He grinned to himself. Then he realized that his whole body was drenched with cold sweat.

Chapter
◆ ◆ TWENTY-TWO ◆ ◆

London had changed, and not for the better. As he walked along the Embankment with Sir Edmond Dixon, Dan saw what Soviet supremacy meant to the nation whose empire had once reached around the world.

Houseboats lined the Thames, stretching past Waterloo Bridge and past the bend in the river as far as Dan could see. Grimy, overcrowded houseboats packed with refugees from all those young nations that once had flown the British flag. And refugees from Europe as well. What would Churchill have thought, Dan wondered, if he'd known that fifty years after his death there'd be more than a million Germans living in Chelsea and Earl's Court? Or that Japanese tourists are the lifeblood of Savile Row?

Beggars lined the Embankment, most of them sitting on the pavement, silent and blank-faced, empty hats upturned beside them. Too hungry to stay on their feet, Dan thought. They were ragged and scarecrow thin. And filthy. That's what shocked him most: London's streets, her buildings, even the grand old Embankment itself, were thick with collected grime, unswept litter. Graffiti in a dozen different languages were scrawled everywhere, even on the statue of Victoria herself.

They've lost it, Dan saw. Heart, nerve, self-respect, whatever it takes to make a people strong and great—they've lost it. He shuddered inside, knowing that America was sliding down the same grimy chute. Jane can coddle them along for now; they can still tell themselves that everything'll work out okay, but the States are going to be like this soon. New York is already this bad. New Orleans is not far behind. It'll get like this all over the States.

Sir Edmond apparently was unbothered by the decay. He strolled through the warm autumn morning alongside Dan as they headed for the Houses of Parliament, ignoring the beggars, paying no attention to the teeming houseboats clinging to the Embankment's stone wall. The river was gray and oily, but the morning air sparkled clean and fresh. The umbrella that Sir Edmond held tightly rolled in his right hand would not be needed. At least the Soviets sell them all the natural gas they need, Dan thought. No coal fumes ruining the air. Then he realized, Of course, that means that Britain isn't in the market for American coal. Score another point for Soviet economic imperialism.

Peddlers' stalls dotted the walkway of the Embankment, offering meager selections of fruits, cakes and an occasional colorful scarf or tie.

"Stolen goods, mostly," warned Sir Edmond. "Wouldn't touch them, if I were you."

He was a slim, slight man in his early fifties with curly reddish hair that was just beginning to go gray and the pinched, nervous face of a rodent. His teeth were very bad, but the suit he wore was new, expensive and perfectly tailored. Gray pinstripe, with pearl-gray vest.

Neither Sir Edmond nor Dan noticed the two other men trying to look like casual tourists as they walked along the Embankment a dozen or so yards behind them, threading their way through the strolling pedestrians and squatting beggars and peddlers' stalls, their eyes never leaving the backs of Dan and the Englishman. They were both dressed in nondescript tweeds. One of the men carried an umbrella, almost identical to Sir Edmond's, except that its tip was needle sharp.

Big Ben tolled the quarter hour, and Dan smiled to himself. Well, there's still that. St. Paul's and Westminster Abbey and that old Gothic tower with its clock. The stones remain, even though the people get shabby.

Sir Edmond checked his wristwatch. "Actually, I've got to be at the committee meeting in three-quarters of an hour."

"I understand," said Dan. "I appreciate your taking the time to meet me face to face."

"Think nothing of it."

"You've read all the briefs, I presume."

Sir Edmond gave Dan a haughty look. "Of course. Fascinating business. Did you actually do what the Russians claim you did?"

Grinning, Dan said, "I sent a mission out to an asteroid. They were bringing samples back when the Russians intercepted them and jailed them. . . ."

"They claim they put your crew in temporary custody pending a ruling from the World Court."

"I know what they claim," Dan said.

"They further claim that the asteroid material found aboard your spacecraft is legally the responsibility of the International Astronautical Council."

"Yes, and they claim that a corporation cannot claim ownership of extraterrestrial materials. I know that. Astro Manufacturing doesn't claim ownership of the asteroid or the samples. But we *do* claim the right to use that material in manufacturing processes. There's nothing in international law that prevents *use* of extraterrestrial material."

"Providing the IAC approves."

Dan stopped short, forcing the English lawyer to stop also.

A dozen paces behind them, the two other men took a sudden interest in the cheap Nepalese jewelry being offered at the nearest peddler's stall.

"No," Dan insisted, jabbing with his forefinger against Sir Edmond's lapel. "You don't need IAC approval. The IAC can prohibit your using certain extraterrestrial materials, but only after they have reviewed all the facts of the matter and only after a formal vote by the full council. I've read that law very carefully, Sir Edmond. So have the best lawyers I could find."

"It's rather a sticky point," said the Englishman, "I grant you."

"The Russians have no right to hold on to that cargo," Dan said firmly.

"Possession is nine-tenths of the matter, you know."

Dan felt a growing exasperation. Sir Edmond had been recommended as the sharpest legal mind in the field of international law. But Dan was experiencing doubts.

"The Russkies are also claiming that you have endangered the entire world by altering the course of the asteroid so that it might hit the Earth."

"Absolute bull—" Dan stopped himself short. "Nonsense. The asteroid will go into orbit around the Earth. It won't get any closer than the Moon does."

"Hmm." Sir Edmond looked unconvinced.

"Any competent astronomer can make the necessary observations and testify."

"Perhaps. If the Russkies don't alter the confounded rock's trajectory."

Dan felt his brows hike upward. "Do you think they'd do that?"

"To beat you in the World Court? Are you serious?"

Suddenly Dan liked this rat-faced Englishman. He laughed. "It's a good thing I've got a few honest astronomers keeping track of the asteroid."

"Yes, quite. They're not all Americans, I trust."

"Two from the University of Caracas, one from the international observatory in Peru, a married couple at the Pic du Midi in the Pyrenees, and the entire Junior Amateur Astronomer's League of Japan. Is that good enough?"

Sir Edmond smiled back at him. "Sufficient. Sufficient."

They resumed their walk toward the Parliament buildings. The two men following them immediately lost interest in Nepalese bracelets.

"Tell me frankly," Sir Edmond said, his voice lowered almost to a whisper. "Did you actually do it?"

"Do what?" Dan asked innocently.

Sir Edmond glanced around at the sparse pedestrian traffic. "No one has a recording device here. There's no need to be reticent. Did you really lead that rescue mission?"

Dan smiled tightly at him. "Sir Edmond, you're a lawyer. Astro Manufacturing Corporation has retained your services to represent us at the World Court against the Soviet Union's claim that the asteroid and its samples belong to 'the peoples of the world.' Which means, effectively, to Soviet Russia."

"Yes, but—"

"The Soviet Union has protested to the government of Venezuela that I personally invaded the Soviet base on the Moon, threatened the lives of Soviet citizens, and abducted eight Astro employees from Soviet custody."

"Did you or didn't you?"

Dan hesitated, then said, "Somebody did. And whoever it was deserves my unending gratitude. Those eight employees were returned to *Nueva Venezuela* unharmed. If the Russians want them back, they're going to have to extradite them from Venezuela. I have another set of lawyers fighting that."

"But did you personally . . ."

"What difference does it make?" Dan asked.

"Well, I'd like to know just what kind of a client I'm dealing with."

"Your client is a corporation," Dan replied. "A large,

213

multinational, soulless corporation. I just happen to be the man who sits at the top of the machine."

Sir Edmond chuckled. "Very well, Mr. Randolph. Have it your own way. Perhaps one day, after this untidiness is all cleared up, you'll trust me enough to tell me what really happened up there. . . ."

They were approaching Westminster Pier. The pedestrian traffic here was thicker, brisker. Men with briefcases and women carrying big shoulder bags strode purposefully. The squatting beggars were scarcer, and a tall, stern-faced bobby paced slowly along in the opposite direction, hands clasped behind his back. The two men following Dan and Sir Edmond quickened their pace and closed the gap behind them.

Dan was asking, "How long will it take the World Court to hear our case?"

"Oh, several months, at least. The Russkies are laying on heavy pressure to get it on the court calendar quickly, but the—"

The two men pushed between them, muttering a "Pardon me, please," as they almost knocked Sir Edmond off his feet. Dan staggered a few steps backward.

"Of all the cheeky bastards," Sir Edmond grumbled.

"Just like New York," Dan said. Briefly he thought about hailing the two men and dressing them down, but they were weaving fast through the crowd, almost running.

"They must be late for an appointment," Dan said, as much to himself as to Sir Edmond.

The Englishman squinted up at Big Ben, its tower standing tall and straight against the bright blue sky. "Which reminds me that I have an appointment of my own to keep."

Dan walked with him past the statue of Richard the Lion-Hearted, up to the front entrance at the Commons side of Parliament.

"I'll ring you up in a few days," said Sir Edmond. "You'll be in Caracas?"

Nodding, Dan said, "If not, the phone will know where to find me."

"Very good. I . . ." The Englishman's eyes suddenly squeezed shut. His mouth dropped open and a strangled groan gurgled in his throat. His knees buckled. Dan grabbed him as Sir Edmond's head lolled back on his shoulders. The umbrella dropped from his nerveless hands. He was dead before Dan could lower him to the pavement.

Chapter
♦ ♦ TWENTY-THREE ♦ ♦

Dan Randolph stood at the head of the lane, turned sideways like a fencer, his arm extended straight from the shoulder. The gun barked as he snapped off four quick shots. The sleek black automatic in his hand hardly bucked at all.

Pete Weston clamped his hands to his ears as the gunfire echoed off the firing range's walls. They were alone in the indoor range; the other nine lanes were empty and dark.

"Aren't you supposed to wear headphones when you shoot, to muffle the noise?" Weston asked.

With a shake of his head, Dan hefted the automatic in his hand, testing its balance. "I want to get accustomed to the noise. I don't want anything to throw me off if I have to use this thing for real."

"You're really serious?"

Weston was wearing his usual Wall Street attorney's uniform: a gray three-piece suit. Dan had on an old pair of tan chinos and a short-sleeved shirt.

"That Russian sonofabitch tried to murder me," Dan told the lawyer. "He sent a couple of KGB goons after me and they got Dixon by mistake."

"You can't be sure. . . ."

Dan silenced him with a look. "Pete, I still have friends in London. The official autopsy report said heart attack. But Dixon's cardiovascular system showed no signs of it. The KGB has used a nerve poison for assassinations since Stalin's time. And there was a scratch on Dixon's leg, where the thugs jabbed him with the umbrella one of them was carrying. Cut right through his pants leg."

Weston said nothing, but the expression on his high-domed face showed that he was not convinced.

"They were after me," Dan said. "Malik's pissed because he can't just arrest me and throw me in a Russian jail. . . ."

"As long as the government of Venezuela protects you," the lawyer pointed out.

"Right." Dan pulled the cartridge clip from the butt of the pistol and began refilling it from the box on the countertop in front of him.

"You'd better be *very* nice to Hernandez," Weston advised. "He's got you by the *cojones* now."

Dan grinned at the light-skinned, freckle-pated lawyer's use of a Spanish term. "You're becoming a real native, Pete. Next thing you know, you'll be taking siestas and playing the guitar."

Weston showed no amusement. "Just the same, if Hernandez wants to hand you over to the Russians . . ."

"I'm being very nice to him, don't worry. I'm treating him with enormous care and affection. My contributions to his favorite charitable causes have risen steeply in the past few weeks."

He slammed the clip back into the gun, whirled and fired five shots at the target down at the end of the lane. Weston clapped his ears again and grimaced. The target, a holographic image of a darkly threatening man holding a gun in his hand, showed bright red dots where the bullets passed through it. Dan's five shots were scattered around the chest and shoulders.

"Five for five," he muttered.

217

"Uh, look, boss . . ." Weston stammered, "I know I don't have to remind you about this, but, uh . . . well . . ."

"Spit it out, Pete! I'm not going to shoot you."

"Well . . ." The lawyer looked miserable. "You probably already know it, but if you want to stay on Hernandez's good side, for God's sake don't mess around with his daughter anymore. Understand?"

An ironic smile flickered across Dan's face. "Yeah, I know."

"There's no surer way to get him sore at you than to—"

"I know!" Dan repeated. "Don't worry about it. She's going to marry Malik; she'll be living in Moscow before the year's out."

"Really?" Weston blinked with surprise.

"I've been invited to the engagement party. By Hernandez himself. Tomorrow night."

The lawyer's eyes blinked again, rapidly. "And you're going?"

His grin returning, Dan said, "You told me to be nice to Hernandez, didn't you? Not to do anything that might upset him?"

"So you're going to her engagement party."

"I'm going."

"Where is it? At Hernandez's mansion?"

Dan shook his head. "No. The Russian embassy."

"The *what*?"

"The party's at the Russian embassy. Tomorrow night at nine. White tie. RSVP."

"You can't go to the Russian embassy!" Weston waved both hands agitatedly. "That's Soviet territory! It'd be like going into the Soviet Union itself. They'll put you under arrest as soon as you step inside the door!"

"No they won't. Malik won't spoil his own party."

Running a hand through his thinning hair, the lawyer said, "You're afraid they're out to kill you, and you're going to step right into their parlor? That's crazy!"

"So I'm crazy," Dan replied lightly. "You wouldn't want me to offend Hernandez, would you?"

"But—"

"All the Third World space operators will be there: Kolwezi from Zaire, Vavuniya from India, al Hashimi from Pan-Arab . . . all of them. I'd be conspicuous by my absence if I didn't go."

"Yamagata?" Weston asked. "The Chinese?"

Dan shook his head. "I doubt it. The Russians aren't being polite to the Chinese this year, and Saito has to worry more about offending his biggest customer than offending the Soviets."

"I still think you're running a helluva risk."

"Malik won't do anything to screw up his engagement party. Don't worry about it. They might try to grab me as I leave, if they can do it quietly, without disturbing the other guests. That's why I'm having my Fred Astaire suit altered to carry my little companion here. . . ." He raised the trim dead-black automatic, pointing it ceilingward. "They won't take me without a fuss, and I'm making certain that they know there'll be a fuss if they try anything."

"How can you make certain of that?"

"Come on, Pete, open your eyes! The Soviets have informers everyplace. Astro is honeycombed with them, no matter how much we try to weed them out."

"But I don't see—"

"Look around! I rented the whole firing range for the entire afternoon, every day this week. Paid enough to make it worth their while to turn away all their other customers. Maybe I'll buy it and keep it exclusively for my own use. Don't you think that will attract their attention?"

"Wouldn't it be safer—and cheaper—just to stay away from their embassy?"

"And miss Malik's engagement party? Not for the world!"

Weston shook his head, a lawyer whose client stubbornly refuses good advice.

"Besides," Dan added, "it may be my last chance to see Lucita."

Turning, he straightened his arm and emptied the gun at the holographic target. Every bullet went through its head and face.

Dan took his new secretary to bed with him that night, and although she was beautiful, willing and even inventive, he found himself fantasizing about Lucita as he made love with her. In the morning, when he opened his eyes he saw that she was already awake, propped on one elbow, watching him. He tried to recall her name: she was a Dane, a leggy, full-bosomed Viking with golden hair cropped short and curly, and eyes as green as finest jade.

"Do you know what you need?" Her tone was very serious; her low, sultry voice devoid of any hint of seduction.

"Vitamin E, perhaps?"

A smile brightened her face.

"Do not joke. What you need is to be married. A good wife would bring you much happiness."

Dan was so stunned that he could find no words to answer her.

"It is the right time in your life for marriage. You should have children. What good is all your money if you have no children to give it to?"

He remembered her name. "Kristin . . . are you volunteering for the job?"

"You are joking again." She threw the bedclothes off and swung her long legs to the richly carpeted floor, sending a wave through the waterbed.

Standing, she turned back to him, a naked Norse goddess with a body that would be worth killing an army to acquire. "I am not trying to capture you, Dan Randolph. You are a good lover. You know how to please a woman. But you do not love me. Perhaps you do not love anyone. If you find a woman you truly love, you must marry her. It will be the only way for you to find happiness."

He grinned up at her. "I'm happy now."

"No, you are not. You have everything a man needs to be happy, but you are not a happy man. Not truly."

He considered that thought for a moment, then asked, "Would you marry me?"

"Without love? No."

"You wouldn't marry me for my money? So that *your* children could be very wealthy?"

She shook her head. "I would only marry you to make you happy, Mr. Randolph."

The idealism of youth, Dan thought. She's young and very beautiful; she can afford to play a waiting game.

He stretched his arms out to her. "Well, you can make me happy right here and now."

She frowned at him. But she climbed back onto the warm waterbed and let him bury his face in her breasts.

Chapter
◆ ◆ TWENTY-FOUR ◆ ◆

No matter how they tried to disguise it, the Soviet embassy still looked like a fortress. A high stone wall surrounded its ample grounds. There was no barbed wire atop the wall, but Dan knew that modern electronic devices and invisible laser beams guarded the perimeter quite effectively. The big spotlights that ostensibly outlined the main building against the night sky also served to illuminate the spacious lawn and wide walks, making it easier to spot possible intruders. The main building itself, designed by a Venezuelan architect to specifications laid down by a Soviet committee that included at least one security officer, looked like a heavy, brooding old hacienda set far out in the wilds where it had to be defended night and day against the possibility of Indian attack.

Feeling slightly foolish in his white tie and tails, and very conscious of the pistol holstered under his armpit, Dan stepped out of his limousine at the embassy's front door. All day long he had toyed with the idea of bringing Kristin or some other date with him, but finally decided to come alone. After his morning conversation with the secretary, inviting her to this function would reinforce her nutty ideas about marriage, Dan thought. Besides, it'll be easier to get a chance to talk with Lucita alone if I don't have a date hanging on my arm.

The trio of servants just inside the front door stopped him. The tallest of them, a cadaverous bald man who might have been anywhere between forty and sixty, spoke to Dan in a hissing whisper:

"Sir, I am sorry, but we cannot allow firearms to be carried inside."

Behind him, his two assistants glowered at Dan. In their evening clothes they looked like bit players from an ancient Hollywood gangster movie.

Dan smiled at the gaunt-faced butler. "The pistol is for my own protection. I was nearly assassinated recently."

"You are under the protection of the Soviet Union in this building, sir. That will be assurance enough of your safety."

"It was a Soviet agent who tried to assassinate me," Dan replied sweetly.

The butler showed neither surprise nor dismay. "It is regrettable that you believe so, sir, but you cannot enter the party while carrying a firearm."

"Then would you kindly inform my host of this problem? I have been invited to this party, I have no intention of leaving it because you say so, and I will not give up my protection."

For a moment the butler hesitated. Then he hissed, "As you wish, sir," and turned his back to Dan. He pulled from his jacket pocket a slim two-way radio, the size of a cigarette case, and whispered urgently into it in sibilant Russian. Dan stood smiling pleasantly at the two glowering goons. They must have a metal detector built right into the goddamned doorway, he mused. Probably an X-ray machine, too. You could get your annual medical checkup just by walking into the place.

223

"Would you step this way, please?" the butler asked with exaggerated politeness. Dan followed him into a small anteroom. The butler left him there without a further word, gliding back to the foyer like a shadowless wraith.

It was a tiny windowless room, holding nothing more than a bare wooden desk, two stiff chairs and the inevitable portrait of Lenin above the desk. The walls were papered in red, with a hammer and sickle design. A small chandelier that could hide all sorts of miniaturized cameras and microphones. A rather worn oriental carpet on the floor.

A husky young Russian stepped into the anteroom. His rented evening suit looked several sizes too small for him; he seemed to be bursting out of it. He was big enough to make the room crowded. His ruddy young face was serious, almost angry.

"I have been instructed to take your gun," he said flatly.

In Russian, Dan replied, "You're just going to get yourself shot, son. Go tell Comrade Malik that I'll talk to him and no one else."

The youngster took a step toward Dan, who snaked his hand toward the holster.

"Come with me," he said, trying to make himself smile. "I will take you to the Comrade Chairman."

Dan let his hand fall away from the gun butt and followed the young man down the main hallway and through the big open doorway that led into the ballroom. It was already filled with guests. Dan spotted Abdus Kolwezi's handsome black face; the tall Zairian stood above the crowd like a dark mahogany tree above a forest of stunted shrubs. A full orchestra was playing sedate dance music. Servants were carrying trays of drinks and canapes through the crowd. Most of the conversations were either in Spanish or Russian, although Dan heard snatches of English—both American and British—as he followed the big security guard through the throng like a small sloop being towed by a massive tug.

Malik was standing at the far end of the room, Dan saw, with Lucita and her father at his side. The admirers crowding around them melted back as the security man guided Dan to Malik's presence.

"Ah, Mr. Randolph. We meet again," said Malik, loud enough for the cluster of people around them to hear him easily over the noise of the party.

Dan nodded, his eyes on Lucita. Her gown was soft pink, cut low enough to display a glittering necklace of rubies and diamonds.

"Señorita," Dan said, making a little bow to her, "you look more beautiful each time I see you."

Her smile seemed mechanical; her eyes searched his. "You are very gallant, señor."

"And you, Señor Hernandez," Dan said to her father. "This must be a very proud moment for you."

Hernandez, looking as patrician as a grandee of old, replied haughtily, "It is my daughter's happiness that brings pleasure to her father's heart."

And rain makes applesauce, Dan answered silently.

"Mr. Randolph, they tell me you are carrying a gun," Malik said, his voice as bright as his smile. "Is it a six-shooter? Do you think you're still in Texas?"

Dan grinned back at him. "I was safe in Texas."

"You're perfectly safe here, I promise you." The Russian looked splendid in his dinner clothes, as if he had been born to them. He wore three small medals on his jacket. Dan recognized the Order of Lenin and the Cosmonaut's Star; the third one was unfamiliar to him.

"I don't feel very safe," Dan said. "Especially when a Soviet agent recently killed a friend of mine while trying to assassinate me."

No one actually gasped, but the crowd seemed to draw in its breath. Lucita stared at Dan, then looked back at the Russian.

Malik's smile never wavered. "Now why would a Soviet agent attempt to assassinate you? That's as silly as my believing you would lead a raid on Lunagrad and threaten the lives of all the Soviet citizens there."

Dan laughed. "Now why would I lead a raid on Lunagrad?

Just because your thugs kidnapped a team of Astro Manufacturing employees and illegally held them prisoner on the Moon?''

Hernandez looked shocked, but Malik merely took Lucita's hand in his as he replied, ''Yes, that would be a ridiculous thing for you to do.''

''There are courts of law,'' Dan said. ''Everyone knows that capitalists use lawyers and bribery to get their way.''

''Of course,'' said Malik. ''Besides, you're too old to go adventuring. All your women and luxury have made you soft.''

Grinning, Dan replied, ''You can't have all those women if you're soft.''

Some of the older women in the crowd did gasp; most of the others snickered.

''But,'' Dan continued, ''I do feel that my life is being threatened. An assassination attempt was made on me.''

Malik kept the smile on his face, but his voice became hard. ''The Soviet Union does not engage in hoodlum behavior, Mr. Randolph. Only in old Hollywood movies do Soviet agents try to assassinate rich American capitalists.''

''Are you sure of that?'' asked Dan.

''Quite certain. I promise you, Mr. Randolph: if a Soviet agent had been instructed to assassinate you, he would not have bungled the job.''

The whole room fell absolutely silent. The band had stopped, all the other conversations seemed to cease and all eyes turned to the two jousting men. Even the smoke seemed to hang motionless in the air.

Dan tried to see what was going on behind the Russian's ice-blue eyes. But they were an impenetrable screen. Then he saw that Lucita's eyes were filled with anxiety.

''You have nothing to fear from assassins, Mr. Randolph,'' Malik said. Then his tone lightened. ''A hangman, perhaps, but not an assassin.''

Laughing, Dan replied, ''I'm very relieved.''

''Then you won't need your six-shooter, will you?'' Malik said.

Still grinning, Dan said, "Oh, it has a lot more than six shots in it."

"But you can bear to part with it while you're here, I trust."

"No, I'd rather keep it. I'm becoming rather fond of it."

"I thought," Malik teased, "that in the Wild West men settled their differences with their fists."

With a slight nod, Dan answered, "Not when one of them is a martial arts champion. I'll keep the gun. In the Wild West it was called 'the equalizer.' "

"You really don't need it," Malik insisted.

Dan asked, "What's the matter? Are you afraid I'm going to shoot you?"

"That would be . . ."

"As ridiculous as leading a raid on Lunagrad."

Malik's smile evaporated.

"Don't worry," Dan said. "You don't have to be afraid of assassins any more than I do. But I'll hold on to my pistol, just the same. For my own protection."

Malik glanced at the looming young man still standing beside Dan. Something passed between them, silently. Then Malik shrugged and put on his smile again.

"As you wish, Mr. Randolph. I wouldn't want you to feel frightened. But if you don't mind, I'll have Georgi here stay close to you for the duration of the party. I wouldn't want your gun to go off accidentally; you might hurt yourself."

"I'm flattered that you care," Dan said.

Turning to Lucita, Malik said, "Would you care to dance, my darling?"

As if on cue, the band struck up a waltz. Lucita gave Dan a fleeting, frightened glance, then allowed Malik to lead her through the crowd to the dance floor.

Hernandez stepped up to Dan's side as the crowd that had clustered around Malik began to dissipate, like a cloud of smoke wafting into nothingness.

"You play a dangerous game," Hernandez muttered.

Dan looked into the Venezuelan's haughty face and dull, mud-brown eyes. "We all do what we must, my friend."

"Do you have any idea of the pressures that Comrade Malik is exerting on the government of Venezuela—on *me*? He wants proof that you led the raid on Lunagrad, and he means to get it."

"How can he get something that doesn't exist?" Dan asked mildly. "I was working night and day in *Nueva Venezuela* to try to get my men released by the Russians. I have tapes of all my calls to the World Court, to the Soviet Council of Ministers, to the United Nations—I even made several calls to you."

Hernandez snorted. "Between three and five in the morning, when you knew I would be asleep and could not answer them."

"I left messages. You could examine them with voice analyzers. It was me."

"Those messages could have been taped before you left for Lunagrad, or even while you were on the way there."

Dan shrugged. "Look, I was just as pleased as you were when my men returned to *Nueva Venezuela*. But they don't know who their rescuers were any more than I know." He could not keep from grinning. "Some altruistic strangers with a love of justice and adventure. Like the Lone Ranger."

"Who?" Hernandez frowned.

"Never mind."

"And you expect the government of Venezuela to sue the Soviet Union over the minerals your spacecraft was carrying when the Russians seized it?"

"I certainly do," Dan said. "They had no right to seize either the ship or its cargo."

Hernandez shook his head. "Madness. If you think that I will recommend we go to the World Court . . ."

"I have an alternative for you," Dan offered.

"Yes?"

"Talk to Malik directly. After all, he ought to do a favor for his prospective father-in-law."

228

Hernandez threw up his hands and stamped away. Dan stood there, laughing.

The waltz ended and the band took up a Latin rhythm. Dan saw Malik still dancing with Lucita, and decided that the only chance he would have to talk to her would be on the dance floor. He threaded through the dancers, with the bulky Georgi following two steps behind him.

Dan approached Malik from behind. Lucita saw him and quickly turned her eyes away from him. Tapping Malik's shoulder, Dan asked cheerfully, "May I?"

For an instant the Russian looked as if he would rather punch Dan, but he released Lucita and stepped back without a word. Dan put his arm around her tiny waist and they whirled away from Malik and the burly security guard.

"You are insane!" Lucita whispered, barely audible over the music.

Dan said, "Your father has the same opinion of me. It must run in your family."

"Are you really carrying a gun?"

"Let me hold you closer and you'll feel it for yourself."

But she stayed a decorous distance from him as they danced.

"That's a beautiful necklace," Dan said. "And the earrings match it. A family heirloom?"

"Vasily's engagement present to me," she said, her voice empty of joy or pride.

"I should have guessed," said Dan. "Some other family's heirloom—a family that died in Siberia, most likely."

Lucita's eyes flashed anger for a second, but it quickly passed. "Did you really lead the raid on Lunagrad? That's all that Vasily talks about. He's furious about it."

"If I did, beautiful one, this wouldn't be the best place in the world to admit it, now would it? The Russian embassy, no less. There must be microphones in every drinking glass. And you're the fiancée of the man who wants to have me hanged!"

Lucita lowered her eyes for a moment. Then, "I'm not his

fiancée yet. Not until midnight, when the announcement is made."

Dan grinned at her. "Shall I steal you away, then? Shoot our way out of here and jump on the fastest steed in all the wide Border. . . ."

"Lochinvar," Lucita recognized. "I read that poem in school."

"Well? Are you game? Shall I rescue you from this engagement?"

She smiled, but there was sadness in it. "And where would we go, my gallant knight? Where could we hide that they would not find us?"

With a shrug, Dan said, "There must be a cave somewhere, an enchanted forest . . . maybe a domed city at the bottom of the sea."

"He wants to kill you," Lucita said, intensely earnest. "He will not rest until you are dead."

"I know."

"You mustn't let him kill you. You must stop baiting him, stop fighting against him."

"Instead of having him kill me, I should lie down and die without putting him to any trouble? No, Lucita. I can't do that."

"I am going to marry him," she said.

He looked down at her lovely face: so serious, so grave. What would Malik do if he just tilted her chin up and kissed her?

"Lucita," he whispered.

"Yes?" She looked up at him, her eyes gleaming with the beginnings of tears. Dan saw sadness in those eyes, a resignation to the inevitability of a life shaped by the ambitions of her father and Vasily Malik. Yet there was something else in her luminous dark eyes, a conflicting emotion: was it hope? A desperate plea for rescue? A silent scream for help?

The music ended, the dance came to an end. Out of the corner of his eye Dan saw Malik pushing his way through the crowd toward them, with giant Georgi right behind him.

"Lucita," he said. "We're all doing what we've got to do. All of us."

She blinked the tears away and took a deep, shuddering breath. "Yes, I see. I understand."

She turned away from Dan, held out her hand to Malik and let him lead her away.

Dan stayed at the party only long enough to invite Kolwezi and the other Third World space industrialists to his office for lunch the next day. They all agreed immediately; they had all expected the invitation.

That accomplished, Dan left the party long before midnight and the public announcement of Lucita's engagement to Malik. Georgi accompanied him to his limousine.

"Sorry to have troubled you," Dan said to the young Russian.

"Not to worry," he replied. "If not for you, I would be standing guard outside and miss the party. Now I can go to the kitchen and inspect the caviar."

Dan laughed. The beefy young man waved good night as the limo pulled away.

The lights were on in Dan's bedroom when he got back there. Kristin must have come back for another session of marriage counseling, he thought sourly. He pulled his tie loose and unfastened his collar as he made his way across the living room. You can't let some women into your bedroom once without them thinking they have squatter's rights. Never let them take a toothbrush out of their handbag, he told himself.

Kristin was lying naked on the waterbed. Her face was a rictus of shock and pain. Her blood soaked the sheets, still bright red and warm enough to drip onto the carpet. Her throat had been slashed very thoroughly, very brutally, very expertly.

Chapter
◆ ◆ TWENTY-FIVE ◆ ◆

Dan leaned back in his leather desk chair and examined the earnest, determined face of Nobuhiko Yamagata. Bright morning sunlight streamed through the big windows behind his desk. There were dark rings under Dan's eyes. He had not slept; the night had been spent with his own security people and the police detectives of Caracas and the Venezuelan national government.

Now, wearing an open-necked tan sport shirt and rumpled chinos, Dan regarded his old friend's son carefully.

"Nobo," he said, "I want you to return to Japan. Immediately. Today."

If the young Japanese was surprised, he masked it successfully. "Has my work failed to—"

"It's got nothing to do with your work," Dan said. "It's for your own safety. Two people who were somewhat close to me have been murdered. I'm not going to take the chance that you might be next."

Nobo shook his head the barest fraction of an inch. "I will not go. Not voluntarily. You can fire me, of course. But I will not quit."

232

With a sigh, Dan replied, "Okay, you're fired."

The faintest hint of a smile crossed Nobo's face. "Very well, then, I shall stay in Caracas to organize a labor union among your engineers and astronauts."

Dan blinked, uncertain he had heard the younger man correctly.

"If you are going to fire valued employees so arbitrarily," Nobo said, his grin widening, "then a labor union is necessary to protect our rights."

"Now look . . ."

"Sir—I know what has happened. I have spoken to my father about it. He predicted that you would try to bundle me off, for my own safety, and he instructed me to use my own judgment in the matter."

"Well, then use some judgment," Dan snapped. "Malik is playing a goddamned cat-and-mouse game. He's trying to terrify me, or make me feel guilty enough to surrender to him. His goons are methodically murdering the people around me. Maybe he's trying to get my key people to run away."

"And your first reaction is to force *me* to run away?"

"You are the son of my closest friend," Dan said. "And in the few months you've been here I've come to think of you almost as my own son—or at least a close nephew. I don't want you to be killed."

Nobo raised a long, slim forefinger. "Point number one: I too have become very attached to you, almost like an uncle." A second finger. "Two: You risked your life to rescue me and the others when the Russians took us prisoner. . . ."

"It was my responsibility. I sent you on that mission."

Ignoring Dan's reply, Nobo lifted a third finger. "Three: You are having a meeting this afternoon with space industrialists from four other nations. My father agrees that it would be a good thing for me to represent Yamagata Industries and Japan at this meeting."

Dan rubbed his chin for a moment, thinking, If Saito can't or won't attend the meeting, it would be a good idea to have Nobo sitting in for him. Then the only power missing would

233

be China, and in a way Yamagata almost represents the Chinese as well as Japan.

"Okay," he said. "You're welcome to stay for the meeting. But then I want you on your way back home, understand?"

Nobo did not bow his head as he would if he agreed with Dan. Instead, he said, "I have often heard my father say that you are rushing toward death, like a Samurai warrior of olden times."

"Your father is sometimes given to exaggeration."

The young man shrugged. "That may be. But we are all moving toward our deaths. Death will come when it comes. It is part of life."

"So's paying taxes," Dan grumbled. "That doesn't mean you can't try to avoid it."

They make a motley crew, Dan thought. Kolwezi as tall and black as an American basketball star. Vavuniya looking like a brown pygmy next to him. Al Hashimi, the hawk-nosed sheikh even in a Western-style business suit. And Chalons, the golden Polynesian, with the blood of at least four different races in him.

They sat around the marble dining table in Dan's apartment. All morning long, Astro security personnel had combed the walls, the floors, the ceilings, even the adjoining buildings for listening devices. Metal mesh curtains shimmered across each window, letting the noonday sunlight in but foiling microwave beams that might catch the vibrations of the windows or the very air inside the apartment and translate them into the words being spoken. Uniformed guards patrolled every floor of the buildings, and half of the men and women in street clothes who roamed through the lobby and hallways were Astro security employees.

More guards covered the roof and still more patrolled nearby in cruising unmarked cars and fluttering helicopters. Maybe Malik's trying to get me to spend myself into bankruptcy, Dan thought as he contemplated the costs of such security. Each man and woman in his security forces had been thoroughly investigated when they had been hired, and checks of their loyalty went on all the time. But Dan knew from his own experience how easily someone could be bribed. And it was not always money that corrupted; just as often it was flattery, or revenge, or naked lust.

One hand grenade in here would wipe out all the Third World space industry leaders, he thought. Malik could achieve his goal at a stroke. There'd be nobody left to operate in space except the Soviet Union.

Luncheon was served by a trio of pretty young women who were trained bodyguards. Each man received a dish prepared especially for him, out of the detailed dossiers maintained by Dan's computers. The aromas of roast goat and curried chicken dominated the room. Dan introduced Nobo, who sat at the far end of the table. The conversation during lunch was light, pleasant, guarded.

But as the meal drew to its close, Dan tapped his fork against his water glass for their attention.

"I think you all know what's going on," he said, putting the fork down on his emptied plate. "If any of you don't, then you ought to fire your director of intelligence."

The men chuckled, somewhat uneasily, Dan thought.

Al Hashimi, seated at Dan's right, said, "I understand that a young woman was murdered here last night."

"That's right."

"Regrettable," murmured Chalons.

"She was a victim of the war that the Soviets are waging against us."

"Us?"

"All of us here at this table," Dan said firmly.

They glanced at one another. Vavuniya, his black eyes darting from one face to another, said in his singsong English, "But what has this unfortunate incident to do with us?"

"Everything," replied Dan.

"I'm afraid I don't understand."

"The Soviet Union wants to be the *only* power operating

235

in space. They have forced the United States and all the members of the old NATO alliance to renounce their space programs. . . .''

"In the name of peace," said Kolwezi, his deep bass voice taking on an edge of sarcasm.

"Sure," Dan replied. "The same kind of peace they imposed in Poland. And Afghanistan. And Greece."

"There are no lovers of the Soviet system here," Kolwezi said. "You need not remind us of their atrocities."

Dan nodded an acknowledgment, then resumed, "The six of us here at this table—together with the People's Republic of China—represent the only non-Soviet space efforts in existence."

Al Hashimi allowed a thin smile to cross his face. "The six of us here at this table are the only private entrepreneurs operating in space," he corrected. "Each of us flies the flag of a nation, but we each represent large corporations more truly than we represent Venezuela, or Zaire, or even Japan."

The others nodded. Vavuniya was somewhat grudging about it, Dan saw. Nationalism was important to the Indian. Nobo easily agreed with al Hashimi: Yamagata Industries and the government of Japan were as thoroughly interlinked as the two twining spirals of a DNA molecule.

"Do you believe," Kolwezi asked, "that the Soviets are opposed to us because we are capitalists?"

"Sure," said Dan. "But there's a hard pragmatic reason behind their philosophical opposition. If they can eliminate us, if they can attain a total monopoly of space industries— manufacturing as well as raw materials—they gain a further stranglehold on the world's commerce."

Vavuniya shook his head in quick, disbelieving strokes, reminding Dan of the nervous movements of a frightened brown rabbit. "But why would Soviet Russia do such a thing? The Russians have no enemies to fear. They have cowed the United States into surrender without firing a shot; America has retreated into isolationism. Western Europe depends on the Soviets for oil and natural gas. Soviet Russia is the world's most powerful nation, no one opposes her."

"But it's not enough," Dan said. "They want more."

"How could they?"

"Greed. Philosophy. The natural momentum of growth. Sure, they've beaten the U.S. and Western Europe. They didn't have to resort to nuclear war; the West just pissed away its power until the Cold War was over and the Russians were the winners. But there's the rest of the world—China, Japan, the Third World nations."

"Russia has nothing to fear from them," Vavuniya insisted.

"I know that. And you know it. But maybe those men in the Kremlin don't know it. Or maybe they want to control the whole world. Maybe they want even more: maybe they want to *rule* the whole world, turn the entire goddamned world into one big homogenized tightly controlled Soviet state."

Al Hashimi took a gold cigarette case from his jacket. "I haven't heard such rabid American anti-Communist rantings in many years." He put a cigarette in his mouth and lit it with a gold lighter. "It's very amusing."

Dan smiled back at him. "It's amusing as long as the Soviets are paying a decent price for Arab oil. What happens when they take over the existing solar power satellites and start building new ones to serve Europe and Africa? Who buys your oil then?"

Al Hashimi leaned back in his chair and blew a long cloud of gray smoke toward the ceiling.

"If and when the Soviets gain total control of space manufacturing," Dan went on, "they will use that power to get total control of the nations we represent. Venezuela's manufacturing and oil exports will be threatened. India's exports of steel and automobiles . . ."

"How can that be?" Vavuniya demanded.

Dan replied, "Because *I've* shown them that they can get high-grade iron ore from asteroids, double-damn them to hell and back! They'll undercut India's prices for steel. And with zero-gravity processing, they'll be able to make steel alloys that are twenty times stronger, weight for weight, than anything you can make on Earth.''

The Indian's swarthy face went ashen.

"As the representative of Yamagata Industries," Nobo said softly, "and Japan, I must admit that I find it hard to believe that the Russians could force Japan out of its space manufacturing operations.''

Kolwezi chuckled, a deep throaty sound. "If Zaire had China's protection, I would feel confident too.''

But Dan disagreed. "China isn't strong enough to challenge the Soviet Union head to head. And the Russians can afford to be patient with Japan. They'll squeeze the smaller nations out first; they're already after Venezuela. Then" —pointing to the men as he spoke—"Zaire and Polynesia will be the easiest to pressure. Then the Pan-Islam factories and India's.''

Nobo cocked his head slightly to one side in a gesture that said, "So?''

"Once they've done that," Dan continued, "they can squeeze Japan gently but continuously. Raise the price of raw materials. Cut down on their supply: after all, they'll have all those newly acquired factories to feed, won't they? Yamagata's space operations will lose profitability; your products will have to sell at higher prices than the competing products manufactured by the Russians. They'll use good old, tried and true, nineteenth-century robber baron tactics on you. And it will work, eventually. They can afford to operate at a deficit for as long as it takes. Yamagata can't.''

The young Japanese pursed his lips.

"China will be the only other nation operating in space, then," Dan said. "At that point the Russians wouldn't be averse to using their muscle. They'll force China out of the game as part of their long-range plan for bringing China under Soviet control here on Earth.''

"The Chinese have not dismantled their nuclear arsenal," Kolwezi pointed out. "Their missiles are still in their silos and still fully armed.''

238

Dan felt his face freeze. With a conscious effort he kept his voice calm and even as he said, "If the Soviet antimissile satellites were good enough to make the American nuclear deterrent useless, how much do you think they fear from the Chinese nuclear force?"

Al Hashimi, holding his cigarette straight up between thumb and forefinger, agreed. "Yes, the Russians still have their lasers in orbit. They can shoot down any missiles launched at them."

Chalons' usually cheerful Polynesian smile had disappeared long ago. Bleakly, he reminded them, "Those lasers can also be used on our factories and space stations."

"That's a comforting thought!" muttered Kolwezi.

"They would not dare!" Vavuniya snapped.

"They wouldn't have to," said Dan. "They won't have to attack our facilities in space any more than they had to launch their missiles at the United States. Once you know that they *can* destroy you, and you have no way to defend yourself, they win. It's like chess; you don't fight to the last man once you've been checkmated."

"You believe, then," al Hashimi said, squinting through his cigarette's smoke, "that the Soviets will try to pressure us out of our space operations through economic and political means."

"Right. This recent price increase of theirs is just the beginning. They have a monopoly on raw materials and they're going to use it to squeeze the life out of us. That's why they illegally stole my asteroid spacecraft and imprisoned the crew. They will not allow anyone to upset their monopoly on raw materials, no matter what they have to do to protect it."

"Then what can we do?" Vavuniya flapped his hands like a helpless man ready to give up. "If they are determined to destroy us, they certainly have the power to do so."

"We fight back."

The three words seemed to immobilize the five other men at the table. For a long moment they sat as if frozen: Chalons

239

looking desperately unhappy, al Hashimi grimly amused, Vavuniya frightened, Kolwezi plainly disgusted with the state of affairs Dan was predicting, Nobuhiko more curious and expectant than anything else.

Al Hashimi broke the silence. "Fight back? Against laser-armed satellites and nuclear missiles? With what?"

"Our wits," replied Dan.

"Explain what you mean," Kolwezi requested.

Dan said, "The Russians aren't supermen. They have weaknesses. The raid on Lunagrad showed that they can be surprised and overpowered by even a very small group of men, if those men are determined enough."

"And now the Soviets are stationing a battalion of armed troops at Lunagrad," said al Hashimi in a bored, sardonic tone.

Dan grinned at him. "There's almost a quarter of a million miles between our factories and the Moon. Dozens of Russian ore freighters trundle back and forth across that distance every day. They are unmanned and unprotected."

"What are you saying?" Vavuniya gasped.

"According to my lawyers' reading of the international regulations, the ore in those freighters does not belong to the Soviet Union. It does not belong, legally, to any nation. Those resources are, and I quote from the law, 'the common heritage of all humankind.' " Dan smiled broadly at them. "In other words, gentlemen, they are ours for the taking."

Chalons laughed. Al Hashimi snorted impatiently and stubbed out his cigarette in the stainless-steel ashtray that had been set at his place.

Vavuniya said, "But we cannot simply take the ores out of the Soviet freighters."

"Why not?" Dan countered. "The Soviet Union does not own the ores. Legally, they can be used by any nation which can obtain them. The fact that we pay the Russians to dig them up from the Moon and bring them to our factories does not give them title to the stuff. Legally, we're merely paying them for transporting the raw materials to us."

"But they would never—"

Dan silenced him with a curt gesture. "The Russians themselves are using that argument in the World Court against Astro Manufacturing. They claim that the asteroid material my spacecraft was carrying did not legally belong to Astro, and they had a perfect right to confiscate it."

"Ah," said Kolwezi, "there's a difference. Astro Manufacturing is a private corporation. It isn't a nation. The law does not allow private corporations the same protections that it gives to nations."

"It's a tricky legal point," Dan admitted. "But each of us operates under the banner of a sovereign nation. Why shouldn't Zaire—or India, or Japan—go out and *take* the ores we need for our factories?"

"Because the Russians would use their lasers to destroy our factories," Chalons said.

"Or they would guard their freighters," suggested Nobo.

"There are a hundred ways they could stop us," al Hashimi said.

"Maybe," said Dan. "But they'd have to exert themselves. They'd have to use force of one kind or another. They'd have to show the world—and the World Court—that they are using their power against the best interests of the smaller, independent nations."

Vavuniya blinked his big, brown, liquid eyes. "I see. I understand. The Soviets would be in the position of obviously bullying the other nations. World opinion would be marshaled against them."

"Right."

"Since when has world opinion bothered them?" al Hashimi countered disdainfully. "Especially when their vital interests are at stake?"

"All I'm saying," Dan urged, "is that we can make it tough for them to squeeze us out of space. We can raise their costs so high that they'll stop trying to get rid of us. We can't overturn the Soviet Union, I know that. But we can prevent them from ruining us, if we act boldly enough."

"At the risk of having our factories destroyed and our nations threatened with nuclear retaliation?" Kolwezi asked.

Dan grinned at him. "You wouldn't be sitting at this table if you hadn't taken some risks during your life."

"True," the Zairian admitted. "But this . . ."

"It's this or we're finished. The Russians are moving to push us out of space entirely. You know that."

From the far end of the table, Nobo asked, "You, sir, have already been personally threatened by Soviet actions. Two persons have been murdered, and it seems likely that you are marked for assassination by the KGB. Wouldn't it be easier for the Soviets to counter any moves we make by eliminating us as individuals?"

Dan looked down the length of the table at his old friend's son. "None of us is exactly defenseless, on the personal level. And I think that the murders have a personal motivation, not a political one."

"Still . . ."

"No course of action is without risks," Dan said. "Personal as well as corporate and national."

"You are asking us to commit piracy," al Hashimi said.

"The Russians will call it piracy," Dan admitted cheerfully. "But we have strong legal arguments to the contrary."

"They'll seize our factories," Chalons insisted. "Or blow them to pieces."

"Not if they don't know which factories to attack," said Dan. "For God's sake, we're not going to *advertise* what we're doing! There are six factory complexes in orbit—seven, if we can bring the Chinese into this. The Russians can't attack them all, and surely we're smart enough to keep them guessing as to who's doing what to whom."

"They'll protect their freighters, put guards aboard or escort them with armed spacecraft."

"In time," Dan admitted, "maybe they will. But it will cost them a fortune. It'd be much easier for them to negotiate a lower price for the ores."

Nobo mused, "They would have a difficult time protecting

every freighter all the time. That would tie up hundreds of men, perhaps thousands.''

Al Hashimi turned his sardonic smile toward Dan. ''And it would reflect very poorly on the new chief of their space programs.''

Dan grinned back at him. ''Yes, it might, at that.''

Tapping both his hands on the tabletop, Vavuniya said enthusiastically, ''After all, the ores are very certainly the common property of all humankind. We have as much right to them as anyone.''

''Are you all mad?'' Chalons asked. ''The Russians won't hesitate for a second to use armed force against us.''

''Then we must have protection,'' said Kolwezi.

''Perhaps China would be willing to back us,'' al Hashimi suggested. ''Not publicly, of course. But a quiet guarantee of protection against Soviet retaliation. . . .''

''Or the United States,'' Vavuniya said.

Al Hashimi sneered. ''The United States would never dare to challenge Russia. The Americans have given up. They don't have the spirit to stand up and fight.''

Dan felt his teeth clench painfully, but he said nothing.

Nobuhiko offered, ''I believe that my father might be willing to contact certain people in the Chinese government and sound them out about this plan.''

''Good,'' said Dan.

''And you,'' Vavuniya urged, turning from al Hashimi's stern visage to Dan, ''you should sound out the American government. You were a close friend of the American President, were you not?''

''Long ago,'' Dan replied.

Kolwezi shook his head. ''We can talk and ask questions and make plans, but the simple fact is that this idea of space piracy is nothing short of insane. It will never work.''

''I agree,'' said al Hashimi. ''Nothing can come of it.''

''It *is* rather like trying to bell the cat,'' Chalons said.

''I wouldn't want to be the one to try to hijack a Soviet ore freighter," al Hashimi confessed. "I can see myself rotting in the Gulag mines on the Moon."

Chalons nodded vigorously.

With a deep chuckle, Kolwezi said to Dan, "It's a bold scheme, but I don't see how it could ever be successful."

Vavuniya's eyes flicked from one man's face to another's. Finally he agreed sadly, "I suppose they are right. It could never come to be."

Dan was silent for several minutes. Then he shrugged wearily. "Okay. Maybe you're right."

Nobo was staring at him, puzzled.

"I'm certainly not going to try it if you're not in the scheme with me," Dan said.

They all shifted uneasily in their chairs and avoided his gaze. After a few minutes more of desultory chat, the meeting broke up. One by one the men got to their feet, shook Dan's hand and, expressing their regrets at being unable to agree with him, they left the apartment. Finally, no one was left except Nobo.

The young Japanese slumped back into his chair at the end of the long marble table. The dirty dishes and crumbs of luncheon were still strewn across it.

Dan grinned at him. "Don't look so glum."

Nobo's chin was on his chest. "I thought . . ."

"You thought wrong," Dan said.

"They have no guts at all, do they? How did they ever get to the positions they're in?"

"By looking before they leaped," Dan said, his grin widening.

"What are you so happy about?"

Dan said, "I want you to go back to your father and tell him what's happened here today. The whole story. See if he'll speak to his contacts in the Chinese government."

"But why? . . ."

Sitting on the edge of the table and leaning toward his young friend, Dan said, "They bought the idea. Don't you understand that? None of them is foolish enough to admit it, especially in front of witnesses. But they're going to go ahead with it—as soon as I start the ball rolling by grabbing the first Russian freighter."

Nobo's mouth dropped open.

Dan laughed heartily. "Don't you understand? They're too cautious to say it out loud. In fact, if any of them *did* agree, I would have suspected that he'd run straight to the Russians and tell them everything."

"Then we're going to do it?"

"I'm going to do it," Dan said firmly. "You're getting the hell out of here and back to Japan, where you'll be safe."

"No! I want to—"

Dan gripped his shoulder. "I can't take the risk with my oldest friend's son, Nobo. I'm sorry, but that's the way it is. The best help you can give me right now is to get back to your father."

Nobo said nothing.

"That's the way it's got to be," Dan said softly.

Finally, Nobo nodded, his face bleak. He got up to leave after a few more moments. Dan walked him to the apartment door. After shutting it behind him, Dan muttered to himself:

"He'll be safe in Japan, with his father." Then he heard himself add, "And he'll be ten thousand miles away from Lucita."

Chapter
◆ ◆ TWENTY-SIX ◆ ◆

As he watched the space station *Nueva Venezuela* slowly turning, like a set of brilliant white wheels nested one within another, hanging against the eternal dark of space, Dan realized all over again what a desperately mad scheme this was.

Piracy. In space. It was enough to make him laugh out loud—almost. The men who sat jammed into the flitter's cramped cockpit with him probably were nervous enough without him suddenly cackling like a lunatic. So Dan held himself in control. But it was madness; they were all insane and he was the craziest of the lot and he knew it.

Then the space station turned far enough for him to see the red, blue and gold flag painted on its flank, and he remembered the method behind his insanity. Shifting in his seat as much as the harness would allow, Dan turned his head to look at the glowing mass of the Earth, so big that it filled the sky with its brilliant blue beauty and swirling bands of pure white clouds. He could make out the coast of California and the Baja, the rugged folds of the Sierras, the wrinkled browns and reds of the deserts that stretched beyond the mountains.

The Earth turned, and the flitter glided deeper into space.

The American coast slid away from his view and there was nothing to be seen but the vast expanse of the Pacific, glittering under the sun. Polynesians had crossed that huge ocean in open outriggers, Dan knew, voyages that made modern sojourns in space look easy and safe.

It was a happy coincidence that the flitters, designed to ferry men and equipment from one orbital facility to another, were built like long thin broomsticks. Usually they were loaded down with bulky cargo pods, like donkeys carrying oversized loads. But their basic needlelike shape gave them a low radar profile; if they were not saddled with bulging burdens, they were hard to spot on a radar screen.

Three other men sat wedged into the flitter's narrow cockpit. Carstairs, the irreverent, irrepressible Australian, was at Dan's left, piloting the flitter. The Venezuelan kid, Vargas, and a quiet, tight-lipped former Israeli, Zlotnik, sat in the two rear seats. They all wore silvered pressure suits and helmets; there was no room inside the cockpit's bubble canopy to squirm into the suits, nor was the cockpit pressurized. Without cargo pods, the flitter was little more than a slim needle bearing small thrusters at one end, the cockpit at the other and a latticework of titanium girders holding the two together.

With a small shake of his head, Dan turned his eyes away from the hypnotic glory of Earth and focused his attention on the task ahead. The Soviet ore freighter was little more than four hours away. Was it truly unguarded, undefended? Or did the Soviets already know about this wild plan to hijack it? Has somebody told them about it? Is Malik sitting there like a spider in the middle of his web, Dan wondered, just waiting for me to step into his trap?

They would love that, Dan thought. Billionaire American capitalist caught in the act of piracy. They'd stage a big trial, get the biggest crowds since the French Revolution. They'd hang me on worldwide television; I'd get the highest ratings ever.

Then he grinned to himself. They'll have to catch me first.

"Injection burn." Dan heard Carstairs' voice in his helmet

earphones as the rawboned Aussie flicked his gloved fingers across the flitter's control panel. The slightest feathery touch of thrust nudged Dan gently against the padded back of his seat. A cold puff of nitrogen gas was being squirted out of the thruster nozzles, pushing the spacecraft into an orbit that exactly matched the path of the Soviet ore freighter.

Dan glanced down at the radar display screen. There was the freighter, a fat dumb blip in the middle of the orange-glowing screen. Computer numbers flickered along the edge of the screen, telling him exactly how far away the freighter was and how long it would take to make the rendezvous with it. Dan started to scratch at an itch on his nose, but his hand bumped the visor of his helmet. He laughed at himself. We're actually going to board that craft and steal its cargo. We're going to be pirates. Yo-ho-ho and all that!

"No escorting spacecraft," said Vargas' soft, youthful voice. Just a touch of tightness in it, Dan realized. Just a bit of nerves.

"Can't tell if it's crewed from this distance," Zlotnik muttered.

"We'll get a computer-enhanced image in an hour or so," Dan said, keeping his voice light and easy. "Nothing to do until then, so relax."

"Sure, boss. And what do we do if the enhanced picture shows a crew pod on the freighter?"

With a laugh, Dan answered, "We wave to them as we go past, then turn around and head for home."

"They won't have any bloody crew aboard," Carstairs said. "Fuckin' Russkies aren't that daft, puttin' crews aboard fryters with nothin' t'do but jerk themselves off for two bloody weeks at a tyme. We're the only madmen in this part of the universe."

Dan heard the others chuckle at the Aussie's evaluation of the situation. But he's right, Dan thought. We're the only madmen in this part of the universe. The others, al Hashimi, Vavuniya and the rest, were waiting to see how this first attempt came out. Nobuhiko and his father were sitting safely in Tokyo, surrounded by loyal retainers who would literally put their own bodies between the Yamagatas and any assassin. And Dan's attempt to win at least a tacit understanding from Jane Scanwell had crashed miserably.

He had realized when the other space industrialists had sat down with him that they would inevitably expect him to gain at least the covert support of the United States. Old habits die hard, and although al Hashimi might sneer at the States openly, even he still half expected some show of resistance from Washington against the Soviets.

And so did I, Dan realized. So did I.

To his surprise, Jane had agreed to see him much more easily than the last time, several months earlier. The American President still would not risk being seen publicly with the expatriate billionaire, but she was willing to spirit him into the White House for a quick, clandestine meeting.

Dan had flown to New York and taken the ancient, crowded, filthy train from La Guardia to Penn Station. Teams of fully armed policemen in helmets and riot armor stood menacingly at each end of every car, glittery-eyed attack dogs beside them. The train was noisy and reeked of sweat and urine. People were jammed in shoulder to shoulder as it lurched and swayed and roared along the elevated tracks. Peering past the shoulders of blank-faced riders who clung to the handbars like immobilized chimpanzees, Dan saw that vast areas of Queens had been burned out, the buildings blackened and hollow, their windows gaping emptily. The Russians didn't have to bomb New York, he thought grimly. The city is self-destructing.

As the train crossed the sewage-choked stench of the East River on the Queensboro Bridge, Dan got a glimpse of Manhattan: the FDR Drive was practically empty except for armored Army personnel carriers and dilapidated city buses; the midtown towers were grimy with soot from the coal-burning power plants; the UN buildings, abandoned for several years now, looked dirty and uncared-for. Then the train plunged into the subway tunnel with a deafening roar.

At Penn Station, Dan saw that New York had finally produced a modicum of public safety and solved a large part of its unemployment problem at the same time. Police were everywhere, in teams of two or three, armed like strike force commandos with everything from snub-barreled shotguns to gas grenades. And Dan quickly learned how the bankrupt city paid its swollen police force. There were toll desks at the entrance to Penn Station: to get in, Dan had to stand in line for ten minutes and then pay a twenty-dollar admission toll. The policewoman at the desk also checked his passport there. Every person in line had to show some form of identification. Dan noted that the policewoman was just as heavily armed as the men who stood behind her.

Even so protected, Penn Station still had hustlers and thieves prowling through its underground mall. Dan was approached by half a dozen panhandlers within fifty feet of the entrance. He plowed past them, clutching his travel bag closely, but then he felt a hand brushing against his side. He grabbed at it, and found himself squeezing the thin wrist of a frightened, skinny, freckle-faced redheaded kid who could not have been more than ten years old.

"That's my pocket you're reaching into," Dan said quietly, not breaking his stride, yanking the boy alongside him.

The kid said nothing. His eyes were wide with fright.

Dan glanced around, looking for others who might be accomplices. "Do you want to go to jail?" he asked the kid.

"Please, mister . . . please lemme go."

A black policeman was watching them, Dan saw, holding a mean-looking electric truncheon and tapping it menacingly into his open palm.

Before Dan could decide what to do about the young pickpocket, a trio of lanky teenagers raced past, dodging through the crowd. In the brief glimpse he got of them, Dan thought they looked Hispanic, or perhaps even Oriental. One of them was holding a shoulder bag by its strap, maybe a woman's bag, flapping loosely as they ran at top speed toward the exits.

The black cop dropped his truncheon and yanked the pistol from the holster at his hip. Dan dove for the floor, yanking the kid down with him. But before the cop could fire, Dan heard the boom of a shotgun. Twisting his head, he saw two of the teenagers staggering backward and collapsing to the floor, their faces and chests torn into ragged masses of bloody flesh. The third teenager, the one with the bag, skidded to a stop and raised his hands. A white policeman raced up to him and belted him across the face with his truncheon. He went down, too, his body thudding heavily against the dirty tiles of the floor.

"On your feet and on your way," the black cop bellowed, stuffing his pistol back into its holster. His face was angry, scowling. "Come on, get up and get moving. All of ya."

Dan got up from the oily, filthy floor, feeling as if he had exposed himself to every disease known to medical science. He released the kid's wrist and made a silent shooing motion. The youngster faded into the crowd. Nobody stayed around to watch what happened to the three purse snatchers. Dan followed the crowd to the train for Washington.

It was almost midnight by the time the train pulled in to the capital, three hours late. Dan was hungry and irritated. He felt dirty, rumpled, soiled. The train's air conditioner had not worked at all, and the bulletproof windows could not be opened, so the only way to get any relief from the heat was to stand in the open, between the cars. But the guards at each end of the car would not let any passenger out onto the platforms. Too dangerous, they said. People throw things at the train. Snipers like to pick off passengers who stand on the platform.

The train stopped for almost half an hour on the outskirts of Washington while special security teams, in smoke-gray uniforms with shiny black belts and boots, searched every passenger and each piece of luggage. "For your own protection," they said, murmuring the slogan over and over again, like a religious chant, as they moved from one passenger to the next. Dan hoped at least that the stern-looking brunette who seemed to be the team leader would be the one to frisk him. Instead he got a sweet-faced young man who searched him so thoroughly that Dan became convinced he was gay and enjoying himself.

Welcome to the nation's capital, Dan said silently to himself.

As he stepped off the train, a pair of slim young men met him. They looked alike enough to be brothers. Both were dressed in conservative light suits, both had thick mops of carefully combed light brown hair, both were clear-eyed and smiling the kind of relentlessly cheerful, dazzlingly toothy smiles that Dan always associated with earnest young evangelists who were determined to save your soul whether you liked it or not.

"Mr. McKinley?" one of them asked, using Dan's prearranged alias. "Come with us, please."

They escorted Dan into an unmarked light gray sedan, where one of them scanned him and his one travel bag with an electronic sensor as the other drove out into the empty, silent, dark street. Instead of heading directly to the White House, as Dan had expected, they drove along the Mall to the garage under the former Air and Space Museum—which had been "closed for renovation" for more than two years. There they transferred Dan to another car, with another team of security agents, two men and two women this time, who searched Dan and his bag still again. Only then was he driven to the White House.

Even though it was slightly past midnight by now, there was a sizable throng of pickets ringing the White House. In the glare of the police searchlights that played on the crowd, Dan could read their placards as they shuffled glumly along:

WE NEED JOBS

A WOMAN'S PLACE IS IN THE HOME,
NOT THE WHITE HOUSE

STOP POLICE TERROR

FARMERS ARE STARVING!

The woman sitting on Dan's left glanced at her wristwatch. "I thought they were going to break this up by midnight," she complained.

"Guess the riot squad's running late," said the man sitting on Dan's other side.

"Or they gave 'em some extra time to disperse," the driver suggested.

"They don't look like they're dispersing."

"They will, once the riot squad opens up on 'em."

All four of the security agents laughed, and Dan felt an unpleasant chill tingle his spine.

The picketers made no attempt to stop the car, and within a few minutes Dan was passed through the most elaborate security check of all, relieved of his travel bag and ushered by a tall, lithe black woman into a tiny elevator that took him to the upper floor of the White House, the President's living quarters. His escort was no household servant, Dan knew. She probably had a gun on her somewhere; Dan amused himself for a few moments, speculating on where it might be hidden. She eyed him coldly, like a snake ready to strike.

The elevator door slid smoothly open and Dan stepped into the long Center Hall, warmly decorated in yellow and white, with bookshelves lining one wall and comfortable soft chairs and sofas scattered about the gold carpet.

"Wait here," said his escort. She went to a door and tapped on it. Dan could not make out the words that came from the other side of the door, but his escort beckoned him with a crooked finger.

She opened the door and motioned Dan inside. Jane was sitting at a tiny wooden desk, talking low and intensely into a telephone, her eyes fixed on the phone's small picture screen. A man's face filled the screen, the beefy, red-eyed, overwrought face of a thoroughly angry man. He looked like a cop to Dan. Jane held the phone receiver to her ear, so that Dan could not hear her conversation. He could read the cop's lips, though: he was complaining about not having enough personnel to do everything that was expected of him.

Dan looked around the small sitting room. It was cluttered with old Victorian furniture, darkish and gloomy. The long windows were completely covered by closed brown paisley drapes. A little chandelier holding seven electrified candles dangled on slim rods from the ceiling. The rosewood coffee table had been set with a tray of liqueurs and two oversized snifters.

"Hello, Dan," Jane said as she put down the telephone. "It's good of you to see me."

She got up from her chair and crossed the room, both hands extended to him. "It's good to see you again."

She was wearing a silk brocade robe of pale pink, almost apricot; very feminine, very alluring as it clung to her tall stately figure. Her rich auburn hair flowed loosely to her shoulders, catching the light from the chandelier with a coppery glow. She looked tired, but her face was almost unlined, her green eyes clear and not as suspicious as the last time they had met.

Gesturing to the settee, Jane said with a slight smile, "I made certain that your favorite brand of Armagnac was brought here."

"You should try it." Dan smiled back.

"All right. I think I will."

They sat side by side on the settee and Jane allowed him to pour a splash of Armagnac into each of the snifters.

"It looks like you've got some troubles tonight," Dan said.

"The picketers? They're here every night. Usually the police clear them out by midnight. They're running a little late tonight."

"Do you think you'll be reelected?" Dan asked.

"I expect to be."

He raised his glass to her. "Well, here's to victory in November, then."

She nodded once, then sipped at the brandy. Dan took a good swig of his, and let it slide down his throat, smooth and warm.

"The Russians stole your ship," Jane said, with no preliminaries.

"Yes, but I got my men back."

"You *did* lead the raid on Lunagrad yourself." It was not a question.

He grinned boyishly. "Yes, I did."

"That was a very courageous thing to do. Foolish, but courageous."

"I got them into the pickle they were in; it was my responsibility to get them out."

Jane leaned back in the settee and swirled the liqueur in her glass. "But the Russians still have your ship, and they're going to claim in the World Court that you've endangered the whole world by altering the orbit of that asteroid."

With a little laugh, Dan said, "They can claim whatever they like. By the time the World Court takes up the case, the asteroid will be in a permanent orbit around the Earth, no more dangerous to us than the Moon is."

"Unless the Russians alter that orbit."

Dan hesitated a moment. "Why would they . . . Oh, sure, I can see why. To discredit me. But they can't push the asteroid into a trajectory that'll impact the Earth. It'd be like dropping a hundred H-bombs on the area where it hits."

"They could drop it into the ocean, couldn't they?"

"I suppose so," Dan mused. "What have you heard? Are they up to something?"

The President shook her head. "My scenario analysts have been playing with their computers. The chances that the Russians would push the asteroid into an Earth impact are very small—less than five percent."

Dan waited for the other shoe to drop.

"But if they do it," Jane continued, "the chances that they will aim the asteroid at an American city are better than fifty percent."

"That's crazy!" Dan snapped.

"Is it? Suppose the asteroid hits New York, or even Washington? What effect would that have on the World

Court? Or on world opinion? Where do you think Dan Randolph could hide from the lynch mobs?''

Dan reached for his snifter and took another long swallow of Armagnac. ''Do you have any evidence that the Russians are planning to do this?''

''None whatsoever. But they could, any time they choose to.''

''It doesn't make sense.''

''It makes perfect sense, and you know it!'' Jane's green eyes flashed. ''That's why it is critically important that neither you nor I do anything to antagonize them.''

''Just let them have their way, huh? Well, I never believed in the Chinese advice to a woman about to be raped. I like the American advice better: Kick the bastard in the balls.''

''Dan, you're such a fool! Why can't you face reality? Why can't you see the world as it is?''

''I do see the world as it is, and I hate it.''

''But don't you understand what's happening? Can't you see that the Russians are going to lose, in the long run? If we can hang on . . .''

Feeling suddenly confused, Dan asked, ''What are you talking about?''

''In the long run, we will prevail,'' Jane said firmly. ''The Soviet system is crumbling, bit by bit, a little more each year, each day.''

''Crumbling? I don't see . . .''

''They're getting fat and lazy,'' Jane insisted. ''Their economy is sinking deeper into the morass every year. They're dependent now on Western goods and Third World raw materials. They buy manufactured items from you and the other space factories. . . .''

''And set the prices for raw materials,'' Dan added. ''And the prices for oil. *And* the prices for foodstuffs.''

''But how long can that go on? They never could compete with a free economy, and they're falling farther behind with every luxury item they import.''

Setting his snifter down on the coffee table, Dan replied,

"They don't have to compete, Jane. They command. They run the world's economy because they have nuclear weapons and a huge army, and we don't. They have the guns, and the power."

She got to her feet and began pacing the little room. "You don't understand. Yes, they have the power—for now. But it's slipping from their fingers, a little at a time. If we can be patient, if we can hang on for another decade or so, the Soviet system will dissolve. The Russians themselves will get rid of it."

"Bullshit!" Dan exploded. "That's the same kind of thinking that got us into this mess in the first place!"

"Don't raise your voice to me," the President said.

"Double-dammit to hell, Jane, I've been hearing that kind of crap all my goddamned life! Don't antagonize the Soviets, they might get angry and start a nuclear war. They're paranoid, so we've got to treat them very carefully. Let's reduce the number of weapons we've got, that'll make the Russians feel safer. Jesus H. Christ! We disarmed ourselves piece by piece and all *they* did was build better weapons and more of them!"

"That's all in the past," Jane admitted. "But now we can outlast them. Socially, politically, economically, we're stronger than they are, Dan. Time is on our side."

"You're just dreaming, Jane."

"It's no dream." She faced him with glaring eyes. "My forecasters have examined every possible scenario. The computers show it quite clearly. The Soviet system will fade away"—a smile lit her face—"just as Marx always said it would."

"And what do we do until that happy day?" Dan grumbled. "Bend over so they can kick us harder?"

"We do nothing to antagonize them," Jane answered. "We let events take their natural course."

With a shake of his head, Dan said, "No, Jane. Not me. I don't care what your forecasters and your computers say. The Soviet system isn't going to fold itself up and disappear.

They have the whole world in their grip, and they're tightening that grip every day."

"For the time being."

"The time being? Jesus Christ, Jane, look outside your own window! This country's falling apart! They're hungry out there. They have no jobs. Their money's worth nothing. They have no future to look forward to."

"I know it's going to be difficult," Jane said, almost in a whisper. "But there's no other way. We've got to walk through the fire."

"Not me," said Dan, getting to his feet. "I'm going to fight those sonsofbitches in every way I can."

"That will just make things worse."

He stared at her long and hard. She really believed what her aides were telling her. She really thought that, given time, the Soviet system would collapse. What they haven't told her, Dan realized, is that the American system is already collapsing.

"Jane," he said, softening his voice, "I came here to ask for your help . . . or at least your understanding."

"Are you going to fly out to another asteroid?"

She was smiling again, smiling at him like a patient schoolteacher or a mother who knows that her boy has been up to some mischief. She doesn't know, Dan told himself. The hijacking scheme hasn't leaked.

"It doesn't matter what I'm going to do," he said, feeling weary of the whole business. "I came here to get your support, but I can see that it's useless."

For a long moment, Jane said nothing. Dan could see uncertainty in her eyes, conflicting emotions playing across her beautiful face.

"Then why don't you give me your support," she blurted. She said it quickly, all in a rush, as if she were afraid the words would not come out at all if she spoke at her normal pace.

They stood facing each other, the little coffee table between them. "What do you mean?" Dan asked.

"Stay here with me, Dan," said Jane. "I need your strength, your courage."

"Stay?" He felt an electrical shock surge through his guts. "You want me to stay—here?"

With three quick strides Jane was in his arms, head nestled against his chest. "I want you, Dan. I don't want to face the world alone. I need you beside me."

He laughed softly. "Jane, do you have any idea of what the media would do to you if you—"

"They can be controlled," she murmured. "They won't get in my way."

"But we never did agree on politics," he reminded her.

"I can trust you, Dan. The others all have their own axes to grind. I can rely on you even when we don't agree."

"We'd be at each other's throats the first day."

She replied, "I was thinking more about the first night."

Dan held her tightly, inhaling the scent of her, feeling her hair brushing against his cheek. Once he had loved her, or thought he had, while she had been married to his closest friend. Now, as he stood with her pressing against him, he saw Lucita in his mind's vision, her dark, somber eyes, her waif's face sad and vulnerable.

"It won't work, Jane," he whispered.

Her body stiffened. She pulled away from him.

"We'd end up hating each other inside of a week," he said. "Besides," he added carelessly, "what kind of a reputation do you think we'd get? You keeping a lover in the White House? And can you see me as a kept man?"

She did not smile. "Yes, I can see you as a kept man. Kept in prison."

Dan realized he was dealing with an explosively volatile woman now.

"I can even see you being shot by the security guards," Jane said, coldly furious. "You came here under an alias. You're determined to undermine everything that I'm working for. Maybe shooting you here and now would be the best thing."

He made himself grin. "It would save the Russians the trouble."

Her green eyes snapping at him, Jane said, "I ought to do it. I ought to get rid of you once and for all. You've been nothing but trouble for me."

"Maybe you're right," he admitted. "Maybe it would save us all a lot of misery."

She huffed angrily, "You're impossible! You've always been impossible!" She stamped to the door.

"Jane," he called.

She turned, bitter rage blazing from her eyes.

"Whatever I do," Dan said, "it's because I still consider myself an American, despite everything that's happened."

"You're a fool," she said. "And I'm an even bigger one."

She left Dan standing alone amid the Victorian furniture in the little sitting room. Within moments, an elderly butler stepped through the open doorway, his parchment-wrinkled face looking sleepy and apologetic at the same time. He was small, bald and slightly bent, as if bowing was a permanent habit with him.

"The President wants you to sleep in the Lincoln Bedroom," the old man said, gesturing stiffly. Dan followed him back into the hall.

The butler opened the heavy door of the bedroom and stood to one side. Dan saw a mammoth rosewood bed, Victorian tables with ornately carved legs, topped with marble, a portrait of Lincoln next to the bed. His travel bag had been deposited on the sofa that sat in the middle of the room.

"Lincoln never slept in this room," the butler said as Dan stepped in. "He used this as an office. He signed the Emancipation Proclamation in here."

The old man showed him the connecting bathroom, the light switches and the television set hidden behind draperies opposite the huge bed. Dan thanked him and was glad to see him leave. Feeling very tired, Dan went to his travel bag and began to unpack his toiletries. Then his eye caught a framed set of three pieces of paper, covered with handwriting. He went to the wall and studied the patient, forceful pen strokes:

"Fourscore and seven years ago, our fathers brought forth upon this continent a new nation . . ."

A dull rumbling sound seemed to shake the room slightly. A roar, almost like the distant thunder of a rocket lifting off. Dan went to the window and pulled the curtains back.

The windows were double-paned with thick shatter-resistant plastic that was almost soundproof. Almost. But the noise from outside leaked through. The riot police had arrived, in squadrons of armored vehicles that were spraying streams of vile-looking greenish gas at the crowds of picketers. People were screaming, running, placards dropped to the pavement as they tried to escape the tracked vehicles lumbering down upon them. Where the gas reached them, they doubled over, fell to the ground retching, coughing, spasming. Blazing searchlights played over the seething mass of people as platoons of helmeted foot soldiers linked arms to form a cordon that stretched far out into Lafayette Square and up New York Avenue.

Dan reached down and picked the remote TV control unit from the bed table. One button drew back the draperies and turned on the set. The tube showed an old movie. Impatiently, Dan clicked from one channel to another. Nothing about the riot. The twenty-four-hour news channel was showing a tape of the President's press conference, from the day before. Jane looked cool and totally in command of herself as she spoke about new government programs that would stabilize employment and revitalize American agriculture.

For half an hour Dan watched the troops gassing and clubbing the picketers, dragging them away into huge waiting vans, while the TV showed nothing of the riot at all. No bulletins broke the regular programming. Looking through the window, Dan could see television trucks out there among the Army vehicles. Squinting against the hard glare of the searchlights, though, he saw that even the TV trucks were painted olive green. Army. There would be no media coverage of the riot. Nor of the arrest and detention of several hundred picketers.

The last of the heavy tracked vehicles rumbled away. Cleaning crews drove up in big garbage trucks to make the area look neat and unblemished before the sun rose.

Dan let the curtain fall and turned away from the window. His eye caught the Gettysburg draft framed on the wall.

". . . testing whether this nation, or any nation so conceived and so dedicated, can long endure."

Jane would be reelected all right. Dan was certain of it. And she would guide the nation down the path of least resistance, telling herself and the American people that time was on their side, that all they had to do was grit their teeth and bear their present pain and humiliation, and someday in the rosy future the Soviets would mend their ways and the whole world would be free and happy.

Dan made up his mind to get out of Washington, out of the U.S.A., as early as possible the next morning.

Chapter
◆ ◆ TWENTY-SEVEN ◆ ◆

"There she is," said Carstairs.

Dan's eyes flicked open. He felt a moment of confusion. "Was I sleeping?" he muttered.

"Snoring lightly," answered the Australian.

Dan tried to rub his eyes and bumped his gloved hands against his helmet visor. Blinking the sleep away, he peered out through the flitter's canopy and saw the Soviet ore freighter, looming huge and close, a giant hollow sphere, a thin shell of metal that could split apart to disgorge tons of lunar rock and soil—the raw materials of all space industries. A massive, perfectly round egg floating through empty space. With a big red star painted on it, above the letters CCCP.

"Soyuz Sovietskiya Socialistik Ryespublik," Dan muttered.

"That's an awful accent you've got," Zlotnik's voice teased in his helmet earphones.

"Sure. And I don't intend to learn any better, either," Dan growled.

Carstairs piloted the flitter close to the bulky ore carrier, then maneuvered their spacecraft to circle all the way around it. This close, it looked to Dan like a world of its own, bright sunlight glinting off its curving flank.

263

"Gawd," muttered the Australian, "it's huge."

"It's almost as if they hung it there to tempt us," said Zlotnik. "Like they want us to steal it."

"We're not stealing," Dan snapped. "We are claiming natural resources that are the common heritage of all humankind, and therefore belong to no single nation."

He heard Zlotnik's answering snicker. "Yeah. And we're doing it when the Russians aren't looking."

Vargas, the young Venezuelan who was usually as silent as a rock, said, "We are expropriating the expropriators."

"Paco?" Carstairs said with mock surprise. "Was that you?"

"Reciting from Marx?" Zlotnik added.

"My father is a member of the Communist party of Venezuela," the young astronaut said. "I learned Marx and the Bible at the same time."

"No time for religion now," said Carstairs. "Or for chat."

The Aussie's gloved fingers played deftly across the control panel keyboard. With microscopic puffs of thrust the needle-shaped flitter matched its speed and trajectory to that of the massive Soviet freighter. Like a tiny pin chasing a fat, round balloon, Dan thought.

"No crew pod in sight," Carstairs muttered.

"No radiator fins or any other signs of a life support system," said Zlotnik. "She's unmanned."

"I pick up two transponders," Vargas added, his eyes on the electronics control panel in front of him. "They are signaling at the usual Soviet frequencies, just as all the others do. Nothing out of the ordinary."

Dan turned the radar scan to maximum range and studied the orange-glowing screen in front of him. "No other spacecraft in view. She's unescorted."

"Ours for the tyking," said Carstairs.

For half an instant Dan hesitated. Then he said, "Okay, let's get to work."

Carstairs pressed his thumb against the button that actuated the canopy release, and the glass bubble silently, smoothly swung up and away from the cockpit. One by one the four astronauts unlatched their safety harnesses, floated out of their seats and clambered slowly, hand over hand, along the grips that studded the latticework midsection of the spacecraft. From the equipment pods there they detached one-man maneuvering units, which looked rather like high-backed chairs minus the seats. Dan strapped himself into one of the jet backpacks slowly, with deliberate care.

"Need any help, boss?" Carstairs chuckled in Dan's earphones. He was already floating free of the spacecraft, ready to jet out on his own.

Dan smiled. "I can do for myself, thanks."

"I just thought someone your age, you know . . ."

"Listen, pal, there are old astronauts and there are bold astronauts—"

The Aussie finished in unison with Dan, "But there are no old, bold astronauts."

The jet backpacks were one-man spacecraft, complete with their own thrusters, electrical power, tool kits and life support systems. They turned an individual astronaut into a one-man spacecraft, independent and free to maneuver for two hours or more.

It took almost a full two hours for them to accomplish their tasks. First all four men checked the freighter's spherical hull for booby traps or alarms. Then Zlotnik and Vargas detached the ship's two radio transponders, electronic beepers that told the mission controllers in the Soviet space station, *Kosmograd*, and back on the Moon at Lunagrad, where the ore carrier was. They linked the two transponders with a length of plastic line, which they unreeled from a heavily insulated container made of foam plastic. The line became as rigid as steel after ten minutes' exposure to vacuum, and ensured that the two transponders would be separated by exactly the same distance they had been apart on the freighter itself. Then they attached angular metallic radar reflectors to the line, so that a radar probe from *Kosmograd* would get a return blip of just about the same intensity as the freighter would yield. To the

Russian mission controllers at their consoles in the space station, it would look as if the freighter were still on course, placidly gliding toward its scheduled destination.

Dan and Carstairs found the freighter's electronic guidance unit, a black box the size of Dan's hand. They disconnected it and replaced it with a black box of their own, preprogrammed to alter the freighter's course by slight degrees until it was heading for *Nueva Venezuela* instead of *Kosmograd*. The freighter was propelled by its own rocket motors, which burned the cheapest and most abundant propellants available: powdered aluminum and oxygen, scraped up from the Moon's dusty soil by the lunar Gulag miners.

The new guidance unit Dan connected to the Russian control system immediately activated the rocket motors. Dan felt a sudden nudge of acceleration, light, but as definite as a tap on the shoulder. They wanted to move the freighter into its new trajectory with as little thrust as possible, both to conserve the freighter's supply of propellants and to make as small a cloud of radar-reflecting exhaust gases as possible.

Don't attract the attention of the mission controllers, Dan warned himself. Let them think everything is so normal that they can take a nice, quiet nap.

The final task the four astronauts had was to make the freighter invisible to Soviet radars. From pouches the size of mailbags, they dug up gloved handfuls of glittering metallic dust and strewed them into the emptiness around the freighter and their own flitter. As he jetted slowly in a widening arc, sprinkling the radar-absorbing dust, Dan suddenly got an image of Peter Pan's Tinker Bell. He laughed aloud.

"You all right?" Zlotnik asked.

"Sure," Dan replied. "Sure."

The growing cloud would absorb radar waves: not completely, but enough to mask the freighter and their flitter so that the normal Soviet radar surveillance would not see the ore carrier change course. If, for some reason, the Soviet controllers directed a high-power radar beam or a laser probe at the freighter, the dust cloud could be penetrated. Dan was banking on the hope that the Russians were not going to be alert enough to use their more sensitive equipment.

As he jetted carefully around the freighter, Dan recalled how the flatlanders back on Earth thought that working in zero gravity was like floating on air, when actually it was more like swimming the English Channel. He was soaking with sweat, and the air circulation fan in his helmet was buzzing its loudest to keep his visor from fogging over.

Finally they were finished. Dan hung in the dark emptiness, the huge glowing Earth spread like an overwhelming vision of beauty, off to his right. The Sun was at his back. The Soviet freighter loomed in front of him, with their flitter hanging alongside it. The cloud of radar-absorbing dust glittered faintly around him, shimmering slightly where the sunlight struck it at the right angle to create a fragile, shifting rainbow. Already the transponders and radar reflectors were too far away for Dan to see.

They jetted back to the flitter, unstrapped and stowed the backpacks, and slid into their cockpit seats. Dan felt bone-tired, exhausted emotionally as well as physically. As Carstairs closed the canopy over them and punched in the course corrections to allow the flitter to stay alongside the ore carrier, Vargas fussed over his electronics console.

"Radio transmissions from *Kosmograd* seem normal," he reported.

"What about Lunagrad?" Dan asked.

Vargas muttered to himself for a few moments, then Dan heard Russian folk music in his helmet earphones: balalaikas and zithers and a mournful baritone voice.

"Christ, that's dreary!" Dan said.

"Must be what they ply to the miners," Carstairs joked, "to cheer 'em up."

For the thousandth time that day, Dan wished he could open his visor and scratch his nose, rub his eyes or just run a hand across the stubble on his chin.

"We've got to pressurize the cockpit next mission," he said. "Sitting in these suits for ten, twelve hours is no picnic."

267

"Don't know about you," Carstairs agreed, "but it smells like a bloody sweat sock in here."

"That's because you don't spray under your arms," Zlotnik kidded.

"And another thing," Dan said, ignoring the banter. "There ought to be some way to dispense the radar chaff automatically. Having us flit around like a quartet of double-damned fairies is ridiculous."

"A quartet of what?" Carstairs quipped.

"Don't get cute."

"You're thirty-six years too lyte with that advice, chum."

"Vargas, can you turn off the Russian music?" Dan asked. "It's damned depressing."

"Yessir," the young Venezuelan said.

For several moments, Dan heard nothing at all except the hum of his suit's air fan and the hiss of his own breathing.

Then Carstairs began crowing, "Yo-ho-ho and a bottle of rum . . . sixteen men on a dead man's chest."

Suddenly they were all laughing.

"We did it!" Zlotnik said. "We're pirates! We stole it right out from under their radar noses and they don't even know it yet!"

Dan laughed with them, but inwardly he wondered what the Russians would do once they found out about his piracy.

Chapter
♦ ♦ TWENTY-EIGHT ♦ ♦

Dan stayed at the *Nueva Venezuela* factory complex for an additional six hours, long enough to see the captured freighter unloaded and then swiftly broken up. He watched from the factory's control center as a picked team of workers used industrial lasers to cut the freighter's spherical shell into long slivers of metal, like a giant clockwork-orange skin being sliced apart. The dismembered freighter was fed into the factory's smelters, together with the ores it had carried. Dan demanded that they get the job done quickly, before the Soviets realized what had happened and sent a team of armed inspectors to the factory.

Satisfied that the evidence had not only been destroyed, but turned into useful raw material, Dan showered quickly, changed into a fresh set of coveralls and rode the next regularly scheduled shuttle back to Caracas. He helicoptered from the landing field to the roof of his downtown building. When he breezed back into his own office, Pete Weston was waiting for him, his usual worried frown wrinkling his high-domed face as he sat in the anteroom, chatting with Dan's new secretary. Weston jumped to his feet as Dan came in, still wearing the sky-blue coveralls he had put on that morning at *Nueva Venezuela*.

The lawyer was wearing a light sports jacket and pale blue slacks. Even his shirt and tie looked less rigid than usual. Dan grinned at him, realizing that Weston was finally learning how to relax and be more comfortable.

"You're looking dapper this morning," Dan said.

Weston forced a quick smile, but raised one hand. A single flimsy sheet of paper was clutched in it.

"We've got troubles, boss."

Dan nodded at the new girl, wondering if she had been told what had happened to her predecessor.

"Come on in, Pete," he said, opening the thick oak door to his private office.

"Financially," Weston said, once the door was firmly closed, "your little hijacking expedition is a big success. The ores alone were worth slightly more than ten million."

Dan slid into the big leather chair behind his desk. "But?" he prompted.

Weston's worried frown deepened as he dropped his slight frame into the chair in front of Dan's desk. "But the Russians are apeshit. They've been burning up the telephone links between Moscow and Caracas all morning. Their satellites have been put on full alert. The Soviet space committee has requested an emergency meeting of the IAC. We've received an official request for an inspection of our facilities, and my spies in Hernandez's office tell me that he's received a request for a complete inspection of *Nueva Venezuela*."

"Which he will grant," Dan muttered.

"We're granting their request, too," Weston said. It was not advice, it was a fait accompli. "Either that or they'll send in tanks and troops."

Dan waved a hand in the air. "Let them inspect! There's nothing for them to find."

"They'll want to interrogate Astro employees."

"No," Dan snapped. "That they can't do. We're under Venezuelan law. The Venezuelan police can interrogate our people, if they arrest one of us for breaking Venezuelan law. But the Russians can't."

"They can if the Venezuelans allow them to," Weston pointed out.

Dan gave him a sour look.

"It works this way," the lawyer said, hunching forward in his chair. "International law supercedes Venezuelan law. If you're suspected of breaking international law—like committing an act of piracy—the nation in which you reside has the responsibility and the authority to arrest you and hold you for trial."

"So?"

"So the locals here could allow the Russians to participate in the interrogation of anyone arrested in this matter."

"Hmm." Dan leaned back in his chair and steepled his fingers. "Looks like I'd better get to Hernandez and make sure he's not too sore at us."

Weston almost laughed. "Not too sore? He's madder than a high school principal in the middle of a food fight."

Dan blinked at the lawyer. "A high school . . ." With a shake of his head, he reached for the phone keyboard. "I'd better give him a call."

"Don't bother," said Weston. "He's already called here. Four times. Wants you in his office at eleven sharp."

"Uh-oh. That sounds grim."

"I'd be willing to bet that Vasily Malik will be there."

Nodding, Dan agreed, "Wouldn't surprise me at all. Maybe you'd better come along, too."

"Okay," the lawyer said. He got to his feet. "I'd better change into a more businesslike suit."

Dan broke into laughter. "Oh, for God's sake, Pete! You look fine. You're not going to a funeral, after all."

Weston looked highly unconvinced.

Lucita had awakened that morning to the sound of a gentle but insistent tapping on her bedroom door. She opened her eyes and saw that it was still dark. With an effort, she

271

focused on the red-glowing digits of the clock on the bedtable: 4:44 A.M.

Feeling more angry than alarmed, she groped in the darkness until she found the silk peignoir she had left on the bed, while the knocking continued, growing louder. As Lucita pulled the robe over her nightgown, she recognized the voice of her maid, Estrellita:

"Señorita, please. Your father told me to wake you."

Lucita clicked on the little lamp atop the bureau as she opened the door a crack. "What is it?" she asked sleepily.

Estrellita was also in her nightrobe, a plain cotton shift. "Your father said to wake you. Your fiancé is coming here. From the Land of Red. He is flying here on a rocket!"

Lucita showered and dressed quickly, but took the time to brush her hair properly and make certain that her face showed no trace of sleepiness. She pulled on a knee-length wraparound surplice of turquoise slashed with bold diagonal stripes. A hint of jewelry at her wrists and ears and she was ready to face her father—and her fiancé.

The breakfast room was filled with fresh new sunlight by the time Lucita came downstairs. Her father was draining a cup of coffee, rigid with tension as he sat in the white wicker chair. He was fully dressed in a gray double-breasted suit. His usual breakfast was spread before him on the glass-topped table, but he had touched none of it. Malik was not there.

"Good morning," she said to Hernandez. "I was told Vasily would be here."

"He is on the way. His shuttle is scheduled to land in a few minutes. Then he will helicopter here to have breakfast with us."

Lucita sat at her father's right, with the sun on her back already feeling warm and enlivening. Her father looked very angry, very tired and—what was most alarming—very frightened.

"What's wrong, Papa? What's happened?"

"It's that damnable Yankee, Randolph!" Hernandez exploded. "He won't rest until he's ruined us all!"

272

Lucita barely suppressed a smile. "What has he done now?"

"Piracy!"

"Piracy?" She laughed; she could not help it.

"This is not funny," Hernandez said sternly. "Piracy in outer space. It's unheard-of. It's madness. He will destroy himself . . . and me along with him!"

Slowly, patiently, Lucita extracted the story from her sputtering father. By the time Malik arrived at their home, she had a rough understanding of what had happened.

Vasily looked grim, his clothes rumpled, as if he had thrown them on hurriedly. His usual smile was gone. In place of the dashing, debonair Russian with the flair for Western style and wit, Lucita saw an angry, urgent man who gave her a peck on the cheek by way of greeting and then plunged into an intense conversation with her father. The two men ignored her. They had only one person on their minds: Dan Randolph.

Lucita sat at the breakfast table and listened, too fascinated by the fury of the hatred her father and her fiancé were pouring out to be upset with them for paying her no attention. The servants felt the rage boiling up from the two men, also. They hung back beyond the doorway of the kitchen, too terrified even to ask if the men wanted coffee.

Pete Weston was still wearing the sports coat and slacks when Dan's limousine pulled to a stop in front of the glass façade of the Ministry of Technology. Dan had changed into an open-necked shirt, tan slacks and a raw silk jacket. He pushed open the limousine's door before the chauffeur could scamper around to it and stepped out onto the pavement. There were two armed policemen flanking the big glass doors of the building's main entrance.

"Holy Mother of God," Weston muttered, ducking out of the limo's door behind Dan. "It looks like they mean business."

Dan grinned at him. "Come on, Pete. Into the valley of death." He started up the steps. "Who's the patron saint of lawyers, anyway?"

273

Weston did not smile.

Dan had deliberately delayed his driver enough so that they arrived at Hernandez's office at seven minutes past eleven. More armed and uniformed policemen were stationed in the halls of the Ministry of Technology building, and in the reception room outside Hernandez's office. A male secretary ushered them into the sanctum sanctorum.

It was a huge office, richly carpeted and handsomely furnished. Hernandez sat stiffly behind his enormous desk, Malik stood to one side of it, hands clasped behind his back, his eyes fixed on Dan. The Russian had chosen to wear a khaki-colored summer suit that looked baggy and unpressed. No jokes and banter today, Dan knew. This was going to be strictly official business.

The long walk from the door to the desk was supposed to intimidate visitors, but Dan grinned easily as he made his way across the thick carpeting and took one of the two stiff-backed chairs placed before the desk.

"Good morning," he said lightly as he sat down. Pete Weston, looking very unhappy, perched on the front two inches of the other chair.

"You obviously know why I have summoned you here," Hernandez began without preliminaries.

"I have a suspicion," replied Dan. Turning slightly to lock eyes with Malik, "I understand that one of your ore carriers is missing."

"Stolen," the Russian snapped. "Hijacked by pirates."

Dan allowed himself a small grin. "Pirates? In space? Isn't it more likely that one of your mission controllers was drunk and simply lost track of the freighter?"

"No, that is not likely," Malik growled.

Hernandez, just as furious as the Russian, said, "Comrade Malik has asked me to allow a complete inspection of the *Nueva Venezuela* facilities. . . ."

"Asked? Or demanded?"

The Venezuelan's mustache bristled. "Asked."

"And you've agreed to cooperate," Dan said.

"Yes, I have."

"Are the other Third World space facilities being inspected?" Dan asked.

Hernandez blinked, then looked up at Malik.

"We see no need for that," the Russian answered. "We are very sure that it is you who led this latter-day buccaneering expedition."

"Buccaneer!" Dan nodded an acknowledgment. "You've been reading up on the subject of pirates, I see."

"Do you deny it?" Malik snapped.

"Deny being a pirate? Of course I deny it. How can anyone be accused of piracy if they're merely helping themselves to materials that no one legally owns?"

Malik waggled a finger at Dan. "No, you can't play with words that way, Mr. Capitalist. We have lawyers in the Soviet Union, too. . . ."

"Yes, I know. Prosecutors who never lose a case."

"The International Astronautical Council assigned the Soviet Union the responsibility for mining and transporting the lunar ores."

"For which you charge exorbitant fees."

"The fees are allowed by the IAC."

"Sure."

"No other nation may mine or transport the ores."

"But you don't own them," Dan said firmly. "The law is clear on that point. You can scoop the stuff off the Moon's surface, you can transport it to space stations in orbit around the Earth, and you can charge outrageous fees for those services. *But you do not own the ores.* They are the common property of the whole human race. Anybody can use them. That's the law."

Malik glowered at him.

"So how can anyone be accused of stealing something that no one legally owns?"

Hernandez said, in a voice that he obviously was struggling to keep under control, "The legal fine points will be settled by lawyers. . . ."

275

"Just like possession of my asteroid will be," Dan interjected.

His fists clenching on the desktop, Hernandez went on, "But the disappearance of a Soviet-owned spacecraft is a serious matter, which must be investigated fully. I have sworn that the government of Venezuela will offer every assistance to the Soviet Union in this affair."

"Fine by me," said Dan. "You can search *Nueva Venezuela* all you want to. But I suggest you search the other Third World facilities, too. I don't see why Venezuela alone should fall under suspicion."

Malik snorted angrily. "We won't find anything in *Nueva Venezuela* or any of the other stations. I know that. But I think some of your people might have interesting stories to tell us. . . ."

"The employees of Astro Manufacturing Corporation are citizens of many different countries," Dan said. "You'll have to get the permission of their national governments to detain or interrogate them."

"You are a citizen of Venezuela," Malik said.

Pete Weston spoke up. "Under Venezuelan law, a citizen must be charged with a crime when he is arrested. To charge a citizen with a crime, you must have some evidence."

Hernandez said, "A citizen can be detained for questioning without being charged."

"Rafael," Dan said, deliberately turning familiar and informal, "do you have any idea of how many judges in this city are very close friends of mine? Would you want to cause a conflict with some of the most powerful men in Caracas, simply because this Russian paranoid thinks I'm responsible for his own problems?"

Malik glared at Dan.

"Think about it for a moment," Dan urged smoothly. "He has absolutely no evidence that I or anyone else at *Nueva Venezuela* had anything to do with his losing an ore carrier. Think of how foolish you would look if you allowed the

276

Russians to dictate to you, and powerful men in the government decided that you had acted wrongly."

Hernandez straightened in his chair. His chin rose a notch. He reached across the desk to the silver cigarette box, took out a long slender cigarette wrapped in light brown paper and lit it with a palm-sized laser lighter—both the box and the silver-plated lighter had been gifts from Dan Randolph. Through all this no one in the room said a word, and Hernandez's eyes never left Dan's.

"You place me in a very awkward position, señor," he said at last, blowing a thin cloud of gray smoke toward the high paneled ceiling.

"I've done nothing at all," Dan replied, holding up his hands in a gesture of innocence. "I've merely come to your office when you asked me to."

"You have stolen the property of the Soviet Union," Malik insisted.

"Prove it," said Dan.

Malik took a step toward Dan, who tensed in his chair, ready to spring at the Russian. But Hernandez put his arm out and held Malik back.

"We must all control our tempers," Hernandez said.

Dan grinned at the infuriated Russian. "This isn't the Workers' Paradise, you know, where you can throw a man into jail and torture him into confessing."

"That is quite enough, Señor Randolph." Hernandez's nostrils flared angrily. "You go too far."

Shrugging, Dan got to his feet. "If you want to detain me for questioning, naturally, that's your privilege. Otherwise . . ."

"You are free to go," Hernandez said. "I would ask, however, that you do not leave Caracas without letting me know beforehand."

"Certainly."

"That includes the launch facility."

"Of course," Dan agreed. Turning to Weston, still tensely

gripping the arms of his chair, he said, "Come on, Pete. Let's get back to the office."

"Good day, Señor Randolph, Señor Weston," said Hernandez.

"Good day to you, Señor Hernandez," Dan said. With a widening grin, he added, "And to you, Comrade Malik. May all your days be as beautiful as this one."

Malik glared pure hatred at Dan. But his lips curled slightly upward in a cold smile. "I look forward to seeing you again, Mr. Randolph. Under more pleasant circumstances."

Dan arched an eyebrow, wondering what the Russian meant by that. But the only answer he gave was a slight cock of his head. Then he turned and marched out of Hernandez's office, with Weston trailing him.

As the security guard led them back down toward the main entrance, Weston pulled a handkerchief from his back pocket and mopped his balding brow.

"Cheez, boss, you really *like* playing with fire, don't you?"

"Why not?" Dan said lightly. "It's never boring."

Lucita was coming into the building, through the heavily tinted glass doors, as they arrived in the lobby. Recognizing Dan, she took off her sunglasses and walked across the echoing marble floor toward him.

"I thought they would have you in jail by now," she said, true concern in her voice.

Dan laughed. "Jail? Me? What an absurd idea."

But she was totally serious. "It is not a joke. My father was furious with you this morning. And Vasily would like to kill you."

"I know," said Dan. Spreading his arms, "Here I am, though, all in one piece."

"Are you still carrying your gun?" she asked.

"No, I left it home. I trust your father; why should I wear a gun to visit him? Besides, the guards here would have taken it away from me."

Lucita glanced at Weston, then stepped slightly away from

278

him, toward the wall of the lobby which was covered with a sweeping mural depicting the advance of Venezuelan technology from Indian hand plows to spaceships plying the starry heavens.

The lawyer took her hint. "I've got to find a men's room," he told Dan. "My kidneys aren't as strong as yours."

"I'll wait for you here," Dan said. Then, turning back to Lucita, he said, "I'm flattered that you're so worried about me."

"He means to kill you," Lucita whispered. "I am certain of it."

"Your fiancé?"

She nodded. "Vasily hates you. You should have seen him this morning. He frightens me."

"And your father? How does he feel about all this?"

"He is very angry with you. He is terribly afraid of Vasily—not for his life, but for his political ambition. You are making things impossible for him."

"That's too bad," said Dan.

"He will side with Vasily, you know. No matter what the Russians want to do, he will go along with them."

"As long as it doesn't bring him into conflict with his own ambition," Dan pointed out. "He can't afford to give in to the Russians at the expense of Venezuela's independence."

"He would be much happier if you were dead," Lucita said.

Dan smiled bitterly. "So would a lot of people."

"Did you do it?" Lucita asked.

"Do what?"

"Did you really steal the Russian spacecraft?"

His smile turned mischievous. "Do you think that I'd commit an act of piracy? Do I look like a pirate?"

Lucita's elfin face bloomed into an answering smile. "Yes, I think you do. You are the only man in the whole world mad enough to do such a thing."

"That's hardly a compliment."

"What makes you think that I was attempting to compliment you?" she said, turning saucy.

279

He bowed his head. "Of course. I should have known better. The daughter of a noble family does not offer compliments to an outlander whom she suspects of piracy."

Lucita giggled. "You are insane. And you draw me into your madness."

"If I am insane," Dan replied soberly, "it's because of the spell that you cast over me."

She grew serious again. "You must not speak to me like that. I am engaged to be married . . ." The realization of it struck her. "To the man who wants to kill you."

Suddenly it hit Dan, too. He ran out of words. There was nothing left to say.

Pete Weston came striding across the marble floor of the lobby toward them. "The limo's outside," he said.

Dan nodded. "Yeah."

He started to turn toward the door, but he could not tear his gaze away from Lucita's sad, beautiful, dark-eyed urchin's face.

"You really mustn't marry him, you know," he said to her, so low he could barely hear it himself.

She said nothing. He started for the door, where Weston was waiting for him.

"Dan!" Lucita ran to him. "Would you come to my home for dinner tonight? With my father and me? Vasily will not be there."

"Tonight?" Dan blinked with surprise.

"Please! I . . . want you to speak with my father, with no one else present. I don't want him to hate you."

He nodded dumbly.

"Eight o'clock," Lucita said. "I will see to it that only the three of us are there."

"Sure," he said. "Eight o'clock. You can phone me if there's . . . any change."

"Yes. Of course."

Weston pushed the glass door open and Dan felt a flood of hot sunlight on his neck and back. He turned and walked outside, looked back over his shoulder at Lucita standing there watching him, like a fairy-tale princess watching a knight going out to face a dragon.

The squeal of a car's tires broke the spell. Snapping his head around toward the noise, Dan saw a black compact car swinging up the driveway in front of the building. He could see two men in the front, one bent tensely over the steering wheel and the other leaning partway out the window on the passenger's side, holding a blocky, bulky gray metal box in his two hands.

Before Dan could react, a pencil-thin beam of searing red light lanced through the morning air, from the metal box. Straighter than any arrow, it caught Pete Weston in the left eye and nearly sawed off the entire top of his skull before it winked out. The car roared away as Weston sagged to the cement paving and tumbled down the steps to the feet of Dan's waiting chauffeur.

Dan stood frozen, his mind a blank, his body unable to move. No blood came from the lawyer's wound. Pete just lay there, arms and legs sprawled awkwardly in death. The chauffeur dropped to his knees, far too late to protect himself from any weapon that might have been aimed at him.

Dan found the strength to turn and look back at Lucita. Through the tinted glass door, he could see that the horror on her face was matched by his own reflection.

Chapter
◆ ◆ TWENTY-NINE ◆ ◆

"I'm going to kill that sonofabitch and I don't care who knows it."

Dan said the words calmly, quietly, to the image of Saito Yamagata kneeling on a woven straw tatami mat, fists on knees, face set in a grim scowl.

"You must remember," Yamagata said, "that I cannot guarantee the security of this transmission."

Dan was sprawled on a sofa in his own living room, wrapped in a sky-blue terry-cloth robe, his hair still wet from a long hot shower, an opened bottle of Jack Daniel's on the coffee table in front of him. He had spent almost the whole day with the Caracas police, describing the car and the two men who had murdered Pete Weston, making arrangements to take care of the lawyer's body and then, the hardest part, calling Pete's wife and breaking the brutal news to her. It was twilight now. Through the windows on the far side of the room, Dan could see the sky flaming with the burning reds and lush violets of a tropical sunset.

Yamagata's holographic image, transmitted from his Tokyo residence, knelt across the coffee table from him, just as

f the Japanese were actually in the living room with
him.

"I don't give a fuck about security," Dan growled. "I
hope the bastard is listening to me right now. I'm going to
kill him, if I have to do it with my bare hands."

"You are understandably upset," Yamagata said.

Dan took a long pull on the tumbler of whiskey in his
hand. There was neither ice nor water in the glass.

"I know what he's doing, that Russian," he muttered.
"He's trying to isolate me: kill or scare off anybody who's
close to me. Maybe he thinks I'll get frightened, too, and
back off."

"Perhaps he is merely trying to warn you," said Yamagata.

"He's the one who needs the warning. Maybe he can kill
me, but he sure can't scare me." Dan took another swallow
of the whiskey and felt it glide down his throat, hot and
smooth. "Nobo's all right?" he asked.

Yamagata nodded. "He is quite safe. But he wants to
return to you."

"No," Dan said. "That's a risk I won't take. Not with
your son, Sai."

The holographic image fell silent for a long moment.
"Nobuhiko does not lack courage. He is very insistent on
returning to work with you."

"I can't allow it, Sai." Dan shook his head. He felt just
the slightest bit woozy. "Not your boy."

"Then the Russian is achieving at least part of his
objective."

Dan stared at his old friend.

"You are too concerned about Nobo to allow him to return
to work for you. If you had known that your lawyer, the man
Weston, was marked for death, would you have allowed him
to remain at your side?"

Dan started to answer, but he did not want to say the
words that formed in his mind.

Yamagata smiled at him. "No, you would not. I know the
quality of the heart that beats inside you, Dan. You think

283

nothing of taking risks that defy the gods, but you would not ask others to take risks one-hundredth as dangerous.''

"If it's me he's after," Dan muttered, "why doesn't he kill me?''

"The Russian is after power, not merely your life. He wants to kill you, but he wants to break you first.''

"How can you—''

Raising a pudgy hand to silence Dan's objection, Yamagata said, "The Soviets want to drive us out of space; you have told me that many times yourself.''

"Yes, I know.''

"Murdering you would not further that aim. Comrade Malik's goal, undoubtedly, is to be able to arrest you and bring you to trial before the eyes of the whole world, to show the world that a capitalist who operates space industries is a pirate, a brigand, a thief and robber.''

Dan nodded grimly. "I get it. And by implication, *every* capitalist operating in space is a pirate.''

"Exactly so," Yamagata agreed. "Your life is merely part of a larger scheme: to allow the Soviets to take over all the space factories.''

Dan sat silently, swirling the half-inch of whiskey left in his glass.

"Moreover," Yamagata continued, "the Soviets are facing some political problems as well. Your asteroid mission— and their seizure of your ship—has opened many eyes. There is talk now of asking the IAC to review the agreements regarding space resources.''

Dan said, "Brazil's asking for changes already. And I've heard rumors that the Organization of African Unity is going to support them.''

"You see?" Yamagata said. "It is not too difficult for the Soviet leaders to believe that if they make a martyr of you, they harm themselves. But if they can bring you to trial and show the world that you are a thief . . .''

"I see.''

"They need you alive—for the time being. They do not

want to stir up the Third World nations. They do not want to encourage resentment or resistance.''

"If only we had some help," Dan muttered. "If China would just—"

"China will do nothing. My contacts there advised me to seek help from the United States.''

"Fat chance! They've got America whipped. Jane's not going to do a thing to help us.''

"But the Soviets must keep the goodwill of the Third World," Yamagata insisted. "The Third World holds most of the resources, the raw materials. And now, with space manufacturing, the Third World is becoming a powerful industrial force as well.''

"And to control the Third World they've got to control us. Or take over our operations and dump us.''

"Exactly!" Yamagata beamed like a teacher whose prize pupil had finally gotten the correct answer. "That is why they cannot murder you.''

"Not yet."

"Not at all. The murders of those near you have been terror attacks, meant to cow you. Or deeds done out of sheer spite. But they will not murder you.''

Draining the last of the whiskey, Dan said, "But they'll bring me to trial and let a judge condemn me to death, if they can.''

Yamagata nodded. "That is the way my analysts see the situation. I agree.''

The madness of it appealed to Dan. Then he thought of something even funnier. "Ah! But suppose, in the middle of all this, the Russian in charge of their space operations gets so jealous of me over his fiancée that he has me murdered anyway? What then?''

The Japanese shook his head. "Either you are drunk or you are trying to confuse the issue.''

"Neither," said Dan. "The young lady who accompanied me when I visited you in Sapporo . . .''

"Señorita Hernandez. The one that Nobo was so smitten with.''

"Yes. Suppose Malik shoots me in a fit of lover's jealousy? He's engaged to her, you know."

"So?" Yamagata's face looked suddenly troubled. "Frankly, she is one of the reasons why Nobo is so anxious to return to Caracas."

"Then that's another reason to keep him away," Dan said.

"I'm afraid he is already on route. His plane took off twenty minutes ago."

"Sai, it's too dangerous."

"He will be protected. I have sent a very special cadre of people to watch over you both."

"How many?" Dan asked.

Yamagata shrugged. "I don't really know. It is of no consequence. Neither of you will know they are there, unless they are needed."

"Ninjas?" Dan wondered.

The Japanese smiled. "Ever the romantic. This is the twenty-first century, Dan. There are no more ninjas."

"I'm going to send Nobo home as soon as he arrives here."

"No!" Yamagata's eyes flashed. "It would shame him, and I will not permit that, even from you, my old friend."

"But he's walking into a dangerous—"

"He understands the danger, and so do I. Permit your friends to display a little courage, Dan. Frankly, I do not believe the Russians will dare to touch him, any more than they would attempt to assassinate you or me."

Dan shook his head in vehement disagreement. "Sai, I think your analysts and your theories are lovely. But if and when Malik decides to, he'll try to murder me, or you, or Nobo, without the slightest hesitation."

Yamagata put on his inscrutable smile. "Death is not to be feared."

"It's not to be sneezed at, either."

"Ah, what a way with words you have!" Yamagata laughed, his whole body heaving and rocking on the woven straw mat.

Dan allowed himself a small grin. "There's only one way

out of this that I can see. I've got to kill that Russian sonofabitch before he kills me—or everybody close to me."

Yamagata's laughter cut off like a rocket motor suddenly run dry of propellant. "No, my friend. That is the worst thing you can do. It would only lead to a bloodbath, murder upon murder. A zero-sum game, as the analysts say."

Dan imitated Yamagata's own shrug. "Death is not to be feared."

"But *results* are what count," the Japanese said. "Whoever pirated the Soviet ore carrier has done more damage to Malik than a hundred assassinations. *That* hit the Russians where it hurts them most. It makes them fear that they will lose control of the space trade."

"A pinprick," Dan said.

"The *first* pinprick," Yamagata countered.

Dan focused on his friend's face with new interest.

"Do not be surprised if other pinpricks come, very soon."

"Really?"

Smiling like a beneficent Buddha, Yamagata said, "Naturally, wise men such as you and I would never engage in such madness. But I would not be surprised if there are more raids on Soviet freighters."

"You think so," Dan said.

"Do not underestimate the commotion this has caused among the space industrialists. The Russians have invoked the suppression powers of the World Information agreements to keep the news out of the media. Perhaps you are too close to the situation to feel its full impact."

Dan put the whiskey glass to his lips, saw that it was empty and put it down.

"Yes," Yamagata said cheerfully. "I would not be surprised at all to see more Soviet freighters hijacked. And sooner or later the news will become public knowledge."

"And that's when the Russians will decide to close us all down, Sai. Or kill us. Or maybe both."

"Whiskey makes you gloomy, my friend."

"No," said Dan. "The Soviets have a simple way to deal

with problems that really bother them: they destroy the problem. Like Godzilla stomping Bambi. Sure, they'd rather keep the space factories working and keep the Third World happy. They don't really want to upset the applecart, not as long as they're getting their pick of the apples. But if and when we cause them enough trouble, they'll stomp us flat and to hell with the Third World, to hell with trade balances and the media and everything else except Soviet domination of the whole world and everybody in it.''

Yamagata searched his friend's face for a silent moment, then said firmly, ''Dan, get a good night's sleep. You will see the world differently in the morning.''

Dan forced a smile. ''Sure. Good advice.''

Yamagata's hand reached forward and his three-dimensional image suddenly winked out, leaving Dan alone. It was almost fully dark now. The living room was deep in shadows. Dan reached for the whiskey bottle and refilled his glass.

''Get a good night's sleep,'' he mumbled. ''Sure.'' He swung his legs up on the sofa and leaned back into the comfortable pillows. He closed his eyes and tried to make his mind a blank. But he saw Pete Weston, his left eyeball an empty socket dripping seared flesh, a thin bloodless line cutting across his high forehead, his mouth still open in a silent, final gasp of surprise and pain.

The robot butler trundled to within precisely ten centimeters of the coffee table's edge. ''Sir, there is a visitor waiting in the foyer, asking to see you.''

Nobo's here already? Dan wondered. He sat up, and the impact of the Jack Daniel's made his temples throb.

''Show him in. And turn on some lights.''

The robot pivoted noiselessly on the thick carpeting and wheeled toward the door. Lamps recessed into the ceiling threw pools of light against the paintings that decorated the walls. Dan got to his feet and tightened the belt of his robe. His slippers were either under the coffee table or under the sofa; he had no intention of searching for them.

But it was not Nobuhiko who followed the butler's stubby metal form into the living room. It was Lucita.

"What are you doing here?" Dan blurted.

She was wearing a simple short-sleeved black frock, as if in mourning. Her hair was loose and flowing. In the subdued light, Dan could not make out the expression on her face.

"I came to see . . . if you are all right," she said. Her voice was low, uncertain, questioning.

"I'm still alive."

Lucita took a few hesitant steps toward the sofa. The robot stood immobile, its task accomplished and no new jobs assigned to it.

"It was so horrible," Lucita said. "Look, my hands are still trembling."

"Never seen a man killed before?" Dan's voice sounded harsh, bitter, even to himself.

"No, I—"

"Your boyfriend did it, you know."

"Vasily? He was trying to murder you, wasn't he?"

"He's not that sweet," Dan said. "He's killed three friends of mine. He'll kill more."

She seemed dazed. "Can I . . . may I sit down?"

Dan could not understand the anger burning inside him. He crossed the space separating them in three swift strides and grasped her by the shoulders.

"What's your game, Lucita?" he demanded. "What the hell are you doing here?"

"I don't know," she said. "I'm frightened!"

Now he was close enough to see her eyes glistening in the faint light, filled with tears.

"You're in no danger. He wants to marry you, not kill you."

"Frightened for you," she said. The tears spilled out and she broke into sobs. Dan pulled her to him. She leaned her head against his chest, crying, and let him fold his arms around her.

"One moment he was alive, and then . . . then . . ."

"Don't!" he snapped. "Don't bring it up again. He's dead and there's nothing that words can do about it."

"But I thought they were trying to kill you. Even as your friend was falling to the ground and the car was speeding away, the only thing in my mind was that they were going to kill you, too."

"No, I'm safe." For the time being, Dan added silently.

"I know that Vasily did it. He hates you. He wants you dead."

"The feeling is mutual."

Lucita pulled away from him slightly. "You must not let him kill you. You must not!"

"Why not? What difference does it make?"

"Because I love you," Lucita said, her eyes widening with sudden realization of the truth of it. "I love you, my *Yanqui*. I could not stand to see you killed."

Dan's mind spun. "Love me? You love me?"

"You are the only man in all the world worth loving. How could I love anyone else?"

"Lucita . . ." He pulled her to him again and kissed her, while a voice inside his head marveled, She loves me! This beautiful, spoiled, fragile girl actually loves me!

"Would you really steal me away?" she asked breathlessly. "Would you build me a palace like the Taj Mahal or a city at the bottom of the sea?"

"Whatever you desire, Lucita *mía*," Dan whispered. "We can go off to the Himalayas and search for Shangri-la together. Or build a spacecraft that will take us out among the stars."

Looking up at him, she smiled, and Dan could feel her warm young body relaxing in his arms.

"I have never seen the Taj Mahal," Lucita said. "Or the Pyramids. Or the Golden Gate Bridge."

"You will," he promised. "You'll see them all. Sugar Loaf, the Parthenon, the Eiffel Tower, Tahiti, Victoria Falls—I'll show them all to you."

"The whole world?"

"Everything. Italy alone can take ten years. And New Zealand: the most beautiful spot on Earth is the South Island. And the Great Wall of China . . ."

"And New York! Can we see the Statue of Liberty?"

Dan felt his blood run cold. "The Statue of Liberty. Sure." But the enthusiasm had drained out of him. "If they haven't torn it down by the time we get there."

She realized that she had touched an open wound. "I'm sorry," Lucita said.

As gently as he could, Dan released his grip on her and gestured toward the sofa. "It's all right, Lucita. Not your fault." He grinned sardonically, remembering an old cliché. "Being in love means never having to say you're sorry."

She sat like a kitten, legs tucked up under her. Dan thought briefly about turning on more lights, decided that he preferred the shadows, then sat wearily beside her.

"Would you really take me all around the world?" she asked, curious as a child on Christmas Eve.

"Forever and ever," Dan said, trying to recapture the elation he had felt so briefly. "We'll make our home in a seaplane, a flying houseboat, so that we can go wherever we want to and never leave home."

"That would be marvelous!"

"Yes," he quoted, "isn't it pretty to think so."

She reached up to touch his cheek. "Dan, I will go with you, wherever you want to go. I do love you."

He took her hand in his and kissed it. "And your fiancé?"

She tossed her head. "I never loved Vasily. No matter how I tried to fool myself, I know that I could never marry him."

More softly, Dan asked, "And your father?"

"I don't care," Lucita said. "He is interested only in his own ambition."

Dan took a deep breath. "You're really serious about this?"

"I love you, *Yanqui*," she repeated. "I have tried not to, but it did no good. I love you."

"Lucita . . ."

"Yes?"

There were a thousand things whirling through Dan's mind,

words that he wanted to speak to her, promises that he wanted to make. But he heard himself say only, "We can have a beautiful life together, Lucita—once I've finished this business with Malik."

Even in the darkness, he could see her eyes widen. Her breath caught, and she pulled back from him.

"Finish your . . . You mean you'll fight against him until he kills you!"

"Or I kill him," Dan said woodenly. "Whichever comes first."

"While I sit and wait for the victor to claim me as booty!" Lucita's voice was hot with sudden anger.

Shaking his head, Dan asked, "Do you think he'd just let us run off and—"

He stopped. The thoughts racing through his mind coalesced into one terrible, overwhelming realization.

"What is it?" Lucita asked.

He stared at her, speechless, numb.

"Dan, what is wrong? What? . . ."

He understood everything now, and the cold numbness that had made him feel so weary, so hopeless, was boiled away in an instant by a rage so intense that his hands clenched into fists and he could feel his heart thundering.

"You're doing it for them!" Dan said, his voice shaking with fury. "You're trying to get me out of the way, out of Caracas, away from Astro."

"What are you saying?"

"While I'm joyriding with you around the world, they'll be taking over *Nueva Venezuela*, Astro, all the Third World facilities. While I'm busy giving all my attention to you."

"No. . . ."

Dan gripped his thighs as hard as he could, forcing his hands to stay away from her. "A lovely little Delilah: that's what you are. Lead me off around the world while Malik and your father wipe out everything I've worked to create."

"Dan, no, that is not what I—"

He sprang to his feet, banging against the coffee table and knocking over the half-empty bottle of whiskey.

"And what did they promise you?" he demanded. "Money? The undying gratitude of the Politburo? A good seat at the Moscow Ballet every year? Would Malik still marry you after you'd done your work on me?"

"You're insane!" Lucita snapped. "How could you think that I would do such a thing?"

"And what happens while we're jaunting around the world? Do I get bitten by a cobra at the Taj Mahal? Or do I have a skiing accident on the Southern Alps?"

Lucita burst into tears. "I swear . . . Dan, you are wrong . . . nothing . . ."

"No, of course not. I'm imagining the whole thing. You just suddenly decided that you're madly in love with me and if I'll just stop fighting against the Russians and run away with you, you'll be mine forever and ever. *Bullshit!*"

She got up from the sofa like a prizefighter lifting himself from the canvas after being knocked down. Sobbing, she ran across the dimly lit living room, toward the front door. The robot butler, sensing a human body in motion, rolled after her.

"May I show you to the door?" it asked.

But Lucita was already there, and through, before the robot could open the door for her.

"Good evening," it said politely.

As the robot gently shut the door, Dan stood silent and immobile. And alone.

Chapter
♦ ♦ THIRTY ♦ ♦

The first snowfall of the year. Vasily Malik looked past the stern-faced men sitting across the table from him and out to the long windows and the pewter-gray clouds that pressed down against the spires and domes of the Kremlin.

His soul felt just as dreary as the wintry scene outside. It was barely October, the parades celebrating the beginning of the Revolution and the anniversary of the first Sputnik had hardly cleared Red Square. And it was already snowing. Thick, wet flakes drifted down, as inexorable as the rotation of the world on its axis, as remorseless as the comrades who sat arrayed around this heavy, dark conference table, their displeasure focused entirely upon him.

He thought of Caracas, how sunny and warm it would be, even in October. Even in December. But that was merely geography, climate. There was no human warmth in Caracas, not for him. He and Lucita were to be married in little more than two months, yet she was as cold and distant as the farthest planet. As far as she was concerned, Malik knew, it would be a political marriage, nothing more. But I will make it more than that, he thought. She won't be frigid with me; I'll thaw her, even if it takes force.

The ornately carved door at the far end of the conference room swung open, and the Premier shuffled in. How ironic, Malik thought, that the youngest man in three decades to lead the government and the Party should suffer a stroke. It almost makes one believe in God, or at least in fate. But the Premier clung to his power like a shipwrecked sailor clutching a scrap of flotsam. All the ministers got to their feet as the Premier entered, dragging his left foot slightly as he came to his chair at the head of the table. A uniformed guard held the chair for him. He sat, and placed his paralyzed left hand in his lap. Once seated and comfortably arranged, he looked almost normal. The stroke had left scant traces on his face, and his speech had not been impaired. The outside world saw him only thus, either already seated or atop the reviewing stand at Red Square, so far distant from the crowds and photographers that not even his limp could be noticed.

"This emergency meeting of the Council of Ministers will come to order," said the Premier. His voice had always been soft, almost dulcet. His face, gaunt and lined just after the stroke, had filled out almost to its former healthy condition. The pallor on his cheeks was hidden by makeup, when necessary.

The ministers sat. Malik was easily the youngest among them, flanked on either side by men of his father's generation. And the ministers across the table from him were even older; especially Marshal Titov, who looked already embalmed, like an Egyptian mummy in a soldier's uniform. Malik wondered how the old warrior found the strength to stand up, especially under the load of medals he always wore. Even among the aides sitting behind the various ministers and secretaries, hardly any were younger than Malik.

The Premier nodded to the council secretary, sitting at his right.

"There is only one subject on the agenda," said the secretary. He was a chubby, balding, pink-faced pig of a man, Malik thought, with tiny beady eyes almost hidden in his bloated face. When Malik had been on the rise, the secretary had been his friend and ally. But the past few weeks he had shown his true colors.

"The depredations caused by these so-called pirates," said the Premier.

Every eye around the table turned to focus on Malik.

He smiled sardonically. "With all respect, Comrade Chairman, they are not merely *so-called* pirates: what is happening is piracy, pure and simple."

"And it must be stopped," growled old Marshal Titov.

The Foreign Minister, who sat at the Premier's left hand and fancied himself next in line for the top position, held up his hands placatingly.

"The position we find ourselves in is neither pure nor simple," he said to the Premier, speaking so low that the others had to strain to hear him. "Officially, the Organization of Latin American States, led by the government of Venezuela, has taken the position in the World Court that the Soviet Union has illegally seized the cargo of one of their spacecraft—the one that was carrying samples of rock from an asteroid. . . ."

"Where is that asteroid now?" the Premier asked, proving that his mind was still quick. "Has it entered a fixed orbit around the Earth?"

"Not yet, Comrade Chairman, but it will," Malik replied. "Our astronomers have confirmed that it will orbit at the same distance as the Moon itself, nearly four hundred thousand kilometers away."

"Then there is no danger of it falling on Earth?"

"Not unless someone pushes it out of orbit."

The Premier nodded, somewhat stiffly, and turned back to the Foreign Minister.

He cleared his throat and resumed, "Our legal position is somewhat . . ." He groped for a word. "Somewhat contradictory. On the one hand, we maintain that we had the right to seize the cargo of the Venezuelan spacecraft and even to detain its crew. On the other, we maintain that no one has the right to seize the cargoes of our spacecraft carrying ores between the Moon and the space stations in orbit around the Earth.''

"Excuse me, Comrade Minister,'' said Malik, "but there is no contradiction at all. The Soviet Union has the approval of the International Astronautical Council to carry all ore shipments between the Moon and the space stations. The capitalist asteroid mission was not approved by the IAC. And certainly no one in the IAC or the United Nations gave permission for the capitalists to move that body of rock out of its natural orbit.''

"It can't fall on the Earth, can it?'' the Premier asked again.

"No, sir,'' Malik repeated. "Not unless the capitalists deliberately alter its orbit once again.''

The Premier's waxen complexion paled even further. "Would they do that?''

Malik spread his hands, the equivalent of a shrug. "My information is that the capitalists brought the asteroid into orbit around the Earth so that they can use it more conveniently as a mining base—a source of metals and minerals.''

The Minister of Industry stirred. "That would compete with our lunar ores,'' he rasped in his dry, aged voice.

"To some degree,'' Malik conceded.

"But they're not allowed to do that! Only the Soviet Union has the right to mine ores in space.''

Malik fought down the urge to remind the Minister of Industry that he had explained the situation at the last two council meetings. Instead, he patiently explained again, "We have the exclusive right to mine ores from the Moon, Comrade Minister, and transport them to the space stations. There has been no ruling by the IAC on mining asteroids.''

The withered little man looked puzzled. He turned to the aide sitting behind him and exchanged a few hurriedly whispered words with him. Malik guessed that he was asking what an asteroid was.

"We are drifting off the subject," said the Premier. "What are we going to do about these acts of piracy?"

"Pirates should be hanged!" snapped the Minister of Transportation, sitting on Malik's left. He was the next-youngest man at the table, and had long been Malik's rival. "Find them and hang them, every last one!"

"It's not that easy," Malik said. "They don't fly the skull and crossbones, you know. They don't show themselves publicly."

"You know who they are," the Transportation Minister insisted. "We all know who their ringleader is. The American—Randolph."

Malik nodded. "He started it, of that I am certain. But over the past six weeks, acts of piracy have grown far beyond what Randolph alone is capable of doing."

Focusing directly upon the Premier, Malik went on, "Six weeks ago, the pirates made their first raid and stole one of our ore freighters. Within a week, two more freighters were looted of their cargoes. On the same day. The following week, it was three freighters."

"On the same day?"

"Two on one day, the third two days later."

The Premier absently rubbed his paralyzed arm as Malik continued, "Since then, not a week has gone past without at least one ore freighter being emptied of its cargo or stolen altogether."

"Outrageous!" snapped the Transportation Minister.

"Yes, it is. And it is the work of more than one organization. Randolph and his group, working from the Venezuelan space station, could not possibly be doing all this by themselves. The space organizations of the other Third World nations are also helping themselves to our ore shipments. Apparently they send the ores to the Chinese space complex, which then exports them to the various Third World factories as excess Chinese material."

Marshal Titov's shaggy white brows knitted together in a frown that would have been ferocious in a younger man. "Then round them all up. Seize all these space stations and send their crews to the lunar mines. That will stop the piracy."

"Seize the Chinese space station?" The Foreign Minister looked startled at the thought.

"Not them! The others."

"And turn the entire Third World totally against us," countered Malik.

"We can't have that," the Foreign Minister agreed.

"Why not?" Titov demanded. "Who's to stop us?"

The Premier smiled wanly at the old soldier. "Gregory Gregorovich, I know that we have the military power to conquer any nation on Earth, but after we conquer, we must rule. It would put too much of a strain on us to try to rule a hostile world. Not only is that contrary to Marxist-Leninist principles, it is simply not practicable. Remember the troubles we used to have with Poland and the rest of Eastern Europe."

Titov glowered at the Premier. "Yes, and I remember that it was our tanks and our inflexible will that brought them into line."

The Premier's smile remained fixed on his face. "But it was our economic and political policies that finally ended the troubles and brought them under control once again."

The Foreign Minister quickly agreed. "Not even the Red Army can be everywhere at once. If all the nations of Latin America, Africa and Asia turned against us, think what an opportunity for the Chinese!"

"We should have crushed them years ago," Titov grumbled. "And of course the Red Army can't take on the rest of the world, now that you've cut it back to a shadow of its former strength."

"Gregory Gregorovich, my dear friend and comrade-in-arms," said the Premier soothingly, "we live in a new era.

The old days, when you commanded those squadrons of tanks and I directed the Strategic Rocket Corps, were glorious days. It was the strength of our arms that brought the capitalists to their knees, we all recognize that. But now that we have no serious rivals for leadership, now that we can work to bring Marxism to every corner of the world, we must not frighten the smaller nations into resisting us. Our policy is to win them with sugar, rather than force them to swallow vinegar.''

"And above all, do nothing to antagonize the damned Chinese,'' Titov mumbled.

"We will win them over, in time,'' said the Premier.

"We should bomb them out of existence, that's what we should do.''

"And their retaliatory stroke?''

"That's what our satellite defense system is for, isn't it? It cowed the Americans, didn't it?''

"The Chinese are not as easily cowed,'' the Premier answered gently. "They are not as afraid of nuclear devastation as the Yankee capitalists.''

"They would fire their missiles at us,'' the Foreign Minister added. "Even with all our lasers up in the satellites, a few would get through. Would you be willing to see Moscow go up in smoke? Or Leningrad?''

"Yes!'' Titov snapped. "If it would eliminate the damned Chinks once and for all, it would be a price well worth paying.''

From the far end of the table, the gaunt, hollow-cheeked, dark-eyed man who was in charge of state security spoke up, his voice surprisingly deep and powerful. "Even if you destroyed China and conquered all the other nations, Gregory Gregorovich, as I'm sure you could, we would then have to control them, administer them.''

The old marshal scarcely hid the contempt he felt. "Are you saying that the KGB could not keep them in line, once the Red Army had shown them who's boss?''

The taunt did not ruffle the Minister of State Security; not visibly, at least. "I am saying that it is better to have these nations cooperating with us, even though their cooperation is far from perfect, than to force them into submission."

"We are not going to use a bludgeon," the Premier said firmly, "when a scalpel is called for."

Marshal Titov made a sour face, but did not reply. The others shifted in their chairs.

"Then just what steps should we take to stop these pirates?" the Transportation Minister asked. He was looking at the Premier as he spoke, but his words were aimed at Malik.

The Minister of Economic Planning spoke up. "The losses are becoming somewhat serious. Almost ten percent of the ores shipped from the Moon over the past six weeks have been stolen. And the rate of loss is increasing."

"Why can't you stop them?" Transportation demanded. "Aren't the freighters under radar surveillance? Can't you see the pirates when they attack one of our spacecraft?"

Malik said, "It isn't that simple. Yes, each freighter is under constant radar surveillance from the moment it leaves the Moon until it arrives at *Kosmograd* or one of the other stations. But the pirates are using very sophisticated electronic systems to trick our radars. We are fighting a battle of electronics."

"If I were you," the KGB chief said, hunching forward in his chair and locking his long-fingered hands together, "I would put troops in a few of the ore carriers. When the pirates went to raid it, the troops would be able to deal with them quite swiftly."

"Yes, but which freighters?" Malik asked. "There are some two dozen in transit on any given day. Which ones will the pirates attack? Should we arm all of them? We simply don't have that many trained men available at Lunagrad. We would need more manpower."

"That can be done, if it is necessary," the Premier said.

"But what if we capture one band of the thieves," Malik countered, "and the others simply hang back, waiting until

301

we stop putting troops aboard the freighters? Then we go right back to where we started.''

"With one band of pirates removed," Titov muttered.

"It would be better," Malik said, "to get the ringleaders. When exterminating weeds, it is necessary to kill the roots.''

"You know who the ringleaders are?" the Premier asked.

"The instigator of these outrages is the American capitalist, Daniel Randolph.''

"Then kill him," said the KGB chief.

Malik shook his head. "And create a martyr?''

The Transportation Minister snickered. "Comrade Malik tried a campaign of terror against the American, but it frightened his fiancée too much. . . .''

"That is not true!" Malik snapped, feeling his face redden. "My personal life has not and never will interfere with my duties." He took a breath and, turning to face the Premier, said more calmly, "We initiated a program of selected violence to isolate and intimidate the American. It was my decision not to assassinate him, since doing so would disrupt the Venezuelan space industry operation in an unpredictable way, and antagonize Venezuela and the other Third World nations.''

"I am aware of your decision, Vasily Maximovich," said the Premier. "I agreed with it, at the time.''

"We wanted to bring the Yankee capitalist to heel, not kill him. We wanted to bend him to our will.''

"But the results have not been satisfactory," the Transportation Minister said.

Malik told himself that this conference room was too small to contain both of them. Sooner or later, either he would do in the Minister of Transportation or he would be done in himself. But he kept his rage under tight control, looked past his rival and addressed the Premier.

"Comrade Chairman, the Minister of Transportation is misinterpreting the facts. When I tried violence against Randolph, his capitalist friends rallied around him. His Japanese associate sent a team of bodyguards. His friends elsewhere in the world not only refused to abandon him, they actually began their piratical raids at that time. Clearly the campaign of terror was counterproductive."

"So what do you propose to do, Vasily Maximovich?" the Premier asked.

"The idea of putting troops aboard the freighters is basically sound," Malik said. "But instead of arming all of them, I propose to arm only one."

"One?"

Nodding, Malik said, "One will be sufficient, if we obtain the necessary intelligence to reveal which freighter Randolph will attack next."

"Ah . . ." The Premier smiled. "A Trojan Horse."

"You grasp the situation immediately," Malik praised, stopping himself at the very last instant from saying, *"as quickly as ever."* It would not be wise to remind the Premier of his recent stroke.

"So you catch one band of pirates," the Foreign Minister said. "How does that differ from what was suggested earlier?"

"In two ways, Comrade Minister," answered Malik. "First, we have no need of greatly increased manpower. We arm one freighter only. Second, at the same time we are eliminating the pirates, we take command of the space station from which they came and arrest their ringleader, the American, Randolph. We bring him to Moscow for a trial, before the World Court and with full world coverage on television. Then we hang him, in accordance with international law. *That* will stop the others."

"Do you believe so?" asked the Premier.

"I am certain of it."

The others around the table nodded their agreement. All except the Minister of Transportation.

"It sounds very good," he said, cold disdain in his voice. "But how do you learn exactly which freighter should be your Trojan Horse?"

"For that," Malik said, "I will need an informer. And I believe I already have one."

"An informer? Is he reliable?"

"The most reliable kind of informer," Malik retorted, smiling at his rival. "She doesn't even know that she will be informing on the Yankee capitalist."

Chapter
♦ ♦ THIRTY-ONE ♦ ♦

Rafael Hernandez sat gloomily at the head of the long, polished dining table, carefully watching his daughter. Lucita sat at her father's right; the massive, high-backed chair dwarfed her, made her look like a little child again in her father's eyes. The long mahogany table, built to take thirty or more, was empty except for the two of them. No candelabras glittered. No musicians played. No laughter or conversation passed across the table. The room was lit only by the chandelier overhead and the wall sconces. The silence was broken only by the occasional sound of fork or knife against plate, and the hollow boom of thunder outside, from a distant rainstorm.

Lucita had eaten practically nothing of her dinner. The servants brought course after course and then carried each dish back to the kitchen, virtually untouched.

His own appetite was failing him as well. He had little stomach for what he was about to do. He tried talking about the wedding, which was barely more than a month away. Still so much to do, so many details to arrange. Lucita replied politely, but clearly without interest.

It is that devil Randolph, Hernandez told himself. She is brooding over him, instead of looking forward to her wedding. For her own well-being, I must do what must be done.

Finally, as dishes of flan sat before them, Hernandez said, "I fear I must invite Dan Randolph to the wedding."

Her eyes flashed at him.

"After all, he is an important personage," her father went on. "Not to invite him would be unpardonable."

"He will not come to my wedding," Lucita said.

Hernandez touched a spoon to his custard. "What makes you say that?"

She shook her head, the way she did when she was a little girl. "He will not come. I know it."

"I agree with you." Hernandez forced a grim smile. "I am quite certain that he will not be able to accept the invitation."

"Not be able to accept?" Lucita asked.

The flan was delicious: cool and firm and sweet. Hernandez savored it as he studied the sudden interest in his daughter's eyes. There was pain in them. And fear. And much more.

"What do you mean, he will not be able to accept the invitation?" Lucita repeated.

"I have received information that Señor Randolph will be locked in a Soviet prison cell by the time of your wedding." Hernandez's smile was unforced now. "He will be arrested very soon, for piracy."

For long moments Lucita said nothing. She picked up her spoon and toyed with the custard dessert, slowly demolishing its quivering gelled mass. Hernandez watched her, waiting.

"Good!" Lucita said at last. "Then we've seen the last of him."

It was his turn to feel surprise. "You don't care that he will be arrested and hanged?"

"Care? Why should I care?"

"I thought you were . . . fond of him."

"I hate him," Lucita snapped. "And he hates me."

"Ah," said Hernandez. "I see."

Lucita struggled to push her chair back and got to her feet. "Excuse me, please, Papa. I can't eat any more."

He nodded to her, and she left the dining room, walking as carefully as a woman who has had too much to drink and does not want to reveal how uncertain of herself she really feels. Hernandez sat at the head of the table, alone. It is for the best, he told himself. It had to be done.

Lightning flashed outside, throwing the majestic old room into a sudden cold bluish light. Thunder cracked loud enough to rattle the dishes on the table. Rain suddenly lashed against the French windows.

Hernandez dabbed his lips with the damask napkin, rose from his chair and walked slowly out of the dining room, through the hallway and into the small study that he used as an office. He did not turn on a light as he went straight to his desk, pulled up the swivel chair and pecked out the number of the Soviet embassy on the lighted keyboard of his desktop phone.

It took a few minutes for the embassy communications center to reach Vasily Malik. It was just after three A.M. in Moscow, but Malik's face looked bright-eyed and alert when it finally appeared on the phone screen.

"The trap has been baited," Hernandez said without preliminaries. It surprised him to realize how heavy his heart felt.

"Good," said Malik.

"I am not sure that this will work," the Venezuelan said. "Her infatuation with the American seems to be finished."

Malik shook his head. "I don't believe so. She will try to warn him."

"You're certain there's no way . . ."

"No way that she can learn you have set the trap for us?" Malik's lips curled slightly. "No, she will never know—unless I deliberately tell her."

"You wouldn't do that!"

"Why should I? That would be a grave disservice to my father-in-law, would it not? To tell his daughter that he used her like bait on a fishhook?"

Hernandez groaned inwardly. Now the Russian had a permanent hold on him. He had made a fundamental error. Malik was not the kind to forget about it, either. They would pull their strings on him as tight as they wanted to, whenever they chose, from now on.

"She won't be in any danger, you promised me that," he said.

Malik's smile broadened. "Of course not. She is to be my wife, the mother of my children. I will not endanger her in any way."

"Good," Hernandez said. Automatically, he added, "Thank you."

"You have done well. Now we wait for the prey to enter the trap. Good night."

The picture screen went blank. Hernandez stared at it for a long time. Yes, he thought, they will help me to become president of Venezuela. On their terms. Only on their terms.

Nobuhiko Yamagata felt puzzled and flattered at the same time.

He had been greatly attracted to the young Venezuelan woman who had accompanied Dan Randolph to his father's ski lodge in Sapporo. At first he had thought she was a servant or a paid companion. It had been during dinner that he'd realized she was merely a friend of Randolph's; not even that, a casual acquaintance. She was very beautiful, very desirable and very independent. It had overjoyed Nobo when Randolph had asked him to come to Caracas to work for him.

But Nobo quickly learned that the relationships between men and women in the West were incredibly complicated. Lucita Hernandez became engaged to the chief of the Russian space program, but she had still been seen from time to time in Dan Randolph's company.

And now, a scant month before her wedding, she had sent word to Nobo that she wanted to meet with him. Was it an honorable thing to do? Nobo wondered. Would he be causing trouble for Dan Randolph by meeting with her? Would his behavior reflect poorly on the Yamagata family, or cause repercussions between the Russians and Yamagata Industries? Just what did this beautiful but unpredictable woman have in mind?

Nobo wrestled with his conscience for almost a full day after reading Lucita's message on the screen of his phone console. His conscience lost. He phoned her and made a date for lunch.

I am still a stranger in this land, he told himself cheerfully. She knows much more about the customs here than I do. It would not be proper for me to refuse her invitation.

Thus reassured, he borrowed an Astro Manufacturing car—a GMota, designed in Japan and built by Japanese robots in a Caracas factory—and drove to the restaurant in downtown Caracas where he would meet Lucita Hernandez.

He took a table on the sidewalk and ordered a Kirin beer as he waited for her. In five minutes he checked his watch seven times, and examined the menu twice to make certain that he was at the right restaurant. It was a pleasant spot, shaded by the tall trees of Bolivar Square, across the street. No automobile traffic was allowed around the square, although several big tourist buses were parked by the hotel up the street. Most of the people strolling past his table looked like vacationers to Nobo; they were clothed in shorts, splashy sport shirts and casual dresses. An occasional businessman strode past, looking tense and wearing a suit with a tie. And then there were the mestizo women: mixed bloods who had the tall, leggy, exotic looks that made Nobo's heart beat fast.

Then he noticed that there was life in the high, moss-covered trees of the square. Not merely birds. Monkeys were squawking and swinging through the trees, racing around and around, burning energy as recklessly as a runaway rocket, just for the sheer exuberant fun of it. And as Nobo looked closer, he saw that the trees also were inhabited by other shapes: hairy, dark sloths were hanging from the branches, barely moving, as the monkeys whipped past them. Nobo laughed aloud. In the time it took a sloth to unhook one clawed foot from a branch and move it a few inches, the pack of monkeys had sped around the whole square twice.

The laughter died away as he thought, How like America and Russia they are. The Americans rushed and raced and exhausted themselves, while the Russians plodded slowly and inexorably to world domination. The comparison somehow made him feel glum.

As he reached for his half-empty glass of beer, Nobo saw Lucita walking up the street toward the restaurant. She wore a sleeveless frock of white and a dramatic, broad-brimmed white straw hat. Sunglasses hid her eyes, but Nobo had no trouble identifying her. His hand bumped into the beer glass, nearly spilling it.

He shot up from his chair and stepped out onto the sidewalk to greet her.

"Señorita Hernandez," Nobo said in his best Spanish. "I am so happy to see you again."

"It was so gracious of you to meet me, Señor Yamagata," she said.

"Please call me Nobo," he replied as he held her chair for her.

She sat and took off the sunglasses. Her eyes were wondrously beautiful. "Yes, I remember from the dinner we had. It was a delightful evening."

"I am pleased that you enjoyed it."

A robot waiter glided to their table and, after asking Lucita what she wanted to drink, Nobo pecked out an order for a Cuba libre and another Kirin on the robot's keyboard.

"You are also Dan Randolph's friend, are you not?" Lucita asked him.

Nobo nodded. "I admire him very much. He and my father worked together many years ago. I have known him for as long as I can remember—the American who worked harder than any Japanese."

She smiled, but he saw that it was tinged with sadness. "Dan Randolph is in great danger."

"He is aware of that," Nobo replied. "He laughs about it."

"It is not a laughing matter."

The waiter returned, bearing their drinks on its flat top. Nobo put them on their table and placed his empty beer bottle on the waiter, then inserted his credit card into the robot's slot. It made a rapid series of clicks, then the card popped out again and Nobo retrieved it.

As the machine rolled away, Lucita said urgently, "The Russians are preparing to arrest Dan. He must stop these hijackings at once, or else they will take him to Moscow and hang him."

"But he's a citizen of Venezuela. They can't—"

"That won't stop them! My father will allow them to do whatever they want. No matter what it costs him, my father has thrown in his hand with the Russians."

"Dan's aboard *Nueva Venezuela* right now. He's not scheduled to return until Friday."

"Have him return to Japan," Lucita urged. "Go to the space station yourself and take him back to Japan with you. He will be safe there, I think. Safer than here."

"That may be possible," Nobo murmured.

"And above all, make him stop these raids on the Russian spaceships. Don't let him do anything that they can arrest him for."

Shrugging, Nobo replied, "Have you ever tried to make him do something he does not want to do?"

Despite herself, Lucita smiled at him. "Yes, I know how stubborn he can be. But you *must* make him stop. For his own good."

Hunching forward over the little table and lowering his voice, Nobo said, "A team of astronauts left yesterday to intercept one of the freighters. They will be back tomorrow."

"Then make that the last one," Lucita whispered. "For God's sake, don't let him do any more or they'll kill him."

Nobo straightened up in his chair. "I will go to *Nueva Venezuela* myself, this afternoon. I will tell him everything that you've told me."

"I will go with you," Lucita said.

311

"I don't think—"

"I must! Please. Let me go to him."

He studied her face, so earnest, so pleading. She loves Dan, Nobo realized. He thought he should feel surprised, or perhaps even a little resentful. He felt neither. It seemed completely logical to him that the most beautiful young woman in Caracas should be totally in love with Dan Randolph, so logical and natural that he could not be resentful about it, no matter how much he wanted this lovely woman to love him.

But out of the corner of his eye, he caught the frantic racing of the monkeys through the trees of Bolivar Square. And saw the patient, plodding, inexorable sloths hanging from their branches like hairy growths. It occurred to Nobuhiko that the sloths must live much longer lives than the monkeys. Yes, he realized, the monkeys must die young while the sloths survive indefinitely.

Chapter
◆ ◆ THIRTY-TWO ◆ ◆

A silver tray bearing his untouched dinner sat on a corner of Vasily Malik's desk. A single lamp burned on the desktop, throwing a pool of light over its surface. The rest of his office lay deep in shadow; chairs and the long conference table that extended from his desk like the upright length of a letter T were lost in darkness. Only the massive silver samovar in the corner by the television set glinted a reflection of the desk lamp.

Outside the curtained windows snow was falling in the evening gloom. Moscow was ablaze with lights, and from these office windows one could see the Kremlin in all its barbaric splendor. But Malik kept the windows tightly curtained. He had no desire to gaze out at the onion-shaped domes and high walls, he took no pleasure in watching the automobile traffic inching through Red Square. Nor did he wish to allow anyone to see through the windows and into his private office. The windows stayed closed and covered, day and night.

There was one other person in the darkened office with him, a small, lean, nervous man of about forty, balding, with a pencil-thin mustache and the long slim fingers of a born pianist. He wore a gray suit. His blue tie was carefully knotted and his collar tightly buttoned. An American cigarette dangled from the corner of his thin lips, and he squinted against the rising smoke as he peered at the computer screen on Malik's desk.

Malik, wearing a comfortable, loose-fitting peasant's blouse over his expensive blue jeans, took a cigarette of his own from the cedarwood box on his desk and fitted it to his ivory holder as he said:

"Where the two lines intersect, Lermentov. That's the freighter that they're after."

Lermentov was the KGB officer assigned to Malik. When the chief of the space program traveled outside his office, Lermentov was his chauffeur, or sometimes his valet. But he was always, in reality, Malik's bodyguard and watchdog— and an unbreakable link that connected directly with the Minister for State Security.

He stared at the graph lines on the glowing computer screen. "How can you be sure?"

Malik lit his cigarette and savored it for a moment before answering. "According to the tape we received from Caracas an hour ago, the Yankee capitalist has already sent out a team of pirates. They left yesterday and are expected back tomorrow. Our radar surveillance of *Nueva Venezuela* fixed the time of departure of four of their small ships—that's this point here." He tapped the screen with his index fingernail.

"I see," Lermentov replied.

"Their ships are too small to track with radar for very great distances," Malik resumed, "but the very fact that four of them together sailed out of radar range is proof enough for me. There's only one ore freighter that they can reach soon enough to be back by tomorrow." He tapped the screen again. "This one."

"Then that will be your Trojan Horse."

"Exactly." Malik reached for the phone on his desktop. "We must get a team of soldiers to that freighter tonight."

314

"Can you get them there in time?"

"It will take a high-energy launch from the Northern Cosmodrome in Plesetsk, but I've had the troops and a launching crew standing by for more than a week. They'll get here in time. There may be a few bloody noses from the launch acceleration, but they'll make it in time."

He spoke urgently into the phone, then hooked it into the receptacle on the side of the computer. Data flowed automatically to Plesetsk in an inhumanly rapid series of high-pitched peeps and squeaks. To Malik it sounded like dolphins conversing.

Lermentov leaned back in his chair. "Won't the pirates see our soldiers coming up to the freighter and be frightened away?"

With a self-satisfied smile, Malik answered, "The pirates have been very clever about foiling our radars, using electronic countermeasures to make themselves virtually invisible to us. Well, two can play at that game. They won't see the troops, I promise you. To them, the freighter will look totally innocent and unprotected."

The KGB officer nodded, apparently content.

"By this time tomorrow, Dan Randolph will be on his way to Moscow, in fetters. And the space station *Nueva Venezuela* will be in our hands. Within a week we will be occupying all the so-called Third World space stations and rounding up all their piratical crews."

"The committee will be very pleased with you."

"I should hope so." Malik thought about breaking out the vodka, but he remembered that this apostle of state security did not drink. Time to celebrate later, after the victory is actually in our grasp, he thought.

"You've been skating on thin ice, these past few weeks," Lermentov said. "People were starting to worry about your future."

"I've been playing for high stakes," Malik shot back. "This has been more than an annoying series of raids, you know. From the very beginning I knew that I had to eliminate

315

the last vestiges of the capitalists in space. It wasn't enough to drive the United States government out of space. The capitalists like Randolph simply went elsewhere. . . ."

"Like cockroaches scuttling away from the fumigator."

Malik laughed. "You should have been a poet. But you're right. Now we can round up *all* of them, take over their orbital factories, and eliminate the last shreds of capitalism from space."

"And from Earth," Lermentov added.

"Ah, yes. From Earth too, eventually," Malik agreed.

Lermentov puffed happily on his cigarette.

"There is one additional thing to be done," Malik said "and I need your help in doing it."

"What is that?"

"I need four hydrogen bombs."

"*What?*"

Raising a hand to placate the man's sudden shock, Malik said, "Not military weapons. The kind that are used in big construction jobs, like reversing the course of the Lena River."

"Whatever do you need them for?"

Malik was enjoying Lermentov's obvious surprise and worry "You know that the American altered the course of a asteroid—a big chunk of rock and metal."

"Yes. It will move into an orbit around the Earth, won it?"

"If we leave it alone, it will."

The KGB man's face seemed to pull itself into a wrinkle frown of curiosity and fear.

"I plan to send a special team of cosmonauts to tha asteroid and use the hydrogen bombs to alter its course sti further—so that it will plunge into the Earth."

"By all the saints!"

"We will drop it into the American Midwest somewhere We can't guide it too precisely, of course. But imagine th impact of a few million tons of rock on one of those midwester American states such as Kansas or Missouri."

Lermentov seemed to be having trouble catching his breath. "It would be like . . . like . . ."

"Like a hundred hydrogen bombs hitting them, all at once. Like the hand of God smiting them."

"A disaster. . . ."

"A calamity," Malik agreed. "Of course, there would be no radiation, no fallout. The calamity would not harm any other nation."

"But why? . . ."

Reaching across his desk to stub out his cigarette, Malik said, "What better way to convince the world that Dan Randolph and all his capitalist ilk should be rounded up and hanged? He will get blamed for the disaster, of course. It will be the final nail in his coffin."

Chapter
◆ ◆ THIRTY-THREE ◆ ◆

Nobo had thought it would be difficult to arrange an unscheduled flight to *Nueva Venezuela* on such short notice, especially when his call to Dan resulted in the phone computer telling him that Mr. Randolph was asleep and not to be disturbed except for an emergency.

Sitting in an office at the launch complex, with Lucita perched on a plastic chair watching him, Nobo debated waking Dan. The room was a Spartan, utilitarian office shared by temporary workers, little more than a desk, a computer terminal and a hook on the back of the door to hang a coat. It was frigidly air-conditioned; Americans were not satisfied with air conditioning until it made one's sinuses ache, Nobuhiko thought. Lucita seemed chilled; she sat with her arms wrapped around herself, even though she had changed into a pair of jeans and a sensible, comfortable long-sleeved blouse, at Nobo's suggestion. Skirts and dresses that looked fine on Earth were out of place aboard a space station, especially in the zero gravity areas, he had reminded her.

On an impulse, he put through a call to Zach Freiberg, at the Astro offices in Caracas. The scientist listened to Nobo's worries about Dan, then agreed to arrange for a shuttle to take him and Lucita to the space station.

"Give me a half hour to talk to the chief of operations out there," Freiberg said. "I've found that once you convince him to go to the expense of flying a shuttle up to the station, he fills it up with all the people who've been pestering him for the past week for an extra flight."

So it was arranged. From the office window, Lucita watched as two van loads of technicians rode out to one of the three double-decker aerospace planes parked in a silent, waiting row across the field. Like inquisitive ants they crawled around the huge craft, and then climbed up a ladder and disappeared inside it. She turned to check the digits of the clock on the bare metal desk, and saw that Nobo was watching her, his face a blank mask of Oriental patience. Slowly the ground crew fueled the massive lifter aircraft and its piggyback orbiter. After nearly two hours had passed, a flight crew of three men and four women drove out to the ship and entered it. The minutes flicked by slowly. At last Lucita heard, even at this distance and through the triple-paned windows, the thundering whine of the lifter's powerful jet engines. The double-decked craft trundled slowly from its parking place across the field to the loading ramp near the office building, with the orbiter perched atop it.

Forty-eight people, including Lucita and Nobo, walked through the boarding tunnel and took seats inside the orbiter. It was an old ship, no longer used for the commercial flights that brought tourists to *Nueva Venezuela*, or even for the regularly scheduled cargo runs from the space factory. It was kept for emergencies, like this one.

"I never realized that Dan had so many Japanese working for his company," Lucita said as they took their seats.

"Space construction is one of the most popular career choices in Japan," Nobo replied. "There are many Japanese working in all the space facilities."

The interior of the shuttle was much like the interior of a well-worn airliner, except that there were no windows. Once, when this craft had been used to ferry tourists to *Nueva Venezuela*, there had been television screens set into the backs of the seats, so that the passengers could see views of the Earth and the station, or prerecorded safety or entertainment tapes. Now the seat backs were blank. Employees had seen the views before, they needed no entertainment and they were required to know the safety regulations before making their first flight into space.

The flight was uneventful, and the zero-gravity portion of it was so brief that Lucita did not have the time to worry about being sick. She rather enjoyed the feeling of weightlessness; it was like floating or, better yet, like the unearthly feeling she had gotten the first time she had smoked a whole marijuana cigarette all by herself, in the darkness of the cellar under her convent school dormitory.

There were no stewards or stewardesses to help her once the orbiter had docked at the space station's zero-gravity hub. The other passengers, Astro employees or technicians of one kind or another, were expected to make their own way through the dock area and "down" the connecting tubes to the station's living and working areas. Lucita, whose only previous experience in orbit had been aboard *Kosmograd*, allowed Nobo to take her hand and lead her gently to the tube hatch.

At first it was like floating through a smooth metal-walled tunnel. It was brightly lit and there were plenty of other men and women, both ahead of them and behind. Lucita was glad she had changed into the slacks and blouse. Before long, Nobo guided her hands to the rungs of the ladder built into the tube's wall, and within moments she was descending, step by step, with Nobo just below her and another Japanese, a stranger, a few rungs above.

They reached the bottom of the tube at last, and Nobo held open the heavy metal hatch there. Lucita stepped through and into a beautifully furnished lounge area, richly carpeted, its curving walls decorated in warm reds and oranges and ochers. A single long window showed a slice of the gleaming blue-

and-white Earth, so beautiful that most of the other visitors were drawn to the window, clustering there as if to a religious shrine.

But Nobo was frowning, Lucita saw. "Why are we being detained here in the reception lounge?" he wondered aloud. "These are all Astro employees, not tourists. . . ."

The far door to the lounge opened, and a short, thick-set man in a tan military uniform entered the lounge. He had a glistening leather holster strapped to his hip. Two grim-faced soldiers stood behind him, carrying machine pistols.

"Ladies and gentlemen," said the officer in heavily accented English. "This facility is now under the control of the Soviet Union's space forces. All regular activities have been suspended, pending the arrest and transportation of certain criminals whom we believe to be aboard this station. You will remain here until further notice. Stay calm and follow all orders given by Soviet authorities. Those who do not follow orders are subject to arrest. My troops have orders to shoot anyone who offers active resistance."

As he repeated the words in even worse Spanish, Lucita turned, white-faced with fear, to Nobuhiko.

"Too late," she whispered. "We are too late."

Major Igor Konstantinovich Ostrovsky always became ill in zero gravity. For the entire duration of the forty-minute flight from *Kosmograd* to *Nueva Venezuela*, he was sick as the proverbial dog. He sat in the frontmost seat in the passenger module of the spacecraft, his back to the thirty other Soviet soldiers of his command, so they could not see his ashen, agonized face or his knobby hands gripping the armrests so tightly that all the blood seemed squeezed out of them.

In front of Major Ostrovsky was the blank bulkhead that separated the flight compartment from the passenger module. Ostrovsky stared at it, studying every scuff mark and scrape on the bare, worn metal. He held himself rigidly motionless. He felt as if he were falling, dropping endlessly into a long dark pit. His stomach was trying to crawl up his throat. If he turned his head even the slightest fraction of a millimeter, the whole world seemed to swim giddily and the nausea threatened to overwhelm him. So he sat as motionless as a dead and fossilized creature, trying to will himself into stony insensitivity.

Behind him, over the whir of the air circulation fans and the incessant hum of electrical equipment, he could hear an occasional groan from his troops. They were all trained men, volunteers from the Strategic Rocket Corps' own special soldiery, but still the queasiness of zero gravity got to some of them. They did not have the major's iron self-discipline, however. Several of them used the retch bags that were part of their standard equipment. Each time one of them vomited, the noise made Ostrovsky's guts churn. He tasted acrid bile in his throat, but he fought it down in silent, grim determination.

Two Soviet spacecraft were approaching *Nueva Venezuela*, both under Ostrovsky's command. Each carried thirty officers and men. Ostrovsky used his position as commander to make certain that his spacecraft got the assignment of docking at the emergency collar on the outermost rim of the Venezuelan space station. It meant some tricky maneuvering for the pilots, but the men in the spacecraft would immediately step into the part of the space station where gravity was normal. The other spacecraft was assigned to dock at the regular landing collar, at the zero-gee hub of the station.

But every advantage comes only at a price. The spacecraft lurched and seemed to sway suddenly. Ostrovsky broke into a cold sweat and heard more gagging and moaning from the troops behind him. The pilots were jockeying the ship toward the station's emergency dock, he knew, a difficult maneuver, especially when no assistance from the space station's controllers had been asked for or given.

They don't realize that we're going to board their station and take control of it, Ostrovsky told himself, hoping desperately that it was true. After this forty-minute bout with the nausea of weightlessness, neither he nor his troops were in any condition for a fight.

With a surge that sent waves of queasiness through him, Ostrovsky felt weight returning. His stomach settled down to where it ought to be. His feet stuck to the floor and stopped trying to float away. He could turn his head without fearing that the world would turn itself upside down.

"Docking maneuver complete," he heard the captain-pilot's voice announce over the intercom. "Hatch locked and sealed."

Gratefully, Ostrovsky unbuckled his seat harness and got to his feet. As he straightened his tan uniform, the squad sergeants bawled orders to the men and the two young, shaven-headed lieutenants—as alike as clones—made their way forward toward their commanding officer. Ostrovsky noted with perverse pleasure that they both looked as gray-faced and shaken as he felt.

The soldiers, under the glaring eyes of their sergeants, scrambled up the ladder at the back end of the passenger module and through the overhead hatch that was now sealed tightly to one of the emergency hatches of the space station. They were under strict orders and knew their objectives. For two weeks they had rehearsed this operation. Ostrovsky had reported to Chairman Malik that his troops could seize *Nueva Venezuela* blindfolded. Malik had merely nodded and told him that they should keep their eyes open. Now he would show the chairman how well his troops could perform.

Ostrovsky stayed aboard the spacecraft. Instead of following his men into the Venezuelan space station, he went forward, ducking through the small hatch that led into the flight compartment. While the captain-pilot and the electronics technicians stayed in their bucket seats, the copilot squeezed past Ostrovsky and stood in the hatchway, allowing the major to use the right-hand seat as a command post.

There was only one communications screen on the control panel in front of Ostrovsky, but the electronics tech was clever enough to split it into four segments, allowing the major to stay in touch simultaneously with the four elements of his command: the troops from his own ship, the troops from the second ship, the team riding out toward the asteroid and Chairman Malik himself, waiting impatiently at Plesetsk.

It took precisely twelve minutes for the troops to seize complete control of the space station. Squads of soldiers made their way to the communications and the life support centers, both located in the outermost wheel of the station. The other two squads, working "downward" from the station's hub, took over the landing docks and the electrical power center. Not a shot was fired. The capitalists were caught completely by surprise. Ostrovsky took in the reports from his junior officers and relayed them immediately to Malik.

"The only surprise," the major concluded, "was that an unscheduled shuttle from Caracas arrived at the main landing dock some fifteen minutes before our own spacecraft rendezvoused there."

Malik's face, tiny in the upper right quarter of the small display screen, scowled suspiciously. "An unscheduled shuttle from Caracas?"

"It posed no problem, sir," the major continued. "Our craft merely docked at the alternate collar and disembarked our troops as planned. The shuttle is still docked there; since our operational plan called for a complete sealing off of the station, I have not permitted it to leave."

Malik nodded curtly. "Who sent this shuttle? Who was aboard it?"

"Apparently the ship belongs to Astro Manufacturing Corporation. I do not have a list of the passengers yet, but I presume they were Astro employees."

"I want the names of the passengers. I will be coming up to *Nueva Venezuela* within the hour. Have the list ready for me when I arrive."

"Yes, sir. Of course, sir."

"And Dan Randolph? Where is he?"

"He is safely locked in a holding cell. He was asleep when my men arrested him."

"Asleep?" A smile crept across Malik's face. "How poetic."

"Sir?" Ostrovsky asked. "May I ask about the other mission? The one dealing with the pirates?"

Ostrovsky had wanted to command that mission, of course. There was always more prestige to combat. But it would have meant long hours of zero gravity and he was thankful when Malik chose another officer for the job.

"Completely successful," Malik replied, his smile broadening. "The pirates have been eliminated, every last one of them."

The captain-pilot nodded, satisfied, and gave his copilot the thumbs-up sign. There would be promotions in the offing, they both knew.

"A very successful operation, sir," Ostrovsky congratulated his superior. "Your plan has worked to perfection."

"It will not be perfection," Malik replied, "until the capitalist Randolph is swinging from the end of a rope."

Ostrovsky permitted himself a small grin. "Well, sir, we have him for you. The rest is up to the prosecutors and the courts."

"Unless," Malik mused, "he is shot while trying to escape."

Chapter
◆ ◆ THIRTY-FOUR ◆ ◆

Dan Randolph sat slumped against the wire mesh wall of his makeshift prison cell. A glance at his wristwatch told him that it had been three hours since the Russians had rousted him from his bunk. He had not seen another human being since the soldiers had locked him into this cage.

Malik will be here, Dan told himself. He'll come up here himself to make sure that they've got me. He'll want to tend to the final details in person.

Dan nodded, certain of what he was going to do. Just let him get within arm's reach, that's all I ask. That smiling sonofabitch won't live to see me executed. I'll kill him with my bare hands.

He smiled. And waited.

Vasily Malik was not smiling. He felt anger smoldering in his guts as he scanned the list of passengers from the Astro Corporation shuttle. Forty-eight names, nearly half of them Japanese. All of them Astro employees, except for one: M. Hernandez.

Maria de la Luz Hernandez, he knew. Lucita.

He was seated at one end of the horseshoe-shaped desk that dominated the space station's flight control center. All the controllers' chairs were empty, their display screens blank. No traffic was coming or going. *Nueva Venezuela* was sealed off from the rest of the world. The factory orbiting nearby was also shut down. No one allowed in or out. According to Malik's plan, as approved by the Council of Ministers, the Soviet space forces would have to occupy and search all the other Third World space facilities in their legally empowered drive to root out the space pirates. Within the week, the space stations of India, Polynesia, Africa and the Pan-Arab coalition would all be under Soviet command. Only Japan and China would remain to rival the Soviet Union, and sooner or later they would be driven out of space also.

But at the moment, the vision of Soviet domination was far from Malik's mind.

He tapped the display screen in front of him. "Who is this Hernandez person?"

Major Ostrovsky, standing at Malik's right, risked a small shrug. "I don't know, sir. There is no listing of his status. Apparently he is not an employee of the capitalists."

"He?" Malik snapped. "Do you know for certain that Hernandez is a male?"

"No, sir, I don't. I can find out for you, of course, within a minute or two."

Glowering, Malik said, "Bring Hernandez here, whoever he or she is."

Ostrovsky started to turn toward the shavetail lieutenant standing at ramrod attention behind him.

"Better yet," Malik said, pushing himself up from the undersized plastic desk chair, "I will go to the reception area where those new arrivals are being held."

"Yessir," said Ostrovsky. As Malik headed for the hatch that led out to the corridor, the major asked, "What should we do about the American, Randolph, sir?"

Malik gave him a look of malicious pleasure, the kind of look a boy might get when he traps a butterfly and pins it, still fluttering, to a tabletop. "Randolph? Leave him where he is. I have seen the television pictures. You have the right man. Let him stew in his own sweat for a while longer."

With the major two paces behind him, matching stride for stride, and the lieutenant three paces farther back, Malik made his way along the corridor that ran the length of the station's outermost wheel toward the reception area. To the eye, the corridor sloped upward continuously, but it felt perfectly flat as they walked along it. Doors on either side of the pastel-colored walls led to offices or living quarters, Malik knew. Occasionally the corridor opened up into a lounge area, a small automated fast-food dispensary or an intimate little bistro. All empty now, quiet, as the visitors and crew of *Nueva Venezuela* had been ordered to their quarters. Capitalist luxuries, Malik told himself. Once we take over these stations for good, we'll run them for the benefit of the workers, not for the profit of the moneygrubbers.

Still, a small voice inside his head observed wryly, the moneygrubbers produce a much better style of luxuries. Once the people's servants get their hands on these facilities, the quality of the food and drink will suffer.

Malik shook his head, as if to drive such thoughts from his mind. There were always places where important men could get the luxuries they desired.

When they reached the double doors that opened into the lounge area, Malik stopped and peered through the glass window set into one of them. He thought he recognized the son of Randolph's friend, the industrialist Yamagata, among the couple of dozen Japanese sitting around the plush sofas and chairs of the lounge. Good! He will make a useful bargaining chip. The process of bringing Japan to heel can begin immediately, perhaps.

But then he saw Lucita, standing by the long curving window, looking out wistfully at the Earth. It *is* her. Malik's heart felt encased in ice. She's come here to be with him, probably to warn him against me. He could feel the cold fury racing through him, spreading along every nerve and blood vessel like an invasion of demons.

328

Turning to Major Ostrovsky, he said coldly, "The woman by the window. That is Hernandez. Bring her out here to me."

Something in Malik's voice frightened the major. He saluted and motioned the lieutenant to come with him. Malik paced away from the doors, wondering why he should feel such rage. She had betrayed him. She had flown to the American. Had he expected anything else? Had he expected her to be loyal to him, to stand by his side, even to love him? And he realized that even though he had never expected Lucita to behave in such a manner, that was exactly what he had wanted. He wanted her loyalty, her love.

My God, he thought. Do I really love her? Have I let my guard down so much that she can make me furious with jealousy? The answer was obvious.

Ostrovsky's soft "Sir?" made him turn again.

Lucita stood before him, the major on one side of her, the young lieutenant on the other. She looked so small, so helpless, standing there between them like a prisoner.

"I didn't expect to find you here," Malik said. His voice sounded tight, almost choked, even in his own ears.

Lucita said nothing, merely stared at him. He tried to determine what was in her eyes. It was not fear, he could see. Nor supplication. Anger. She was burning with suppressed anger, just as furious with Malik as he was with her.

He reached out and grasped her by the arm. Leading her away from the two officers, he walked slowly back down the long sloping corridor in the direction from which he had come. Lucita came along with him, not willingly, but not resisting him, either.

"You came to warn Randolph, didn't you?" Malik said.

"I came too late," replied Lucita.

For an instant he wanted to tell her that she herself had sprung the trap on Randolph, that it was her fault he was now under arrest. But he could not bring himself to say the words.

"How quiet everything is," Lucita said. "It's as if the whole station has died."

"I only have sixty men to control the entire station," Malik said. "More will be sent, but for the time being we must keep everyone in their quarters."

"When I was here before, after visiting *Kosmograd*, this place was so alive, so busy and bustling," Lucita said. "I remember that it shocked me. I was bringing Teresa's body home . . ."

Malik felt his jaws clench.

". . . and it shocked me that all these people seemed so busy and happy. Now—it's dead."

"Only for a short while."

She shook her head. "No. Once you put your hand on something, Vasily, it dies. You are an agent of death. I don't think you mean to be, but you are, just the same."

"That's very unfair!" he snapped.

She smiled wanly. "But true."

It made no sense. This was supposed to be victory, yet he felt no triumph. He heard himself say:

"You came here to see Randolph. I will take you to him. You will be the first to visit him in his imprisonment. And the last."

Without waiting for her to reply, Malik took Lucita by the wrist and led her off toward the storage area where Dan Randolph was locked in a cage. Major Ostrovsky and his lieutenant hurried to follow them.

Nobuhiko paced the length of the lounge, feeling the utter frustration of an energetic young man who has been forced into idleness. There must be something I can do, he told himself over and again. Something.

Each time he reached the wall at one end of the lounge, he eyed the Russian soldiers standing by the doors. Two of them at each end, armed with stubby machine pistols that fired flesh-ripping fléchette darts.

With an impatient snorting sigh, Nobo turned away and began pacing again. He was stopped by another Japanese, a wiry, short man with a thick mane of iron-gray hair. He wore an ordinary business suit of dark blue. His tie was decorated with the flying heron symbol of the Yamagatas.

"Yamagata-san," he said, bowing slightly to the son of the family's head.

Nobo returned a curt nod.

"Forgive my clumsy lack of manners for greeting you so informally," said the man in low, swift Japanese, "but I thought it best not to be obvious to the barbarian soldiers."

"You are . . . ?"

"Isoru! At your service, Yamagata-san."

Pacing the lounge in a more leisurely manner now, with Isoru at his side, Nobo asked, "Are you a member of my family, or an employee of Astro Manufacturing?"

"I am both," the older man replied. "Your father arranged for my team to become employees of the American, so that we could be close to you and protect you from assassination."

"Ahh!" Comprehension began to dawn on Nobuhiko.

"My team and I have been at your side for many weeks. My orders were to remain invisible, so that you would not know who we were, or why we were here."

"My father feared for my life."

"Most truly."

"Now I understand. You have done well, Isoru."

The man hissed with pleasure.

"How many men do you have?"

"Ten, including myself. Eight men and two women."

"Women?" Nobuhiko felt startled.

Isoru shrugged. "The times have changed. But they obey orders, and they have a certain surprise value."

"Are they all here?"

"They are all in this room, Yamagata-san, awaiting your orders."

"Can they disarm the soldiers swiftly and silently, without allowing them to fire a shot?"

"Easily."

"I don't want the soldiers killed," Nobo said. "They must be taken prisoner."

Isoru nodded. "It can be done."

Nobo hesitated only a fraction of a moment. He had no clear idea of what to do after disarming the soldiers, but he knew that nothing else could be done until they had been disarmed.

"Very well," he said. "Do so."

Isoru bowed again; only the smallest and least noticeable of bows. His face was as impassive as a rock wall. He walked away from Nobo as casually as a man would after a harmless friendly conversation. Nobuhiko resumed his pacing, but now he watched to see what his father's appointed guardians were going to do.

Though he watched intently, he could see nothing. Isoru gave no obvious signal to anyone else. The man merely strolled off to one of the long observation windows and seemed to stare out at the Earth. The minutes ticked off slowly. Nobo grew tired of pacing and went to the window where Isoru stood, his hands clasped behind his back. But, as if he had eyes in the back of his head, Isoru turned away as Nobo approached and moved off toward one end of the lounge.

Briefly, Nobo debated following him. But it was clear that the man did not want Nobo near him. Then he noticed that a good-looking young Japanese woman was chatting and smiling with the pair of Russian soldiers guarding the door at that end of the lounge. Turning toward the other end, Nobo could see no Japanese within twenty paces of the two soldiers there.

Isoru was still walking slowly down the room. He unclasped his hands and flexed his fingers slightly.

The slim young woman smiling up at the two burly Russian soldiers suddenly struck one of them on the point of his chin with her cupped hand, and drove her other hand blurringly fast into the solar plexus of the other. If Nobo had blinked, he would have missed it. A thud, a choked grunt, and the two soldiers were collapsing to the carpeted floor, their guns slipping from their numbed hands.

332

Swinging toward the other end of the lounge, Nobo saw the two soldiers there slumping to the floor, a pair of wiry Japanese young men crouching over them.

As calmly as a man strolling through a garden, Isoru came to Nobo, made a bow that almost put his forehead on the carpeting and said, "Yamagata-san, the task you ordered has been done."

Nobo looked around the lounge. It was easy now to pick out his bodyguards; ten Japanese men and women, lithe and lean, standing at rigid attention. The others, Japanese and Westerners, were open-mouthed with surprise.

"You have done well," Nobo said, loudly enough for all his people to hear. Ten hisses of pleasure scintillated through the lounge.

Lucita was walking beside Malik through the long narrow corridor of a storage area. Wire mesh screens rose from curving floor to ceiling, where bare fluorescent tubes lit the passageway. Strange crates and boxes were stacked behind the screens, neatly and carefully, their flanks bearing stenciled legends in Spanish and English. It felt chilly here, the kind of cold that Lucita imagined she would feel in a mortuary.

Malik had a pistol buckled to his hip, Lucita realized. The flap of the holster was unfastened. She could see the dead black butt of the gun, ugly and menacing.

Behind her, the two officers matched them stride for stride. They both were armed, too. A sudden fear rose in Lucita's chest; she could feel its electrical currents burning inside her.

"Vasily," she said in English, hoping that the other two could not understand, "you're going to murder him, aren't you?"

Malik did not alter his stride, did not turn his head to meet her gaze. "My orders are to bring him to Moscow for trial. They want the whole world to see that pirates will be brought to justice—and then hanged."

"But you're not going to let that happen, are you?" Lucita had to hurry to keep pace with Malik. He seemed to be

333

walking faster as he got closer to Dan's cell, eager to reach the American. "You intend to kill him yourself."

Still staring straight ahead, Malik replied, "It would not be such a tragedy if he were shot while trying to escape."

"But you can't do that!"

Now he slowed slightly and turned his head toward her. "Why can't I?"

Lucita stammered, "Your orders . . . your superiors . . . they would be angry with you."

Malik's lips curled into a humorless smile. "What difference would that make to you? Tell me why you don't want me to shoot him. The real reason."

"It would be wrong. . . ."

"The real reason," Malik repeated.

Lucita knew that the time for evasion and pretense was over. "I don't want him to be killed," she said. "I love him."

Malik's smile turned cold. "All the more reason."

"If you kill him," Lucita said, "you might as well kill me too."

"Now you're speaking like a romantic child."

She reached out and grabbed at his sleeve, forcing him to stop. The two officers behind them stopped also, and even drifted back away from them a few paces.

"I mean it," Lucita said firmly. "If you kill him, you kill me also. You remember what Teresa did to herself. I can do that, too."

He stared at her, and Lucita could see in his ice-blue eyes the same cold, probing calculations that she had seen in her father.

"You wouldn't. . . ."

"I would rather damn my soul to hell forever than live with a man who had murdered my love."

For an instant Lucita thought she saw a flicker of warmth in Malik's eyes, a hint of honest emotion, a slight momentary dropping of his guard. But it was only for an instant. His eyes glittered hard as diamonds as he asked:

334

"If I don't kill him . . . if I allow him to face trial in Moscow . . ."

"You must let him escape," she said.

He almost laughed. "To where? He is a doomed man, Lucita. Even if I could allow him to escape, where could he hide? There is no place on Earth or in space that could harbor him."

Lucita knew he was speaking the truth. She herself could not evade this single Russian male. Dan Randolph could never escape the power of the entire Soviet government. He is a doomed man. Vasily is speaking truly now. Dan Randolph will die.

She drew in a shuddering breath, then said slowly, "If he must die, then let it be done legally, and not by your hand."

"And you? . . ."

"If you do not kill him yourself," Lucita heard herself saying, "then I will go through with our wedding. I will become your wife."

"And you will stop this talk of suicide?"

"Yes," Lucita murmured. "I will live my life with you." But her mind was racing wildly as she said the words. Perhaps Dan can escape somewhere, somehow. Perhaps my father can intervene and they won't kill him. Perhaps they'll exile him, send him to the mines on the Moon. That would be better than killing him.

"You will be my willing and loving wife?" Malik demanded.

"Yes," Lucita replied, so low that she could barely hear her own surrender. "Your loving wife."

Chapter
◆ ◆ THIRTY-FIVE ◆ ◆

Dan heard footsteps. The bare plastic-sheeted floor of the corridor outside his makeshift cell clicked with the sound of several pairs of boots. He scrambled to his feet.

Malik's coming! He knew that the Russian was among the men approaching. With a grim smile, he waited.

A shock jolted his guts when he saw Lucita walking beside the Russian. What's she doing here? Dressed in jeans, like a woman who was prepared to spend some time in zero gravity. With Malik. She's come up here with him!

Malik looked pleased with himself. Smiling handsomely in his tan uniform, the Russian had every reason to be pleased. He had won, Dan knew. He had beaten Dan and now was enjoying the fruits of his victory. Enjoy it all you can, you murdering sonofabitch, Dan growled silently. In a couple of minutes you're going to be dead.

Malik saw the expression on Dan Randolph's face and knew instantly that the American was going to force them to shoot him. Like a wolf caught in a trap, he will snarl and fight until we have no choice but to kill him. Good! thought the Russian. Let the Yankee attack me. Ostrovsky and the lieutenant will riddle his body while I save Lucita from harm. Then she can't blame me for his death.

Malik brought their little procession to a halt in front of Randolph's cage. He already had the look of a trapped beast about him: unshaved, wild-eyed, as tense as a coiled steel spring.

"Well, Mr. Randolph," he said in English. "We meet again."

Dan looked them over carefully. Damned clever of the bastard to bring Lucita along. If I do anything to start them shooting, she might get hurt.

"My men," Dan said to Malik. "The men who were out at the freighter . . ."

"The pirate crew you sent to steal our ore shipment?" Malik's grin bared his teeth. "I'm afraid they were all killed in the battle."

"Battle? They didn't have any weapons! How could there be a battle?"

Malik shrugged. "They were all killed. Every last one of them."

Dan was not surprised at the news. But the molten surge of fury that erupted inside him was a surprise. He fought to control it. Wait until they unlock the door, he told himself. Knock Lucita out of the way and then break that smiling sonofabitch's neck.

"You have done us a very great favor, you know," Malik went on, making no move to take Dan out of the cell. "Within a week the Soviet Union will control every one of the Third World space facilities. We intend to root out all of your pirates, every last one of them."

"And shoot them down in cold blood," Dan said.

"Oh, no. We will do everything strictly according to international law. There will be trials in Moscow, with television coverage. The whole world will see Soviet justice in action." Malik motioned for the young lieutenant to unlock the cage door. "I have even arranged for your trial to be delayed until after my wedding, so that Lucita and I can sit in the front row and watch."

The lieutenant fished a plastic card from his tunic pocket and came up to the door. Dan tensed, waiting to spring at Malik the instant the lock clicked.

"We will be married the first Sunday in December," Malik said, sliding his arm around Lucita's slim shoulders. "Isn't that right, my darling?"

The lieutenant slid the card into the electronic lock's slot. Nothing happened. He withdrew it, squinted at it, then turned it around and tried again.

Lucita looked from Malik's gloating face to Dan's. Her lovely face looked as lost and forlorn as a waif's. Dan heard the lock click open, but something in Lucita's eyes held him riveted where he stood. She was trying to tell him something, trying to warn him.

"We will be married," she replied to Malik in Spanish, while still fixing her gaze on Dan, "only if my beloved *Yanqui* has not been murdered by you or your soldiers."

Dan reached out and pushed the wire mesh door open. It swung easily. The lieutenant backed out of its way. The major was standing several paces to the left. Both were armed with pistols, holstered at their hips. As was Malik.

Dan took a step out of the cage, every nerve hyperalert, every muscle tensed for action, like a jaguar released after hours in captivity. Lucita moved slightly, barely a step, but she placed herself between the smiling, tormenting, baiting Russian and Dan himself.

He finally understood. Malik wants me to attack him. He's trying his damnedest to make me go for his throat. Then his aides can shoot me down and make an end of it. Lucita's trying to keep me out of the trap.

"Why are you here?" he asked her in Spanish.

She knew that Malik understood the language, but the other two officers probably did not. "I came to save your life."

Dan shook his head. "It's too late for that."

"Far too late," Malik broke in. Looking disappointed, he gestured down the passageway from which they had come.

338

"A shuttle is waiting to take you to Moscow. We have no time to lose."

Dan shrugged, let his muscles relax, even allowed his head to droop slightly. He walked between Lucita and Malik, with the two other Russians behind.

"I'll be a worldwide television star, eh?" He tried to make himself laugh. "Will I get a chance to tell my side of the story, or will I be so buzzed out on drugs that I'll say whatever the prosecutors want me to say?"

Tight-lipped, Malik replied, "You will get a fair trial."

"Fair? I want a *great* trial!"

"It will be difficult to keep world opinion from demanding your immediate execution," Malik said, "once the asteroid strikes."

"The aster—" Dan felt his breath catch in his throat. He stopped in his tracks and whirled on Malik. "What the hell have you done?"

Out of the corner of his eye, Dan could see the two officers reaching for their pistols. Lucita was behind him, Malik's smugly grinning face only a few inches away.

"Your asteroid, Mr. Randolph. It is about to undergo a change in course."

"That can't happen. . . ."

"But it will happen," Malik said. "I guarantee it. Your asteroid is going to strike somewhere in the state of Nebraska. Between the cities of Omaha and Lincoln, I am told."

Dan's fists clenched.

"The asteroid will strike just a day or so before your trial begins," Malik added. "The explosion will destroy everything for at least a hundred miles around the impact site, and leave a crater like the one in Arizona. It will also destroy any shred of sympathy the Americans or anyone else might have for you."

Dan could feel Lucita's hand on his sleeve, but he yanked free of her. Malik took an involuntary half step backward, away from him.

339

"Attention!" crackled a voice from the intercom loudspeakers, set up in the ceiling of the passageway, alongside the fluorescent light tubes. "Attention! Mr. Dan Randolph, your attention, please!"

It wasn't until he saw the puzzled expression on Malik's face that Dan realized the voice was speaking in Japanese.

"This is Nobo, Mr. Randolph. We have taken control of the entire area between the visitors lounge and the communications center, including the Russian shuttle that is docked to the visitors lounge emergency hatch."

Malik pulled the pistol from his holster. "Who is that? What is he saying?"

"Stay put!" Dan shouted in Japanese. "Hold tight until further orders."

Malik pointed the gun into Dan's face. "What did you say? Tell me or—"

Without even thinking about it, Dan grabbed the Russian's wrist, twisted the gun out of his hand and swung Malik around to shield him from the guns of the other two men.

"Get behind me!" he commanded Lucita. Holding Malik's pistol to the Russian's temple as he twisted Malik's arm in a hard hammerlock, he shouted to the other two in English "Put your guns down and your hands on top of your heads or I'll blow his damned brains out!"

They stood frozen, uncertain, guns held tightly in their outstretched hands.

Dan cocked the pistol and rammed its muzzle against Malik's ear. "Drop them! *Now!*"

Ostrovsky and the lieutenant let the guns slip from their fingers. They clunked against the floor.

Dan backed toward the hatch that he knew was only a few dozen feet away. Every passageway and corridor in the station was studded with airtight hatches which would close automatically in case of a drop in air pressure in one section of the station.

"You can't get away," Malik muttered, grunting as Dan dragged him by his twisted arm. "My men control the entire station and more are on their way."

Dan snapped, "Save your breath. It might be your last."

With Lucita slightly behind him and the two disarmed Russians standing immobile, hands atop their heads, Dan pulled Malik across the metal strip that marked the hatchway.

"Lucita, see the panel on the wall to your left? Press the red button."

She did, and immediately a hooting horn began to wail. Dan pushed Malik away from him as the heavy metal hatch slid swiftly shut, clanging into place between him and the staggering Russian.

He reached for Lucita's wrist with his free hand. "Come on! We don't have a second to lose!"

Ostrovsky and the lieutenant scooped up their pistols and rushed to Malik's side.

"He's taken the bait after all," Malik said with a smile. To Ostrovsky, the smile looked somewhat forced.

They heard Randolph's voice gabbling over the station intercom in Japanese.

"What is he saying?" Ostrovsky wondered aloud.

Malik seemed fully in command of himself. "It doesn't matter. We control the station and there is no place he can hide—for long. Get this blasted hatch open, quickly."

Ostrovsky bent over the control panel built into the wall beside the hatch. He began tapping on the various buttons.

To the lieutenant, Malik said, "You will persuade one of the station's personnel to translate this Japanese talk for us."

"Yessir!"

The hatch slid back, revealing an empty passageway.

"Major Ostrovsky, you will assemble a search party of ten men and go hunting for Randolph."

"He is armed," the major said, "and will undoubtedly use your fiancée as a hostage."

"Undoubtedly," Malik agreed. "But hostage or not, I want him found and taken. Dead or alive."

"We have taken a total of eight soldiers," Nobuhiko said. In the small display screen of the telephone, he looked both pleased and anxious. "They must have at least fifty more in the station."

Dan R̶̶̶olph nodded grimly at him. "And from what Malik said, reinforcements are on the way."

"What should we do?"

Dan was standing in the equipment bay of the station's lunar section. When *Nueva Venezuela* had first been built, this wheel was designed to rotate at a speed that exactly duplicated the gentle tug of the Moon's gravity, so that personnel could adapt themselves to walking, lifting, pouring liquids, working and living at one-sixth the weight they experienced on Earth. But even before the station's construction was finished, the Soviets had established their exclusive domination of the Moon, and the lunar wheel became just another area in which to store equipment. Dan thought of it as a large garage or attic, dimly lit, stuffed with dusty old relics and long-forgotten crates of junk.

It was a good place to hide in, and now he and Lucita were there in the shadowy netherworld where an experienced man could jump twenty feet high and turn half a dozen somersaults before touching his feet lightly to the floor again.

Thinking out loud while Nobo watched, Dan said, "We've got several hundred Astro employees and visitors aboard the station, but they're noncombatants. They'd just get themselves hurt if they tried to help us."

"They have been ordered by the Russians to stay in their quarters."

"Yeah, I know. But pretty soon now Malik's going to hit on the idea of dragging them out and using them as hostages. If we don't surrender, he'll start shooting them, either one at a time or in bunches."

"He wouldn't dare!"

"Wouldn't he?"

"Those people are citizens of many different countries," Nobo said, "Venezuela, the United States, Japan . . ."

"How many fighters do you actually have?" Dan asked.

"Eleven, including myself."

342

"And I make it an even dozen. Against at least fifty armed Russian soldiers."

"What about the security personnel aboard the station? Surely they—"

Dan waved him to silence. "They're guards, not soldiers. They'd be cut down in minutes."

"Then I don't see what we can do."

"I do," Dan said. "First, get word to your father. Tell him to alert all the other space leaders that the Russians intend to seize their stations within the next few days. Second, tell him that there's a Russian spacecraft on its way to our asteroid. They intend to alter its course and have it strike the United States."

Nobo flinched with shock. "Madness!" he blurted.

"That spacecraft's got to be stopped," Dan said. "I don't know how, but it's got to be stopped."

"Yes. Of course."

"Third, get yourself and everybody there with you, including your Russian prisoners, into that shuttle and fly it back to Caracas. . . ."

"And leave you here?"

Dan scratched at his stubbly jaw. "You're not going to be able to do battle with fifty trained soldiers. Get the hell out while the getting's good. Alert the others. Tell them what's going on here. Get the word out! We'll hold on here as long as we can."

Chapter
♦ ♦ THIRTY-SIX ♦ ♦

"But what will you do?" Nobo asked.

Glancing at Lucita, standing beside him utterly calm, her fate entirely in his hands, Dan asked in reply, "Have they taken the factory yet?"

"No, I don't believe they have even tried."

"Good. We'll go there. It's more easily defended."

"The Soviets could destroy it with their antimissile lasers."

"Not while I've got Malik's fiancée with me."

Nodding, Nobo said, "Then I will go there, too."

"Get yourself home. That's an order."

Before Nobuhiko could reply, Dan clicked off the phone connection and turned to Lucita.

"Ever used a jetpack before?"

She shook her head.

With a grin, he said, "You're in for a thrill."

He led her down to one of the emergency airlocks and helped her climb into a Day-Glo orange pressure suit. It hung on a wall rack next to a row of equipment lockers like a headless empty suit of armor, the bulky jetpack and life support tanks already fastened to its back. Lucita virtually

344

disappeared inside the suit; it swallowed her right up to the chin. Dan laughed at the sight of her peering out of it like a child wearing a grownup's outfit.

"Are your hands inside the gloves?" he asked. "Can you move your fingers?"

He saw that the fingers of the gloves wriggled.

"Good."

"But my feet are not inside the boots, I think," Lucita said.

"That's not important."

He fitted the helmet over her head as she watched, silent and wide-eyed. Then he checked out all the suit's seals and connections. The maintenance label on its left leg said it had gone through a complete inspection only a week earlier. Still, Dan took the time to check everything thoroughly.

There are bold astronauts and old astronauts, he repeated to himself as he worked, trying to forget that the Russians were ransacking the station to find them. No sense doing them the favor of killing ourselves.

He was less thorough with his own suit, satisfied to rely on the inspection tag. From the equipment lockers he took a tether and clipped it from a ring on the waist of his suit to a similar ring on Lucita's.

"Whither I goest, so goest thou," he said, his voice sounding muffled inside the helmet.

He saw her nod and heard in his earphones, "Won't they shoot at us, once we are outside the station?"

"If they see us, they might. But they won't know which one of us is me, and which is you."

"Vasily would take that risk."

Dan looked at her. She was serious, but not afraid.

"Would you rather go back to him? . . ."

"Never! I want to be with you."

"Even though we might both be killed?"

"I would rather die with you, my *Yanqui*, than live with him."

Dan felt a wave of blazing, brilliant warmth surge through him. His knees felt suddenly weak. His spine tingled.

Clumsily, inside the bulky space suit, he reached out for Lucita and pulled her close. They could not kiss; the helmets made it impossible. But Dan held her for a long moment.

"I love you, Lucita," he said.

"And I love you, Daniel."

Suddenly the ludicrousness of it struck Dan. He laughed aloud. "We must look like a pair of abominable snowmen trying to make love."

She laughed too. "Do they make space suits big enough for two?"

"I'll have one built," he said, "just as soon as we . . ." The laughter died on his lips as he remembered where they were and what they were facing.

But Lucita seemed totally unafraid. "I am ready to go with you."

With a nod, Dan opened another equipment locker and pulled out something that looked almost like an old-fashioned blunderbuss: a long slim rod with a flared nozzle at one end. The rod was taller than he was, even in his helmet and suit. Handgrips studded the upper half of its length, and there was a cluster of small cylinders fastened to the end near the nozzle.

"They call this a broomstick," he told Lucita as he tapped the control pad on the wall next to the airlock hatch with his free hand. "We'll ride on it faster than the Wicked Witch of the West."

They stepped into the metal-walled airlock, Lucita clumping clumsily in boots that were far too large for her. Dan cycled the lock; the inner hatch closed, the air was pumped out and then the outer hatch slid open. They were not facing the Earth at the moment. All Dan could see were the unblinking pinpoint lights of the stars: the distant eyes of heaven watching him.

He heard Lucita gasp.

"Don't be afraid," he said, reaching for her gloved hand.

"I'm not afraid," she replied. "It is so beautiful! It takes my breath away."

He smiled inside his helmet and they stepped out into nothingness. Like a swimmer, Dan kicked away from the top of the hatch, the broomstick in one hand and Lucita in the other. He helped her to get a firm grip on the broomstick, then flicked open the safety catch that protected against accidental ignition of the rocket motor at its far end.

Using the jetpack thrusters to maneuver, Dan turned himself and Lucita until they were facing the factory. Off in the distance it hung like a floating scrap heap, all angles and projections.

"To the Emerald City," he muttered, and thumbed the ignition button. The rocket flared soundlessly and they were suddenly hurtling toward the space factory.

Malik crouched behind a flimsy partition, mentally ticking off ten seconds. The blast came at nine, loud and sharp as an unexpected clap of thunder.

He got to his feet as twenty armed soldiers rushed, yelling, into the smoke where the doors to the visitors lounge had been blown apart.

Gripping a machine pistol firmly in his right hand, Malik followed the soldiers. Their shouts died quickly. Waving at the lingering smoke as he entered the lounge, Malik saw that it was empty.

"They've gone!" said a beefy-faced sergeant.

"Check the airlock," Malik ordered.

Several of the soldiers began to pull grenades from their belts.

"No explosives!" Malik roared. "If the outer hatch is open to space, we'd all be killed in a flash."

Ostrovsky came pounding up behind him, red-faced and perspiring. "Sir! Word from the communications center . . . was empty when we stormed it." His voice tailed off as he saw that the lounge was also empty.

"Has anyone had the sense to check outside and see if our shuttle is still linked to this airlock?" Malik put acid into his

voice. He knew he had been outsmarted. The devils ha
stolen his own ship and escaped.

Ostrovsky's tongue flicked across his lips before he re
plied, hesitatingly, "I'll . . . I'll check on that, sir."

Malik handed him the machine pistol with an angry snor
"They've slipped out of our fingers. And probably Randolp
was with them."

"I don't see how—"

"You were going to check on where that shuttle might be
weren't you, Major?"

"Yessir! Immediately, sir!" Ostrovsky scuttled away.

He's gone, Malik realized. I don't know how he did it, bu
he's escaped. And taken Lucita with him. Burning wit
anger, he strode down the corridor toward the communica
tions center. Halfway there, he saw Ostrovsky racing towar
him, still red in the face and sweaty, but looking mor
optimistic.

"Sir! The Yankee capitalist is at the factory. We hav
picked up his communications transmissions. He is trying
contact the President of the United States."

Jane Scanwell was aboard Air Force One when the me
sage came through to her. Dan Randolph. Urgent. From th
factory at *Nueva Venezuela*. Life and death.

The President was returning to Washington after a drear
depressing campaign swing through the West. No matt
where she went, no matter how carefully her aides manip
lated the crowds, no matter how tightly her security peop
controlled her route, she still saw the gaunt, empty-eye
specter of hopelessness among the people. Hordes of unem
ployed. Whole cities decaying. Tent cities of hungry fam
lies, ringed by barbed wire and hard-eyed, helmeted speci
security police.

There were no demonstrations against her. No angry voic
interrupted her optimistic speeches. She saw no rage or vi
lence in the streets when her motorcade drove through th
barren, grimy cities. She almost wished she had. The hea

had been taken out of these people. Even in Salt Lake City, her own spiritual home, the people were weighted down with a sullen, unremitting despair.

There was no doubt of her reelection. The opposition was scattered and weak. The people had no faith in their promises. Nor in mine, Jane knew. I'll win because they have no other real choice. And if I want to ram through a constitutional amendment that will allow me to run again in four years, they'll let me do that, too. But do I want to? Do I have to?

Her secretary interrupted her bleak ruminations by standing before her. He was a frail, almost effeminate young man who seemed to have an affinity for self-abasement.

Jane looked up into his soft, worried face. "What is it?"

"Mr. Randolph is still trying to reach you, ma'am. He is calling from—"

"I know where he's calling from."

"But he says that the United States is being threatened by an attack. Something about a strike in the Midwest, worse than a nuclear missile."

Frowning, Jane snapped, "I told you to have his call channeled through State. If Dan Randolph has anything to say to me, it can go through normal channels."

"Yes, ma'am. But they—State, that is—they seem to feel you ought to talk to him."

Startled, annoyed, Jane swiveled her commodious chair to the curving console built into the plane's bulkhead. Through the window above it she could see the brilliant fleecy white of clouds lit by the sun. Down below, on the ground, she knew that the weather was wet and gray and gloomy. But up here it was a beautiful, sunny, blue-skied afternoon.

"Put him on," she snapped. When Dan Randolph's face appeared on the display screen, she smiled in spite of herself. Until she saw that he was unshaven, grim-faced. And there was a very sultry looking Latin girl standing behind him.

Lucita knew that she was standing upright, even though her stomach was telling her otherwise. She stood behind

Dan, who was seated in front of a small display screen in the factory's communications center. It was a crowded, narrow little room, barely as wide as an aisle, with electronics consoles lining the walls and hardly enough space in between for a few small plastic wheeled chairs. Even though Dan had ordered all the technicians out of the room, it still felt stifling and hot to Lucita. Her insides felt as if she were falling; she knew that was because the entire factory was in zero gravity and she was weightless. She forced herself to control the nausea that bubbled uneasily within her. She gripped the back of Dan's chair tightly and tried to press her slippered feet onto the Velcro surface of the floor's carpeting. Still, her palms were sweaty and her stomach fluttered.

"That's as much as I know," Dan was saying to the American President. "Have your people check with Zach Freiberg at my office in Caracas. He's been tracking the rock since we first went out after it."

Lucita studied the older woman's face. She was just as beautiful as all the photographs had shown her to be, but it was the remote, imperious beauty of a woman who allowed her head to rule her heart. And in the little screen of the factory's communications center, the President's cold green eyes flashed with anger, anger that was directed not at the Russians, but at Dan.

"I told you it would cause trouble," *La Presidenta* stormed. "I warned you against doing it."

Dan seemed angry too, but his temper was more from exasperation than hatred.

"Jane, it's done and those bastards are going to shoot that rock into the middle of the country just as hard as they can. But you still have time to do something about it."

"Do something? Do what? You've destroyed us, Dan. You've destroyed everything!"

"Wake up, dammit!" Dan snapped. "You still have troops, don't you? I have rockets. I can put a dozen shuttles down at airfields in the States. You can load them with troops and

350

send them off to catch the Soviet spacecraft. You can overtake them, if you act fast enough."

"And they'll bomb us with their missiles instead," the President said.

"Not if you get the other nations to act with you. Venezuela, Japan, China, for Chrissake! The Africans, India—they'll all act together on this, if you take the lead. They're all threatened."

"You've rigged this, Dan Randolph!" she accused. "It's all your fault!"

"Even if I did, what difference does that make now?" Dan argued. "You've got to act, Jane. You've *got* to!"

The arm and shoulder of a man appeared to one side of the President, leaning over her. She looked up. Lucita heard swift, muttered words. As the two of them talked and Dan sat tensely, hands gripping the edge of the communications desk, Lucita pondered what she was seeing and hearing.

La Presidenta loves Dan, she realized. She could not be so angry and stubborn with him if she did not. She loves him, but knows that she cannot bend him to her will. And Dan, does he still love her? He did once, that is clear. Is it true that a man can love more than one woman at the same time? Lucita wondered.

She knew many men who claimed to love both their wives and their mistresses. But Dan and *La Presidenta* were different. She would have to be the dominant one; he the kept man. He would have none of that, Lucita knew. But did he still love her, nevertheless?

Dan was leaning forward in the flimsy plastic chair, straining to hear what was being said by the President and her aide.

Jane Scanwell finally turned her face toward him again. "I've called a meeting of the Cabinet to convene as soon as I land in Washington," she said, her face grim, bleak. "And I've instructed the Secretary of State to request an emergency meeting of the General Assembly in Geneva. . . ."

"The United Nations?" Dan snorted.

"I know what you think of the UN, but it's got to be done."

"And military measures? Shall I send shuttles to—"

"No!" the President snapped. "We are not going to turn this into a military confrontation between the United States and the Soviet Union. Those days are gone."

He smiled wanly. "In that case, good-bye, Jane. I'll be dead within a few hours, and so will everybody here."

"Not if you surrender."

"They won't take any prisoners. Any more than they took prisoners among the unarmed men who were hijacking the ore freighter."

The President's frown deepened. "Dan, I can put a call through to Moscow . . ."

The picture on the phone's small screen suddenly wavered and broke up into a wild scramble of jagged colored lines. The voice disappeared into a harsh grating hiss of static.

Dan pushed several buttons on the console's keypad, to no avail. He looked up at Lucita.

"They're jamming all the frequencies. We're cut off from the ground."

Lucita placed a hand on his shoulder. "Then he knows we are here."

Dan nodded. "They'll be coming here for us."

Chapter
◆ ◆ THIRTY-SEVEN ◆ ◆

Malik was already in a pressure suit when the message came through from Moscow. Frowning, he carried his helmet under his arm to the spartan room that had been Dan Randolph's personal quarters aboard *Nueva Venezuela* and had the communications technicians feed the call to the phone there.

It was the General Secretary himself, his face so gray and waxy that Malik feared he was about to suffer another stroke.

Unable to sit comfortably inside the bulky space suit, Malik tilted the display screen upward and bent as far as he could to face his country's leader.

"What is happening up there, Vasily Maximovich?" asked the General Chairman.

"Sir, we have destroyed the band of pirates who were attempting to steal our ore freighter, and we have taken control of the Venezuelan space station, all according to plan."

The General Secretary did not look pleased. "And the Yankee capitalist, this man Randolph?"

"He has fled to the factory complex, a few kilometers

from this station. I was just about to lead my troops there when your call came."

"Is it true that some of the capitalists managed to escape from the space station in one of our own ships?"

Malik felt his jaws clench. His enemies had obviously placed an informer among the troops here. Perhaps Ostrovsky. More likely one of the junior officers.

"A few of them did get away, after illegally stealing one of our shuttles, yes, sir, that is true. But they are of small consequence. Once we take Randolph, the others will fall into our hands quickly enough."

With a shake of his head, the General Secretary replied, "We are receiving messages from many governments, comrade. Angry messages. Demands, even." The older man's eyes flicked downward and Malik heard the rustle of papers. "Japan, Zaire, Angola, India, Indonesia, Britain, Canada . . . even the Americans have had the temerity to demand that we abandon our occupation of *Nueva Venezuela*."

"But the government of Venezuela has not objected, has it?" Malik countered. "As long as they do not object, we are well within our rights—"

The General Chairman waved his good hand to silence him. "The Americans claim that we have altered the course of this asteroid, and that we are going to attack them with it. They have called for an emergency session of the United Nations' General Assembly."

"Our men have not reached the asteroid yet."

The General Chairman stared at Malik wordlessly.

"Sir, our plan is succeeding. In an hour or less we will have the capitalist Randolph in our hands. The protests from these other nations can be dealt with from a position of strength."

"I agree, Vasily Maximovich. The business of the asteroid bothers me, but I agree that we must put an absolute and final end to the pirates. We must occupy all the so-called Third World space facilities and make certain that they can never again be used as bases for piracy."

354

"That is our plan, sir."

"If necessary, Vasily Maximovich, I am prepared to use our antimissile lasers to destroy those facilities."

Malik felt a pang of alarm. "That won't be necessary, sir!"

"But if it becomes necessary, my young comrade, I will authorize it."

"Our plan is to occupy and utilize the space facilities, not to destroy them."

"I know, I know. But better to destroy them than to allow these thieving marauders to continue their depredations."

A vision of the space factory flashed through Malik's mind. He saw the powerful deadly beams of antimissile lasers lashing out from Soviet satellites, slicing through the factory, burning through its flimsy metal walls, exploding the very air inside the modules where people lived and worked, where Lucita stood beside the Yankee capitalist. He saw her dying, burning, exploding, her skin bursting in a shower of blood.

"It will not be necessary, I assure you, Comrade Secretary. Not necessary at all."

The room was filled with smoke and nervous, frightened men. Rafael Hernandez surveyed them carefully, forcing himself to maintain at least the outward appearance of calm in the midst of the stormy emotions raging about him. A dozen men, the leaders of Venezuela, were arguing at the tops of their voices.

They are terrified, Hernandez realized, watching them gesticulating wildly and pacing across the big, formal office of the president of Venezuela. It was an ornately decorated room: heavy, stiff brocade curtains at the windows, an elaborate chandelier dripping crystal from the paneled ceiling, portraits of heroes and statesmen lining the walls. But the frightened dozen men took no notice of the trappings of rank. The Russian bear was growling at them, and they were bewildered and afraid. It was well past midnight; they had been storming at each other for more than an hour, and still no one could agree on how to react to the Soviet seizure of *Nueva Venezuela*.

The President, puffing fitfully on a Havana cigar, finally rapped his knuckles on the top of his desk.

"Gentlemen!" he called out loudly. "Arguments and recriminations are of no use now. We must decide on a course of action."

Hernandez eyed the President through the haze of smoke from his own cigarette. A small man, soft and overweight. He enjoyed the good life that Hernandez had made possible for him. His face was bland and bloated. The man was weak, he always had been weak, and he always tried to cover up his weakness by demanding some form of action.

"What action can we take?" shouted the Minister of Trade. "The Russians have troops up there. Soldiers armed with guns!"

"We have troops," said the Defense Minister. "And we have rockets to carry them to *Nueva Venezuela*, too, don't we, Rafael?"

Hernandez took the ivory cigarette holder from his lips before replying, "The Soviets might shoot down our rockets with the lasers they have in their satellites."

"They wouldn't dare! That would be an act of war!"

Trying to keep himself from sneering at the former general, Hernandez said, "Would we declare war on the Soviet Union?"

The Defense Minister turned toward the President, who still stood behind his huge, curved desk.

"That is out of the question," the President said, shaking his head hard enough to make his jowls quiver. "Out of the question."

"Then what can we do?"

"We can send Moscow a formal protest," said the Foreign Minister, "and ask for an emergency session of the General Assembly to consider this matter. After all, that is Venezuelan national territory they have invaded. It is just the same as if they had landed an army on our own soil."

"We must not allow our emotions to blind us to the facts," Hernandez countered. "The Soviets are *not* invading our country. They are searching the space station for the pirates who have been stealing their ore shipments."

"Why did they pick *Nueva Venezuela*?" demanded the Minister of Trade. "Why not attack the Indian space station, or one of the Japanese?"

"Because they suspect the American, Randolph, to be the leader of the pirates," Hernandez said.

"How could they believe that?"

"Because it is true."

"Nonsense! Impossible! Why would the Yankee billionaire stoop to such a thing?"

The others began to chime in and the room filled with a dozen separate clamoring voices once more. The President waved his hands and banged on the desktop again, in vain. But then the phone on his desk buzzed softly, and every voice instantly went quiet.

In the sudden stillness, the President picked up the handpiece: "Yes?"

The others stared at him, trying to decipher what he was hearing from the expression on his face.

"Very well," said the President. "Send him in."

Hernandez turned to the leather-covered door. It was swung open by a tall, stern-faced military policeman in a polished steel helmet and spotless uniform. He held the door wide, and a small, wiry Japanese dressed in baggy blue coveralls stepped into the office. He was young, but his face looked haggard, strained. Still, there was a crackle of energy about him, an air of determined purposefulness.

He walked quickly across the smoke-filled room to the President's desk. There he bowed from the waist, arms clamped to his sides.

"I am Nobuhiko Yamagata, Señor Presidente. I thank you most humbly for granting me this opportunity to speak with you."

Hernandez was surprised at the quality of the man's Spanish.

"Señor Yamagata," responded the President, "I understand that you were aboard *Nueva Venezuela* when the Soviet troops seized it, and that you captured one of the Russian shuttles and rescued several of our citizens."

Nobo dipped his head in a brief bow of acknowledgment. "I did not act alone. I was helped by a team of my countrymen."

"You stole a Russian ship?" gasped the Minister of Trade.

"And captured eight Soviet soldiers. They are in custody at the Astro launching center." Nobo reached inside his coveralls and pulled out a Russian machine pistol. A murmur of shocked surprise wafted through the room. He placed the gun carefully on the President's desk; it looked grim and deadly.

"We are trying to decide what must be done," the President said, almost in a whisper.

"The Russians will kill all those whom they believe oppose them. They have already killed a dozen unarmed astronauts, several of whom were native citizens of Venezuela."

"What?"

"My duty," Nobo went on, ignoring their frightened, questioning faces, "is to return to *Nueva Venezuela* and try to help rescue the others from the Soviet troops."

"We have prohibited all space launchings," Hernandez said.

"Precisely why I am here," Nobo countered. "That prohibition must be lifted, or many more citizens of Venezuela and other countries will be slaughtered by the Russians."

"I find that difficult to accept," said Hernandez.

The young Japanese turned to face him directly. "Sir, your daughter is there. Her life is in as much danger as the life of Dan Randolph."

Hernandez felt his knees buckle. "My . . . Lucita?"

"Yes," said Nobuhiko. "If we do not act swiftly, she will be killed along with all the others."

Chapter
♦ ♦ THIRTY-EIGHT ♦ ♦

Zachary Freiberg's face looked drawn and grim in the small screen. He's aged since he's come to Astro, Dan thought. Then, correcting himself, No, he's matured.

The scientist was in his office in Caracas. Dan was still at the communications console in the space factory, his legs unconsciously wrapped around the pedestal of his chair to keep him anchored in the zero gravity. The Russians were jamming all radio frequencies, but Dan could talk to his Astro headquarters by laser, linked by a pencil-thin beam of light as long as the factory was above Caracas' horizon.

"They're on a high-energy burn," Freiberg was saying. "It'll be a week before they reach the asteroid."

"They've got to be stopped," Dan insisted.

"How, for God's sake?" Freiberg snapped. "The Venezuelan government has forbidden all launches. Rumors are flying around here that if we try to launch anyway, the goddamned Russians will shoot us down with the lasers from their antimissile satellites."

Dan glanced at the clock digits ticking off in the lower

right corner of the screen. Only a few more seconds before the factory's orbit carried it out of range of Caracas.

"Even if we could launch a team after them," Freiberg was saying, "they'd have to go at such high gees that they'd all have hernias or hemorrhoids by the time they caught up with the Russians."

"You've got to do *something*, Zach. It's up to you. I'm depending on you. The whole country's depending on you. That fucking piece of rock is going to wipe out a helluva lot of the Middle West. Millions could be killed."

"I know. The computer projections—"

"Then do something! Get on the horn with President Scanwell and make her see that she's got to act!"

"I'll try," Freiberg promised. "I'll try my best."

The picture in the display screen suddenly wavered wildly, then broke up. The screen went blank.

Dan leaned back in his seat, exhausted, drained physically and emotionally. In the faint reflection of the darkened display screen he saw his own face: haggard, hollow-eyed, unshaved, his hair matted and tangled. He suddenly realized that Lucita was gone; he was alone in the cramped little cubicle of the communications center. Before he could think of what to do, the door swung open and she entered, stepping carefully in her Velcro slippers, carrying a small tray laden with plastic containers.

"I could not find much in the galley," she said. "Only some soup and something that was labeled soyburgers, whatever they are."

He smiled weakly at her. "I don't feel hungry. . . ."

"You will eat," Lucita said, fastening the tray onto the console desktop in front of him. "To keep up your strength you must eat."

He took the cover off a plastic bowl: the hot soup hung in a perfect weightless sphere, surrounded by a faint mist of steam. The aroma made Dan suddenly ravenous. He jammed the cover back onto the bowl and put its spout to his lips. The soup felt burning hot and invigorating.

For several minutes he ate and drank, saying nothing. Finally:

"I've done everything I can," he said to Lucita.

She nodded.

"There's only one other thing I can think of," he added.

"What is that?"

"We can put you back into a suit and send you back to *Nueva Venezuela*. Malik doesn't want to hurt you. You could get out of this."

"Not without you," Lucita said.

"I could surrender to him," Dan pointed out. "He won't kill me. He'd rather put me on trial in Moscow, put on a big show." He made himself grin at her. "It would be a big help to have you testify in my defense. You could be my character witness and tell them all what a great guy I am."

She did not smile back. "He will kill you as soon as he can."

Before Dan could say anything more, someone tapped at the door.

"What is it?" Dan called out.

The door opened wide enough for a man to stick his head in. It was Kaktins, the scarecrow-lean Latvian with the wild hair. His long, lantern-jawed face was somber.

"They are coming," Kaktins reported. "The shuttle that was at the loading dock has disconnected and is coasting this way."

Dan pushed himself to his feet, automatically letting his slippers grip the Velcro carpeting. "It's filled with their troops, no doubt."

"No doubt," Kaktins agreed.

With Lucita trailing behind him, Dan trudged down the long tubular corridor that led to the factory's main airlock.

"They must have left some troops aboard the station," he mused aloud, "to keep it in their grip."

Kaktins nodded vigorously enough to make his whole body bounce weightlessly. "Can't be more than twenty soldiers coming over here. Thirty, maybe."

"And how many men do we have?"

"Sixty-three technicians and machine operators in factory," said Kaktins. "Nineteen are women. Not counting you and the lady."

Dan turned slightly toward Lucita. In the flat shadowless lighting of the metal-walled tunnel she no longer looked like an elfin little waif. She was a woman, Dan realized, as brave and determined as any woman who chose to stand beside her man in the hour of mortal danger. Unsmiling, her dark eyes searching his, she seemed totally unafraid of whatever fate was approaching. And totally beautiful, desirable, a woman worth fighting for, worth risking everything for.

"We have laser cutting tools," Kaktins was saying. "Maybe they are clumsy to handle, but they could slice a man in half—like that." He snapped his fingers.

"And slice through the factory's walls while we're at it," Dan countered.

"We could get them when they come in airlock."

"Yeah, we could kill some Russian kids in soldier suits. They'd just send more of them up here. In the end, we'd get every one of us killed."

"They kill us all anyway," Kaktins said. "You think they let me go free?"

"We're not going to fight them," Dan said firmly.

"But—"

"Not with lasers or pistols. Not the way they expect."

"What do you mean?"

Without taking his eyes off Lucita, Dan told the Latvian, "We'll try a strategy the Russians have used on invaders since the time of the Mongols. I don't know if it'll work, but it's the only chance we have."

Willem Quistigaard took a deep breath of clean Alpine air as he stood at the top of the run. The wind had died down after blowing away the clouds. The sky sparkled freshly blue, and the snow beneath his skis felt good: dry powder, in perfect, unspoiled condition. The dismal gray rain of Paris had turned to new snow here in Switzerland. Being chairman of the International Astronautical Council had its benefits, the best of them being that he got preferential treatment at his favorite ski resorts. Later in the day this run would be filled with bureaucrats from other UN agencies who were taking the afternoon off, and clumsy tourists from Bulgaria and similar backwaters. But this morning it was all his.

He lowered his goggles over his eyes, took in the spectacular Swiss scenery once more, then pushed off and headed down the clean, empty slope. He felt the bite of the cold wind in his face and the exhilarating, half-frightening thrill of racing down the mountainside. This must be something like the feeling they get in zero gravity, he thought as he bent forward into the wind. Perhaps one day I will let them take me up to one of the space stations and see what it's like.

They were waiting for him at the bottom of the slope. As he rushed along on the final leg of the run, he could see his responsibilities gathered down there. A long black limousine, several of his assistants standing by the car, looking as out of place here on the ski slopes in their fur-trimmed overcoats and homburgs as he would look in the IAC offices in his stretch pants and windbreaker.

He braked to a stop in a swirl of powdery snow just a few meters from where they stood.

"What's the matter?" he asked. "What's happened?"

His chief secretary, a fellow Swede, tall, rawboned, as blond as a Norse god, crunched across the snow in his expensive Italian shoes.

"All hell's broken loose. The Soviets have seized *Nueva Venezuela* and apparently killed a dozen people."

"My God!"

"They claim they were pirates, caught in the act."

"Of course. Why else would they do it?"

"The Japanese government has asked for an immediate emergency meeting of the General Assembly. So has the United States."

"The Americans?" A tendril of fear crawled up Quistigaard's

spine, a fear he had not felt for more than a decade. The Americans claimed that they had dismantled all their nuclear bombs. The Russians claimed that they could shoot down any missiles fired at them. But was it all true? Could there be a nuclear war, now, after all these years of peace?

"There's more," the secretary said. "We just received a protest from the government of Venezuela against the Soviet seizure of their space station. More protests have come in from several other Third World nations."

Quistigaard felt his hands trembling inside their gloves. "And the Chinese? What do they say?"

"Nothing—as yet."

He leaned on his ski poles and felt his heart racing, pounding inside his chest. It is all Dan Randolph's fault, Quistigaard told himself. Everything was going along peacefully until the damned American began to rock the boat. I hope the Russians find him and hang him from the Kremlin walls.

But to his secretary he said, "Help me get these damned skis off. We have a thousand things to do and only a few hours in which to do them."

Chapter
◆ ◆ THIRTY-NINE ◆ ◆

One of the ungainly projecting arms of the space factory ended in a bulbous pod that housed a large industrial laser, a complex jumble of electrical power machinery and massive slabs of copper polished so finely that a giant could use them as shaving mirrors.

Dan Randolph hung weightlessly amid the thick cables and long rows of capacitor banks. The laser pod was unlighted except for the glow of the gleaming Earth revolving below, huge and bright and so close that Dan felt he could almost touch it with his outstretched hand. Silhouetted against the Earth's daylit blue was the bull's-eye structure of *Nueva Venezuela*. And hanging between them, looming larger every second, was the approaching Soviet space shuttle.

It looked very much like any nation's shuttle, Dan thought, and for the totally pragmatic reason that they were all designed for the same task. Form follows function, and except for the red star painted on the shuttle's raked-back tail fin, the aerospace craft might have been built in Japan or India or California.

Dan looked at the gleaming aluminum column next to him

before reaching for one of the handgrips set into it. Signs that warned DANGER—HIGH VOLTAGE were stenciled everywhere and he had no intention of frying himself before Malik arrived. He half climbed, half swam in the weightlessness of zero gravity until he was hovering alongside a short, swarthy, potbellied technician in the olive-green coveralls of a laser operator. The man smelled faintly of oil and sweat and something acrid that Dan could not identify. I imagine I must smell pretty much the same, Dan thought. The technician was bending intently over his control board, his short legs dangling in midair as he checked out the electrical circuitry. He grunted and nodded to himself as he clicked color-coded buttons across the length of the long panel.

Holding on to one of the handgrips studding the edge of the control board, Dan nudged the technician.

"Everything ready?" he asked.

The tech looked up, and Dan saw that he had the butt of an unlit cigar clamped in his teeth. "Sure. Ready to go. Checks out one hunnert percent."

Dan noticed a handful of fresh cigars in the tech's chest pocket. "You don't smoke those things in here, do you?"

He broke into a ragged-toothed grin. "Don't smoke 'em at all. Useta. Smoked a dozen a day, years ago. But I made a bet with a guy—whole case of Glenlivet. Ain't smoked one since then. Nobody says I can't chew 'em, though."

Dan was glad that his back was to the Earthlight and the tech probably could not see the expression on his face too clearly. Then he turned slightly and pointed toward the approaching shuttle.

"See the tail cone, back at the end?"

"Sure. Where the rocket nozzles poke out."

"All right," said Dan. "I want you to make a cut just forward of those fairings that house the nozzles."

"I can saw 'em right off for you."

Dan tapped him on the shoulder. "Just a deep slice will do. Just enough to cut the electrical connections between the thrusters and the cockpit, so they can't move the bird once she's docked with us."

"Gotcha. No sweat."

"How long will it take?"

"Coupla minutes."

"Fine. Wait until she's docked. I'll tell you when to start."

"Sure." He reached across the control board, flipped open a protective covering and clicked on the master power switch. From somewhere deep in the bowels of the machinery, Dan heard a generator begin to whine.

"That's all you want me to do?" the technician asked.

"That'll be plenty," said Dan.

"I could saw that bird into jigsaw pieces at this range, you know. Cut 'em up for good. They'd never know what hit 'em."

"And then one of their antimissile lasers would do the same to us," Dan said.

The tech grunted as if he'd been hit in the solar plexus.

"No," Dan said. "I just want to cut off their retreat. The less bloodshed, the better." Except for one particular Russian, he added silently.

"You're the boss," said the technician.

The two men watched silently as the Russian shuttle maneuvered toward the factory's main airlock. The delta-winged craft rotated ninety degrees, so that the hatch built into its top, just aft of the flight deck, locked onto the factory's airlock. To Dan and the laser operator, the shuttle appeared to be below them; it was as if they were floating a few hundred yards above it.

The whine of the power generator was almost beyond the range of human hearing as Dan murmured to the technician, "Okay, now. Slice his balls off."

The tech grunted once, took the wet, chewed cigar butt out of his mouth and jammed it into a pocket on the leg of his coveralls, then began tapping on the buttons of his control console as delicately as a church organist playing a Bach fugue. High overhead, Dan saw one of the big copper mirrors, thick and square as a coffin, swing silently in its jeweled mounting. He knew it was his imagination, but he thought he could feel the air inside this pod crackling as the mirror began to shimmer, like a desert landscape in the heat of the burning sun.

Turning his head so quickly that it spun his body about, Dan saw a scalpel-thin line etching itself slowly across the top of the Russian shuttle, angling across its white body just forward of the root of the rakishly angled tail fin.

"Inner airlock has been opened," Kaktins' voice reported over the intercom grill built into the control board. "They are entering main section."

"Are they in suits?" Dan asked.

"No space suits. Only soldier uni— Ah! One of them shot out the camera. Barbarian thugs!"

"Have you taken all the space suits out of the lockers?"

"Yes, yes," Kaktins replied, sounding almost miffed at the question. "Just as you ordered. All suits here in control center with us. No suits anywhere else in factory."

"Good. Fine. We'll be back there with you in about five minutes."

"Better hurry. There are about thirty of them, and they are shooting out TV cameras as they spread through factory."

"We're done here," the technician said, pulling a fresh cigar from his chest pocket.

Dan saw that the dark-edged cut had sliced completely across the shuttle's rear end. That should do it, he thought. When they try to light up their engines to get back home, they'll find out that they're stuck here. They can limp back to *Nueva Venezuela* on their maneuvering thrusters, if they have enough fuel left in them. But they can't retro-burn and return to Earth.

"Okay," Dan said, clapping the technician on the back hard enough to send his new cigar spinning out of his mouth. "Let's haul ass back to the control center."

* * *

Vasily Malik stood uneasily in the vast, echoing, gloomy expanse of the space factory's main workshop. The machines were still and silent. The big, high-vaulted chamber was only dimly lit; most of the lamps set up among the curving ribs of the ceiling had been turned off.

Malik was accustomed to weightlessness, but he did not enjoy it. He was not an astronaut or engineer who had to learn how to work in zero gravity; he was a government official who experienced zero-gee when he traveled into space and much preferred to feel some solid weight, even the feather-light pull of the Moon, and to know in his guts that up was up and down was down. Now he stood alongside a huge pile of machinery, heavy metal beams and grasping arms that looked like a giant robot's workbench. The chamber felt chilly to Malik, as if the cold and darkness of the void outside were seeping into it.

Nonsense, he told himself. Randolph thinks that he has me at a disadvantage here. But he will soon learn that I can ferret him out here or anywhere else that he tries to hide from me.

One of the young lieutenants came gliding up to him and stopped himself only by grabbing at the edge of the aluminum beam next to where Malik stood.

"They have evacuated every section my men have searched, sir," said the lieutenant, a little breathlessly. "The place is empty."

"They are *here*," Malik insisted. "They must have retreated farther, into those pods on the far side of the factory."

"Yessir," agreed the lieutenant.

Malik saw that more than a dozen soldiers were milling around the outer areas of this big, shadowy chamber, bobbing slightly in the weightlessness. He pulled a flat, slim portable computer about the size of a hand from his back pocket and touched a button at its base. Its display screen glowed to life.

"According to the plan of this place," he said as the lieutenant peered over his shoulder, "we have entered the factory from here, the main airlock, and worked our way to here, the machine shop.''

''Yessir.'' The lieutenant pointed with an extended finger. ''My men have come along this section, past the control center and living quarters, while the other squad has come through this way, where the communications and life support centers are.''

''And they are all empty. No one in them.''

''That is correct, sir.''

''You left men at the communications and life support centers?''

''Yessir! As you ordered.''

Malik studied the computer screen. ''Good. They must be hiding out in these arms, where the smelters and lasers are located.''

''If they're here at all, sir,'' ventured the lieutenant.

''Oh, he's here,'' Malik said. ''I can smell him. He's here, cowering in some dark corner like a trapped rat.''

''Malik!'' The word boomed through the sepulchral chamber like the voice of God. ''Vasily Malik, can you hear me?''

Looking up into the eerie shadows of the steel-ribbed ceiling, Malik shouted, ''Randolph! Where are you?''

''I'm at your jugular vein, Malik.''

Without thinking about it consciously, Malik pulled his pistol from the holster at his hip. ''Give yourself up, Randolph. Surrender yourself and there will be no more bloodshed. Let Lucita go. There's no reason for you to hold her as a hostage.''

''You've got it all wrong, friend,'' Randolph's voice boomed from the loudspeakers in the ceiling. ''You're the one who has to surrender. You've led your men into a trap.''

''Don't try to bluff your—''

''Haven't you noticed that it's getting cold in there? I've turned down the air pressure.''

The young lieutenant stared at Malik, his mouth hanging open.

''Your shuttle is crippled and all the passageways leading

back to the main airlock have been opened up to vacuum, as of . . . *now*."

Malik heard the clang of airtight hatches slamming shut and the distant, muffled Klaxons that warned of air pressure loss.

"It's an old Russian strategy." Randolph chuckled. "Lead the enemy into your territory and scorch the earth behind him. You're trapped, pal. If I want to, I can pop open the emergency hatches in there. Ever see what happens to a human body when it's suddenly exposed to vacuum? It's called explosive decompression. Not pretty."

"You're bluffing! We have occupied the control center, the life support center. . . ."

"Sure you have. But I had the equipment in them disconnected before we retreated back here. We're running everything from the emergency backup equipment out here in the smelter pod."

"I don't believe you!"

Randolph's laugh grated against Malik's nerves. "You don't believe me? Then go pry open one of the hatches. Blow open with a grenade, if you're carrying any. I only wish I had a working camera in there so I could see you when your skin bursts and your eyes blow out of your head."

"You've killed my men?"

"Not yet. They're locked into the communications and life support centers. The airtight hatches will keep them safe, as long as they don't try to get out."

Malik fought down a wave of fear-driven fury that threatened to engulf him. He took a deep breath and looked down at the pistol in his hand until he was quite certain that it was not trembling. Still, his palms felt slick with perspiration.

"This delaying action won't prevent the inevitable, Randolph," he said, feeling frustrated at having to talk into the shadows. "Soviet spacecraft are on their way here with more troops. . . ."

"Are they?" Dan's voice cut in. "You'd better come up here and take a look."

371

"What do you mean?"

"Go to the airlock hatch labeled number four. Enter it. We'll cycle the hatch from here. Follow my instructions when the other side opens and I'll lead you here to the smelter pod."

Malik's eyes scanned the perimeter of the big, darkened chamber. He saw a hatch with the numeral four glowing in white above it.

"Come alone," Dan's voice warned. "And leave your gun behind."

Chapter
◆ ◆ FORTY ◆ ◆

From the control station high above the main smelters, Dan watched the TV monitors as Malik made his way along the long tubular passageway from the main machine shop to the smelter pod. As far as he could see, the Russian was unarmed. His holster flapped emptily. But there were plenty of places to hide a weapon inside the tunic, pants and boots of his uniform.

And he claims to be a martial arts expert, Dan reminded himself. "You'll have to search him," he said to Kaktins.

The Latvian nodded, a lopsided grin on his face. "It will be new experience for me for Russian to be prisoner."

Most of the men and women of the factory complex were gathered down in the smelter area where, ordinarily, raw ores from the Moon were melted down and separated into their constituent aluminum, titanium, silicon, oxygen and other elements. But now the smelters were cold and quiet, their huge maws gaping blankly, the conveyor belts that fed them unmoving.

The control center was a curving tube built above the big, blackened smelters. Row upon row of consoles and monitoring panels lined its length and wrapped themselves all around the circular inner walls, except for a long slit of a window that looked out on the smelters themselves. Built for zero-gravity operation, the control center contained no chairs at all, only occasional posts jutting out from the consoles, like perches for birds, where the technicians could roost and anchor themselves for a while. Dan hovered weightlessly in front of a set of display screens, like a man floating before a giant insect's segmented eye. Behind him, half a dozen technicians watched the panels that now controlled the entire factory's air, heat, electricity and communications.

Far down the long line of consoles, almost lost to Dan's sight by the bend of the curving room, Lucita stood in front of a communications screen, her blue-jeaned legs wrapped around an anchor post. Dan could make out her father's face in the screen, drained almost white, eyes bleary.

He put out a hand to steady himself as his body drifted slightly. Over his head, another set of screens showed the sight that he still found almost unbelievable: eight spacecraft, ranging in size from little flitters to big, delta-winged shuttles, converging on *Nueva Venezuela*. They bore the markings of the Pan-Arab Federation, Polynesia, the United African States, India and Japan: every space-faring nation or group of nations.

"A message for you, boss," called one of the communications technicians, a woman. "It's from the Japanese shuttle. Sorry I can't switch it to one of your monitors."

"That's all right." Dan pushed away from the monitors, which showed Malik entering the airlock that opened into the smelter pod, and let his body glide up to the communications screen. Looking down toward Kaktins, he said, "Take a couple of the biggest men you can find and search him thoroughly before you let him out of the airlock."

Kaktins grinned and glided for the exit at the end of the control room.

Dan bobbed up to the big communications screen and blinked twice when he saw Saito Yamagata's face beaming at him.

374

"I request the honor of docking at your factory complex, old friend," said the Japanese industrialist.

"Permission granted," Dan said immediately. "What the hell are you doing up here?"

Yamagata's laughter rocked his head back and made his eyes squeeze shut. "I thought you would be surprised. When Nobo told me what was happening, I immediately embarked for *Yamagata One*, bringing a trained squad of security troops with me. I thought you might need help."

"We can use all the help we can get. Thanks, Sai."

"A pleasure."

Dan briefed him quickly on what was happening, then ended the conversation and turned back to the TV monitors. Kaktins and two other men were escorting Malik from the airlock toward the control center.

He glanced back at Lucita, saw her still deep in talk with her father's image. It could still all blow up in our faces, he told himself. We're not out of the woods yet.

Malik looked grimly defiant when they brought him into the control center.

"You might as well surrender," were his first words to Dan. "More Soviet troops are on their way."

Taking him by the elbow, Dan turned the Russian slightly so that they were both facing the bank of communications screens.

"Look," he said. "Spacecraft from every space-faring nation, heading here to help us. You've jammed our radio links with the ground, but we've been getting news from the other space stations, relayed by commsats over laser links. All hell's broken loose down there. The General Assembly is going to meet in emergency session in another twelve hours or so. The chairman of the IAC has threatened to suspend the Soviet Union's license to mine lunar ores if you don't withdraw your troops from here. The government of Venezuela has protested your seizure of *Nueva Venezuela* and the killing of Venezuelan citizens."

Malik's face went gray.

"If I were you, I'd get in touch with Moscow and see what they have to say about all this." Dan grinned his broadest, happiest grin.

"I know what they'll say." Malik's voice was as heavy and dull as lead.

"Yeah. I think I do, too. You're finished, Vasily. They're going to throw you to the wolves. If they get the chance."

The Russian's brows rose a scant millimeter. "What do you mean by that?"

"You murdered twelve of my men. Good men. You ordered them killed, slaughtered without a chance."

Malik's handsome face broke into a crooked, bitter smile. "I see. And you are going to execute me. Like the sheriff in the Wild West."

Dan shook his head. "You still don't understand how we do things, do you? The sheriff just arrests the bad guys. A judge and jury tries him."

"You're not going to—"

"Yes, I am, pal. Right here. We're going to pick twelve good people and true and try you for mass murder. We're going to give you a fair trial. And then we're going to hang you."

Malik lashed out at Dan with both hands, blurringly fast, without warning. The force of the blows slammed Dan back against the communications console. Glass shattered and Dan felt a stabbing pain in the back of his neck. Kaktins kicked against the console and launched himself after Malik, who was pushing himself hand over hand along the rows of electronics gear past the startled technicians, toward Lucita.

The two smelter operators who had been with Kaktins stared dumbly, unsure of what to do. Dan grabbed one of the perch-poles and hurled himself after the Latvian, feeling blood trickling down his neck.

Kaktins grappled for Malik's booted feet, but the Russian suddenly turned, the slim blade of a knife gleaming in his right hand, and slashed at Kaktins. Blood spurted and the Latvian howled with pain, doubling up.

376

"Lucita!" Dan shouted. "Look out!"

She turned from the screen just in time to see Malik rush up toward her, the reddened knife in his upraised hand.

"I'll kill her!" Malik screamed. "If you come any closer I'll kill her!"

Dan reached for Kaktins, who was clutching his shoulder and moaning.

"I thought you searched him, for Chrissake," Dan growled.

The Latvian blinked pain-fogged eyes. "I thought I did, too."

Dan pushed himself past Kaktins to confront the Russian. Malik was holding Lucita around the waist, keeping her in front of him, like a shield. He pressed the point of the knife against her throat. The other technicians had flown in the opposite direction, away from the danger. A couple of them pulled Kaktins back as Dan faced Malik and Lucita.

"I'll kill her, Randolph!" Malik snarled. "I'll kill her!"

Dan hovered weightlessly a few feet in front of them. Lucita was wide-eyed with shock, gasping, her hands gripping the Russian's arm with white-knuckled intensity.

"It's all right, Lucita. He's not going to hurt you," Dan said calmly. "It's me he wants, not you."

Malik's eyes narrowed slightly.

"That's right, isn't it, Vasily? You don't want to kill her. You want to kill me. Well, you'll never have a better chance than now." Lapsing into Russian, Dan said, "Come and get me, you cowardly son of a whore!"

With a strangled roar, Malik flung Lucita to one side and dove at Dan, knife first. Dan stretched one arm up, his fingers touching the panels overhead just enough to give him some traction, and pushed himself sideways to evade the Russian's thrust. As Malik dived past, Dan kicked with both feet at his chest and face.

The Russian grunted and spun crashing into the consoles. Dan glided effortlessly between Malik and Lucita.

"You're hurt," he heard her say.

But he kept his eyes on Malik, and the knife still in his hand.

"I'm not a kung fu expert, Vasily, but I've fought in zero gravity before," Dan taunted. "It's been a long time, many years, but it's like riding a bicycle: it all comes back to you when you try it again."

Malik glanced over his shoulder. A solid mass of technicians loomed behind him, blocking his retreat.

"Come on, Vasily. Cut my heart out. I'm just as defenseless as the men you had murdered. I'm an old man, and you're a trained expert in the martial arts. Right? You told me so yourself. So come and get me, shithead."

Warily, cautiously, Malik advanced on Dan. He kept his left hand out, groping against the consoles for balance and support. Dan refused to move, refused to be maneuvered out of his position in front of Lucita.

Malik came closer. Dan hung motionless, his eyes on the knife. As Malik hunched himself together to launch another attack, Dan turned slightly, away from the knife, offering the profile of his body as a target. Malik lunged, but Dan side slipped and wrapped his left arm around the Russian's throat. Ramming both his knees into Malik's spine, he yanked hard. The two bodies tumbled wildly in midair. Dan suddenly let go and grabbed Malik's arm, twisting it and forcing the knife from his suddenly numbed fingers. Then, planting both feet solidly against the consoles, Dan launched a straight right fist against Malik's jaw with every ounce of strength in him.

The crack of bones breaking sounded loud enough to make the others in the control center flinch. Dan felt pain shoot up his arm as Malik's head snapped back and his eyes rolled up blankly. The Russian floated unconscious, arms lolling, jaw hanging open. Blood filled his mouth and drifted in tiny globules.

"Jesus Christ," Dan muttered, grabbing for a handhold with his left hand and wringing his right. "I think I broke my double-damned knuckle."

He saw the knife hovering, and reached out to take it with good hand.

Lucita was suddenly at his side. "Don't kill him, Dan! n't. . . ."

He laughed. "I'm not going to kill him. I won't have to. comrades in the Kremlin will do that. Breaking his jaw s good enough for me."

Sudden understanding filled her eyes. "You provoked him attacking you!"

He nodded sheepishly. "I didn't stop to think he might aten you, though. I'm sorry about that." Throbbing pain de him grit his teeth. "Didn't think I'd bust my hand, er."

Lucita tried to frown at him. "You deserve it. For fright- ng all of us."

Chapter
◆ ◆ FORTY-ONE ◆ ◆

Despite the Novocain and the plastic cast, Dan's hand s
throbbed. He was laughing, though, as he sat sprawled on
bunk of his utilitarian compartment aboard *Nueva Venezu*
and lifted a glass of amontillado with his left hand.

The little room was crowded with visitors. Saito Yamag
had just offered a toast to victory. Lucita, perched on
little plastic desk chair next to the bunk, looked radia
happy. Dan ignored the others, men from half a dozen
ferent nations, and reached out to touch his glass aga
hers.

"You have won a great victory," Yamagata repeated.

The slim, gaunt-cheeked Egyptian colonel who was re
senting the Pan-Arab coalition nodded in agreement. "
the first time in thirty years the Russians have been force
back down. A new day is dawning, I can feel it."

Dan tried to shrug, but the movement sent a tendril of
along his right arm. "We've won a battle—maybe. Not
war."

"The battle has been won definitely," Yamagata said.
was sitting on a stool commandeered from one of the w

shops, next to the cabinet where Dan kept his meager supply of sherry.

The Indian representative, a tall, turbaned Sikh with a handsome curly gray beard, said in the deep, authoritarian tones of an experienced diplomat, "The General Assembly will insist that the Soviet Union pay reparations for this outrage. And the IAC will undoubtedly move to allow competition for lunar resources."

"I'll believe that when I see it," Dan countered. "The Soviets won't give up their monopoly on the Moon that easily."

"At the very least," the Sikh insisted, "the IAC will approve your claim of the asteroidal materials."

"And allow future expeditions to collect more asteroids," Yamagata added.

"Under IAC control," Dan added.

"Of course. No nation should be allowed to claim ownership of a natural body of the solar system. And the orbit of such a body should be altered only after the IAC has approved of such a maneuver."

Lucita asked, "What will happen to the Russians who are on their way to Dan's asteroid?"

The Sikh frowned at her, whether because a woman had the temerity to interrupt the men's conversation or because she granted a private individual ownership of the asteroid, Dan could not tell.

Yamagata answered, "They have been ordered by Moscow to return without altering the asteroid's present trajectory. A UN mission will be sent to the asteroid within a few days."

"They'll claim possession of it," Dan muttered.

The Japanese grinned at him. "Naturally. But the materials of the asteroid will be available for mining by Astro Manufacturing Corporation—and its partner in the venture."

Dan drained the last of his amontillado. "Do you really think," he asked, "that we've gained anything? That we've broken the Russian stranglehold?"

"Yes!" Yamagata said immediately. "Definitely. We have opened up the solar system for all the nations of the world. *You* have done that, Daniel. We all owe you a very great debt of gratitude."

"I'll accept a small percentage of your profits," Dan quipped.

Yamagata laughed. The Sikh raised his stern white eyebrows.

They chatted for what seemed like hours. Dan's mind drifted, their voices became a blurred background, like the hum of electrical equipment or the soft lapping sound of waves at the beach. He was bone-tired. His eyes closed.

Suddenly realizing that he was being impolite, Dan snapped his eyes open again. The room was empty, except for Lucita, still sitting beside the bunk.

"What happened to everybody?"

"You fell asleep," she said softly. "They left."

Seeing his empty liquor cabinet, Dan said, "They took the rest of the sherry with them. I'll bet that was Sai's idea."

"No," Lucita said. "I told them to. I didn't think they would leave without it."

He grinned at her. "Come here."

She sat on the edge of the bunk and leaned over him. He kissed her, gently.

The phone buzzed.

Holding Lucita close to him with his good arm, Dan clumsily snapped his fingers. It took two tries before the phone's little screen on the desk lit up and showed the face of a communications technician.

"Mr. Randolph?" she asked.

"Yes, I'm here."

"Oh. Hard to see, your room's dark."

"What is it?" Dan demanded.

"The President, sir. She wants to talk to you."

"The President of the United States?"

"Yessir!" The technician was an American, Dan could see from her attitude. "She's calling from Washington."

Dan hesitated a moment. Then, "Tell her I'm resting. Doctor's orders."

The technician's eyes went wide with disbelief.

"Dan," Lucita whispered urgently, "you can't make the President wait. . . ."

"I'll call her back," Dan said to the phone screen. "Tell her I appreciate her call, and I hope she takes advantage of what's been accomplished today. And give her my thanks for her help."

"Yes, sir," the technician replied. "Is that all?"

"That's all for now." He snapped his fingers and the phone screen went dark.

Lucita looked alarmed. "Dan, *La Presidenta* . . ."

He pulled her closer and covered her lips with a kiss.

"You're much more important to me," he said. "America's an old nation, Lucita. Maybe she'll become great again, maybe not. We've given her the chance, now it's up to the people and their leaders. You and me, though, we have other places to go, other worlds to see."

"But I thought . . ."

He smiled at her. "You're the only woman I'm interested, *amada*; I've found what I've been searching for."

She nestled her head against his shoulder. "Truly?"

"Truly." He nuzzled her dark, fragrant hair. Then he laughed softly. "How would you like to spend your honeymoon on Mars?"

Ben Bova

☐	53200-7	AS ON A DARKLING PLAIN	$2.9
	53201-5		Canada $3.5
☐	53217-1	THE ASTRAL MIRROR	$2.9
	53218-X		Canada $3.5
☐	53212-0	ESCAPE PLUS	$2.9
	53213-9		Canada $3.5
☐	53221-X	GREMLINS GO HOME	$2.7
	53222-8	(with Gordon R. Dickson)	Canada $3.2
☐	53215-5	ORION	$3.5
	53216-3		Canada $3.9
☐	53210-4	OUT OF THE SUN	$2.9
	53211-2		Canada $3.5
☐	53223-6	PRIVATEERS	$3.5
	53224-4		Canada $4.5
☐	53208-2	TEST OF FIRE	$2.9
	53209-0		Canada $3.5